To T... as gen... tleman as ever graced the streets of Vallejo.

Pat Manley

AN HONEST MAN

Owen Chaffee
9166 A Hubbard Court (like old mother
Elk Grove Ca. 95624

775-544-9807
Pats telephone #
@ Chaffee at Com.net

Patrick Manley

Serial II
4514670649
954 320

patrickwmanley
@gmail.com

775-544-9807

Published by Populist Press

Reno, Nevada

To the memory of Nels Solander who taught me how to bait a hook and do an honest day's work. Forty years later, the smell of his Copenhagen, the sound of his easy laugh and the reassurance of his kind smile are still clear in my memory.

FOREWARD

"To most Europeans, I guess, America now looks like the most dangerous country in the world. Since America is unquestionably the most powerful country, the transformation of America's image within the last thirty years is very frightening for Europeans. It is probably still more frightening for the great majority of the human race who are neither Europeans nor North Americans, but are Latin Americans, Asians and Africans. They, I imagine, feel even more insecure than we feel. They feel that, at any moment, America may intervene in their internal affairs with the same appalling consequences as have followed from American intervention in Southeast Asia.

"For the world as a whole, the CIA has now become the bogey that Communism has been for America. Wherever there is trouble, violence, suffering, tragedy, the rest of us are now quick to suspect that the CIA had a hand in it. Our phobia about the CIA is, no doubt, as fantastically excessive as America's phobia about world Communism; but in this case, too, there is just enough convincing guidance to make the phobia genuine. In fact, the roles of America and Russia have been reversed. Today America has become the world's nightmare."

British
Historian Arnold Toynbee

INTRODUCTION

The following is an account of a chance acquaintance that I made with an old man up in Montana in the summer of 1998. He was staying at the Moseby cabin next to my grandfather's place on Flathead Lake in western Montana. I guessed that he was in his mid-seventies, and he appeared to be on his last legs. While we were fishing he began to make all kinds of wild accusations about everything from the assassination of John Kennedy to CIA mind control experiments. He seemed to have inside information on everyone from Richard Nixon to George Bush and even more obscure characters like Howard Hunt. At first it was confusing as he made repeated references to The Beast and the Shadow Elite. He also talked about a Shadow Government that had made most of the military decisions since World War II. His knowledge seemed to come from his background with the Agency or the Company which were terms he used for the Central Intelligence Agency.

At first I thought Jim Quinn was a little crazy or maybe he was feeling the effects of some medication for his failing health. He indicated that his days were numbered due to his advanced stage of emphysema. Over a period of six days he tried to explain to me, from an insider's point of view, what had happened in this country since World War II. The names and events were confusing to me in the beginning, but by the time the seminar was over I had a pretty good understanding of the key players in Jim's story. At first I was suspicious of everything I was hearing. I even wondered if Jim Quinn was his real name. As the week wore on, I began to accept the sincerity of an old man without much time left.

Jim had a beat-up leather suitcase full of papers. It contained documents that were organized in manila folders. Some were hand-written notes and some looked like official documents. He would refer to this pile of information as he carefully explained what he considered to be the most important events of the Cold War era. The first night I wrote down everything I could remember after Jim went back to his cabin. After that, I openly scribbled down his strange story as he told it. I was the only student in this bizarre political science class. Jim approved of the notes. He wanted to make sure that I got it right.

When I said goodbye to Jim Quinn at the end of the week, he handed me the old leather suitcase and wished me luck. I had become the curator of these documents. It was clear that Jim expected that I would somehow make his story public. I knew that I was in over my head. He had been journalism major in college, and I thought that he intended to write this story but he had run out of time. My ability with the English language was much more limited, but the task had fallen to me.

When I returned to Nevada, I opened up the old suitcase and spread the folders out across the dining room table. There was a folder on every key player of the era like Lyndon Johnson or J. Edgar Hoover.

There were other folders with "classified" written across the top. Other folders were labeled "witness statements" or "damage control" or "suspicious deaths". There were summaries of books that Jim had read on the subject. When I finally decided that I would try to put all this information in a book, I tried to use Jim Quinn's own words and phrases. I could still hear his raspy voice as he talked for hours. With the notes I had taken and the papers he had given me, I thought that I could write an accurate account of his story. Whether all this information was true would be up to the reader to decide.

I never saw Jim Quinn after those six days in Montana. Our parting was somewhat of a mystery. It still makes me nervous to think about it. When I began to lay out the background material, the story began to make more sense. It was like a ten-thousand piece puzzle. At first all you had were the corners and part of the border. As you filled in the center, a picture began to appear. I got so involved with trying to put the whole thing together that I decided to go to Dallas in November of 98. It was the thirty-fifth anniversary of John Kennedy's death. What I learned in Texas made my hair stand on end.

Patrick Manley

FINLEY POINT

A MARKED MAN

"Dulles never got to move into that new office. Imagine the humiliation. Some snotty nosed Irishman ends his distinguished career about the time he's going to see the rewards for years of hard work. A state of the art office complex with its own dining room for entertaining the who's who in espionage and he never gets to set foot in it. McCone moves in before the paint's dry. Dulles would have wandered the inner sanctum in his favorite slippers, smoking his pipe, feeling good about the contribution he'd made to making the world safe for American corporations. Then the master is taken down by a young punk Irishman who never did understand the system that Dulles had put in place. It never was about communism. It was about making the world profitable for his well-healed friends. Permindex, the dummy companies, government overthrows. It was nothing but a scheme to enrich U.S. businesses overseas.

"A friend of his, an old client named Edward Durrell Stone, had designed the entire complex. Congress put up the money to build the new CIA headquarters in the woods at Langley, Virginia. Allen Dulles would have his own suite of offices on the seventh floor, but he never saw it finished. It was going to be a monument to his legendary career. Everything was falling nicely into place. Forty years of cultivating the favor of this country's most powerful businessmen had put Dulles in a position of considerable power. Now it was time to put his feet up on the desk and enjoy the Agency that he had created. Pull on his pipe and look back at his accomplishments.

"Then came the Bay of Pigs. A lot of us in the Agency predicted it would fail, but Dulles and Bissell were determined to run with the idea. They thought they could force Kennedy into using military air power to support the invasion. They were wrong. Kennedy had made it clear that the only way he would approve the operation was that it be limited to Cuban exiles fighting to get their country back. No U.S. involvement. He had no choice due to the Neutrality Act. We weren't at war with Cuba. The operation had gotten too damn big. Castro knew about it. The Russians knew where and when it would take place. Dulles figured he had Kennedy both ways. If he didn't approve last minute air support, he would take the blame for the failure. If he went along with the program, he would be blamed for naked aggression. If they couldn't have Nixon, at least they could compromise Kennedy.

"Dulles and Kennedy had been at odds since the day that self-assured Irishman set foot in the oval office. Kennedy was making speeches in support of Patrice Lamumba while Dulles was implementing a plan to have him killed. Two foreign policies. There was one thing Dulles hadn't counted on. Kennedy took the blame for the Bay of Pigs and then fired Dulles, Bissell and Cabell. The hierarchy of the Agency had been given their walking papers. And Kennedy wasn't finished. He threatened to break up the CIA and scatter it to the winds. There was talk that Bobby Kennedy might be DCI in a second term. So Dulles never moved into his new office, and Kennedy became a marked man. It was only a matter of time."

Our fishing trip had gotten off to a strange start. I had asked the old man in the cabin next to mine if he would like to go out in the boat and catch a few silver salmon. We had no sooner eased away from the dock when he started this lecture. He chose his words carefully as if he had practiced this speech.

"Ever wonder why the great men of peace are always killed? Go all the way back to Jesus Christ. If a man is talking peace or spirituality instead of materialism and greed, and he's gained a serious following, his days are numbered. More recently it was Ghandi and Martin Luther King and Anwar Sadat. These were men of peace. Humble men who disavowed violence. Why were they such a threat? Because the biggest concern to those in power is a populist movement that challenges their control and their profits.

"I would say that eighty percent of Americans are honest, hard working people. Would you agree with that? They keep their creditors happy. They pay their taxes. They raise their families. That may be their biggest accomplishment. When that first shovelful of dirt hits the lid of the casket, they may own a home or a piece of property. They never had much, and they never complained much.

"At the low end you have your ten percent bottom-feeders who refuse to pull their weight under any circumstances. They're involved with street crime or they've learned how to beat the welfare system. They choose not to participate. They're not going to shoulder their responsibilities under any circumstances. Some have no choice. The disabled or retarded. They've been wandering the streets since Reagan's budget cutbacks turned them out of the mental hospitals.

"At the top you have your corporate criminals. CEOs who make their multi-million dollar bonuses by laying off people or cancelling their health benefits. These are the white collar vultures. They pick the carcass clean and always want more. They do the bidding of their masters without asking questions. The apex of this group is the Shadow Elite. The blue-bloods and bankers who buy politicians who will fix the system in their favor. To these people, the rank and file are a sub-species who do the work and consume their products. As long as we have diversions like television and new cars to keep us complacent, we won't pose a threat to their control.

"To me, it seemed to turn ugly during Reagan's watch. That's when the Holy Trinity became I, ME and My. Every man for himself. Fuck the other guy. No more talk of the underdog. The disadvantaged. The dispossessed. They all disappeared. They're the ghosts living under the bridges. The battalion in rags with their pathetic belongings in shopping carts. Or the families living in run down motels with dirty faced kids playing in the parking lot. America's strange collection of lost souls. Casualties of budget cutbacks and corporate greed. The Reagan Legacy. Some are drunks or old fashioned hobos. Most couldn't hold a job under any circumstances. Criticize the Catholics, but at least they keep a few soup kitchens open. We've all learned to walk by without seeing them."

Our twelve-foot fishing boat glided smoothly over the waters of Polson Bay. The morning was clear as the sun rose over the Mission Mountains behind us. I had high expectations for catching some fish as I guided the boat toward Finley Point. Jim Quinn sat facing me as he continued his strange monologue. I had the feeling that he had already written this story in his head.

"Remember when a man's greatest honor was to die for his country. Reveille. Military Honors. Your coffin comes home wrapped in a flag. We saw plenty of coffins during Vietnam. A brass band whipping up those patriotic feelings. It all changed after Dallas. The Agency had been bumping off people all over the world, but we crossed the line with Kennedy. A president was shot down at mid-day in front of a crowd of his admirers. That's a stark scene. A scene that I guess I'll never get out of my head. We had perfected the art of removing uncooperative leaders wherever it was necessary, but I never figured we'd use that apparatus in our own country.

"After Dallas, it seemed that a man's greatest honor was to be killed by his country. It was an impressive group. King was removed in Memphis. Then Bobby in L.A. I'd include Wallace but he wasn't killed and he wasn't that impressive. But his paralysis sure changed the election in 1972. It was a three way split at the time, if you recall. Nixon, Wallace and Mcgovern. If Wallace stays in the race, nobody gets a majority of electoral votes. The decision goes to The House of Representatives which was controlled by the Democrats at that time. McGovern is the next president. Totally unacceptable to the Shadow Elite. So they go back to the lone nut formula.

"Walter Bremmer was an unemployed dishwasher for Christsake. He was flying all over the country waiting for an opportunity to shoot Wallace. He was staying in fine hotels and eating well, but he hadn't worked in months. Who was bankrolling him? Within hours of Wallace being shot, Chuck Colson asks Howard Hunt and the boys to plant McGovern campaign material in Bremmer's house. The FBI had already sealed off the place so Hunt refused. It turns out that Bremmer may have been treated by an Agency psychologist by the name of William Bryan who later worked with Sirhan Sirhan. Just a coincidence, right? If anyone ever compared the movements of Oswald, Bremmer, Sirhan, and James Earl Ray, the lone-nut theory would be laughable.

"At the time of the attempt on Wallace, Chuck Colson's nickname with us covert types was 'The Assassin Master'. Did it ever seem odd to you that people were always dropping dead around Nixon? If Jack and Bobby aren't killed, Nixon never gets close to the White House. Nixon was the Black Heart of the Beast in those days. He was a guy the Shadow Elite could work with. George Bush was another. Pro-business, pro-military. I hear good old Chuck Colson has found religion these days. I can't decide whether to laugh or puke. At the time, Colson was Nixon's right hand man in charge of any and all dirty tricks. He and Gordon Liddy and that little weasel, Segretti, ran a dirty tricks operation for Nixon on a scale that will never be seen again. And Dick Nixon, the would-be statesman, controlled the entire operation out of the Oval Office. He reveled in every little detail."

Jim Quinn stared south across the lake toward Polson. He coughed and spit over the side of the boat. As I steered the outboard toward Finley Point, I saw blood in the saliva as it floated past me on the calm water. I studied the old man as he sat facing me with his canvas cap pulled low across his eyes. His jaw was covered with uneven gray stubble and his skin was sickly pale. His shoulders looked pointy and frail.

"You were involved in the Kennedy assassination?" I tried not to sound too surprised by what I had just heard.

Jim looked up from under his cap. His eyes narrowed as he stared at me. "You people will never get it right. We've been removing leaders of countries all over the world since WWII. If you wouldn't play ball with American business, you were a communist and you were out. Coup d'état. Strip away a man's protection and there's always another faction ready to take over. Sometimes the new guy turns out to be no more amenable to our business or military interests than the man we just got rid of. So we repeat the process. Iran, Guatemala, Indonesia, Vietnam, Laos, the Philippines, the Congo, Peru, Chili, Bolivia, the Dominican Republic, Haiti. On and on and on. Changing the monkey. That's what we called it.

"At the time of Kennedy's removal, we were set up in over one hundred countries. Usually through our ambassadors. Sometimes with oil companies. About a third of American diplomats around the world were CIA. We were a world power unto ourselves. With our own foreign policy dictated by our benefactors. If you were the head of a small country, you had two choices. You could accept bribes and become wealthy or you could be a hero and get your ass shot off. Kennedy was just another head of state who wouldn't knuckle under to our military and corporate masters. He couldn't be bribed, and he couldn't be intimidated. He was stubborn about ending the Cold War. He had this vision that he could change our lives for the better. The men who paid the bills liked things just the way they were. As Kennedy became more popular, it began to really worry these people. Their fortunes were in jeopardy. That left only one solution, which was accomplished in Dallas.

"Kennedy was an intelligent guy who was interested in everything. If you had a conversation with him, you felt like you were being interrogated. He wanted to know everything that you knew. He craved knowledge. He had the most restless, energetic mind of anyone that I've ever been around. You hear all this crap about him being a poor student, but he graduated with honors from Harvard. No one seems to remember that. His senior thesis became a book called, WHY ENGLAND SLEPT, about England's failure to prepare for the war with Germany. When his father was ambassador to England, Kennedy traveled all over Europe. He got a firsthand account of fascism. He'd pick up hitchhikers and interrogate them about the quality of life in their country. How did they like Mussolini? What was their opinion of Franco? He would interview anyone who would talk to him. He wasn't as surprised as most Americans when Germany invaded Poland or Mussolini sent troops into Ethiopia. When America was finally dragged into the war, Kennedy joined the Navy, bad back and all.

"Oddly enough, Kennedy was recruited by Naval Intelligence as was our friend, Lee Harvey Oswald. Kennedy might have spent the duration of the war stateside if he hadn't taken up with a Danish journalist who was one fine looking woman. Inga Arvad. Our crime-fighter at the FBI was sure that Inga was a Nazi spy. So J. Edgar had her phone tapped. He bugged every hotel room where Inga and young Kennedy would spend a weekend together. The old pervert was probably jealous of her. Anyway, Joe Kennedy got wind of this potential scandal and arranged for his son to be shipped overseas on a PT-boat assignment.

"Kennedy was very savvy on foreign affairs. When he was in prep school, he subscribed to the New York Times so he could follow world developments. In other words, John Kennedy had more interest in international affairs when he was in high school than young Bush has while he's being considered for president. That's typical of the Bush family. You don't have to be brilliant when you are being told what to do. George Sr. was with us from the time he stumbled out of Yale and allegedly went into the oil business in Texas. If you look at the ledgers for Zapata Oil during those years, you'll see that you couldn't stay in business with those kinds of numbers. Bush looked very heroic during The Gulf War, but that was little more than a training exercise. Use up some military hardware. Keep our defense contractors happy. If you want to know the meaning of genuflect, watch the Bush family when the Shadow Elite comes to call. They're like jackals following a pride of lions. They're content with the scraps.

9

"It wasn't long after Kennedy became President that he realized the Agency was out of control. We had become nothing more than a private army to serve our corporate interests overseas. We were accountable to no branch of government. We didn't have to disclose our budget or our activities. Is that a prescription for treachery? Our corporate benefactors would put up the money and we'd do their dirty work. We'd rig an election or make sure bribes got into the right hands. If all else failed, we had what we called an Executive Action. EA. That was our Plans Division. Most of the rank and file at Langley had no idea what went on at Plans. Kennedy was just one of a series of Executive Actions. He was no different than Patrice Lamumba or Salvador Allende. These guys were all bad for business. Visionary types.

"The Bay of Pigs was the turning point for Kennedy and the Agency. The operation had been set up during the Eisenhower administration through Vice President Nixon. He was the Action Man at the White House. He worked closely with Allen Dulles, Charles Cabell, and Richard Bissell. Nixon knew all our dirty secrets. He had no problem getting rid of people who refused to play ball. He thought like an Agency guy. Pure expediency. In 1960, it was a foregone conclusion that Nixon would be the next president. We were confident we had a guy that we could work with. Hell, he'd worked on the details of Arbenz and Lamumba. Later, as President, he had Allende removed. Nixon's philosophy was the same as ours. Win at any cost. It served him well in politics. Nixon wasn't the least bit shy about sacrificing a few people here and there. Then Kennedy throws a monkey wrench into the deal by winning the election. We were in shock. The good old boy network at the Pentagon and Intelligence, along with our defense contractors and overseas corporations, could not believe what had happened. Our hand-picked guy, Nixon, was out. We were not prepared to work with Kennedy.

"I'll give you an idea of what a threat Kennedy was perceived to be to the military industry. At the time of his election, there was a multi-billion dollar defense contract set to go to Boeing for the development of a new military aircraft. Kennedy put this contract on hold. He later awarded the contract to General Dynamics of Fort Worth, Texas, where it would be more politically advantageous. It looked like these Kennedy boys were going to play good old fashioned hard ball. I can't tell you how many pissed off people there were over at the Pentagon. You did not dare bring up the subject of the Boing contract. Kennedy had completely circumvented the system for his own political advantage. And he had made some serious enemies.

"We decided to force Kennedy's hand at the Bay of Pigs. The whole thing was set up to fail. The Soviets knew where and when the invasion was to take place. Allen Dulles was out of the country on vacation at the time. Does that sound a little suspicious? That the Director of the CIA would choose to be out of the country during the most important Agency operation since WWII? Unless he wanted to distance himself from what he knew was going to be a disaster.

"Two days before the invasion, our B-26s knocked out seven of Castro's T-33 fighter jets. Three planes escaped. Later that day our spy satellite photographed the planes parked wingtip to wingtip at a small airfield near Santiago. We had five B-26 bombers with Cuban pilots ready to leave Nicaragua the night before the Bay of Pigs invasion. They would arrive at dawn and knock out Castro's last three fighter jets. Without these planes, there would be no resistance to our landing force. Just before our planes were set to take off that night, McGeorge Bundy, unbeknownst to Kennedy, calls off the mission. There was talk among our Cuban pilots of ignoring orders and taking off to carry out their assignment. They knew that their mission was critical to the success of the invasion. It was their best chance to take their country back.

"McGeorge Bundy's brother, Bill Bundy, had been an asset of the Company for years and was close to Allen Dulles. Anyway, by the time Kennedy found out that the mission had been aborted, it was too late to get the planes into the air. So General Cabel spends the rest of the predawn hours begging Kennedy to authorize military air support to protect our landing force. Kennedy refused. He had made it clear to the Agency when he signed off on the operation that there would be no U.S. military involvement. He had no choice. It was against the law. He would have been condemned around the world for naked aggression. We thought we had him. If he refused, he would be labeled as a traitor by the Cubans and our covert troops. Kennedy would be exposed as being soft on communism.

"There was another aspect of the Bay of Pigs that is never mentioned. The night before the invasion, a ship called the Santa Ana, under a Costa Rican flag, sailed from the port of Algiers on the Mississippi River. It was headed for the Cuban port of Baracoa which was near America's Guantanamo Naval Base. There were a couple hundred Cuban exiles on board outfitted in Cuban military uniforms. The idea was to create a diversionary strike against our naval base that would force Kennedy to launch an all out invasion against Cuba. The commander of the mission learned from a landing party that the beach was already lined with Cuban military personnel. Diaz decided to abort the mission. He was ordered to proceed. He refused. He said to land would be suicide. Unknown to Diaz and President Kennedy, there was a Marine battalion on a nearby ship that was ready to engage Castro's troops. The Agency had involved the Pentagon without the President's knowledge or approval.

"As it turned out, many of our men who were captured at the Bay of Pigs were brutally tortured and killed. Some were decapitated right there on the beach. Needless to say, this caused a deep hatred of Kennedy throughout the Agency and the Cuban groups. You might say throughout the entire defense establishment. Allen Dulles sacrificed hundreds of loyal warriors for a chance to expose Kennedy. With Dulles, it was always about positioning the Agency to gain more power. Dulles figured that Kennedy had been seriously discredited and his political future was in doubt. The Agency might not have to worry about a second term.

"Then a funny thing happened. Kennedy went on TV and took full responsibility for the entire incident. Americans rallied behind him and he became more popular than ever. Our plan had backfired, but we had another plan. In essence, Kennedy's political recovery after the Bay of Pigs had sealed his death warrant. Kennedy knew he'd been set up. He had Bobby conduct an investigation. It was at this point that rumors began to circulate about Bobby being put in charge of the Agency. Talk about some nervous spooks. If Bobby becomes the new DCI, the fun and games are over. Even more nervous are the companies that relied on us to fix things for them overseas. The whole set-up would collapse if Bobby Kennedy was put in charge.

"John Kennedy now had a better understanding of our tactics. With Mac Bundy's treachery, he also knew that members of his own administration had loyalties other than to him. Averill Harriman helped pick the Kennedy cabinet. He had been a business partner with Allen Dulles. Another of Dulles's close friends was Douglas Dillon, the Secretary of Treasury. Dillon had served as Ambassador to France for John Foster Dulles when he was Eisenhower's Secretary of State. Dillon was a Wall Street guy who was part of the Dulles inner circle. Mac Bundy was Kennedy's Director of National Security. His brother, Bill, was an Agency guy. That's how it works.

"Allen Dulles had placed loyal members of his own team in every branch of government, including state governments and even police departments. Roscoe White, who fired the fatal shot from behind the picket fence in Dallas, was Agency. He had joined the Dallas Police Department two months earlier as part of a liaison program between the CIA and metropolitan police departments. White was a sharpshooter. He was trained to kill people. He and Oswald had gone through Marine training together and both had been recruited for intelligence work. Dulles didn't miss a trick. His moles were everywhere. All along the line there were

14

* Roscoe white killed Kennedy

cut outs so these guys couldn't track back to the Agency. This probably wasn't what Harry Truman had in mind when he set up Central Intelligence after WWII. We had no accountability. The Company answered to no one. Except maybe our wealthy corporate benefactors. We would politely decline to provide information to Congress by saying that it would compromise our National Security."

Jim coughed and spit into the water. He tapped a Pall Mall out of the pack and fired up his lighter. It was hand-carved ivory and more elegant than anything else about the man. I glanced over at the red gas tank a few feet from where he smoked. I just shook my head. It would be a waste of time to point out the danger. Jim was totally caught up in his story. The boat could have been on fire and he would be talking about Allen Dulles.

As we passed through the narrows between Finley Point and Bird Island, I cut the throttle to trolling speed and started to get the fishing gear ready. I baited a hook and threw the spinners over the side. Jim looked less than excited as I handed the pole to him. He was fighting some unknown war in the Congo. He finished his cigarette and flicked the butt far onto the water. I baited my hook and threw the line over the opposite side of the boat. There we were. As unlikely a pair as ever set sail on Flathead Lake. As we trolled toward Wild Horse Island, the sun was getting hot on the back of my neck. Jim was determined to continue the discussion, with or without my participation.

"Kennedy knew he'd been set up at the Bay of Pigs. The guy was a lot more mentally tough than you might think. He fired Dulles, Cabell and Bissell. These guys were icons in intelligence circles. Sacred Cows. This was strike two for Kennedy within the military establishment. Kennedy made one of his typical smart-ass remarks to the effect that if this was Great Britain, his government would be out, but this was the United States, so you three are out. I'll tell you, this did not sit well with the Director and General Cabell. These guys were lifers. They'd lost their titles, but not their power. They continued to maneuver within the Agency. The only difference was they didn't show up at the office. There was a continual stream of us going to Dulles' estate for briefings. He had worked too hard to establish the power of the Company to let Kennedy destroy everything.

"Kennedy said he was going to scatter the CIA to the winds. He realized how powerful and out of control we had become and he was going to put a stop to it. There was the rumor that Bobby would be the new DCI in their second term. That would be the end of our free hand overseas. Believe me, Dulles was as emotionally tied to the Agency as Hoover was to the FBI. The CIA was his lifetime achievement. He was not about to let Kennedy destroy it.

"When Kennedy began to make peace overtures to Khrushchev and Castro, everyone within the loop agreed that he had become dangerously soft on communism. It almost became our patriotic duty to stop him. When he signed an order to begin withdrawing military personnel from Vietnam and indicated that he would undertake a full withdrawal after his re-election, our defense contractors were running scared. We had this massive military apparatus in place after Korea. We needed an outlet for all that

16

hardware. Vietnam was our best hope. Some of our close associates would go belly-up if the Vietnam effort were to end. A lot of Americans would be out of work. It was bad for America and bad for business. Patriotism has always been profitable. That was H.L. Hunt's favorite saying.

"Both of Kennedy's kids had birthdays coming up after Dallas," Jim stared off toward the trees. "That bothered me for awhile. It probably shouldn't have, but it did. Dallas was just business. Like the other EAs. Maybe because he was Irish. I don't know. Maybe that's why Dallas bothered me for quite a while. Shooting a man down in the street before a crowd of people. It was a bold move. The finality of it wasn't lost on Lyndon Johnson, either. He was very cooperative with us for the next five years. Don't screw around with the Company and don't cross the Military.

"We lost 50,000 men and half a trillion dollars in Vietnam. Remember that interview at the LBJ ranch with Walter Cronkite shortly before his death? LBJ said that he thought that a rogue element of the CIA had been involved in Kennedy's murder. This was a former president talking. Someone with access to the most sensitive information. Don't you think this was quite a revelation from the man that the assassination put in the White House? He knew what the hell he was saying. He was letting us in on a secret. A few years later, Dan Rather is back on the air saying Oswald did it. He knows better.

"Most of our goons were in a mood to celebrate after Dallas. Sturgis and that bunch. Alpha 66. Sociopaths, if you want the clinical term. One of our pilots in Dallas was a guy named Chuck Rogers. He was from

17

Houston. Very bright guy. Genius type IQ. Chemical engineer, I believe. He fronted with Shell Oil while he did contract work for us. After the assassination, he went home to Houston and was confronted by his elderly mother about the phone bill for the month leading up to the assassination. She thought it was very suspicious and threatened to go to the authorities. So Rogers kills his mother and father in a bloody rage. He hacks them up and packages their remains and stores them in the refrigerator. I'm not kidding. It was weeks before they were found. Of course, Rogers was long gone. He knew we would cover for him. He was a damn good pilot. Besides, there is no more dedicated employee that one who has nowhere else to go. That's why we liked to use the Cubans. They were men without a country. They had no choice but to do what they were told."

THE BEAST

I watched an osprey with its huge wings laboring as it flew back to its nest on Rocky Point with a good sized fish. At least somebody was having some luck. Jim and I had not had so much as a nibble. He looked like a lost soul as he stared across the lake. His wheezing and coughing were not encouraging. The palms of his hands were a light purple. Probably bad circulation. I had no idea why he was so determined to discuss his intelligence background. Maybe it was the end of the line and he needed to get rid of some baggage. I was a sophomore in high school when John Kennedy was shot. Thirty-five years later, the events were still surprisingly clear in my mind. It seemed like the mood of the country had changed after Kennedy was killed. I began to appreciate the fact that I was fishing with a man who might have some answers.

"What really happened in Dallas?" I pressed the issue.

"I'll get to that," Jim sounded irritated as he waved me off with his left hand. "You can't understand Dallas until you understand what preceded it," he paused and spit into the lake. "About the time WWII was ending, a German general named Reinhart Gehlen, who was in charge of Nazi Intelligence, sent word to Allen Dulles, who was head of OSS operations in Europe, which he would surrender to Dulles and turn over a dossier with profiles of his top agents throughout Europe and Russia. To Dulles, this was an Intelligence coup. A chance to greatly broaden our intelligence capabilities. So he met with Gehlen and the two of them flew directly to Washington. Shortly after that, we began to blackflight German intelligence officers, scientists, doctors and psychologists to the United States. We would provide them with new identities as refugees from Lithuania or Latvia or some other Eastern European country and place them in safe-houses. This was a sensitive matter because some of these Nazis could have been prosecuted as war criminals. Among them were doctors and psychologists who had conducted experiments on the Jews. These Germans were filtered into jobs with government hospitals, state mental institutions, even universities. Dulles never agonized over moral questions. This was high stakes poker and he always dealt from the bottom of the deck.

"Dulles saw these Nazis as a valuable resource. Nothing more. He later used Gehlen to set up espionage behind Soviet lines. Gehlen helped instigate the Hungarian uprising in 1956. Power and expediency were the cornerstones of any correct foreign policy. I think Dulles admired the Germans. They were forceful and decisive. The Director used to ridicule Kennedy and his Harvard pals, as he called them, for wasting so much time debating the morality of foreign policy issues. He thought they were soft. Make the tough decision and carry it out efficiently. It was as simple as that. Nixon understood. Dulles thought Kennedy had

20

no backbone for the tough decision, but I would have to disagree.

"Everywhere Kennedy looked he saw the need for change. Who, but a cocky young Irishman, would prosecute the mob on a scale that no one has ever dared? He made mortal enemies in H.L. Hunt and Clint Murchison and the rest of the Texas billionaires when he threatened to cut their fat twenty-seven percent oil depletion allowance. Kennedy publicly called it a subsidy for the wealthy. He pissed off the steel companies when he went on TV and criticized them and forced them to roll back their prices. These were heavy hitters with a lot of clout and they were lining up against JFK. He alienated most of the South when he became the first president since The Civil War to enforce civil rights laws. His people went through the South and encouraged minorities to register to vote. This had all the earmarks of a populist uprising.

"It's the same reason that the Shadow Elite set out to destroy Bill Clinton after he was elected. The thing the Blue-bloods of Banking and Industry fear most is a popular president who has the ability to rally support for causes that are unprofitable. Remember Clinton's early push for national health care? The only way you are going to have universal health care is to control the rising costs in the health industry. The American Medical Association and the pharmaceutical companies and the insurance boys didn't like that idea too good. So here comes Richard Chafe, a wealthy Virginia publisher. He sends a couple of his lawyers out to Arkansas to dig up anything they can on the Clintons. After mucking around in the garbage for a few months, they come up with Paula Jones and Whitewater. The

Obama could do
the same thing with
the Oil Co's... on the price of gasoline!
If he wasn't afraid to."

idea is to compromise the president. Take his focus away from national health care and the like. And don't think for a minute that Monica Lewinski was an accident. She was nothing but a tool like our boys Lee Oswald and James Earl Ray. Linda Tripp was her handler as sure as I'm sitting here. Tripp had high level clearance with the Department of Defense. But I'll have to say we are getting more civilized. Clinton had only his character assassinated. He also showed plenty of bad judgment which made the job a lot easier.

"Kennedy made his biggest mistake when he openly threatened to destroy the CIA. He began by firing our top men. Then there was the rumor of Bobby as the new DCI. But what got him killed was his decision to pull out of Vietnam. That was strike three. The Cold War meant billions of dollars to those of us in the defense establishment. We weren't going to let this rich kid destroy everything we stood for. Too much of our economy depended on keeping the Cold War in high gear. Not even Lincoln had made as many enemies as John Kennedy did in his first three years in office. If one is to be judged by the caliber of his enemies, Kennedy would rank right up there. He was going to do what he thought was right and damn anyone who got in his way. He seemed totally unconcerned about his own safety. He was very cavalier about it. That's why he made such an easy target. I've always had this nagging feeling that he sensed his life might come to a violent end."

There was no action from the fish. Probably too hot. I suggested that we reel in and have some lunch. I opened the thermos of iced tea and poured us each a tin cup full. I handed Jim a ham sandwich. He did not seem to care if he fished or ate. He just stared past me toward the blue Mission Mountains to the east.

"You think Kennedy knew he might be killed?" I tried to keep up my paltry end of the conversation.

Jim nodded slowly. "A man who feared for his safety would not have taken on so many enemies. Kennedy had some serious physical problems. He had a chronic bad back that he had injured in college. He also had Addisons Disease or some dysfunction of the adrenal glands which required constant medication. He had already cheated death several times. Certainly in the South Pacific. His PT-boat was cut in half by a Jap destroyer. The thing exploded in flames. They swam five miles to a small island. Kennedy towed one guy with his teeth. They held out for several days, but no one came looking for them. They were given up for dead. The other boat that had witnessed the explosion couldn't believe anyone had survived. Kennedy couldn't stand to lay around on that island so at night he swam through those shark waters to look for help. He found two natives and carved a message on a coconut shell and convinced them to take it to his outpost. Sounds unbelievable. Ask the men of Kennedy's PT-boat crew if he was a coward.

"John Kennedy seemed like a guy who was in too big a hurry to worry about inconsequential things like his health or safety. As President, he had become obsessed with world peace. This put him on a collision course with The Beast. He was in constant turmoil, even with members of his own administration. He was often a minority of one in his effort to make peace with Russia and not to get involved in Vietnam. He said in his second term that a lot of people might hate him, but

23

he didn't care. He had a plan that he thought would make life better for most Americans and he was determined to see it through. I doubt that he gave too much consideration to growing old. He and his wife were building a new home in Virginia at the time of his death. He talked about publishing his own magazine when his presidency was over. Or maybe return to Congress like John Quincy Adams. Mostly, he wanted to make his contribution as president. He wanted to be known as the man who had kept the peace. That's all. He had big plans for his second term when he wouldn't have to worry about being re-elected.

"When Harry Truman signed the bill that created Central Intelligence, he thought we would be an information gathering agency. Allen Dulles, Gordon Gray and Bob Lovett had another idea. They lobbied hard to keep the clandestine option alive. That was the only way they could set up a private military force with secret funding from their benefactors. Our activities couldn't be controlled by the president or congress. The Beast won that round and our country was changed forever. The powerful group of businessmen that Allen Dulles represented had formed a parallel government with its own foreign policy, it own budget and its own private military. To his dying day, Allen Dulles thought he had done this country a great favor when he built the power of the Agency. Even though Americans had no idea of our fun and games overseas, Dulles thought he was acting in our best interests. A very paternal attitude. Maybe arrogant is a better word. He and his brother had all the answers. Two very self-righteous men.

"When Eisenhower was elected in 52, Allen Dulles was appointed as Director of Central Intelligence. His brother, John Foster Dulles, became Secretary of State. Along with Vice President Nixon, they conducted their own foreign policy. Poor old Ike was usually the last to know what was going on. Nixon was right up to his eyeballs with our covert operations. Like I said, Nixon was The Black Heart of the Beast during that era. He was not at all reluctant to have people killed. It became an early option with any uncooperative foreign leader. In the time I had been with the Company, Executive Action had gone from last resort to early option. Nixon always wrapped himself in patriotism with that tense smile, but he was the most ruthless opportunist that I have ever known. He was absolutely desperate to get ahead by any means available. He figured that the Agency would be a valuable tool on his journey to the top so he ingratiated himself with us at every turn. We fit like spoons. Our goals were his goals. His enemies were our enemies. I'll tell you, Nixon and the Dulles brothers were a deadly combination in those days. Ike didn't stand a chance.

"Do you remember the U-2 incident? When Gary Powers was supposedly shot down over Russia? This will give you an idea how the military boys had their own agenda. On May 1, 1960, Eisenhower was meeting with British Prime Minister Harold MacMillan at Camp David. Charles De Gaulle had just left Washington for Paris. They were preparing for a peace summit with Khrushchev that was to take place in two weeks. Ike, the old warrior, wanted to move toward ending the Cold War before he left office in January. He, better than anyone, knew that an arms race was not the answer. He had forbidden that we undertake any reconnaissance flights over the Soviet Union or do anything that might jeopardize the upcoming peace talks. The problem was that Nixon, the Dulles brothers and Richard Bissell had a plan of their own.

"While Eisenhower was concluding talks with MacMillan, Gary Powers left Turkey for Norway on the longest spy flight ever attempted. His fuel tanks were full. One look at the huge droopy wings would tell you that. What Powers didn't know was that he didn't have enough raw hydrogen. It was necessary to mix the hydrogen with jet fuel at such high altitudes. Powers had only enough raw hydrogen to make it half way across Russia. That's exactly what happened. His engines quit and he had to glide down in wide circles and then parachute to the ground. If his plane had really been shot down at such a high altitude, he wouldn't have survived, and the plane would have disintegrated.

"There was another surprise. It was against regulations to carry any kind of military identification on a spy flight. Anybody knows that. A plane on such a sensitive mission, against the expressed orders of the President, would have been thoroughly sanitized so that we could claim that it was a civilian weather flight. That was absolutely basic. When Powers was captured in Russia, his plane was carrying several pieces of military ID. Why? It was totally against policy. I will guarantee you that Powers was not aware of any identification on that flight. Years later, Allen Dulles admitted in a congressional hearing that Powers had not been shot down. He admitted it was engine failure. The American people have never been told the true story. It's the way they dumb us down. Why was this flight set up to fail? Why was the Bay of Pigs set up to fail? War is money.

"Our Shadow Government had its own agenda which had strictly to do with profits. The answer is simple. We needed an international incident of sufficient proportions to ruin the upcoming peace talks. If the Cold War ends, the cash dries up. It's as simple as that. Imagine the news in Russia when they captured an American spy pilot on May Day! That's the Soviet version of The Fourth of July. Later I saw pictures of the plane. There were no signs of bullet holes or rocket fragments. It was in fairly good shape. At the time, we didn't know Powers was alive. We released a statement that a high altitude weather research plane was missing and might have violated Soviet air space.

"Khrushchev was waiting in the weeds. Old Hog Jowls had us by the nuts. We didn't know that Powers had been captured. It was unlikely that he would have survived a crash from that altitude. On May 7th, a week after the plane had been lost, Khrushchev announced that the pilot had been captured and was in good health. Then he did a very strange thing. He gave Eisenhower a graceful way out. Khrushchev said that it was possible that the American President might not have been aware of the spy mission. He said that he thought that elements within the CIA might have wanted to sabotage the upcoming peace talks. He suggested that if this was the case, the American President could show good faith by firing some of the Agency hierarchy. It seems that the Russian Premier had a better grasp of what was going on than Ike did.

"Eisenhower stood behind The Agency. He should have done what Kennedy had to do a year and a half later. He should have canned their asses right then and there. Cut loose those arrogant bastards. The U-2 incident was the primary reason why Ike warned the American people about the growing power of what he called the military-industrial complex. The Beast. In other words, the old general could clearly see that those who made their living from the Cold War were running their own foreign policy."

FUN AND GAMES

Jim finally finished his sandwich. I had never seen a less enthusiastic eater. It was like work to him. You could see by the way his clothes fit so loosely that he had lost a lot of weight. His old leather belt had been cinched up three notches. I guessed he was in his mid-seventies. The fishing was a lost cause so I suggested that we go take a look at the Indian petrogliphs on the other side of Wildhorse Island. I told him that we could pull the boat right up next to the drawings. Jim's sickly eyes stared blankly at me. I was pretty sure that I hadn't broken his train of thought. I eased open the throttle. The breeze in my face was refreshing.

"You've read about that forty-year civil war that ended a few years ago in Guatemala? We started that sonuvabitch in 1954. It was our first major success in this hemisphere. This will give you a little more insight into the Dulles Brothers. A guy by the name of Jacobo Arbenz had just been elected. Unlike so many Latin American leaders, he decided that he wanted to better the lot of his countrymen. Eliminate a little poverty and malnutrition. Big mistake. Take the corporate bribes and don't screw with the system. Why stir up trouble when you can be a wealthy man? Dress in tailored suits, lie your ass off and then move to Europe when your term in office is over. Like most countries south of the border, a few people control all the wealth. Hell, who am I kidding? It's gotten that way in this country. Ever see so many people living on the streets? Twenty years ago there was no such term as homeless. A few bums and hobos was all. Now look at them. In some parts of town, the vehicle of choice is the shopping cart. Tell those folks how well things are going these days. But try to raise the minimum wage and some politicians will squeal like stuck hogs. They'll give you eighteen reasons why we can't pay a person a living wage.

"Land reform was the obvious solution in Guatemala. The problem was that not only did United Fruit own most of the land; they owned the railroads and the telephone lines. To make matters worse, John Foster Dulles, our Secretary of State, was a major stockholder in United Fruit. The wife of United Fruit's PR Director was Eisenhower's personal secretary. See how the game works? Walt Bedell helped us plan the coup and he later turns up on United Fruit's Board of Directors. This is how the Good Old Boy Network operates. It's an inside game. If you're on the inside, the Agency is at your disposal. If you're an outsider, you spend most of your time trying to sort through the layers of disinformation. All that's required to become part of The Beast is to sell your soul.

"Anyway, Arbenz decides to build his own power plant and some new roads to reduce his country's dependence on United Fruit. He draws up a plan to nationalize Guatemala's resources and he offers United Fruit a settlement. By all accounts it was a pretty fair offer, but United Fruit was highly offended. This was their land and railroads and telephone lines. Throw in the dirt cheap labor and everything was fine. This was the way things worked in the Third World and this guy, Arbenz, had better get used to it. United Fruit had just about had their fill of democracy in Guatemala. As a token gesture, they offered to deposit a large sum of money in a Swiss bank if Arbenz would agree to step down. Arbenz was a proud man. He wouldn't go for the deal. He stood his ground. This set the wheels in motion.

"We begin to work behind the scenes with a few corrupt right-wing generals. Slip them a little cash and these guys would turn on their own relatives. I remember a guy named David Phillips, who later became head of intelligence in the Western Hemisphere. He spoke up at a meeting and asked if we could overthrow a democratically elected government. That caused smiles around the room. Of course we could. Arbenz would not listen to reason. That meant he was a communist and had to be removed. That's always been our position.

"We got our great and good friend, Cardinal Spellman, to contact Archbishop Arellano in Guatemala. Shortly thereafter, a pastoral letter was read in all the Catholic churches that called for parishioners to rise up against Arbenz, who we called the 'Communist Devil.' You mix a little patriotism with religion and you're hard to stop. Two months later, we start bombing the National Palace, government fuel tanks, ammo dumps, airports, etc. Make it look like a major rebel uprising. When Arbenz went on radio to rally the people, we jammed his broadcasts. Then we put out false reports that a rebel army was advancing on Guatemala City. This was excellent theatre. We

31

created stories about mutilated journalists and other atrocities committed by the Arbenz Government. It was convincing as hell. Nixon's old buddy, Howard Hunt, was right in the middle of it. He later liked to take credit for the whole operation. Like Teddy Roosevelt at San Juan Hill.

"Now it was time for our bribed military generals to come to the fore and convince Arbenz to resign. This opens the door for our new hand-picked guy, Castillo Armas, to take charge of the government. As a final touch, we take foreign journalists on a tour of the National Palace where we've planted all sorts of Russian and Chinese communist literature. They took the bait. There was righteous indignation in the reports that they fired off to their editors. The operation was a fine success all around.

"To solidify his position, Armas arrested many of those on the suspected communist list that we provided for him. He tortured and killed a good many of them. United Fruit was given their land back. The Banana Workers Union was broken. Some of the union organizers turned up dead. Armas then abolished all opposing political parties and imposed strict literacy requirements. Kind of like we've always done in the South. This effectively eliminated most Guatemalans from voting. Armas then shut down the newspapers and burned subversive books. The killing went on for about forty years. United Fruit was back in business and there wasn't a communist in sight."

As we neared the east end of Wildhorse Island I could see the fallen down remains of the old lodge. A stone fireplace stood prominently amongst a pile of gray boards.

"Mind if we stop?" Jim motioned toward the shore. "I've gotta take a leak."

I looked for a place with gravel to land the boat. I found a good beach a couple hundred feet past the ruins. I eased the boat into the gravel and then hopped out to throw the rope around a drift log. I could still feel the vibrations from the outboard motor in my right arm as I helped Jim out of the boat. He seemed weaker than when I had met him the day before. His hand was cold and had very little grip.

"They used to run ferries out here in the thirties and forties," Jim explained. "They had dances on Saturday night. Hiawatha Lodge, I think they called it."

I walked up the shore to look at the fallen down remains of Hiawatha Lodge while Jim took care of his business. When I got back, he was sitting on the bleached white log as he smoked a cigarette.

"Sorry to hear about your uncle," he said flatly as he stared at the east shore of the lake.

I had driven up to Montana earlier that week for my Uncle Al's funeral. The June weather was so nice that I had decided to spend the rest of the week at my grandfather's old cabin on Finley Point. The boat and all the fishing gear were still in the boathouse. While I was trying to get the old Evenrude started, Jim had wandered over and introduced himself.

"You knew Al?" I was surprised to learn that this old CIA man had known my uncle.

"I knew all the Solanders. Vic and I rodeoed together. That's how he got that bad scar on his lip. A saddle bronc kicked him square in the face. Al was younger, but I knew the whole family."

"I guess it's the passing of a generation," I explained. "Al was the last of the kids. He was always an entertaining guy to be around. I went fishing with him up at Lone Pine Reservoir one time, and he bet a guy in Red's Bar twenty bucks that we'd catch a dozen fish. By late afternoon, I think we'd caught seven pike. So we're walking back to the car and Al sees a kid down the shore and walks down to talk to him. All I see from a distance is Al take out his wallet and hand the kid some money. Then the kid hands Al a string of fish. When Al catches up with me, he's got that big red-faced grin on his face and he says, "Spending five dollars to make twenty has always been good business."

I looked sideways at Jim. For the first time in two days he showed some emotion in the form of a weak smile. He pulled out his pack of Pall Malls and offered me one. I hadn't smoked a cigarette in years, but I thought I'd better have one with the old guy.

"I knew your father too," Jim said as he lit my cigarette. "We went through ROTC at Fort Missoula together. He was a very amusing guy. Academically, he said he always strived for 'a gentleman's C.' Most of his energy was devoted to the girls. Typical Irishman. He called your mother his Sunday night girl, meaning he would take her someplace respectable like the movies. He was a pretty decent welterweight. Couldn't punch worth a damn. He liked to show off his footwork and his jab. He was a southpaw as I recall. I saw him play drums at Yellowstone Lodge one summer. He was no Gene Krupa, but he beat on them pretty good." Jim laughed and spit off to the side.

"You spend much time in Montana?"

34

Jim shook his head, no. "I've known the Mosebys for years. Eileen was your mother's best friend when they were kids. She was a foreign correspondent until recently. She once interviewed Oswald in Russia of all things. I ran into her at a cafe in Paris in the late sixties. She was a nice looking woman. When the doctors gave me six months, tops, I figured this was a pretty nice place to spend some time."

I loaded Jim back into the boat. We made our way around the north side of the island. Some gray clouds had formed over the west shore as we approached the cliffs with the petrogliphs. As near as I could tell, the pictures seemed to depict a hunting party that got caught in a thunderstorm. I let the boat idle in along the rocks. Jim wasn't the least bit interested in the paintings. As we left the west shore of Flathead Lake, Jim continued to educate me about the abuses of his former employer.

"Here's some background to understand what happened to Kennedy in Dallas. Those of us who know about these things aren't talking and I won't be around much longer. What I told you about Guatemala was by no means an aberration. A Company guy I had known for years told me that he drove around the Congo for several days with the body of Patrice Lamumba in the trunk of his car while he looked for a safe place to dump the corpse. In fact that's where I got this lighter. Charlie brought it back from Africa."

Jim handed me the hand-carved piece of ivory with a bowl large enough to hold a metal lighter. There was a detailed elephant head carved on each side. Most of the ivory had turned a light brown with age and some of the features were worn smooth.

"They were afraid that some journalist would see how badly Lamumba had been mutilated. He was the first elected Prime Minister of the Congo and he was so popular that we knew if he was deposed, he was sure to resurface. We were confident that Tshombe would allow us access to the minerals we wanted in Katanga. We were already entrenched there with the British and the Dutch. Tshombe was greedy and therefore controllable, but he was hated by his people. We were spending over a million a day fighting that civil war to prop him up.

"After Mobutu took over, Che Guevara was fighting on the side of the rebels. We came up against that guy all over Latin America and even in Africa. Chuck Rodgers said he was there when we caught up with Guevara in Bolivia. His hands were cut off before he was killed. Souvenirs for somebody back at Langley. If the truth was known, I think everyone at the Agency respected that guy. We hated him but we respected him. In hindsight, he truly was a freedom fighter. Anyway, Mobutu became probably the richest man in Africa while his people rotted in poverty. You wonder why Americans are hated in some parts of the world. The American people had no idea what the Company was doing in these Third World countries, but the poor bastards who suffered the consequences sure knew what was going on.

"The Shah of Iran was another dandy. He was a privileged man who was well hated throughout his country. When Mossadegh was elected and decided to nationalize Iran's oil fields, the Shah fled to Europe. The big losers in Mossadegh's plan were the British oil companies. We came to their assistance so a precedent would not be set in the Middle East. We bribed students and created riots and helped orchestrate Mossadegh's overthrow. We then brought the Shah out of hiding, but he was so unpopular that we had to set up a secret police to protect him. The SAVAAK developed some of the most creative torture techniques that we've ever seen. Like the human hot-plate where the interviewee is strapped to a slab of metal that is equipped with heating elements. Very few detainees remain silent when their flesh begins to sizzle.

"Maybe one of the most offensive stories I ever heard was told to me by one of our Cubans who had witnessed the incident. We had a station chief in Montevideo, Uruguay, named Dan Mitrione. Good Italian boy. Former police chief from somewhere in Indiana. Anyway, he taught torture techniques in the soundproofed basement of his home. He would find homeless men on the outskirts of the city and use them in his seminars. The Cuban told me that he watched Mitrione hook up four of those poor beggars to demonstrate how much electricity a body can tolerate. He killed each one of them in turn. Of course they were nameless indigents who were never missed, but that was the mindset at the Agency. We could dress up an atrocity in terms of making the world safe for Democracy. It always had more to do with keeping a corrupt or unpopular regime in power.

"Whenever you hear that we're giving economic aid to one of these small countries, it usually has to do with training their police in interrogation and torture techniques in order to prop up our man in office. These days most of it is handled through the DEA. I believe that Uruguay still has prisons full of political prisoners.

That's the only way to prop up a phony government. A group of rebels finally caught up with our boy, Mitrione. I think they made a movie about the guy. He was a real American hero. I heard that Frank Sinatra sang at his funeral. No kidding.

"To show you the cost of doing business in the Third World, we dumped twenty million into the 64 election in Chile to try and stop Salvador Allende. We used every tactic imaginable including letters from the Pope. We had posters made up showing children with a hammer and sickle stamped on their foreheads. Subtle stuff like that. The problem with Allende was his push to redistribute the wealth in Chile. Sound familiar? Two percent of the people own all the wealth. Numbers like that might appeal to the Shadow Elite, but Allende had a medical background and all he saw was malnutrition. I remember a cornerstone to his campaign was to provide milk for every child in Chile. Well, this was communist as hell. To accomplish his objective, he would have to nationalize the country's mineral resources. Anaconda Copper was not amused. Nor was IT&T.

"A helluva lot of American cash was made available to try and defeat Allende. President Nixon told Dick Helms, who was CIA Director at the time, in no uncertain terms, that assassination was an acceptable alternative. If a simple killing could accomplish their goal, it was a small price to pay. Why not? It had worked in many countries including our own. Nixon's entire career was paved with the bodies of his enemies. Allende was just another name on the list.

"We put Chile's economic balls in our corporate vice and tightened down hard. We closed off their seaports so no food could get in. Starvation is a powerful tool. Unrest is guaranteed. Riots, violence and finally, the military coup. I think Chile was one of the low points for the Agency, but Nixon and Kissenger were very satisfied with the result. I've heard there are half a million retarded Chileans due to malnourishment during that blockade.   Allende never had a chance. He had a simple goal of feeding his people, but you don't take on Anaconda Copper and IT&T. After the coup, we kept the country sealed off for about a week so the executions could be done properly."

THE PLOT

I'll have to admit I was getting a little depressed by these stories. I didn't question Jim's inside knowledge about these sinister affairs, but his sledgehammer approach had kind of worn me down. Enough. I get the point. I looked over my shoulder to the west. The sky had gotten much darker. A strong wind had started to kick up a few whitecaps. I realized that unless we moved as fast as this little trolling motor would take us, we might be in trouble. Flathead Lake can get dangerous in a hurry. When we cleared Wildhorse Island and got out into the open lake, the waves were considerably larger. Fortunately we were going with the wind and moving about as fast as the waves. It occurred to me that we might have a problem when we tried to turn south through the narrows with the waves hitting us broadside from the right and the rock cliffs to the left. If we were lucky enough not to get swamped, we might still get carried into the rocks.

I studied Jim's face. He was completely unconcerned. The noise from wind and the waves hitting the boat had cut short his dissertation. As we approached Bird Island, I could see the spray from the waves blasting against the rocks to the west. It began to seem foolish to try and get through that narrow strip of water. I decided to head straight into the gravel bank on Bird Island. It was mid afternoon. If the storm passed, we would have time to reach our cabins before dark.

I slowed the engine and tried to ease in, but a wave turned us sideways and rolled us onto the bank. As I helped Jim out of the boat the rain let loose. We were drenched before we could make it to the trees. I went back and secured the boat the best I could by pulling it up on the gravel and lashing a rope around a small stump on the shore. I reached under the bow and got the canvas tarp that we used to cover the boat. It had ropes on all four comers and I thought we could fashion some sort of shelter with it.

As I made my way into the trees toward Jim, I heard the first crack of thunder to the west. Being under a tree in a lightning storm wasn't recommended, but we had little choice. If we went to the other side of the small island, the woods might block some of the wind and rain.

I finally got the four ropes tied to trees with the back ropes lower so the rain would run off behind us. The lake in front of us had three or four foot swells and was all whitecaps. We got settled in and Jim offered me a cigarette. This time I felt like I needed one.

"This thing isn't going to get over any time soon," I stated the obvious.

"Are you with me so far?" Jim hammered away.

"The truth is there were damn few small countries where we didn't get involved. It was always about making the world safe for American corporations. That was precisely our function. The formula was always the same. If you wouldn't do business with us, you were communist and you were in trouble. The Dulles brothers got the Beast moving and it's been stirring up trouble in these small countries ever since.

"In the mid-fifties, Cambodia was thought to be important enough that both Dulles brothers paid a visit to Prince Sianouk. They tried to bring him into the fold by forcing him to accept SEATO protection. Sianook was a Buddhist and wanted to remain neutral. Big mistake. We eventually closed off his borders and began bombing raids which forced him to accept aid from Russia and China. While we were planning his overthrow, Ike was honoring him in Washington with a 21 gun salute. Two foreign policies. One public, one private. Two governments. One public, one private.

"The Cold War was the golden goose for those of us in the defense business. There were fortunes being made across the country. Any serious defense cutbacks would have resulted in corporate failures and huge layoffs. A good part of our economy was dependent on defense spending and still is. We could not let Jack Kennedy kill the golden goose. Or Martin Luther King. Or Bobby Kennedy. Or the United States Congress for that matter.

"Consider what happened in 1983. I was retired by then. Congress was in a mood to make substantial cuts in defense spending. There was a thaw in the Cold War and Congress intended to turn more of our resources toward domestic problems. Then a Korean jetliner with about 300 aboard was reported missing near the Soviet island of Sakhalin. The first reports said that it had been shot down for violating Soviet air space. Japanese radar had tracked the passenger plane until it disappeared near Hokkaido, far from Sakhalin. Japan immediately sent out twelve rescue vessels. Japan has state of the art coast guard craft. Best in the world. While they were closing in on the location, the Agency sent a message to Seoul and Tokyo that the plane had landed safely on Sakhalin Island. The Japanese called back their rescue boats. By the time the Agency announced that the plane had indeed gone down in the deep waters of the Kurile Trench, it was too late to search for survivors or the aircraft itself.

"The next thing you know our Secretary of State, George Shulz, goes on national TV and berates the Soviet Union for shooting down the passenger plane. The Russians deny everything. For the next week, all you hear is sabre rattling about the Evil Empire. Americans are angry as hell. We see it as a despicable act by a country that will never be civilized. The thaw in The Cold War is over. Congress falls in line and passes the largest peacetime defense department budget in history. Reagan signs the bill, and we're back in business.

"I'll show you how confusing these events can be to outsiders. Georgia Representative, Larry McDonald, had been on that flight. The evening the plane went down, a State Department official had phoned McDonald's family and assured them that the plane had landed safely on Sakhalin Island and passengers and crew were safe. Their information was based on the Agency's first report and was nowhere near the truth. Two questions. Why would the Soviet Union risk war with the United States to shoot down a defenseless passenger plane? Why would the Agency put out a false report that the plane had landed safely?"

We used the lifejackets as headrests as we waited out the storm under our canvas shelter. The lake in front of us was very rough. The sound of the wind through the trees was interrupted only by an occasional crack of thunder. I commented on how clean the air smelled as Jim offered me a Pall Mall. I was now a chain smoker.

"Oswald was the perfect fall guy. Lonely kid. Broken home. Fairly bright. Took the military seriously. Always followed orders. Read everything he could get his hands on. It wasn't that he didn't like people, but he would rather spend his time reading. It's funny. The marines that were interviewed by the Warren Commission said he would spend entire days on his bunk reading. The one thing that all these marines agreed on was that Oswald was not a violent person. They also agreed that he was a very poor shot. How about that? The man accused of killing the President and a police officer was described by his fellow marines as a passive guy who liked to read books. No matter how clever we were in our attempt to frame him, you cannot change the essential fact that Oswald was not the type of individual to shoot anyone.

"When a kid enters the Marines with a thorough knowledge of Marxism, Naval Intelligence takes notice. After it was determined that Oswald was loyal to our country and he would follow orders, he was recruited for intelligence training. In 59, we had a defector program run by Bill Harvey, I believe, that we ran in conjunction with ONI. We would give them language training and provide them with a background that the Soviets might consider useful. In Oswald's case, we stationed him at Atsugi Air Base in Japan which was a take off point for our U-2 fights over Russia. Oswald was a radar operator who had access to codes that would be useful to the Russians. When he defected to the Soviet Union a year later and the codes were verified by Russian Intelligence, we simply changed the codes.

"The Russians soon discovered that Oswald would be of little use to them, so they put him to work in a factory in Minsk. That's where he met Marina. When we called him back in the summer of 62, the Russians were happy to be rid of both of them. The fact that a defector who had given military secrets to the Soviets could return to this country so easily tells you all you need to know about Oswald's connections. The State Department even loaned him money for his return trip. Here's something you've never heard. Over the next year, Lee Harvey Oswald paid back every cent he had borrowed from the State Department in forty and fifty dollar amounts. Does that tell you something about his reliability? If he really had defected and given classified information to Russia, he could have been shot for treason. Instead, we provided him with money for his trip home. Was he detained or debriefed when arrived in The United States? Absolutely not. Instead, he was turned over to George DeMohrenschildt.

"We called DeMorhrenschildt, 'the Chinese.' He was one of those charming and intelligent guys who seemed comfortable in any social situation. He was like Allen Dulles in that regard. He had worked with the Nazis in France during WWII. I believe his father had been an officer in Czar's army in Russia. Very colorful background. Spoke several languages. Anyway, DeMorhrenschildt had settled in Dallas. He ran some of Clint Murchison's businesses and was an asset of the

Agency. He led a group of White Russians in Texas who were violently anti-Communist. This was the group that embraced Oswald the defector and his Russian wife. This would be a contradiction if these people were not aware that Oswald had been on a government assignment and continued to work for us.

"It was about this time that the FBI recruited Oswald as a security informant. That sounds odd, but there were many of us at the time who were working both sides of the street. It was a chance to pick up two paychecks. It was also a way for Hoover and Dulles to keep an eye on each other. There was never any love lost between those two. Oswald was given an FBI number and was paid about two hundred a month to report on activities of communist groups, Cuban revolutionaries, etc. At the same time, he was on our payroll on a contract basis. That is why his tax returns were classified and never made public. If Oswald was what we said he was, why would his tax returns be classified? They would be a matter of public record. It's not necessary to ask the tough questions. Start with the easy ones. Why were Oswald's military records destroyed after his arrest in Dallas?

"In the spring of 63, Oswald was sent to New Orleans to be handled by Guy Bannister. He was supposed to infiltrate pro-Castro Cuban groups. With Oswald's communist credentials from his stay in Russia, it should have been an easy fit. While Oswald thought he was gaining information for the Company, we were sheepdipping him as a Castro sympathizer. It's a world of mirrors. Up is down, right is left. As an operative, you have no idea who you're working for or what the objective is. You learn to follow orders and not to ask too many questions. That was Oswald. The New Orleans assignment was certainly no more unusual than his trip to Russia. By hooking up with Bannister, he ended up right in the middle of Operation Mongoose which was our latest attempt to assassinate Castro.

"After the Cuban Missile Crisis, John Kennedy promised Khrushchev that the United States would end our attacks on Castro and Cuba. That was the official policy. The Agency had its own plan. Operation Mongoose was so secret that President Kennedy was not informed. It was centered in New Orleans. It was run by Ed Lansdale and supervised by Clay Shaw. It was a continued attempt to train Cuban exiles to overthrow Castro. This same apparatus was used in Dallas in the fall of 1963. Planned by Lansdale, funded through Clay Shaw, directed by Guy Bannister, Howard Hunt and David Phillips. The focus was merely shifted from Havana to Dallas.

"Despite the new directives by the President, the Agency maintained camps in Florida, Louisiana and Guatemala where we continued to train Cuban mercenaries. The operation reminded me years later of Iran-Contra. In both cases, the CIA decided that it knew more than public officials. Mongoose and Iran-Contra were illegal operations in total disregard for public policy. In 1963, Claire Booth Luce, who had befriended young Kennedy when he was trying to publish his first book, was sponsoring raids on Cuba in total disregard for President Kennedy's orders. It's bizarre and confusing. That's why nobody has ever put it all together. We called it the onion skin theory. You have to peel away so many layers of disinformation that you never arrive at the truth.

47

"So Oswald was turned over to Guy Bannister in New Orleans. Bannister was a hothead who had been forced to retire from the FBI for drunkenness or violence and now had a private investigation business in New Orleans. He was our gun running conduit to the Cuban rebels in that city. He also oversaw a training camp at Lake Pontchartrain. He had been with Naval Intelligence during WWII and had also been an asset of ours over the years. He was an ultra-right winger who we could count on. Bannister was involved with the John Birch Society and the Minutemen. He also published some racist magazine. If there was one person who hated everything that John Kennedy stood for, it was Guy Bannister.

"Bannister staged several incidents that summer that would later convince the American people that Oswald truly was a communist. We had Oswald arrested while handing out leaflets for The Fair Play for Cuba Committee. We had him appear on a radio talk show defending Castro's brand of socialism so the record could be used to incriminate him after the Kennedy was killed. Oswald thought he was establishing his credentials as a Castro sympathizer for a later assignment in Cuba.

"Late that summer Ruth Paine shows up in New Orleans to pack up a pregnant Marina and her daughter and move them to her home in Dallas. An awfully nice gesture, don't you think? Especially when you consider that it was a two bedroom house which meant that Mrs. Paine would have to share a bedroom with her children. That's a true friend. Drives all the way to New Orleans as a humanitarian gesture. Actually, she was returning from the East Coast where she had received updated instructions. To make things more cozy for Marina, Mrs. Paine's husband moves out so that Marina can have a little more elbow room.

"Ruth Paine had graduated from an eastern language school where we recruited people for intelligence work. It was necessary at the time of the assassination that we have a secure place to plant incriminating evidence against Oswald. It was in the Paine's garage that they found that silly picture of Oswald with his communist paper in one hand, his Mannlicher-Carcano rifle in the other hand and a pistol strapped to his waist. We didn't do a very professional job of superimposing Oswald's head on the body in the picture because we had shadows going in different directions. In another picture, we used the same head but the body was at a different distance. It looked pretty odd. A third pose showed up in Roscoe White's possession after his death. His was the body beneath Lee Oswald's head.

"Dulles and Lansdale were pretty sure that the American people would buy our story. For the most part, they have. It makes it much easier when we have a fraud like Dan Rather who is willing to go on the air every few years and look the American people square in the eye and assure them that all the evidence still points only to Oswald. That guy has made a living by misleading the public ever since he rushed onto the air out of breath after viewing the Zabgruder film. He described the President's head as being violently thrust forward from the impact of the fatal shot. In truth, Kennedy's head snaps violently backward at the point of impact. Rather figured that the Zabgruder film would never see the light of day. It wouldn't have if it had not been subpoenaed in New Orleans by Jim Garrison.

"When Oswald returned to Texas, the stage was pretty well set. Ruth Paine, always the helping hand, suggested that he get a job at the Texas School Book Depository. Oswald must have felt a great deal of gratitude toward Mrs. Paine as he moved those heavy boxes around for a buck and a half an hour. Dealey Plaza was an absolutely perfect ambush site and now we had our fall-guy in place.

"As soon as Kennedy's visit to Texas was made official, we began to apply the finishing touches. In fact, it was at this time that Ed Lansdale retired from his career in intelligence work to devote full time to Dallas. Also, Roscoe White shows up in Dallas to join the police force. Actually, we had looked at Chicago and Miami where we could expect cooperation from Sam Giancana and Santos Trafficante, but when Oswald got the job at the book depository overlooking a perfect ambush site, everything shifted to Dallas.

"That spring we had mail ordered the Manlicher-Carcano rifle and the .38 revolver to a post office box in Dallas under the alias of Alik Hidell. Oswald knew nothing about this. Why would he incriminate himself by mail ordering guns when he could walk into any sporting goods store in Dallas and buy them under a fictitious name? And he probably would have chosen an accurate weapon without a defective scope. As a matter of fact, in a rapid fire situation, there would have been no time to use a scope. These are the small details that the official version has chosen to ignore.

"In November, we shifted into overdrive to frame Oswald. We had a guy in Dallas named John Masen who was an absolute dead ringer for Oswald. He had a sporting goods business and he'd been involved in gun running activities with Jack Ruby. He was probably the guy that several people mistook for Oswald in the Carousel Club. He had sold a lot of guns to Manuel Rodriguez and that Alpha 66 bunch. They kept the cache of weapons at Rodriguez's place on Harlandale Avenue. Masen went to Downtown Chevrolet and posed as Oswald to test drive a car. He told the salesman he'd be coming into some money soon. When he was quoted a price, he blew up and said maybe he should buy a car in Russia. A car salesman would tend to remember an incident like that. Then we had Masen at a firing range shooting at another man's target saying that he was practicing for Kennedy. Then our boy shows up at Redbird Airport trying to rent a plane for a flight out of the country. Lansdale wasn't looking for subtlety. He wanted a pile of circumstantial evidence.

"We had Loren Hall take Masen to visit Silvia Odio, who was well known in anti-Castro circles, and introduce him as Oswald. Later, Hall tells Odio that Oswald said the Cubans had no guts or they would have already killed Kennedy. At this exact same time we have Chuck Rogers, who resembles Oswald but is considerably smaller, in Mexico City going back and forth between the Cuban and Russian embassies trying to get a visa to return to Russia by way of Cuba. Rogers argued with a woman in the Cuban consulate who later refused to identify Oswald even though she was under considerable pressure to do so. She kept insisting that the man she had argued with was a smaller man who stuttered. Our boy Rogers. The reason the Agency couldn't release pictures of Rogers going into the embassies was that he was an asset of ours.

"We had Oswald getting a scope mounted on a rifle that already had a scope. We had him trying to get a firing pin repaired. We had him cashing checks and bragging that he would soon come into a large sum of money. The impersonations were a bit heavy handed and sometimes we had Oswald in two places at once, but Landsdale felt that the weight of evidence would bury Oswald. He was correct until all the independent researchers began to pick apart our story. Overall, it was a pretty clever setup.

"While Masen and Rogers were busy impersonating Oswald, the real Oswald was attending meetings of the John Birch Society, the Minutemen and dissident Cuban groups. He was reporting back to Central Intelligence and the FBI as he was paid to do. As Kennedy's visit grew closer, Oswald's warnings to the FBI and the Agency became more frantic. He even sent a telegram to the Secretary of the Navy. In early November, Oswald hand delivered a detailed plan of the assassination to James Hosty at the Dallas FBI office. He had one detail wrong. He thought the ambush site would be the Trade Mart where Kennedy was to speak at a luncheon. That's where most of the Dallas cops were on November 22nd. Imagine Oswald's surprise when Kennedy was shot in front of the building where he worked.

"At the time of the shooting, Oswald was in the second floor lunchroom waiting for a call from Howard Hunt, who was his handler at that time. They had met two weeks before and Oswald had tried to impress upon Hunt that there was a very real chance that Kennedy could be shot in Dallas. What Oswald didn't know was that Hunt was doing everything in his power to assure the success of the assassination.

"Oswald never got the call that day. When his boss rushed in and told him that the President had been shot, Oswald knew he was in danger. He knew too much about the plot. It was prearranged that if anything went wrong, he was to meet Chuck Rogers at the Texas Theatre. Rogers would provide him with cash and fly him out of the country. That's why Oswald made the Thursday night trip to Irving to see his wife. The next morning he left his wedding ring on the dresser. He knew if he left the country, he may never be seen again. That's what Lansdale wanted. The suspect apparently flees to Cuba with all the circumstantial evidence left behind. The American people would demand an invasion of Cuba.

"Oswald was probably at the Texas Theatre at the time J.D. Tippet was shot. He made one big mistake. He called too much attention to himself as he hid in doorways and then went into the theatre without paying. Waiting in the alley behind the theatre was Assistant District Attorney Bill Alexander and three Dallas cops who had been bought off by Jack Ruby to silence Oswald. That was the backup plan if Oswald refused to go with Rogers. That idea fell apart when so many police officers surrounded the theatre. The last thing Lansdale wanted was for Oswald to be paraded in front of the news media where he could proclaim his innocence. At this point, Oswald feared only the group behind the assassination. He knew he was in danger, but he did not realize that he was the fall guy.

"When Oswald was arrested, he was still trying to protect his cover as an agent for us and an informant for the FBI. When he was charged with the murder of a policeman and, later, the President, he must have been tempted to spill his guts. Imagine if he had given his FBI informant's number and disclosed his history with the Agency. Still, he protected his intelligence background. That was ingrained in him. He was smart enough to know that it would be difficult to convict him of two crimes that he did not commit, and he probably thought that the government would have to come to the aid of someone who possessed so much sensitive information. He had no idea that he had only two days to live."

It was getting dark. The rain had stopped, but the lake in front of us was still whitecaps. To the south we could see the lights of the small town of Polson. Along the east shore there was the occasional light from a cabin. We had settled into our makeshift tent. I was the original captive audience. The storm had let up, but Jim hadn't. It was odd to consider that the man who was supposed to have shot John Kennedy might have been the guy who was trying the hardest to prevent his death.

THE PLOTTERS

It was peaceful as we lay under our canvas shelter and smoked Jim's Pall Malls. The sound of the waves was quieter. They lapped the gravel shore as the lake became calmer. The wind had stopped and there was nothing but the sound of crickets and frogs. Jim produced one pack of cigarettes after another from his jacket and we fired them up with his fancy ivory lighter. As I listened to his deep, raspy voice, I remembered listening to radio dramas as a kid. The clomp of cowboy boots on the board sidewalks of Dodge City was much more impressive than watching Gunsmoke on television. I was beginning to buy into Jim's story. It all sounded crazy at first, but he had no reason to misrepresent the facts. His accusations were as uncomplimentary to himself as anyone else. The size of the thing was hard to accept as well as the involvement of our own government.

"The money for Dallas was put up mainly by H. L Hunt and Carlos Marcello. Clint Merchison and Santos Trafficante also chipped in. Dulles always said we were nothing more than an agency. We acted on behalf of our clients. In this case, our benefactors were oilmen, mobsters and the military industry. We would assist them with our covert apparatus. Calvin Coolidge used to say, 'The business of America is business.' This was pretty much the case in the removal of John Kennedy.

"In 1963, H.L. Hunt was the richest man in the world. If ignorance is bliss, he might have also been the happiest man in the world. A billionaire with a fifth grade education. If you went to the far right of the political spectrum, H.L. Hunt would be a little to the right of that. If you weren't white and Texan, you were probably a communist. He funded the John Birch Society and the Minutemen. Most of the Dallas cops were members of one or both. Hunt also funded a weekly radio program that ran throughout the South. The show spent most of its time railing against the Kennedys and Martin Luther King. It was an earlier version of Rush Limbaugh. Mindless, bigoted stuff. Hunt genuinely felt that King and the Kennedys were communists. He believed they were a real danger to this great country that had made him so wealthy. He really felt he was doing all of us a favor in Dallas. The cheap s.o.b. actually took his lunch to the office in a brown paper bag. A billionaire with a sack lunch is a dangerous man.

"Hunt was head of the Dallas Citizens Council where he would hand pick candidates for sheriff, mayor, police chief, etc. The way they kept everyone in line was a low salary plus bonuses. If you cooperated with your masters and were willing to do their dirty work, you could expect a sizable bonus at the end of the year. If you were too independent, you might be laid off or terminated. Roger Craig was the deputy sheriff in Dallas who insisted on telling what he knew about the Kennedy assassination. He wound up dead.

56

"Hunt was a cantankerous sonuvabitch and nobody crossed him. A few days before the assassination, he said that the only way to get those traitors out of office was to shoot them out. He wasn't kidding. The day of the motorcade, his son ran a full page ad accusing Kennedy of treason. Hunt feared no reprisal. A regular visitor to his ranches in Texas was our old pal, J. Edgar Hoover. After the assassination, Hoover flew H.L. Hunt and General Walker out of Dallas, supposedly to protect them against death threats. It's more likely that Hoover was afraid that the old man might say something that might get them all in trouble.

"Hunt was Lyndon Johnson's primary money backer throughout LBJ's career. When Kennedy won the presidential nomination in 1960, Johnson's lifelong presidential aspirations were gone. Finito. As a peace offering, Kennedy offered Johnson the vice presidency. Johnson wanted no part of it. Who in his right mind would give up a powerful position like Senate Majority Leader for a crappy job like vice president? If Kennedy won, Johnson would be too old to run in 1968. Besides, Bobby would be waiting in the wings.

"Enter the crusty old billionaire. He took Johnson aside and more or less forced him to accept the vice presidency. Hunt explained to a very depressed LBJ that many presidents had failed to live through their term in office. From that moment the idea of getting rid Kennedy became an option. That's the only way that Hunt could convince Johnson to accept the vice presidency. The Kennedys were shocked when LBJ accepted. They were sure he would turn it down. The positives for Kennedy were that Johnson could help them in the South and Mike Mansfield would become

57

Senate Majority Leader. John Kennedy had a very high opinion of Mansfield, and he thought he was the perfect guy to help JFK pass his domestic programs.

"Clint Merchison held a party the night before the assassination. A gathering of snakes. Nixon was there. J. Edgar Hoover was there. George and Prescott Bush were there. After the Kennedys had retired for the evening in Fort Worth, Lyndon Johnson joined the group. They all met behind closed doors. Everything was in place. None of these men were involved in the organization of the plot, but they had an idea what was about to take place. Each of them would benefit greatly from Kennedy's death. The next morning, Nixon was off to New York. Hoover left for Washington. Hoover had just finished lunch when he learned of the assassination. The first person in Texas that he called was George Bush.

"Merchison was an old wildcatter who made fortune moving oil illegally across state lines. He had done business with Carlos Marcello in New Orleans and Jimmy Hoffa in Chicago. George DeMorhrenschildt oversaw his business interests in Haiti. Oilmen. Mob. Agency. These people made their own rules. The Beast was a strange combination of forces that wanted to make sure that our system served their own interests. They would eliminate anyone who stood in their way, here or abroad.

"Merchison owned a resort called Del Charro near San Diego. He also owned Del Mar Racetrack . Every summer, Hoover and his companion, Clyde Tolson, would spend a month as guests of Clint Merchison. Everything was on the house including the boys that were brought to them. Merchison used to say that money was like manure. Spread it around and good things happened. He could certainly breathe easier about all his illegal business deals when he owned a piece of the FBI.

"Carlos Marcello had more personal reasons for sponsoring Kennedy's murder. He had been in a two year battle with Attorney General Robert Kennedy. Bobby was trying to deport him, and it had gotten real nasty. At one point, Bobby had Marcello plucked off the street in New Orleans and dumped in Guatemala. From there he was taken on an all day bus ride and dropped off in the mountains of Honduras. He was lucky to make it out alive. Broken ribs. Dehydration. He was very pissed off at Bobby Kennedy. When he got back to New Orleans a few months later, his criminal empire was a mess. The territory ruled by Marcello included Louisiana and Texas. Jack Ruby worked for him. Marcello was supposed to be worth a couple hundred million dollars. This was in 1963. He was determined to keep the Kennedys from deporting him. As he told one of his goons, if you cut off a dog's tail, the head can still bite you. But if you cut off the head, the tail will quit wagging. This was in Sicilian, but the idea was that if they killed Bobby, John Kennedy would avenge his death. If Giovanni was killed, Bobby would lose all his power under Lyndon Johnson.

"Marcello put up two million dollars for the hit on Kennedy. It went through Clay Shaw. He was the Agency cutout in New Orleans. If the plan fell apart and Shaw was eliminated, nothing could track back to the Agency. Shaw was also on the board of directors of Permendex which was a Swiss corporation that laundered money for the Agency and the Mob. It sponsored assassinations of foreign leaders who got in the way of our right-wing agenda. There were a half-dozen attempts made on the life of Charles DeGaulle. Like Castro, he managed to survive. Clay Shaw was the guy Jim Garrison went after several years later in New Orleans. Garrison was very close to solving the case, but the news media picked up our bait and portrayed him as an egomaniac who was starved for publicity. We tried everything imaginable to discredit the guy.

"Santos Trafficante was the biggest loser when Castro threw the mob out of Cuba. He still controlled Florida, but Cuba was everything from gambling to drugs to laundering money. The mob had funded both sides of the revolution in Cuba. They wanted to be in good favor with whoever won. They had no idea that Castro would go communist and throw the Yankees out. Trafficante was desperate to get back into Cuba, and John Kennedy's new hands off policy was unacceptable to him.

"Another factor involving Marcello, Trafficante, and Sam Giancana was Bobby Kennedy's vendetta against Jimmy Hoffa. Kennedy was fully aware of Hoffa's misuse of the teamsters' pension fund and was determined to put him away for racketeering. These mobsters and guys like Clint Merchison benefited from Hoffa's liberal loan policies towards his friends. They had a rooting interest in seeing him stay out of prison. There was a consensus that Kennedy had to go. Months before Dallas, Trafficante was telling his associates not to worry. Kennedy was not going to make it to his re-election. He was going to be hit.

"By involving the Mob and the oilmen, we had our onion skin working. First we blame Cuba and Russia because of Oswald's ties to those countries. With luck, we invade Cuba and step up the Cold War against the Soviet Union. You peel away that layer and you have the Mafia. It was important to have Jack Ruby and guys like Jim Braden on the scene. The next layer was the Texas oilmen which would also point the finger at Lyndon Johnson. If Johnson had been involved in the plot, would he have wanted it to take place in his own back yard? The final layer would be that a rogue element of the CIA had acted out of hatred for John Kennedy over the Bay of Pigs and had acted without knowledge or approval from Langley. By the time Americans peeled through these layers of disinformation, the perpetrators would be long gone. The murder of President Kennedy would be nothing but an historical footnote."

I excused myself and walked partway around the island and relieved myself. It seemed like I had been on this little piece of land for weeks. I took some cold lake water in my hands and threw it on my face and neck. It sounded like every frog in Lake County was trying to talk at the same time. There were no longer any lights from the cabins along Finley Point. I figured that it must be after midnight. The sky had broken up. What looked like a full moon was trying to break through clouds.

As I inhaled the clean air and watched the sky, I remembered my father telling me about something that amused him in a poem by Omar Khayyam. A character by the name of Diogenes was walking through the center of town in the middle of a bright, sunny day and he was carrying a lantern. People shied away as he passed by until one individual had the nerve to ask him what he was doing with a lamp at midday. " I'm looking for an honest man", Diogenes replied. Maybe that was Jim Quinn. Maybe he was the last honest man who was willing to talk about the Kennedy assassination.

When I got back to the shelter, Jim was stretching his legs down by the lake. The old guy was tough as nails. He was sick and exhausted, but he was determined to finish his story.

"You think I should try to start a fire?" I suggested.

"Hell no," Jim cut that idea short. "You might burn down the whole island. It'll be daylight soon enough."

"It's not that cold out," I backed away from my fire suggestion.

"It doesn't get any better than this," Jim rolled his shoulders inside his jacket as he stared out at the lake.

I was happy for Jim and his jacket, but I had on a damp t-shirt and it was getting chilly.

"Allen Dulles was the key," Jim said with his back to me. "Without his approval, it never would have happened. Our group in New Orleans never would have gotten involved. Even though he'd been fired by Kennedy, he still was a force within the military industry. He was on a first name basis with all the eastern bankers going back to his days as a Wall Street lawyer. He had established a powerful network, and he was at the center. There must have been a consensus among the Shadow Elite that Kennedy was a threat to their best interests. A consensus that he had to go. When Dulles gave Ed Lansdale the green light, things began to fall into place. Lansdale was a creation of

Allen Dulles. He'd been recruited from a successful run as a Madison Avenue advertising executive. He was steeped in the art of deception. What better guy to work up a cover story when there was a government in need of overthrowing. Lansdale was the best, and Allen Dulles trusted him like a son. When we were setting up Magsaysay to take power in the Philippines after WWII, Lansdale actually staged battles in villages where the Huks would be driven off by the government soldiers. It was like a damn movie the way he set it up. He was very creative and Dulles loved him for it.

"Lansdale was in Vietnam from the get go. In 54 he helped set up the Saigon Military Mission which gave the Agency a good foothold in Vietnam and allowed us to help defeat the French at Dien Bien Phu. This was the start of our involvement. We moved in with an almost unlimited amount of money and supplies in support of whatever group we wanted to see in power. We escalated the conflict and then asked the Department of Defense for support. Vietnam started out as a clandestine CIA operation and grew out of control. The benefit to those inside the military loop was that we spent billions of dollars in Vietnam. Finally our country wouldn't allow us to spend any more money or sacrifice any more men. It was an unwinnable civil war, but it was good for business for the thirty years that it lasted.

"Anyway, Lansdale helped orchestrate the election of Diem in 54 in the brand new country of South Vietnam. We knew for certain if the elections were held in all of Vietnam, Ho Chi Minh would have won in a landslide. He was a student of our history and our constitution, and he was very respected. He would have done a fine job as President of Vietnam, but we needed a war. Korea was over, and the military hardware was stacking up. We finally forced Ho Chi Minh to seek aid from Russia and China in order to survive. We dropped more bombs in that war than in the history of all wars combined. We cleared out millions of acres with herbicides like agent-orange. I can't believe that anything will grow there today.

"Incidentally, Eisenhower was against the introduction of our military in Vietnam. So the Dulles Brothers again had to work their magic behind the scenes. Before public life, Allen and John Foster Dulles were Wall Street lawyers, and they answered to a higher authority than presidents. To these supremely arrogant men, a president was merely a nuisance. Someone you paid lip service to while you concentrated on making the world profitable for your close circle of friends.

"By coincidence, the same day our Cuban brigade was slaughtered at the Bay of Pigs, General Lansdale initiated his counterinsurgency program in Vietnam. At the time, all we had over there were Green Berets, Army Special Forces, and Air Commandos who were training Diem's military. It was at this time that Kennedy sent National Security Action Memo 55 to his Joint Chiefs of Staff making them responsible for all covert military operations. The order basically stripped the Agency of its authority to conduct clandestine operations. This sent shockwaves through the Pentagon. It was a whole new ball game. No more secret operations. Those who had benefited from overthrown governments around the world did not like these restrictions.

"Three weeks before Kennedy was killed in Dallas, Diem and his brother were killed in Saigon. Diem had not successfully rallied his country in the war effort against the North. It was decided that General Mihn had more popular support, and he would replace Diem. Kennedy was told that the Diem brothers would be flown to safety in France. Instead, they were murdered in their palace. I'm told that when Kennedy heard that the Diems had been killed, his face turned white. He had no stomach for murder. Political chicanery and affairs with women, but not murder. On the other hand, Nixon did. He had helped plan a number of Executive Actions when he was Vice President.

"Lansdale's last slight of hand in Vietnam was the removal of the Diem brothers. I had had a long talk with Lansdale about Vietnam about a year earlier. He told me the most effective interrogation technique he had developed was to take a group of Vietnamese up in a helicopter and throw them out one at a time until someone talked. He thought it was amusing. That's what this type of work can do to you over a period of time. One month before Kennedy was killed, General Lansdale retired from his distinguished intelligence career so he could devote full time to Dallas. It was essential that nothing go wrong at Dealey Plaza. Had John Kennedy survived, Bobby would have destroyed us."

DEALEY PLAZA

The east shore of Flathead Lake was completely dark. It was lonely being stranded on that small island while everyone else had gone to bed. It had gotten colder. I had no trouble staying awake as I was freezing in my damp t-shirt. Jim had painted a disturbing picture of how the forces around Allen Dulles had decided to eliminate John Kennedy. I had waited more than twelve hours to find out what had really happened in Dallas, so I put the question to Jim.

"Who all was involved in Dealey Plaza?"

Jim lit his cigarette and slowly blew out the smoke.

"Ask yourself this. Why was the group from Fort Sam Houston asked to stand down? Normally they would have provided protection along the parade route. Why were the only available Secret Service men in the car that followed the President? Why was there no Secret Service presence along the motorcade route? Why hadn't the Secret Service ordered that windows along the route be shut? Why had the Secret Service agreed to a last minute change in the route requested by Major Cabell? It was against regulations to make that hairpin turn from Houston onto Elm Street. The President's car would have to slow down to about ten miles per hour. He was a sitting duck.

"The Dallas Times Herald had printed a map of the motorcade route that showed the parade going straight down Main Street and onto the Stemmons Freeway. If you look in the Warren Report, that part of the page is blacked out. How would a lone assassin know that there would be a last minute change that would bring the President beneath the building where he worked? For that matter, how would a team of assassins know about the last minute change that would bring the President into their crossfire?

"Who was in charge of the Secret Service at the time? The Secretary of the Treasury. Who was the Secretary of the Treasury? Douglass Dillon. Who was Douglass Dillon? A Wall Street banker who had served as Ambassador to France for John Foster Dulles and had become part of Allen Dulles' inner circle of powerful friends. Why was the Secret Service so negligent in their protection of John Kennedy in Dallas? Because Allen Dulles had someone in place who could compromise the Secret Service.

"Several days before the motorcade, Police Chief Curry had driven Secret Service Agent Sorrels on the motorcade route. Curry had insisted that the best location for the luncheon would be the Trade Mart which was larger and more modern than alternative sites. It would also take the motorcade through Dealey Plaza where the ambush would take place. When Curry and Sorrels reached the corner of Main and Houston, Curry pointed ahead and said, it's all freeway from here. Instead of turning right on Houston as he would when he lead the motorcade on November 22nd, Curry turned left and back to the police station.

"They had to bring the motorcade under Oswald's window. If you ever visit the Texas School Book Depository, look down from the sixth floor window. As you look up Houston Street, John Kennedy would be coming slowly toward you at point-blank range. It would be an easy shot. If you missed, you would have time for a second shot. Why would Oswald wait until the limousine was halfway down Elm Street where his vision would be blocked by trees? There's no way he would have waited. He would have taken the easy shot. The reason that the shooting didn't start until the limo was part way down Elm Street was that was where Kennedy was in the crossfire of our four shooters.

"Oswald had been told to wait in the second floor lunchroom for a call from Howard Hunt. Hunt was stationed in Mexico City at the time, but he was in Dallas to oversee the operation. There was no margin for error. We had our best people on hand.

"Oswald was told to expect a call at 12:15. We needed Oswald to be isolated. Unfortunately, one of his co-workers saw him eating his lunch shortly before Kennedy was shot. Needless to say, the call never came. When Oswald heard that the President had been shot in front of the School Book Depository, he must have been afraid for his safety. He had given warnings to Hunt. He might have started to realize that he was being set up. All his warnings had been ignored and the President had been shot in front of the building where he worked. He knew Ruby and Roscoe White and some of the other plotters. He now thought they were his main danger. If anything went wrong and his cover was in jeopardy, Hunt had told Oswald to go to the Texas Theater where Chuck Rogers would provide him with money and fly him out of the country. This is exactly what Oswald did.

"On the sixth floor of the book depository, our old friend, John Masen, was posing with a rifle so he could be seen by people waiting for the motorcade. When the President turned onto Elm Street, Masen fired a blank to get everyone's attention. This was the signal that set our four teams in motion.

"Team one was on the second floor of the Dal-Tex Building directly behind the limousine. Our Cuban shooter had a .30 caliber M-1 equipped with a silencer. His position was a side window where he would not shoot directly over bystanders. He would have been too obvious if he shot from the front window. We knew nobody waiting to watch the motorcade would be standing on the side street. A silencer or suppressor was necessary so that shots would not be heard from that direction. The problem with a suppressor is that it reduces the speed of the bullet. Each of our shooters had a spotter with a radio. All agency and Cubans.

"Team two was on the sixth floor of the book depository, at the other end of the building from Oswald's window. We wanted shots coming from that location, but we wanted a better angle than we could get from Oswald's window with the trees in the line of vision. A fatal shot from that location would have been ideal. It would have made the frame-up on Oswald much easier. Shooter number two had a Mauser with open sights. This was a weapon similar to the Mannlicher-Carcano, but it was much more accurate and reliable. The first weapon found in the book depository was actually the Mauser. A deputy named Roger Craig made himself very unpopular when he kept reminding investigators that the first rifle found in the book depository was a Mauser. The problem with this location was still the obstruction from the trees.

"Roscoe White stood behind the crook in the picket fence. He was in police uniform so he would not attract any attention. Sergeant Patrick Dean protected his back. White was our best sharpshooter. He would have the best possible shot with his high velocity pistol. We couldn't have a rifle barrel sticking over the fence. It would have been too awkward to get into position. This was pistol range. Probably no more than thirty yards and almost level ground. White was an Agency sniper who we used before and after Dallas. He did a lot of clean-up work for us. Damage control, we called it. Like I say, he was in uniform that day. No one is going to question a police officer behind that fence. White had come down from Chicago two months earlier and joined the Dallas Police to teach surveillance techniques and help root out subversive elements. Dulles had set up this program so the Agency would have its own people working inside these city police forces. White was a deadly shot. He had a calm temperament.

"In a storm drain farther down and behind the fence was little Chuck Rogers. In addition to being a mathematical genius and an ace pilot, he was also a crack shot. He could have succeeded in almost anything he wanted to do, but I guess he had been rejected by the girls so he joined our little group of misfits and psychopaths. His lower body was in the storm drain as he aimed through an opening in the fence. He would have to wait for the limousine to clear the fence and a row of trees before he would have a good look. Rogers also had an M-1 with a silencer. He was too close to the bystanders on the railroad bridge for the muzzle blast to be heard. He was our last opportunity if Kennedy had not been mortally wounded.

"Each shooter could only count on one good shot. Secret Service Agent Kellerman might throw himself over the President. The driver would be expected to accelerate which would make a second shot unlikely. The crossfire was to commence when Kennedy reached the Stemmon's Freeway sign next to the sidewalk. They took the sign down after shooting. Supposedly there was a bullet hole in it. That would have been hard to explain.

"Roscoe White shot early because he was about to lose Kennedy behind the sign. His shot hit Kennedy in the throat. Then the other three fired. Our Dal-Tex sniper hit Kennedy in the back. The wound did not penetrate more than a few inches due to the reduced velocity with the silencer. Shooter number two shot from the book depository and hit John Connelly in the shoulder. Rogers had to contend with the corner of the fence and a tree. His shot might have hit the edge of the freeway sign. Kennedy had survived our best volley. He had been hit in the throat and the back, but he was definitely alive.

"What happened next was kind of surrealistic. Instead of roaring off to safety, Kennedy's driver put on the brakes. Agent Kellerman sat dumfounded. When Agent Ready jumped off the backup car, Agent Roberts ordered him back. What the hell was going on? Two cars back, Lyndon Johnson was already covered and protected.

"Kennedy's steel back brace held him upright. Since the driver had nearly stopped, there was time for a second volley. Dal-Tex had to shoot over the Secret Service Agents who stood on the running boards of the car behind Kennedy. He missed high and hit the curb near the triple underpass. A fragment hit a bystander named James Teague. Our book depository shooter led Kennedy too far and hit Connelly in the wrist. Roscoe White's shot was point blank and hit Kennedy in the right temple. That frangible bullet at such close range caused the President's brain to literally explode. Blood and brain matter left the back of his head with such force that Bobby Hargis thought for a minute that he had been hit. Hargis was the motorcycle officer to the left rear of the limousine. Rogers never had to fire his second shot.

"That was it. One blank. Seven shots. Three with silencers. If Kennedy would have slumped over after the first volley, he would have lived. His back brace got him killed. Along with the slow reaction from the Secret Service and the unbelievable mistake of his driver.

"We had our own Secret Service impostors all over the railroad yard and behind the Dal Tex building and the book depository. Sturgess and his bunch. Bernard Barker. Alpha 66. None of the shooters would be taken into custody. We didn't have to worry about that.

"Sheriff Decker wasn't in on the plan. He was kind of a loner who we couldn't count on. He ordered all of his available men into the railroad yard, but we had blocked the radio transmission. Just like Guatemala.

"There was one order of business left. We wanted to implicate Oswald in a second murder.

"J.D. Tippit was sacrificed for two reasons. We wanted to divert attention away from Dealey Plaza. What better way to do it than with the shooting of a cop? We also knew that if it appeared that Oswald had killed a cop, it would be much easier for the public to believe that he had killed the President. Circular logic, Lansdale called it. If Oswald hadn't shot the President, why would he shoot a cop? If a man would shoot a cop, he would also be capable of shooting the President. Oswald was the patsy. Tippit was the sacrificial lamb."

Jim walked to the lake and flipped his cigarette into the water. He looked worn out. His boney shoulders slumped badly. He had been talking all day and halfway through the night. He was sick and tired, but he was determined to tell his story. I wondered why no one else in his line of work had the same need to talk. In Jim's case, time was running out.

MARY

I was listening to the birds when I opened my eyes. It was beginning to get light outside. I looked over at Jim. He was snoring with his mouth open. His pale skin was pulled back so I could see the outline of his skull. The old guy was near the end. I wanted a cigarette, but I didn't want to wake him. I had become tobacco addicted in one day.

I quietly got to my feet and walked into the trees to take a leak. I could see that the boat had been pushed sideways up on the bank. I looked it over and saw no damage. I started to bail the rainwater out of the boat with a coffee can when I saw Jim approaching through the woods.

"I couldn't sleep," he said as he watched me bail out the boat.

"You could've fooled me," I said.

"I might have dozed off for a minute," Jim conceded. "You think it'll start?"

I looked at the two oars inside the boat. The thought of rowing that boat across Polson Bay was depressing. We had gotten a couple hours of sleep and my energy was pretty low. The story Jim had told also made me feel lousy.

"It's hard to believe that they killed the President and got away with it." This time I brought up the subject.

"I've thought of a hundred things that might've gone differently," Jim sounded tired. "If he hadn't worn that back brace, he might have slumped forward and not been hit with the second round of shots. If Mayor Cabell hadn't been able to get away with the change in the parade route. If Kennedy's driver had reacted quicker to the gun shots. If he hadn't gone to Dallas in the first place. If the whole city wasn't in H.L. Hunt's back pocket. If General Cabell's brother wasn't the mayor. If the Secret Service had taken normal precautions. If most of the agents hadn't stayed out drinking the night before, they might've reacted faster to the first gun shots. If the rain hadn't stopped that morning, they would've used the bubbletop on the limo.

"Who the hell am I kidding. There was a contract on John Kennedy in 61 when he visited deGaulle in France. They had given the job to an asset named Luis Romero. The idea was to make it look like deGaulle was the target with Kennedy hit by mistake. French security was too tough and Romero backed out. They would've gotten Kennedy somewhere else. He never would have lasted through a second term. "

I finished bailing out the boat. "I hope this damn thing kicks over," I muttered as I got ready to yank the starter cord. I can't describe the relief I felt when the motor started on the first pull. It seemed like a good omen.

We loaded up the canvas tarp and the life jackets and eased the boat toward the narrows. The outboard motor had a beautiful sound as I pointed the boat toward the cabins. We paid little attention to the early fishermen as we crossed the calm lake. The sun had not yet cleared the blue mountains to the east. I thought Jim had a peaceful expression as we slowed toward the dock.

The stale air of my grandfather's cabin never smelled so good. Jim and I drained a pot of hot coffee as I made some hotcakes with bacon and eggs. I found a jar of homemade raspberry jam in the cupboard, and we had ourselves quite a meal. Jim thanked me as we went outside to smoke a cigarette. We placed two wooden lounge chairs in the morning sun facing the lake.

"Mary loved this place," Jim began in a low tone. "She was here twice. She'd talk about this lake to anyone who would listen. The way the evening sun reflects off the water. The sound of the waves when you go to sleep at night and the first thing you hear when you wake up in the morning. The smell of the evergreens after a rain. She was an eastern girl, Boston Irish, and she thought this place was heaven. We talked about moving out here, but I guess we were settled in Virginia.

"She always wanted me to quit the Agency. She didn't know that you don't quit the Agency. It doesn't work that way. When you're involved, you're useful. When you're not involved, you know too much and you're a liability. Like any other business, the Agency liked to reduce its liabilities. Only in this case, the liabilities are people. It was very difficult to leave the Agency. They watch you carefully even when you retire.

"You heard the news about former DCI, William Colby? He disappears while rowing on Chesapeake

Bay. They called it an accident. Possible, but unlikely. There was one oversight. The first thing Bill Colby did every morning was raise the American Flag in front of his house. On the day he disappears, he forgets to run up the flag. Very unlikely. Like any former intelligence chief, Colby had a lot of baggage he carried around. Dirty laundry. I think he was due to testify in front of a congressional committee.

"Remember when Bill Sullivan had a falling out with Hoover and quit the FBI? He was quoted in the press saying very uncomplimentary things about the Bureau and Hoover's failure of leadership. I think he was also due to testify. Maybe the Church Committee. Sullivan was also working on a manuscript and he supposedly had left the Bureau with a truckload of documents. He had handled the Oswald matter for Hoover after Kennedy's death. He was a danger not only to the FBI but the CIA as well. That fall, Sullivan was killed in a hunting accident by the son of a New Hampshire state trooper. He was mistaken for a deer.

"Mary didn't understand all that. I never burdened her with the details of the job. She knew some of what we did was unpleasant, but her faith in me never wavered. My faith in me did, but hers didn't. You couldn't break her spirit. She was one of those people. Upbeat. Full of hope. The only time I really saw her down was when she found out she couldn't have children. It took her a while to get over that.

"She used to say there are money people and there are people people. You were one or the other. You either put people first or you put money or material things first. She worried that the wealthy were becoming genetically inferior. She thought there might

77

be a little too much inbreeding among the rich. What was needed was an infusion of that good peasant stock. Mary and I were both first generation Americans and she placed a high value on our hard working ancestors. The 'salt of the earth' was what she called honest, hard working people who accepted their responsibilities without complaint. What I'm trying to say is that Mary didn't have much use for the lazy or the greedy.

"She had a sister, Kathleen, whose husband inherited a lot of money. After a few years, Kathleen told Mary that money was a curse. She said she missed the struggle when going out to dinner or buying a new couch meant something. She said that she even found herself treating people differently. As if they were there for her comfort and convenience. Mary said she would like to try it for awhile and decide for herself. She was just being sarcastic. She didn't put much value on material things. She spent most of her time worrying about the underdog. That's why she liked Kennedy. Plus being from Boston. She was sort of bitter after he was killed. An Irishman finally gets to the top and seems destined to accomplish quite a bit as President and then he gets shot down in Dallas. Mary said it was just the latest sad chapter in Irish history.

"Mary was high energy. Always involved in fund-raisers at the church or trying to raise money for a battered women's shelter. The Humane Society. We always had a half dozen stray dogs and cats around the place. She did all the projects around the house. Painting, wallpapering, landscaping. I just stayed out of the way. I was gone a lot. Maybe all those projects were how she combated loneliness. She was the most loyal companion a man could ask for. We had great years together but it would have been better with kids.

"Last November, I got home on a rainy day after I'd been duck hunting. I found her on the floor of the living room. She had made a fire and collapsed in the middle of the room. When I felt for her pulse I could tell she'd been dead for a few hours. There was still a fire burning. I closed her eyes and laid down next to her. I didn't want to let her go. I knew I should call an ambulance, but I couldn't make myself do it. I wanted a little more time with her. That was all. She's all I really ever cared about, and I wanted a little more time. Finally, the fire burned down and I called for an ambulance. When they carried her out of the house they might as well have torn my guts out. It was all over at that point."

I wouldn't look sideways at Jim. He was a proud man. I figured he didn't talk about himself this way very often. I wanted to leave him some privacy as I stared ahead at the lake. He might not have ever confided his feelings about his wife to anyone before. And he couldn't tell his wife the details of his covert activities. For some reason, I was the guy who would hear the whole story. I didn't know whether it was a burden or an honor.

I called work that afternoon and told them that I had to stay over a few days. I didn't feel right about leaving the old guy alone. I figured that a few more days of him getting rid of his burden might allow him to die in peace. Maybe I was giving myself too much credit, but it seemed like the thing to do.

COLD WAR 101

The next four days the routine was the same. Jim would be pounding on the door at first light. He had an old leather suitcase full of papers that he would study as if he was preparing a lecture. Some of the stuff looked like official government documents and rest was a pile of hand written notes. We'd drink a pot of coffee while I made breakfast. He seemed to recover pretty well from our fishing experience. He said it was that good peasant stock. That's how he explained his durability. He said his people had to be resilient to escape that potato famine. Hell, my relatives might have been on the same boat. I guess that was the kinship between us. Plus, he knew my father.

After breakfast we would sit outside and drink iced tea and smoke Pall Malls. Jim had no use for card games and the like. He preferred to stare at the lake and talk. Often he would pause for minutes at a time to gather his thoughts or to give me time to catch up on dictation. We'd break for a sandwich in the afternoon and then back to the seminar. This would go on until sunset. Then Jim would raise his right hand to signal goodbye and slowly walk back to his cabin. I'd go inside with my stack of notes on Jim's lecture for the day. If I worked until ten or eleven, I could organize everything. Later, when I decided to try to write his story, I could still hear his voice. Sometimes he would use slang and sometimes he'd use the King's English. He had been journalism major at the University of Montana before the war. The poor guy now had a carpet salesman writing his book for him.

Jim said that he had ordered the twenty-six volumes of the Warren report and read them cover to cover. He said that Mary couldn't understand his fixation on the subject. The real challenge for the members of the Warren Commission was that they had to isolate five percent of the evidence that supported Oswald as the lone gunman. The report itself was a closed case against Oswald, but the support volumes were a massive contradiction. If all the witnesses who had come forward with information that pointed to a conspiracy had been allowed to testify, Jim said everyone would have laughed at the conclusions of the Warren Commission. With what he knew and the contradictory testimony he had read, Jim said he could not believe that there were still people like Dan Rather or a guy named Posner, who would be foolish enough to say that Oswald had acted alone. He called Posner's book, the second Warren Report. Outside of Nixon, there didn't seem to be anybody that Jim disliked as much as this guy, Posner.

When Jim had learned the Warren Report frontwards and backwards, he started to read all the books by critics of the report. He said the best he had found was by a woman named Sylvia Meager who had surgically dissected the volumes paragraph by paragraph. Jim said her book was nearly impossible to find. There was always Agency money available to buy up controversial books to keep them off the market. If the publisher was tempted to put out a second edition, pressure would be brought by the FBI or IRS and the publisher would usually back down. He said that other trouble makers like Mark Lane and Bill Turner had run into similar problems. He also mentioned a newspaper publisher in Midlothian, Texas, named Penn Jones, who had documented all the suspicious deaths that occurred after the Kennedy assassination and during the hearings of House Select Committee on Assassinations. Jim went through the list of dead witnesses one by one.

As hard as these writers had worked to destroy the Warren Report, Jim said that Oliver Stone had accomplished more than any of them with one movie. He shook his head in disgust when I told him that I hadn't seen JFK. He said that if I was too lazy to read all the literature, if I would watch the movie a few times, I would have a pretty good idea of what happened in Dallas in 1963. I put it on my list of things to do when I returned to Reno.

Jim's class on the Cold War covered all the key participants from John Kennedy to Allen Dulles to Richard Nixon. He would give me a thumbnail biography on each character, but his main emphasis was Kennedy. Whether it was guilt or being Irish, Jim had clearly developed an affinity for JFK. By the time he was finished with Kennedy's story, I must admit that I had a fairly high opinion of the man. We've been saturated with books on failings of his private life to where I had lost track of his many accomplishments. It was at this point that Jim admitted that he had intended to write a book under a fictitious name but he had run out of time.

82

After Jim had gone through the key figures of the postwar era, he explained the cleanup work after the Kennedy assassination. Damage control, he called it. The elimination of witnesses. Corruption of government officials. The behind the scenes control by what he called the Shadow Elite. Greed was the common denominator. What continually amazed me was how easily people could be compromised. How cheaply they could be bought off. That's what differentiated men like Kennedy and Jim Garrison and a deputy sheriff named Roger Craig. These guys stuck to their ideas even if it put them in danger. On the other side were Dulles and Nixon and Hoover. These men would sell their souls for power and personal gain.

By the time the four days were over, I certainly had a different view of recent American history. If Jim Quinn was right, I had been pretty well fooled my whole adult life. I needed time to digest all this new information and see if everything fit. When I got back to Reno, I was determined to organize Jim's story as best I could and see if anyone was interested in publishing it.

AGENCY TYPES

My crash course in Cold War history had finally come to an end. In order to keep my creditors happy, I had to return to Reno. Selling carpet was the cornerstone of my financial empire. It was a more mundane livelihood than overthrowing governments, but I could wait no longer. For six days I had listened to Jim Quinn's explanation of how America had fallen into the hands of the Shadow Elite. These were bankers and heads of corporations and families who controlled most of the wealth in the country. They combined with the military industry and the CIA to form The Beast. Jim saw this alliance as the root of all evil in America since World War II.

I had learned to like the old guy as we spent the week together. He had a hard edge that you would expect from someone in his line of work but he also had a conscience. He was dying and did not have much time to explain the events that troubled him. Other than the years with his wife, he seemed to feel that his life had been a complete waste. He seemed to regret his career in intelligence work. He certainly had nothing nice to say about The Central Intelligence Agency. He had been a loyal soldier but as he looked back he questioned everything that the Agency stood for.

It was finally time to say goodbye. Jim walked across the clearing toward my truck. I was surprised to see that he was carrying his leather suitcase.

" I hope we can set the record straight," he said as he handed me the heavy suitcase.

We shook hands. He looked at me carefully. My guess was that he was wondering if he had told his story to someone who was capable of passing it on. You couldn't read his eyes. The emotion had gone out of them a long time ago. I nodded my head and thanked him for all the information. I wondered how long he would live out there at the Moseby cabin. He certainly had nowhere else to go. I had an empty feeling as I drove up the gravel road. As I looked back, Jim was standing there with his hand raised.

As badly as I felt about leaving the old guy there to die by himself, I felt a sense of freedom as I drove toward the main highway. Jim had laid his burden on me for six days. I felt relieved to drive with the window down as the clean smell of evergreens filled the truck. I knew that my life had been changed because of my chance acquaintance with Jim. I needed time to digest all the information and figure out what I was going to do with it.

I decided to stop in Polson and have breakfast at Price's Cafe. I had been eating my own cooking for a week. It was time for a store-bought meal. Price's had been open as long as I could remember. There were other good places to eat, but I patronized them out of loyalty. My family had always eaten there.

"Sorry to hear about your uncle," the woman behind the counter said as she handed me a menu. There were no secrets in this small town.

"He was the last of their family, you know," I felt that it was only courteous to respond to her comment.

"How long are you here for?" she smiled. Her name tag read, BEV. She was a few years younger than me. She had reddish hair and a look that sort of dared you to flirt with her. I noticed that she wasn't wearing a wedding ring. If you're single in a small town, you have to always be at the ready.

"I have to head back to Reno today. I've been out at Finley Point for a week. It's time to get back to work. I have to keep those bill collectors happy."

"Well, what can I get you?" she smiled, but the flirtation was over. I had been crossed off the list.

I ordered breakfast and looked at the Missoulian sports page to see how the Giants had done over the past week. They had just beaten the Dodgers three straight at Candlestick which was enough to put me in a good mood.

"You know there were two guys in here earlier asking for directions to the Moseby place," Bev said as she set the ham and eggs in front of me. "They were well dressed but they weren't very friendly. I told them it was on Finley Point. It couldn't be too hard to find."

"You know who they were?"

"They kind of rubbed me the wrong way. Kind of rude. Pushy types. They weren't from around here. They had some kind of out of state plates."

"Did they say what they wanted?"

"I didn't ask. I decided I wasn't going to be very helpful. These guys were kind of arrogant."

Bev went about her business and I began to worry about the two men who were asking about the Moseby cabin. They might have been looking for Jim. What had he told me? They keep an eye on you even when you retire. The out of state license plates bothered me. What could they want with Jim? The poor guy would probably be dead within weeks. It seemed like too much of a coincidence that two guys from out of state were looking for the Moseby place.

I was no longer interested in the sports page as I finished my breakfast. I was worried about Jim, but I wasn't sure why. I decided to drive back out to my grandfather's cabin and see what was going on.

It took about twenty minutes to drive out to Finley Point. I kept trying to figure out what these two men might want with Jim Quinn. I couldn't come up with an idea that made any sense.

As I drove down the hill to my grandfather's place, I could see that Jim's car was gone. I had just left him an hour and a half ago. Maybe he had gone into town to get groceries or something. After all, his cook had left for Reno.

I parked my truck in the clearing and got out. For some reason, I was nervous. I looked over at the Moseby place which was probably forty yards away. I couldn't see any activity, but Jim's car was definitely gone. I slowly started up the path to the Moseby cabin.

When I went around to the other side of Jim's cabin I could see a second set of tire tracks in the dirt. Those out of state boys had found the cabin. I must have just missed them. The question was whether Jim had left before them or with them. I walked up to the door. It was locked up tight. If Jim had gone into town for groceries, he probably wouldn't have locked the place. There was not another cabin in sight to the south. I had left for Reno. There was no one else around.

I started to walk down to the lake when I saw it. On the side of the wishing well opposite the cabin was Jim's ivory lighter. I got a chill through my shoulders. That piece of ivory was Jim's most prized possession. He wouldn't have left it there. I wondered if he had left it there as a warning sign. Except he wouldn't have known I was coming back.

I put the lighter in my pants pocket and walked up the shore to my grandfather's place. I decided to wait and see if anyone returned. All kinds of crazy ideas went through my head. What if these were Agency guys and there was some kind of trouble? Why had they left in such a hurry? Maybe they were worried that Jim was talking too much. In that case, they might know about me. Except they had asked for directions in town so they couldn't have known about me. It didn't make sense, but I was nervous.

Then I remembered the suitcase full of documents behind the seat of my truck. It wouldn't have been a good idea for them to find me with all that information. I decided not to wait by the cabin. I would have been too visible. I drove up to the main road and turned north. I drove about a quarter of a mile and pulled off into the trees. From there I could see anyone coming from the direction of town that turned onto the Moseby driveway. It was a Thursday and there was no traffic. I felt pretty well hidden in the shade of the trees.

I waited about an hour. Two cars went by. Locals. I was trying to decide how long to wait when I saw a beige sedan coming up the road. It slowed down like it was going to turn into the Moseby driveway. Instead, it went a little further and turned down toward my grandfather's place. There were three men inside. I recognized Jim's canvas hat on the man in the back seat.

My mind was racing. I had all those damn documents. It would take about five or six minutes for them to get down to the bottom of the hill and turn around and come back. They couldn't see the main road until they got back to the top of the hill. This bought me some time.

I jumped into the truck and closed the door softly. It wasn't shut tight but I didn't want them to hear anything. I started the engine and eased my pickup onto the road. I kept my head low as if that was going to do any good.

I drove slowly to the bend in the road about a half mile to the south. Then I stomped on the accelerator like there was no tomorrow. I figured I was at least three minutes ahead of them. I turned onto the highway and drove about seventy miles an hour to the Turtle Lake cutoff. I decided to take the back roads out of Polson.

I thought about waiting until dark, but I figured they might wait for me along the highway somewhere between there and Missoula. I'll admit I was full blown paranoid at this point. Jim had told me enough about these covert types during the last week. I had no desire to meet these guys or find out what was going on. I felt bad for Jim, but I was already in over my head.

I drove the farm roads south of Ronan and then cut across Highway 93 toward Charlo. This was some of the most peaceful country anywhere, but my adrenalin was still pumping. I passed the Bison Range and turned west along the Jocko River. When I reached

The Clark Fork, I turned south where I could catch the interstate to Spokane.

I was in the clear now, but I kept wondering what was going on back at Finley Point. Why were these guys bothering an old man who only had a few weeks to live. Why had they gone down to my grandfather's place? I was sure that Jim wouldn't tell them any more about me than he had to. He certainly didn't have any loyalty to the CIA. What could have been so urgent? Maybe Jim had talked to someone else and they had just caught up with him.

Whatever was going on, I had no ability to change it. My best hope was to get back to Reno and never hear from these guys. It wasn't until about a month later that I quit looking over my shoulder.

There was no way to get in touch with Jim. I figured he wouldn't call me for fear of giving me up to these Agency guys. By now he was probably dead or very close to it. It was strange to get to know a person so well in such a short time and never be in contact again. Maybe most of Jim's life had been this way. It would be hard to establish any close relationships in his line of work. All I had to show for that week in Montana was an old leather suitcase and an ivory lighter. I guess that was the sum total of Jim Quinn's life.

The remainder of this narrative is from Jim Quinn's manuscript. I have organized a suitcase of material, but I have not changed any of Jim's sarcastic discourse. In the end, these are the final words of an honest man.

COLD WARRIORS

JOHN F. KENNEDY

All you ever hear is that Lyndon Johnson lured President Kennedy to Texas for the purpose of getting him killed. That's the fourth layer of the onion skin. First, we blame Castro, then the Russians, then The Mob, then LBJ and the Texas oilmen. Recently, in Bob Morrow's book, I see layer five. That would be a rogue element of the Agency out of New Orleans with no direction from Langley. The next step is the truth. A covert apparatus from New Orleans, organized by Ed Lansdale, approved by former DCI Allen Dulles, paid for by Marcello, Trafficante, Murchison and H.L. Hunt through the bag man, Clay Shaw. Garrison had just about nailed it down and no one wanted to believe it.

John Kennedy went to Texas because it was one of two big southern states that he thought he could win in 1964. Florida was the other. Kennedy had been in Florida the week before Texas. His motorcade in Miami had been called off because of an assassination threat. At the time of his Texas visit, there was a rift among the Democrats. Big John Connelly on one side. Ralph Yarborough on the other. Kennedy knew he could smooth it over. The main thing was that he wanted to get the 64 campaign underway.

It's sort of ironic. Kennedy was feeling better that he had in years. His back pain had been reduced and he was getting along well with his wife. When their son, Patrick, had died a few months before, it seemed to bring them together again. Jackie would meet him for lunch in the Oval Office. She had also volunteered to campaign for him in 64. Kennedy acted like he was worried about Goldwater, but he knew he would be reelected.

The first item on his agenda was to get out of Vietnam. JFK had spent time with Mike Mansfield and General Douglas McArthur and they told him in no uncertain terms to get the hell out of Vietnam. They convinced Kennedy that a ground war in Southeast Asia was unwinnable. Our military industry wanted that war, but Kennedy didn't. He had signed an order to pull the first thousand men out of Vietnam. Action Memo 256. Two days after he was killed in Dallas, that order was reversed. Lyndon Johnson was two cars behind Kennedy in the motorcade. He saw the President killed and the message was not lost on him. This is what happens when you take on the Beast. Johnson had always been a friend of the military and he was likely to give them their war in Vietnam. There were some big defense contractors down in the Lone Star State.

I wouldn't say that John Kennedy and Lyndon Johnson were great friends, but they respected one another. They had worked together in the Senate and respected one another's abilities. The reason that Kennedy offered the vice presidency to Johnson was not only to try to win southern votes. JFK was weak in the South because of his Catholic background. Kennedy was afraid that as senate majority leader,

Johnson would oppose many of Kennedy's favored programs such as urban renewal and low cost housing. With Johnson as vice president, Mike Mansfield of Montana would become the new senate majority leader. Mansfield was a guy Kennedy knew he could work with. Having said that, Kennedy expected Johnson to decline the offer. It was a step down from senate majority leader to vice president. The offer was an olive branch to the conservative wing of the Democrats and if LBJ accepted, Kennedy figured that his domestic programs would have a better chance in Congress.

Probably the funniest story about Johnson and Kennedy that showed their mutual respect was after the convention when Johnson insisted that Kennedy come down and spend a weekend on his ranch so they could go deer hunting. Kennedy wanted no part of it, but LBJ insisted. Kennedy decided he would deliberately miss when his turn came, but when he saw Dave Powers drop a deer on the first shot, his Irish competitiveness took over. Kennedy got his deer and he figured when the story circulated around Texas, it might help him carry the state. On election night, Johnson called Kennedy to assure him that they would carry Texas. He reminded JFK that together they had carried Pennsylvania. LBJ then asked Kennedy what had happened to him in Ohio.

Kennedy always tried to include Johnson in decision making sessions during his administration. He very much valued Johnson's complete knowledge of Congress. Johnson always knew what the vote count would be on any pending legislation. That was valuable information. Whenever LBJ got fed up with Bobby, John would patiently hear him out. There wasn't the animosity between these two men that the rewriters of history would have you believe. Johnson was actually reluctant to go to Texas in 63 because his popularity had fallen so much in his home state. He was taking the heat for Kennedy's enforcement of Civil Rights, which was not a popular cause in the South. After JFK's death, Lyndon Johnson dedicated himself to civil rights and racial equality. This was a big move for a Texas politician.

Another thing that the disinformers conveniently forget is that Jackie Kennedy and Lyndon Johnson were close friends before and after JFK's death. They would talk regularly and have lunch. Another little known item is that Mrs. Kennedy hired two of the best investigators on the East Coast to look into her husband's death. When she read their report, she sent it on to Johnson. He told her not to release the information because it might put Mrs. Kennedy and her children in jeopardy. That's why she raised her children in Greece. She had a general idea of the forces behind her husband's assassination and she didn't feel safe in this country. Robert Kennedy's murder proved to Mrs. Kennedy that her fear was justified.

Do you think that Jackie Kennedy would have turned over that sensitive report to LBJ if it had incriminated him in any way. Not a chance. His warning to her was as a friend. Don't anger the Beast. It will stop at nothing to maintain its power and its profits. LBJ had gone from being a friend of the military to being a prisoner of it. The Shadow Elite had made him President and he was in no position to deny any request that they made. This was the reason for the grotesque escalation of the war in Vietnam. Johnson could not say no. As much as the presidency validated his whole life, LBJ decided not to run for reelection. His hands were tied. In a strange way, Nixon, who had been an early champion of the Beast, later became a victim as well. He had outlived his usefulness.

After he was buried at Arlington, Mary accused me of developing a fixation on John Kennedy. She didn't understand why I was reading everything I could get my hands on about his younger days. Why was I so interested in the man after his death when I hadn't shown much interest in him while he was alive? Of course, she had no idea that the Agency was involved in Dallas. I had a feeling in my gut that we had gone too far that November. We had made a science of overthrowing governments all over the Third World. Most of us in the Company never figured we'd be called on to overthrow our own government. I wasn't alone in thinking we'd crossed the line. A few other guys I served with retired after Dallas. They didn't site that as the reason for retiring, but it seemed like morale wasn't so good after Dallas. Not that many people at Langley really had any idea of the plot. Lansdale was careful to isolate the operation to our outfit in New Orleans.

Bannister and Shaw were the cut-outs. Bannister was a drunk. He was closely watched until he died of a heart attack less than a year after Kennedy was killed. I have no firsthand knowledge, but my guess is that his death might have been assisted. A heavy drinker with sensitive information is a bad gamble. We were very good at assisting death long before Kevorkian arrived on the scene. When Garrison brought Shaw to trial in New Orleans, the hierarchy at Langley was worried as hell. We did everything in our power to keep Shaw's background under wraps. He was a successful businessman, but he'd been with us since WWII. He was also a big-shot with Permindex which I guess you could call a right wing paramilitary group that operated in Europe. They had put out several contracts on Charles de Gaulle before Kennedy was killed in Dallas. It's odd when you think that Castro and de Gaulle were at the top of the list and they survived. Kennedy dodged situations in Chicago and Miami before he went to Texas. It was only a matter of time. He would have been killed somewhere.

Kennedy understood the limitations of military solutions. So did Eisenhower and McArthur. He also found out that those of us within the military and intelligence establishment were willing to mislead the president as well as the American people in order to pursue our own agenda. Money has always been and will always be the bottom line. The very rich are never satisfied. It becomes an obsession. In 1960, H.L. Hunt was the richest man in the world, but he was threatened by Kennedy's intention to cut the oil depletion allowance. Of course, like Rockefeller, he profited greatly from defense spending. Kennedy was independently wealthy due to his father, but he didn't seem to care about the business end of it. He lived in the world of ideas. From the time he was a teenager, he loved to argue about ideas. History and politics were his obsession. He was determined to know how everything worked.

Kennedy was smart as hell. I think his IQ was close to 150. He had that great sense of humor. That's why the press loved him. Kennedy's jokes were usually at his own expense. Self-deprecation, the college boys

97

would tell you. It was easy for people to be comfortable around someone who had enough self confidence that he could make fun of himself. If you watch the old press conferences from Kennedy's three years in office, you'll see a communication between the President and reporters that you'll never see again. While Kennedy was very serious about being President, he didn't take himself too seriously. In that regard, he was a little bit like Lincoln. They were both detached.

His other asset was his energy. When his PT boat was sunk by a Jap destroyer, Kennedy towed one of his men who couldn't swim five miles to the nearest island with a rope in his teeth. Then at night he'd swim from island to island while he looked for help. He finally found two natives who spoke pidgeon-english. He carved a message on a coconut husk and convinced these guys to row all day and all night and deliver the note to PT headquarters at Rendova. Kennedy swam back to where his men were and they were finally rescued. To a man, they said they would've died without Kennedy. They'd been given up for dead. Kennedy wasn't satisfied waiting to be rescued. They didn't have enough food or water and some of the men had been badly burned when fuel exploded as their boat was cut in half by the destroyer.

When Kennedy was President, he sent for the two natives who had saved his life to visit him at the White House. He was killed before they got there. I saw an article a few years back about one of the guys. His name was Eroni. He named his first boy John Kennedy. That's the effect Kennedy had on people. His PT boat crew knew it. The American people knew it. There was something different about John Kennedy.

Eroni said that he had been sad every day since he heard that Kennedy had died.

Kennedy never had to go to Southeast Asia. He was offered a job as a training instructor at the PT boat school at Melville. Joe Kennedy was doing everything he could to keep his son out of combat, but Jack outmaneuvered him. He had traveled all through Europe and Latin America and he was determined to get to the South Pacific. Kennedy had seriously injured his back on the football team at Harvard and he should have never gotten into the Navy, let alone combat. During the war, he often had to sleep on the floor because of the pain in his lower back. He had covered up the injury in order to enlist in the Navy. It was the back brace that held him upright in Dallas. If he had slumped forward when he was hit in the back, he would not have received the fatal head wound. For whatever reason, Kennedy was able to put the tremendous back pain out of his mind. I think the most important part of his life took place in his head. The body was secondary.

Oddly enough, Kennedy had begun his military service with the Office of Naval Intelligence. This is the same group that recruited Lee Harvey Oswald when he was in the Marines. Kennedy hated that duty. He was in a little office in Charleston, where he spent the day trying to decipher codes. That was definitely not his style, but what got him sent overseas was an affair with a married Danish reporter named Inga Arvad.

Inga worked for the Washington Post and I think she was separated from her husband at the time. Kennedy met her through his sister, Kathleen. I think the reason that Kennedy fell so hard for Inga was that she was smart as hell and sort of unimpressed with him. She stood up to him intellectually and he found that he liked that. She was also a very good looking woman.

Before Inga had left Europe, she had developed some friendships through her journalism with some individuals in Hitler's government. There was never any serious indication that she was working for the Nazis, but when J. Edgar Hoover found out that she was dating Joe Kennedy's son, he went straight to the old man with the information. Together they decided that it would be best if Jack was transferred out of the area. To satisfy his curiosity, Hoover bugged Inga's phone and any hotel room where she and JFK would spend the weekend. The old closet-queen was ever vigilant.

I guess the breakup with Inga was painful for Kennedy. If he had remained stateside, they might have wound up getting married. Joe Kennedy didn't want that to happen. He wouldn't allow a scandal with a married woman to be on his son's resume. As it turned out, Papa Joe's need to control his kids almost got John Kennedy killed.

The PT-boat service was a joke in the Navy. The U.S. Mosquito Fleet they called it. The PT-boats were an outdated torpedo boat made out of plywood. They used high-octane aircraft fuel which was highly flammable. They were a damn floating powder keg. Their advantage was supposed to be speed and maneuverability, but the engines often failed. They had no radar and the crew had no idea where the torpedoes were going. The idea was to patrol at night and try to sink Japanese destroyers. This was all done in the dark using only sight and sound. The US government actually sent men out to risk their lives on these little shit heaps.

The night Kennedy's boat was cut in half was very dark. You couldn't see five feet in front of you. That big Jap destroyer was on top of them before they could maneuver out of the way. To Kennedy's credit, he positioned the boat to fire on the ship before the ship changed course at the last minute and hit the small boat broadside. The fuel exploded. By some miracle most of the crew survived the blast, but two men were killed. It took Kennedy a long time to get over the fact that he had lost two men. There were damn few successes by the PT-boats and a lot of causalities. Just another case of the decision makers back home not being too concerned about the lives of the men overseas. None of this was lost on young Kennedy. He had a very low opinion about the strategy of war by the time he returned to the States. Ask anyone who's been through it. Do they feel patriotic? Not likely. You hope to stay alive and you try not to psycho out. That's it. Every day above ground is a good day. Let the politicians sound patriotic. The soldiers know better.

While all this was going on with the boat wreck and all, you have to wonder about Kennedy's back. Before he went into the Navy, his back would get so bad that he would regularly end up in the hospital. He lied about his condition to get into the service. How many guys lately have lied to get out of the service? Kennedy had ten ways to keep from going overseas. That may tell you something about the guy. Or maybe it was family pressure to do something outstanding. Anyway, you have to wonder what the impact of being hit by that destroyer and the events that followed had on his chronic back injury. I guess under the circumstances, he didn't have the luxury to worry about it.

The other problem Kennedy always had was with his stomach. From the time he was a kid, he'd had a bad stomach. That's why he was always so damn skinny in those pictures when he was young. They'd run a bunch of tests to find out why he was sick and his blood count was so bad but they could never find the cause of the problem. I think they had him in the Mayo Clinic a couple of times. He spent so much time in the infirmaries at boarding school that his best friends were the nurses. He was always comfortable in the company of women. I guess there's been a fairly wide reporting of that. If you read comments of those nurses years later, they remembered that scrawny little Jack Kennedy was amusing and sort of charming even at age twelve or thirteen.

He'd be laid up for weeks in these boarding school infirmaries and no one would come to see him. Rose was in Florida and Joe was in New York or California. Finally his dad would show up at the school. Rose would never come. Instead she would send a newsletter to all her children to tell them how the others were doing. This impersonal form of communication went on for years and it began to aggravate John Kennedy as he got older. Rose had spent time in a convent as a girl and she had an ability to keep unpleasantries out of her world. Her newsletters were very cheerful and often entirely missed what was going on. About the time Joe Kennedy had an affair with Gloria Swanson, Rose put all the children in boarding schools and left for Florida. The family would see each other on holidays. For all his faults, I think Joe Kennedy was affectionate toward his kids and he encouraged them to depend on each other. The fact that Papa Joe was a notorious womanizer probably set a poor example for his boys.

Probably the blackest moment for whole family was the decision to have a lobotomy done on Rosemary. She was the oldest daughter and she was retarded. When you read accounts of family gatherings, it was Jack Kennedy who would ask his friends to dance with Rosemary so she wouldn't feel left out. Despite his problems in his own relationships, there was always that side to the guy. Anyway, Rosemary had been put in a convent. When she was younger, Rosemary was the most affectionate of the Kennedy children, but when she hit puberty, her sexual frustration caused her to sometimes become violent and hard to control. Her parents would hear that she would leave the convent at night and wander the streets. For her own safety, they decided on what Rose would later refer to as "a form of neurosurgery".

There are so many myths floating around about the Kennedys. You always hear that John Kennedy was a poor student. Even when he was getting mediocre grades in secondary school, he was reading the New York Times every day. He had one of those restless minds that soaked up everything he read or observed. He finally got his grades up to where he was accepted at Harvard. His classmates at Harvard voted him most likely to succeed and his senior thesis was published as a book called, WHY ENGLAND SLEPT. John Kennedy wasn't short on the grey matter.

JFK II

When John Kennedy was about twenty, he and a friend named Lem Billings, spent the summer bumming around Europe. Everywhere they went, Kennedy was questioning people about Hitler or Mussolini or Franco. He wanted to find out firsthand how people felt about fascism. Billings later said that they stopped at every old church and art gallery in Europe. That was Kennedy's love of history. It was mostly a pleasant experience until they got to Germany where they were spit on as Americans. Kennedy decided that the German people could be a little bit arrogant and aggressive.

About the time Kennedy and his pal were wandering around Europe, Joe Kennedy was putting pressure on the Roosevelt Administration for the ambassadorship to Great Britain. FDR was never comfortable around Joe Kennedy, but he finally gave in and the Kennedys were off to England. While Hitler was annexing Czechoslovakia, Joe Kennedy was filing complementary reports on British Prime Minister Chamberlain's refusal to get involved. Rose Kennedy seemed pleased with their new social status at the Court of St. James's. She concentrated on preparing her daughters for upcoming debutante events.

While Joe Kennedy and his oldest son, Joe, were making a case for isolationism and excusing Hitler's aggression, John Kennedy wasn't so sure. He had heard complaints about fascism while he traveled around Europe. Not only did he distrust the political framework of fascism, but he doubted that the aggression of Germany and Italy could be ignored. In his capacity as secretary to the Ambassador, John embarked on another trip through Eastern Europe and Russia and down through the Middle East. He pried information out of anyone who would talk to him. There seemed to be great anxiety in everyone he talked with. When he met with the American Ambassador to Germany, he was given a note to deliver to his father in England. The note predicted there would be war within a week. This was quite an introduction to world politics for a kid of twenty-two.

When John Kennedy later heard England's declaration of war against Germany, it was not Chamberlain, but Winston Churchill who left a lasting impression. The Old Bulldog's air of confidence in the face of war was something Kennedy never forgot. If you compare his speeches as President with the sad bunch of pretenders we've had since Dallas, you can see Churchill's influence. In fact, since Franklin Roosevelt, John Kennedy and Martin Luther King are the only two Americans that you would walk across the street to listen to.

A week after England declared war on Germany, Kennedy was sent as an emissary to Scotland to help with a group of American survivors from a passenger ship that had been torpedoed by a German submarine. He really wasn't prepared for the situation, but reporters at the scene gave Kennedy high marks for his compassion and willingness to listen to the survivors. That was a characteristic that would endear him to people the rest of his life. He would rather find out about the other guy than talk about himself.

When the bombing started in England, the Kennedys returned to the United States. Joe Kennedy had always placed a very high value on his own hide. John used his experience to write his book on England and graduated from Harvard with Honors. He then went out to California and took some graduate courses at Stanford, but he seemed out of his element there. Palo Alto seemed a little too refined for a Boston Irishman. He hadn't seen much of the Western Hemisphere so he decided to take a trip through Central and South America. I told you earlier that Jack Kennedy was always a man in a hurry. His trip to Latin American was just another chance to fill up his head with new information. After Pearl Harbor, he joined the Navy. When he was sent to the South Pacific, he welcomed the opportunity to experience another part of the world.

After his PT-boat was sunk and his crew was finally rescued, Kennedy was sent to sick bay for a couple of weeks. He was really beat to hell. Exposure. Coral infection in his feet. Stomach disorder. Severe back pain. Skinny as a rail. It was one of the many times in his life when it looked like his body was ready to give out, but his mind was full of energy.

It was customary in the Navy that if your vessel had been lost, you got reassigned stateside, but Kennedy wanted to stay in the South Pacific. He felt very guilty about losing two crew members. One of the men had been shell-shocked when a bomb had narrowly missed their boat a few weeks earlier. The man had three children and Kennedy had intended to have him transferred off the boat. That situation haunted him. He blamed himself for the man's death.

Pappy McMahon, the man that Kennedy had towed with his teeth from the PT-Boat to Bird Island, had survived and was recovering from his burns. His wife wrote Kennedy a long letter and personally thanked him for saving her husband's life. It did little to cheer him up. He brooded for weeks because he had lost two men and no one had come to look for his crew. It didn't occur to him that without his leadership and his swimming at night in those deadly waters to look for help, none of them would have survived.

John Kennedy wanted revenge against the Japanese. The more he thought about that night in Blackett Straight, he knew that the Jap destroyer deliberately veered to ram his boat. He was determined to avenge the deaths of his two crewmen.

The Navy had converted two old PT-boats into gun boats. Kennedy should have been back in the States, but he talked his way into commanding one of the gunboats. He spent the next few months trying to sink Jap barges. Some of his crew thought that his determination to get even with the Japs was causing him to take too many chances. He was wearing a back brace and walking with a cane and his stomach ulcer was so bad that he couldn't eat most of the time. Not a very threatening figure. All he had was Irish stubbornness.

Kennedy's physical condition continued to deteriorate. He was the hobbling avenger. With his plywood boat and a nervous crew, he was out to destroy the Japanese Empire. The decision was finally made to send him back to the States. This time he didn't argue. He had become cynical about the war effort in the Pacific. Not much of it made sense to him. The planning was poor. The equipment was bad. There were many lives lost while little was accomplished. I think he later applied what he had learned in the Pacific to the conflict he inherited in Vietnam. Unless there was a clear goal and a plan that could achieve victory, it was not fair to ask men to lay down their lives.

Shortly before he died, Kennedy told Walter Cronkite that this was Vietnam's war to win or lose. He meant it. He wasn't going to lose American lives in a quagmire in Southeast Asia. He signed a directive to begin to withdraw our advisors, who were nothing but Agency guys. He said he'd have everybody out of Vietnam following the election. He didn't care who thought he was soft on communism. The Beast could not accept Kennedy's directive. They had a massive effort planned for Vietnam. McGeorge Bundy, who was Kennedy's National Security Advisor, was actually working on a plan to reverse Kennedy's policy in Vietnam while John Kennedy was in Dallas. That's how treacherous it can be when you take on the Beast.

When Kennedy returned from the Solomon Islands, he had no idea of the run of bad luck that awaited him. He first went to Los Angeles to try to renew his relationship with Inga Arvad. She was the only woman who he had taken seriously and, like many enlisted men overseas, her memory helped sustain him through his dark hours in the Solomon Islands.

Inga had taken over Sheila Graham's syndicated column and was doing very well in Hollywood. She was rubbing shoulders with all the big-shots. She had also taken up with a Jewish doctor. When she saw Kennedy, she couldn't believe how unhealthy and worn out he looked. She told some of her friends that he would never recover from the war. She set up two meetings with Kennedy in LA. The first was with the wife of his PT-109 engineer, Pappy McMahon. Inga said that she got pretty choked-up when Mrs. McMahon told John Kennedy how thankful she was for saving her husband's life. She said to a man, the crew thought they would not have survived without his efforts. She told Kennedy that he would never understand the admiration these men had for him. Whatever else happened, she wanted to personally thank him.

The second meeting was a lot more painful. Inga introduced John to William Cahan, her new boyfriend. The two men talked about football and show business and finally, John Kennedy excused himself. He did not want to give up Inga, but he still had his pride. The Inga Arvad part of his life was over. Some of his friends said that he never really got over her.

When Kennedy returned home, he found himself in the middle of a family controversy over whether his sister, Kathleen, should marry an English Protestant nobleman named, Billy Cavendish. Kathleen had John's blessing, but Rose Kennedy considered it a tragedy. She went into seclusion. She denied to the press that the story was true. When Kathleen was finally married, Rose could only apologize for her daughter. A short time later, Cavandish was killed at

Normandy. Kathleen chose to stay in England rather than face the hypocrisy in Massachusetts.

Kennedy then underwent a back operation that almost killed him. Once again the body failed. His lower back went into constant spasms which required heavy doses of pain killers. His stomach ulcer would not allow him to eat and his weight went down to about one hundred and twenty pounds. His friends who visited him in the hospital with his yellow skin and emaciated body were sure he was not going to make it. After two months in the hospital with little improvement, he was told he might be better off at home.

While John was trying to recover his health, the blackest news of all arrived. His older brother had been killed in England. Joe had flown his quota of air missions in Europe, but he kept volunteering for more. He was all too aware of his younger brother's war hero status. He seemed to need to upstage John before he returned to the United States . Finally, Joe volunteered for a hair-brained secret bombing mission. Get this. They loaded about ten tons of TNT into the fuselage of Joe's converted Liberator. After the plane had taken off and reached proper altitude, Joe and his co-pilot were to bail out and two following Venturas were to radio control the flying bomb to crash at a German target near Calais, France. Joe had been warned that the electronic circuitry might be faulty, but he was determined to win the Navy Cross. He had been in the air about twenty minutes. When he switched over to remote control, the plane exploded. No piece of Joe Kennedy was ever found in the New Delight Woods.

Papa Joe Kennedy's plans to be President had ended with his failed Ambassadorship in England. He had second guessed Roosevelt and the American war effort. He had become persona non grata in Washington. Now his plans for his oldest son to become president were gone. His next oldest son, John, was clever, but he wanted to be a writer or a teacher.

Joe and John Kennedy had always been very competitive. From sports to women to arguing politics. As John thought about his older brother's death, he realized that Joe's recklessness in England might have been due to his need to outdo his own publicity from PT-109. Instead of wallowing in self- pity, John decided to interview Joe's old friends and classmates. He put together a little book called, AS WE REMEMBER JOE. Papa Joe could never bring himself to read the book. His highest hopes had always been with his oldest son.

By the time John Kennedy was discharged from the Navy, his father had decided to make him a politician. Papa Joe was the ultimate control freak. He had learned that a Massachusetts congressman named James Curley was having financial difficulties due to a fraud conviction. Mr. Kennedy stepped in and offered Curley twelve thousand in cash if he would vacate his congressional seat and run for mayor. Call it a campaign contribution. Old Man Kennedy was at his best when probing for a weakness. Curley agreed. Now Papa Joe only had to convince John to run for the open seat in Congress.

"John agreed to consider the possibility of running for Congress in Massachusetts. He had no idea that his father had already financed the arrangement. John had always been interested in politics, but he didn't know if he wanted any part of small-time Boston back room politics. He had a lot of ideas about international relations, but he wasn't sure he wanted to spend his days shaking hands outside the factories.

Kennedy went out west to Arizona to rebuild his health. He took a crateful of books on labor law. He had about had his fill of those tedious books and being surrounded by octogenarians when he caught a tremendous break. He was asked by The Chicago Tribune to cover the first session of the United Nations in San Francisco. Despite his seriously damaged health, Kennedy threw himself completely into the assignment in San Francisco. His enthusiastic mind always allowed him to overcome his broken body. Once again he found himself rubbing shoulders with the movers and shakers in world politics.

It became clear from the start of the San Francisco Conference that The Soviet Union was going to be America's biggest post-war problem. They were belligerent and secretive. It was clear that they were not anxious to give back any of the territory in Eastern Europe that they had taken from the Germans. Poland, Hungary, Czechoslovakia, Bulgaria, Latvia, Lithuania, etc. The Iron Curtain. I think Churchill originated the phrase. Anyway, as John Kennedy watched the Russians and filed his reports with the Tribune, he got an early indication of what the Cold War would be all about.

Stalin would not be any more humane with his captives in Eastern Europe than he was with his enemies or his imagined enemies in the Soviet Union. He eliminated millions of the old guard Bolsheviks in prison camps after the war. Gulags, they were called. Stalin was careful to the point of being paranoid. A decorated officer like Solzhenitsyn was convicted in some kangaroo court and sent to prison. In his own way, Stalin was every bit the monster that Hitler was. He was a cold, cunning, bloodthirsty sonuvabitch. The closest American in terms of pure treachery was Richard Nixon. He and Stalin would use any means available to neutralize or eliminate anyone in their way. No need to rationalize. These were two totally dishonest, deceitful men. In terms of dead bodies, Stalin was the champ.

After the Germans had surrendered, the Secretary of the Navy, James Forrestal, invited John Kennedy to accompany him on a tour of Berlin. Kennedy stopped in Ireland on his way to Paris. There he got a firsthand account of the division between the twenty six counties of the Irish Catholic South and the six counties of the Protestant North. The Northern Irish did not want to be ruled by Catholics and England did not want to lose control of the island. The men that Kennedy talked with were survivors of the uprising of 1916. Most of them had spent time in prison. He saw in their faces that these were serious men who would be satisfied by nothing less than a free and united Ireland. All of this travel and conversation was being filed away in his head. When he became President, Kennedy had a pretty good understanding of the crisis areas throughout Europe. He had also gotten a close-up look at the Soviets in San Francisco

Nixon always said after Dallas that Kennedy wasn't ready to be President. Nixon's background was with the military establishment. Kennedy had traveled the world and discussed important events with those who were involved. Nixon saw everything as it affected him and his political future. The ascendency of Richard Nixon was always the first priority. He was a little man who was bitter about the cards he'd been dealt. He had come into this world homely and humorless. His bitterness became his determination to succeed. Kennedy was more detached. He could stand back and see the bigger picture. He understood his charisma, but he took it for granted. He didn't have to shamelessly promote himself like Nixon did. Confidence gives you the ability to leave yourself out of a situation. I've read that Lincoln could see himself in third person. In other words, he could stand back and watch himself as if he was someone else. I think Kennedy could also do that.

On the flight from Paris to Berlin, Forrestal grilled John Kennedy about the situation in Ireland as well as Churchill's defeat by Britain's Labor Party. Here was The Secretary of the Navy picking the brain of the young world traveler. Kennedy was twenty-eight. Anyone who listened to him in those days appreciated his ability to objectively break down a situation. Where his father and older brother could only see things in terms of what was good for America, John could stand back and be more unbiased. This ability made him a hero around the world while he was President. He fought to give the small countries of Africa and Latin America a chance to survive. That brought him face to face with the old colonialists. These powerful and greedy men did not want to lose their footholds and their investments in the Third World. Kennedy always came down on the side of the underdog. It was the Irish in him.

When he landed in Berlin, Kennedy could not believe the level of destruction. He had stayed in the Excelsior Hotel one week before the start of WWII. Now everything was rubble. He was also disturbed by the Soviet presence in Berlin. Kennedy understood their reluctance to give up any territory that they had seized during the war. He could see that it would be America who would have to stand up to Russians. Our European allies were in bad shape and someone would have to oppose Russia's clear intention to expand its territory.

The group visited Hitler's bunker and a submarine plant at Frogge. The assembly line was set up to build one submarine every three weeks. It made Kennedy realize how close Germany had come to winning the war. They visited the I.G. Farben complex in Frankfurt where American investors like Prescott Bush and Averell Harriman had helped supply the German war effort until Pearl Harbor. There was good reason why some Americans wanted this country to remain neutral. There were tremendous profits to be made feeding these war machines. Finally, it was up to Congress to publicly scold these companies and order them to cease their supply of material to Germany. It seems clear to me that the wealthier the individual, the more likely his loyalty will be to his pocketbook than to his country.

The final leg of the tour of Germany was Hitler's mountain retreat at Berchtesgaden. The Eagle's Nest. As they traveled through the German countryside, Kennedy was struck by how normal and healthy the rural areas were compared to the total destruction of the cities. Crops were planted. Livestock was being cared for. At the same time, the Russians were looting everything they could haul out of the territory that they occupied. Forrestal commented that Russia was trying to reduce Germany to their own standard of living.

Before Kennedy and Forrestal left for London, they had breakfast with President Truman and General Eisenhower at Potsdam. The current President and the next two Presidents of The United States sat at the same table. Truman was very calm. He said that the war with Japan would soon be over. He also asked Ike to join the Democratic Party and run for President in 1948. Truman offered to run as Vice President if Ike would accept. That tells you something about Truman's humility. In his late twenties, John Kennedy had witnessed a piece of history.

JFK III

John Kennedy's run for Congress in Boston in 1946 was very awkward from the start. Unknown to John, his father had bought off James Curley not to run for reelection. Although he had been born in Boston, Kennedy had spent a good part of his life in New York, Florida and California. He was considered an outsider to many in the district. He was nearly thirty, but he was so skinny that he looked more like a kid from college. He refused to wear a hat and his low-key manner of speaking was unlike anything the Boston Irish and Italians had ever seen. His strongest asset was his ability to attract volunteers. They piled into his small campaign office every day and the ones who stayed were totally dedicated. People believed in him and wanted to work for him. Kennedy was surrounded by the bright and talented people from his first Congressional campaign to his administration as President.

There were a lot of stories that his friends liked to tell about Kennedy's early days in politics. It could be pretty rough in some of those Irish blue-collar wards. One night at a rally a guy stood up and shouted, "Are you here to tell us how your father is buying you a seat in congress?" Kennedy shouted back, "I'm here to talk about this election. If you want to talk about my family, I'll meet you outside!" The hard working guys from the shipyard liked that answer.

Another time there was a long line of people waiting to meet him and shake his hand. An elderly lady had gotten tired and walked over to the side of the hall and sat down. Kennedy excused himself and went over and had a conversation with her. He probably won the vote of every elderly person in the meeting hall that night. That was Kennedy. He was ready to fight one night and showed consideration for an old lady the next. He could do this in a way that didn't look phony. He always had the ability to read people.

His detractors like to say that it was his money that made him President. What those critics ignore is that John Kennedy worked fifteen hours a day in that first congressional campaign. He would go door to door throughout the district and introduce himself. If he saw one of his campaign stickers on a house, he would seek out the individual and thank him. It surely didn't hurt to have Joseph P. Kennedy's money behind you, but Papa Joe's backroom manipulations could be an embarrassment. John Kennedy had the right instincts. The more people saw him, the more they seemed to like him. Once he got started in politics, he didn't need his father or anyone else to grease the wheels. He was a little bit different and everyone could see it.

Kennedy won a hard fought primary because he worked harder than his opponents. It was that simple. People who work the hardest are the ones who achieve success. The ones who take short-cuts fall by the wayside. Kennedy was no different, but he sounded different. He had discovered that people like direct

118

answers. If a politician sounded halfway honest, people might vote for you even if they disagreed with you on a particular issue. Boston politics had always been about backroom deals and bribery. Papa Joe knew how to work that side of the street. John's style was to speak bluntly about problems and offer possible solutions. This more candid style caught the voters' attention, but it occasionally got him in trouble.

During his first session in Congress, Kennedy had worked to organize veterans groups to support a bill on low-cost housing. The American Legion, who took a lot of money from real estate and construction, continued to oppose the bill. In a debate on the floor of the House, Kennedy said that the American Legion had not done anything to benefit this country since 1918. This was a shocking statement against a powerful lobby. Members of the House rose one by one to go on record against Kennedy's statement. Kennedy's friends urged him to retract the comment. John considered their advice and asked for the floor. Instead of an apology, Kennedy denounced the American Legion again. Afterwards, he joked to his aides that he was finished in Washington, but there were voters who respected this kind of independent thinking.

There was another humorous incident during Kennedy's first session of Congress. Our old friend, James Curley, was circulating a petition to suspend his sentence that he was serving in federal prison for construction contracts fraud. You'll remember Joe Kennedy had bribed Curley to give up his congressional seat and run for Mayor of Boston. Curley had won election as Mayor, but he was doing time at a federal facility in Danbury, Connecticut. He had appeared in court in a wheelchair with a neck brace and complained of serious health problems. It seemed that the most severe ailment was an impending brain hemorrhage. Some of the spectators noticed that Curly had pretty good movement within the neck brace. Others wondered how one might predict a brain hemorrhage.

John Kennedy wouldn't buy it. He thought Curley was in good health and he refused to sign the petition. Curley was larger than life in Kennedy's district in Boston and many influential members of Congress had signed the petition. Even President Truman supported it. Kennedy was staring down the gun barrel, but he refused to sign the petition.

Curley finally got his pardon. When he arrived at City Hall in Boston, gone was the wheelchair. Off came the neck brace. Curley announced to a crowd of supporters that he felt better than he had in ten years. Even Kennedy had to laugh. He had risked alienating his constituency in Boston, but he had stood his ground. Kennedy used to like to say, when you do the right thing, it usually turns out to be the right thing politically. He often spoke out against his own party's bills in the House if he thought they were flawed. He was also not averse to criticizing President Truman if he disagreed with his foreign policy. Some Democrats thought that the young congressman from Massachusetts was a little too independent. Kennedy didn't care. He would follow his own ideas.

In 1948, while John was listening to a recording of the musical comedy, FINIAN'S RAINBOW, a call came that his favorite sister, Kathleen, had been killed in a plane crash in France. As if he hadn't understood the news, John commented that Ellen Lagin had the sweetest voice. Then he broke down in tears. Kathleen had taken up with the Earl of Fitzwilliam and had recently told her family of her intentions to marry him. Rose had threatened Kathleen with banishment from the family and eternal damnation. Those years in the convent made for some severe mothering. This was the third of the long line of tragedies that would befall the Kennedys.

The biggest myth about John Kennedy was that everything came easy to him. He liked to make it look that way. After he had won a second term in Congress, he was looking for a greater challenge. He began to set up a state-wide network for a run for the U.S. Senate in 1952 against Henry Cabot Lodge. In 1951, Kennedy spoke in seventy different communities around the state of Massachusetts. He would take the commute train from Washington and meet with two or three of his aides. He was on crutches due to the deteriorating condition of his back. The group would drive across the state to their destination and the men would help Kennedy out of the car. He would then walk into the assembly hall smiling and shaking hands as if nothing was wrong. His goal was to be known in every part of Massachusetts before he announced his campaign for the Senate.

When Kennedy turned in his nomination papers in July, he had over a quarter of a million signatures. Only 2,500 signatures were required by law. So much for doing things the easy way. They decided to send thank-you letters to each of the two hundred and sixty thousand people who had signed the petitions. Where they had the manpower, they hand-delivered the letters. Several weeks later, Kennedy and one of his men

121

stopped in a local tavern. As they shook hands around the bar, one of the longshoremen pulled the thank-you letter out of his shirt pocket. He told Kennedy that after twenty years of signing these petitions, Kennedy was the first sonuvabitch to ever send him a thank-you letter. It became Kennedy's all-time favorite compliment.

On election night, 1952, Eisenhower carried Massachusetts by two hundred thousand votes. He carried all the Republican candidates with him except Henry Cabot Lodge who was so confident of reelection that he had spent most of his time campaigning for Eisenhower. The vote was close, but Kennedy's instincts told him he had won. That night before the results were final, he wondered out loud what kind of job Eisenhower would give to Lodge. Kennedy later told Tip O'Neill, who had won his first congressional seat, not to make the same mistake he had made when he joined the House. Be nice to John McCormick, he advised. When Kennedy had gotten to Washington in 46, McCormick had demanded that Kennedy get right over to his office. Kennedy said something to the effect that John McCormick had gotten along for thirty years without him. He could get along for another thirty minutes. Let's get some breakfast.

1954 might have been John Kennedy's toughest year. He had gotten married that spring and his life was falling into place, but his back was worse than ever. He was fed up with the crutches. He decided on another attempt at spinal fusion. It had almost killed him before, but he was willing to gamble. The complication was that his malfunctioning adrenal gland created a high risk of infection or shock. The operation failed.

Twice he was given last rites. This was nothing new for Kennedy. The second spinal operation had left a hole in his back the size of a baseball.

Kennedy couldn't stand to waste time convalescing even though he would be bed ridden for weeks. He started to put together notes for an idea that the writer in him had about politicians who had turned their backs on political expediency and stood up for what they believed. The idea had been taking shape in his head for several years and became a book called, PROFILES IN COURAGE. It won Kennedy the Pulitzer Prize. Compare that to the resume of the tired political hacks that we've seen in recent years.

I don't think John Kennedy ever gave himself a serious chance to be President until the Democratic Convention in 1956. He had wrestled control of the Massachusetts delegation away from McCormick and the old guard Boston politicians, but he was still unknown on a national level. He was asked to give the nominating speech for Adali Stevenson. That's when the country got its first look at JFK. He threw away the speech that he'd been given and stayed up all night writing his own speech. When he went on the stage the next night, he took the convention by storm. All of a sudden there was a big push to have him on the ticket as vice president. Kennedy was completely surprised. His father immediately told him to forget the idea. Ike was going to win by a landslide. Why associate yourself with a loser?   Kennedy saw it as just another challenge. Stevenson was in a dilemma. Kennedy was the popular choice, but he had already promised the spot to Kefaver. Kennedy wasn't well known to the power brokers in the delegations and Kefaver got the nod.

Even thought Kennedy had lost the vice presidency, he had learned two important things. He had the ability to appeal to voters outside of Massachusetts. If he was going to make a serious run for the Presidency, he would have to travel across the country and get to know all the important party leaders on the local level. Just like he had done in Massachusetts in 1952, he decided to organize his run for The White House in 1960. Once again he would out work and out organize the opposition. Of course, the good looks and money didn't hurt.

Idaho, Wyoming, Nevada, Oregon, Iowa, Alabama. Kennedy was everywhere. He was on a first name basis with the guys who ran the Democratic party at the local level. When the primaries kicked off, he was in Wisconsin to take on Hubert Humphrey in his own back yard. Kennedy won handily. Then it was West Virginia which was about one hundred percent Protestant. It had long been assumed that a Catholic could never be elected President. West Virginia would be the first arena where Kennedy's religion would become an issue. One day in some small town in West Virginia, Kennedy got tired of dancing around the issue. His Irish temper kicked in. He threw away his speech and just started talking. They didn't keep him from joining the Navy because he was Catholic. They didn't prevent his brother Joe from flying bombing missions over Germany because he was Catholic. When he was baptized, had he given up his right to be President? Was there not a division between church and state? Were his ideas to improve this country worthless because he was Catholic?   If Lyndon Johnson and Adlai Stevenson were concerned with the dangerous conditions of the mines in West Virginia, why weren't they out there campaigning? Kennedy was angry and the people listened.

Kennedy was beginning to win the hearts of the people of West Virginia as he visited all the poor communities.   Meanwhile Jackie was speaking at grocery stores and hospitals where miners were dying of black lung. In desperation, Humphrey challenged John Kennedy to a televised debate. Kennedy showed up at the studio with a box of food rations that the unemployed miners' families were living on. Kennedy had trailed Humphrey by forty points when he had started his campaign due to the religious issue. He knew in his gut that he was starting to get through to the people of West Virginia, but he was afraid he was still going to come up short.

Kennedy had underestimated the fairness of the working people of West Virginia. When the results were in, he had won sixty percent of the vote. A thirty percent gain in a few weeks. This was the Kennedy magic at its best. If you have a concern for people and you talk straight, they might just listen. If you're nice looking and have a sense of humor, they might find you likable. Throughout his short life, the closer people got to John Kennedy, the more they responded to him.

After Kennedy had settled the religious question in West Virginia, support came from everywhere. All those contacts he had made during the previous three years were jumping on the bandwagon. Everybody likes a winner and Kennedy looked like a guy with coattails long enough to get a lot of people elected.

One of his strongest backers was Mayor Daley in Chicago. The two men couldn't have been more different. Daley was blue collar and crude. Kennedy, well-mannered and educated. But the two were comfortable with one another from the start. Each admired the other's strengths. While Kennedy was President, Daley asked him only one favor. He knew a boy who had been raised by his widowed mother. The boy wanted to go to Harvard. His grades were good enough that Kennedy was able to get him admitted. He graduated from Harvard with Honors, but was later killed in Vietnam.

The only obstacle that remained to the 1960 nomination was former President Harry Truman. The old haberdasher went public just before the convention and said that he thought John Kennedy was too young and inexperienced to be President. Kennedy answered that his fourteen years in the House and Senate gave him more experience in national politics than any president in that century. That included Woodrow Wilson, FDR and Truman himself. Kennedy said that he was older than George Washington when he commanded the Continental Army and older than Jefferson when he wrote The Declaration of Independence. No matter. Kennedy was nominated on the first ballot.

The 1960 election was typical Kennedy. He outworked the other guy. He spoke in seventy more cities that Richard Nixon did. The popular vote was close, but Kennedy won by eighty electoral votes. Nixon later implied that Richard Daley fixed the election for Kennedy, but Daley said that in some rural counties in Illinois, Nixon got more votes that there were registered voters. Nixon had every opportunity to win. He benefitted from being Eisenhower's Vice President, even though Ike couldn't stand the guy. Ike wanted to dump Nixon for his second term, but Nixon had gone on TV with the Checkers speech and the nation bought it.

By the time Kennedy and Nixon squared off for their first televised debate, Kennedy had lost all respect for Nixon as a candidate and a person. He thought Nixon was shallow and dishonest. When he had watched Nixon make his acceptance speech at the Republican Convention, Kennedy remarked that he owed it to the country to keep that guy out of the White House. During the debate, you can see Kennedy looking at Nixon with a derisive expression. Kennedy couldn't hide his dislike for that puffed-up phony.

After the first debate, Nixon asked to meet with Kennedy. The two men talked for a short time and Kennedy came away angry. He said all Nixon talked about was the weather and his lack of sleep, but every time he saw a photographer raise his camera, Nixon would point his finger at Kennedy's chest like he was straightening him out on some issue. Kennedy came away disgusted. He said if he had to resort to methods like that, he didn't want the job.

The last week of the campaign may be something that we'll never see again. Kennedy had been putting in eighteen hour days, but he pulled out all the stops during that final week. Los Angeles, San Francisco, Phoenix, Albuquerque, Amarillo, Wichita Falls, Oklahoma City. Pennsylvania, Virginia, Ohio, Illinois, New York, Connecticut, New Jersey, Maine and

Massachusetts. Not more than four hours sleep on any given night. That's how you win an election.

On the next to last night of the campaign, Kennedy landed outside Waterbury, Connecticut. It was past midnight. All along the twenty-five mile route from the airport to Waterbury, people stood with coats over their pajamas. They held torches and flashlights and cheered as he went by. They had stood in the dark until 2:00 AM. They wanted to see Kennedy. When he got to his hotel, there were forty thousand people gathered in the city square. Kennedy went out on the balcony and made a short speech and thanked them for their support. They would not leave. He returned to the balcony and made a second speech. It was almost dawn.

JFK IV

The American people knew they had something different in John Kennedy. He was not your typical politician. He talked straight and he had convictions. The depth of his speeches made you forget that he was young and Catholic. He had one serious personal weakness and it would become a greater problem after he became President. John Kennedy was obsessed with beautiful women. Whether he got the personal feedback or emotional gratification that he didn't get as a child, we'll never know. The fact is that he couldn't say no to an attractive woman. After he became President, they were waiting everywhere. It didn't help that he had Frank Sinatra and Peter Lawford pimping for him.

On the night of the inaugural ball, Kennedy had promised Sinatra that he would stop by a party that was being held in the same hotel. Sinatra had Angie Dickenson waiting for the President. She was a pretty young actress. Half an hour later, Kennedy returned to the ball. Jackie was not amused. No one had to explain to her what had happened. Her father had been a womanizer and now she had to endure the same humiliation from her husband. She later had her own involvements with a New York millionaire and an Italian race car driver.

Evidently, the Kennedys were promoting a more European tradition. Our puritanical background does not allow for such things. When John Kennedy went to the West Coast, Marilyn Monroe would be waiting. There was also a long running affair with Judith Campbell. The problem was that she was also involved with mobster Sam Giancana. It put Kennedy in a vulnerable position which wasn't lost on our top crime dog, J. Edgar Hoover. Of course Edgar had affairs of his own, but never with women.

When you consider this weakness in Kennedy against his compassion and tenacity, it means that he was human. There aren't too many saints amongst us. There are plenty of self-righteous types, but not too many saints. Kennedy certainly wasn't one of them. In the years since his death, there has been so much written about his affairs with women that many people seem to have forgotten his accomplishments. With the exception of Lincoln and the Civil War or FDR and the Great Depression, no other president had ever faced so many problems on Inauguration Day.

In 1960, we were at the height of the Cold War. We were in a nuclear arms race with the Soviet Union. There were enough intercontinental ballistic missiles armed with nuclear warheads to kill everyone in the World several times over. To the old colonialists who were determined to protect their foreign investments, it was convenient to blame Russia or Communism for any threat to their overseas profits. These hard-liners would risk nuclear war with Russia in order to continue their exploitation of Third World countries. Kennedy could not accept war as a viable solution. In this regard, he was in agreement with old military pros like Douglas MacArthur and Dwight Eisenhower. Kennedy also thought that these smaller nations ought to have a chance to govern themselves with a minimum of outside interference. From day one, this put him at odds with the Shadow Elite and the military establishment. The vehicle that these powerful forces had used to control governments throughout the Third World was the CIA. Their motives or actions did not have to be explained to Congress or the American people. This apparatus was later turned on Kennedy.

Organized crime was another juggernaut facing the new President. Kennedy's work on the McClellan Committee in the Senate had made him aware of the extent to which the Mob had taken over labor unions and entire sections of the inner cities. A loan of three million dollars from the Teamster's Pension Fund would be given to Pick Hobson's Riverside Hotel in Nevada. Two months later the hotel would declare bankruptcy. The pension fund was out three million dollars. Retiring truck drivers would then be denied their pensions on technicalities to make up the loss. That was the scam. Kennedy understood the problem and was determined to do right by the union members who were being exploited. With his brother as Attorney General, Kennedy declared war on the Mafia. There were more prosecutions of organized crime during the three years of the Kennedy Administration than at any time before or since.

With Martin Luther King leading marches across the South, the Civil Rights Movement had reached a crucial point. Black people were willing to die in order to achieve equality under the law. Conflict over Civil Rights in the South had reached a higher level than at any time since the Civil War. With all the other problems facing his new administration, John Kennedy was reluctant to get mired down in the problems in the South. As the violence escalated, he realized that the full force of the Federal Government would have to be brought to bear. He sent in the National Guard to back down southern governors and enforce the law. This made Kennedy more hated in the South than any president since Abraham Lincoln.

Kennedy was spread so thin that he had trouble finding time for his favorite programs. He had arrived in Washington with ideas for low-income housing and improved education. He wanted American kids to be more physically fit and healthy. He wanted to pass legislation on something called Medicare. He wanted to start a military alternative that he called The Peace Corps. He was sure if he could send the more idealistic young people to the poorest countries, America might not look so much like the international bully. Kennedy also thought that we could progress much faster in the exploration of outer space. He thought we could put a man on the moon by the end of the decade. He was soon overwhelmed with the Cold War and Civil Rights. In his effort to deal with these problems, he was often opposed by members of his own administration. There were times when only he and his brother, Robert, were in agreement.

Kennedy had enough self-confidence that he decided to surround himself with men whose views were different than his own. His cabinet was filled with conservatives like Dean Rusk and Douglas Dillon.

Kennedy wanted people around him who would challenge his own point of view. What he didn't realize was that some of these men had loyalties other than to the President. He was like Caesar surrounded by men who were a danger to him. As Kennedy reached his third year in office, he had decided to withdraw from Vietnam. He signed an order to bring the first thousand "advisors" home. He had initiated the nuclear test-ban treaty with the Soviets and he had promised Khrushchev that we would stay out of Cuba. To the hawks around him, Kennedy had gone soft on communism.

From the time John Kennedy travelled to Vienna to meet Khrushchev, the two men developed somewhat of an understanding. Kennedy was afraid that the huge crowds that turned out for his motorcade might embarrass the Russian Premier, but it was the kind of reception he received everywhere he traveled. At first, Khrushchev was very intense and threatening. Kennedy was more laid-back and reflective. He would often answer Khrushchev with a humorous remark which would put the Russian leader more at ease. When Khrushchev warned Kennedy that the Russians were going to unify the city of Berlin under Soviet Rule, Kennedy assured him that America would use any means available to see that West Berlin remained free. British Prime Minister Harold Macmillan later said that Kennedy's greatest accomplishment as President was calling Khrushchev's bluff concerning Berlin.

By the time Kennedy left Vienna, he and Khrushchev weren't fast friends but they understood one another. When Kennedy got back to Washington,

Khrushchev sent him a whaling vessel carved out of a walrus tusk along with a friendly letter. From that point, the two leaders corresponded off the official record. Kennedy saw a possibility for a thaw in the Cold War, but he was at odds with men whose livelihood depended on military escalation. Kennedy used to say that if they only said one thing about him after he was gone, it was that he kept the peace. I'm told that when Khrushchev got word of Kennedy's death, he broke down and cried.

On the way to Vienna, Kennedy had stopped in Paris to meet with Charles De Gaulle. Kennedy had been warned that De Gaulle was aloof and arrogant. Fortunately, Jacqueline Kennedy spoke fluent French and had a good working knowledge of French history. De Gaulle spent most of his time flirting with Jackie which was fine with the President. Anything to improve international relations. Kennedy would later refer to himself as the man who accompanied Mrs. Kennedy to Paris. Unlike most politicians, Kennedy did not feel the need to be the center of attention. He would much rather sit back and observe. Before he left Paris, De Gaulle took him aside and warned him not to get bogged down in Southeast Asia like the French had. This supported the advice that Kennedy had gotten from Douglass MacArthur and Mike Mansfield.

The Cuban Missile Crisis was the biggest test for Kennedy as President. Our reconnaissance flights had photographed missile sites being built in Cuba. They were a few weeks from being operational. When completed, they would threaten everything east of the Mississippi River. Kennedy had less than two weeks to defuse the problem. His military advisors were united in wanting to bomb Cuba. Kennedy worried that that would cause the Russians to move against West Berlin or China to invade Taiwan. A bombing of the Cuban missile sites would result in the death of Russians. Kennedy had surmised that Khrushchev was opposed by hard-liners in Russia much the same way he was often at odds with his own military advisors. If Khrushchev was forced to retaliate against Berlin, Kennedy had promised to defend that city. The next step would be the use of nuclear weapons.

The Pentagon assured Kennedy that we could win a nuclear war with the Soviet Union. They conceded that millions of lives would be lost, but they were certain of our superiority. Kennedy saw that alternative as insane. He also felt that he knew Khrushchev well enough to think that the Russian Premier wanted no part of a nuclear conflict. He wanted to offer Khrushchev a way out of the conflict that would allow him to save face with the hawks in his own government. Against the advice of the Pentagon and his military advisors, Kennedy decided on a naval blockade of Cuba. Khrushchev sent word to Kennedy that the price for Russia taking its missiles out of Cuba would be America's agreement to stay out of Cuba. Then Khrushchev demanded that we take our ballistic missiles out of Turkey. Kennedy guessed that the additional demand came from the military hard-liners in the Soviet Union.

While Kennedy weighed the offer, an American spy plane violated Soviet airspace. Kennedy figured that someone in our military was trying to provoke Russia against his orders. Then one of our gunships left the blockade and threatened a soviet ship. Kennedy was trying desperately to control his own military while he tried to reach an agreement with Russia.

Several months earlier Kennedy had ordered that our missiles be removed from Turkey because they had been made obsolete by the Polaris missiles that could be launched from submarines. If he agreed to both of Russia's demands, it might help Khrushchev save face and retain power. Kennedy knew that there were more aggressive and dangerous men who might come to power if Khrushchev was deposed. Kennedy sent word of our agreement and war was narrowly averted. Kennedy felt that the United States had lost nothing, but many people within the military establishment felt he had backed down from Russia. They were angry that we didn't bomb Cuba and seize the island. There were some who advised the bombing of Cuba even after we had made the agreement. For the second time in his presidency, John Kennedy had come face to face with the enemy. Both times, it was his own military.

The first confrontation was during the Bay of Pigs fiasco. The only way that Kennedy would sign off on the mission was with the clear understanding that no U.S. military personnel would be involved. It would have to be Cubans liberating Cuba. When the bombers with Cuban pilots were not allowed to leave Guatemala the night before the invasion, the mission was doomed. The five unmarked jets would have taken out Castro's last three fighter jets and left the landing force with no resistance from Cuba. Once again, a higher authority than the President came into play. The CIA tried to force Kennedy's hand by grounding the planes in Guatemala. Kennedy would have to authorize U.S. air support for the landing force. Kennedy was angry when he realized that the CIA assumed that he would give in and authorize the use of American forces. He stood his ground, much to the surprise of the Pentagon and the CIA. Many Cubans were slaughtered on the beaches of Cuba that day. Kennedy publicly accepted the blame, but he knew the failure was the fault of Allen Dulles.

Dulles was conveniently out of the country on a vacation at the time of the Bay of Pigs. Kennedy thought it was odd that the Director of the CIA would choose to be out of the country during the most important mission that the Agency had attempted since WWII. Kennedy wondered if Dulles knew all along that the objective was to force him violate the law or see the mission fail. Kennedy rounded up Dulles and his two top assistants, Charles Cabel and Richard Bissell. He said he didn't appreciate the deception and poor planning of the Cuban invasion and he fired the three of them. Kennedy also said that he was going to break up the CIA and scatter it to the winds. From that day forward, John Kennedy was a dead man.

While the President was battling with his own military and trying to avoid nuclear confrontations, he was angering much of the South by enforcing civil rights laws. To Harry Truman's credit, he had overcome his conservative southern upbringing and put forth civil rights legislation. Then in the mid-fifties, the Supreme Court unanimously outlawed segregation in public schools. When Kennedy took office in 1960, he was considered sympathetic to the equal rights movement, but he was not a leading advocate. Kennedy had a lot to prove in the area of civil rights.

137

He finally decided to use executive action rather than rely on Congress.

From the time Kennedy helped get Martin Luther King, Jr. out of jail in Georgia, his political career was tied to the civil rights movement. The right thing was usually the right thing politically, but Kennedy's support of civil rights alienated a good part of the South. His approach would be a greater number of blacks appointed to jobs in the federal government and a vigorous protection of civil rights from the Department of Justice. He added five black federal judges to the existing three. He filled high level housing and labor posts with black appointees. Kennedy requested a study to determine the number of black people in government jobs. He was shocked by the results. He ordered his cabinet to remedy the situation by finding qualified black people for civil service jobs. At the higher levels of the federal government, the number of black employees doubled during the Kennedy Administration.

Kennedy formed a committee to rectify job discrimination and appointed Lyndon Johnson to run it. Johnson had always been proud of the support he had gotten from blacks and hispanics in Texas, and being from the South, he would not be as easy to attack by southern conservatives. Bobby Kennedy, for his part, raised the number of black attorneys in the justice department by five times. He also warned that if court orders are circumvented in any part of the country, the Justice Department would act. This would be the arena of serious conflict.

The first area of contention was black voting rights. In 1960, only fifteen percent of eligible black voters were registered. In most counties in Mississippi, there was not one registered black voter. The Eisenhower Administration had filed a few suits on the matter, but none in Mississippi. In his first two years as Attorney General, Bobby Kennedy filed over forty suits including eight in Mississippi. He also worked behind the scenes with black leaders to organize a massive black voter registration drive. This was not appreciated across the South.

Encouraged by the progress, CORE sent out its first group of "freedom riders" in 1961 to challenge segregation in interstate bus terminals. When they got to Alabama, they were beaten and the bus was burned by an angry white mob. President Kennedy called Alabama Governor John Patterson. The governor refused to return the call so Bobby Kennedy sent in six hundred federal marshals to protect the freedom riders. The civil rights movement had escalated. There was no way to put the genie back in the bottle. The President announced that anyone who travels, for whatever reason he travels, would receive full protection under the Constitution.

The next challenge came when James Meredith applied for entrance to the University of Mississippi and was rejected on the grounds of race. He went to court and eventually won the right to be admitted to the university. Mississippi Governor Ross Barnett announced that he would not surrender to the evil forces of tyranny. When Meredith arrived on campus escorted by federal marshals, Barnett read a long proclamation as students sang, "Glory, glory, segregation". Meredith was not allowed to enter.

Bobby Kennedy cited the three top officials at the University of Mississippi with contempt of court and Meredith again tried to gain entrance. Governor Barnett physically blocked him while students yelled, "communists" and "go home nigger". Bobby called the Governor. Barnett said that it was best if Meredith not go to Ole Miss. Bobby replied that Meredith liked Ole Miss. Barnett then told Kennedy that the only way he could save face on the matter was if the federal marshals drew their guns and forced Barnett to step aside. The problem was that the situation had gained so much attention that red-necks from all over the South were on their way to Oxford, Mississippi. Leading the charge was a retired right-wing general by the name of Edwin Walker.

When Meredith tried to enter Ole Miss for the third time , the crowd was so large and aggressive that Bobby Kennedy decided not to escalate the situation with the use of guns. Barnett was cited with civil contempt but he still wouldn't yield. The Kennedys couldn't believe that no one from the academic community at Ole Miss had shown the courage to challenge the Governor. The next step would be the use of federal troops.

Barnett agreed to stay out of the way as Meredith was registered and taken to the dormitory. Federal officials waited in the administration building. As the sun went down an angry mob had gathered chanting, "two, four, one, three, we hate Ken-ne-dy." You have to realize that this was the Deep South where even college students were not the sharpest tools in the shed. They started to pelt the building with bricks and bottles yelling, "kill those nigger loving bastards". Okay you crackers, here comes the tear gas.

Kennedy had gone on TV to explain to the nation what was happening in Mississippi. He said that America cannot tolerate a situation where a man or group of men can use force to defy the Constitution. He said we can't have a situation where a citizen would not be safe from his neighbors. Kennedy hoped to unify public opinion against racism in Mississippi.

In the darkness at Ole Miss, up steps General Walker who announces that he had come all the way from Dallas, Texas. Behind him is a mob outfitted with rifles and shotguns. As the tear gas begins to run out, the first rifle shots are heard along with Confederate war howls. The National Guard and regular Army units moved in to disperse the crowd. The battle raged for hours. President Kennedy was on the phone monitoring the situation until dawn. Two men were killed and hundreds were wounded in a scene right out of the Civil War. Meredith was greeted the next day with, "was it worth two lives, nigger?" His family was threatened. Their house was shot at. In the end, James Meredith got his degree.

Next stop was Birmingham, Alabama and Police Commissioner Bull Conner. When King's freedom marchers tried to end discrimination in stores and restaurants, Bull Connors' boys went at them with police dogs and fire hoses. There was a scene on the news where a blind man was standing on the sidewalk with chaos all around him. You could hear Bull Conner yell, "Get that blind nigger and put him in a car." Then Governor George Wallace stepped forward and announced that he was not willing to compromise on the issue of segregation. This encouraged the white bigots to bomb houses and businesses in the black neighborhoods of Birmingham. The mayor complained of Martin Luther King, Jr. that "This nigger has the blessing of the Attorney General of the United States." Once again it was time to call in the troops. Throughout Kennedy's three years in office, he was caught in the middle of the civil rights tug-of-war. He had a deep sympathy about the inequality that had been institutionalized since the beginning of this country, but he needed help from southern democrats for the domestic legislation he was trying to pass. Low income housing, Medicare and a higher minimum wage were long overdue. Kennedy felt that he had to protect the constitutional rights of all citizens, but he knew that if he alienated the South, his programs were doomed. Although black leaders admitted that Kennedy had done more for their cause than any president since the Civil War, they were not content with a piecemeal approach. Men like Malcolm X and Elijah Muhammad demanded full access and they demanded it now. Blacks had waited for more than a hundred years for equal rights. They were tired of waiting.

In the spring of 63, a federal judge ruled that two black students must be allowed to enroll at the University of Alabama. George Wallace assured the citizens of Alabama that he would personally bar the entrance of any negroes who attempted to enroll at that fine institution. The National Guard escorted the honorable governor off the steps and no bloodshed occurred. Two months later while John Kennedy was delivering a speech that would put civil rights at the top of his priorities, James Meredith's friend, Medgar Evers, was killed in the driveway of his home. The South had issued its own statement on civil rights.

JFK V

John Kennedy had pointed this country in a new direction. No one can argue that point. In the fall of 63, he was putting together a program he called "the war on poverty." He was still bothered by those miners' families in West Virginia that he had visited in the 1960 campaign. They seemed to be beyond the scope of normal economic solutions. They had fallen behind and they needed help to catch up. Along with the widespread poverty among blacks, Kennedy had decided make an all-out effort in 64 to focus on the problems of the poor. To Lyndon Johnson's credit, he carried out these policies with as much determination as Kennedy would have.

The other focal point was to be peace with Russia. Kennedy had developed a good rapport with Khrushchev that culminated in the signing of the Test-Ban Treaty. He wanted to continue to de-escalate the rhetoric as well as the military hardware. This put him at odds with the Old Guard. When Kennedy made his famous speech at American University where he called for an end to the Cold War, there was a lot of grumbling at the Pentagon. Not only did these old warriors think that you could not make peace with communists, they felt their whole reason for existence was in jeopardy.

People around the world rallied behind Kennedy's words, but many powerful people in his own country did not like them. He was thinking beyond himself and his own country. He was thinking in terms of what was best for peace in the world. He was moving way too fast for the lumbering Cold Warriors who sought to control him.

When Kennedy went to West Berlin in June of 63, he was received by the largest crowds ever to welcome an American president. When he attended mass with Conrad Adenauer in Cologne, four hundred thousand people gathered around the old cathedral for a chance to see Kennedy. Similar crowds welcomed him in Bonn and Frankfurt. When he finally drove through West Berlin, more than a million people lined the streets. A German official told the surprised President that not even Hitler had ever drawn such crowds. The people of West Germany were determined to see a man of peace. Americans may have forgotten what John Kennedy stood for, but the message was not lost on the people of West Berlin. Kennedy was their champion. He had defended them from Soviet annexation and now he was trying to end the Cold War.

When the President arrived to make his speech at City Hall in Schoenberg, people were jammed shoulder to shoulder as far as the eye could see. As Kennedy began to speak, the crowd roared its approval. They leaned forward to get every word. When he told them that free men everywhere were citizens of Berlin, the crowd erupted and the noise was overpowering. Every time the President repeated, "Ich bin ein Berliner," the place went nuts. You have to wonder how Kennedy felt as he listened to the deafening approval from these people in another country. When he finished, he told an aide that they would never have another day like this again.

From Berlin, Kennedy went to Ireland to visit the home of his great-grandfather and the grave of his favorite sister, Kathleen. The city of Dublin turned out to welcome their favorite son. O'Connell Street was jammed like everywhere else Kennedy traveled in those last days of his presidency. Irish women yelled, "Bless you," as he drove by. There wasn't a dry eye in the crowd. It was a proud day for the Irish as they showed their affection for the man who had become the world's best hope for peace.

Near Duganstown on the River Barrow, a group of school children sang one of Kennedy's favorite Irish songs called, "The Boys of Wexford." It was about the long fight for freedom in Ireland. When they had finished, the nun asked the President if he would like them to sing another song. Another verse of "The Boys of Wexford" would be fine, Kennedy told her. This was his sentimental side. He was proud to be Irish and he suffered with their long history of disappointment. When the singing had ended, Kennedy pointed across the river and told the crowd that if his great-grandfather had not left New Ross, he would probably be working at that fertilizer plant. Humor was always his way to shake off the sadness.

Sixteen years earlier when Kennedy had last visited Ireland, he had been given directions by a man named Robert Burrell. Kennedy had appreciated the man's kindness. He sent some of his people out to find the man that he had met on the road years earlier. When a Secret Service Agent finally located Burrell, he asked him if he would like meet President Kennedy. Burrell answered that he had already met him sixteen years ago.

Another hundred thousand people greeted Kennedy at Cork and then it was on to Dublin to make a speech to the combined houses of parliament. The speech was carried on Irish national television. Kennedy used most of the speech to discuss Ireland's long fight for freedom while he quoted James Joyce and George Bernard Shaw. After the speech, while Kennedy was shaking hands in the crowd, a woman pointed out two Irish legislators who were having a lively conversation off to the side of the room. Those two men hadn't spoken to each other in twenty years, she told Kennedy. Then she said that Ireland's love for Kennedy was the only thing her country had agreed on since the British Conscription Bill of 1918. Kennedy told her that he held the greatest affection for Ireland and he would return soon.

Later that summer, John Kennedy endured his last personal tragedy. In early August, his son Patrick was born prematurely after Jackie had undergone emergency surgery. The baby developed a lung infection and died two days later. Kennedy was more openly grief-stricken than any of his friends could remember. After all his recent success with the Test-Ban Treaty and his trip to Germany, the loss of his son seemed to make him a more humble man. He found more time to spend with John and Caroline. In the afternoon, Jackie would meet him for lunch.

That fall he went to the Harvard-Columbia football game. At halftime, Kennedy and two of his friends left the game and got an Irish cop to block the parking lot so the press could not follow them. They drove to the cemetery in Brookline to visit Patrick's grave. As Kennedy knelt down to pray, he commented that Patrick seemed to be so alone there. He had no way of knowing that a short time later his son would be buried next to him at Arlington National Cemetery.

When you look at what John Kennedy accomplished in less than three years in office, you have to wonder how the world might have been different if he had lived to serve a second term. No Vietnam. An end to the arms race with Russia. An end to American interference in Third World countries. Bringing the CIA back under the control of government. A new respect for America around the world. A push to end poverty and improve educational access to all Americans. Encouragement of the arts. Confidence in our government. A new respect for public service. An optimism that the American Experiment would only get better. Most of this was lost on November 22, 1963.

While America was shocked by the death of President Kennedy, other parts of the world were devastated. He might have been more important to others than he was to us. In Algiers, socialist President Ahmed Ben Bella told our ambassador that he would rather it had happened to him than to Kennedy. He thought Kennedy was more important to world peace. In Guinea, Sekou Toure said he had lost his only true friend in the outside world. In the back country of Nzerekore, a group of natives gave their American pastor a small sum of money to buy a rush mat for John Kennedy's burial. Ugandans sat in silence for hours on the lawn of the American Embassy. In Mali, militant President Modibo Keita brought his honor guard to the American Embassy and delivered a eulogy. An African magazine editorialized that Kennedy's death ended the first real chance for intelligent new leadership in this century. Africans had spoken. The man who tried to protect them was gone.

In Moscow, Khrushchev broke down and cried. Kennedy's honest dialogue had given him hope that an end to the Cold War was possible. He had prepared a program to drastically cut Russia's military budget in favor of domestic programs. That possibility ended in Dallas. The Russian Premier was first to the American Embassy to sign the book of condolence.

In West Berlin, people lighted candles in their windows as three-hundred thousand lost souls marched by torchlight. In Poland, university students filled the streets to mourn the American President's death. In London, the big bell of Westminster Abbey tolled solidly for one hour. Thousands of people gathered in Grosvenor Square and lined up to sign the condolence book. Prime Minister MacMillan said that John Kennedy had single-handedly carried the hope of the new world. On a Friday evening in Paris, the shops along the Champs Elysees were closed and the street was deserted. Ireland shut down. Radio programming was cancelled. Their young champion was dead. An Irish poet said that the whole country of Ireland was destroyed that night. In Yugoslavia, Marshal Tito read a eulogy over state radio.

All over Latin America, Kennedy's picture was torn from newspapers and tacked up in huts and shacks throughout the barrios. Shrines were set up in his memory. Streets and schools soon bore the name of Kennedy. In Cuba, Castro told a French reporter, "This is bad news. Everything has changed." Halfway around the world in the Solomon Islands, a native who had rowed his canoe for twenty-four hours to deliver a message written by John Kennedy on a coconut husk, heard the news of Kennedy's death. He said that he would never be happy again.

Why did John Kennedy affect people around the world this way? He treated the leader of the smallest nation in Africa the same way he treated the Prime Minister of Great Britain. He had an honest look in his eye while he listened to their problems. As an Irishman, he had a natural sympathy for the underdog. He had a lively sense of humor that was often at his own expense. He took the Presidency very seriously, but he didn't take himself too seriously. Even when he was busy, he would take time to talk to any group of kids who were touring the White House. He had a deep appreciation for literature and poetry. He wanted to be a writer. He considered public service an honorable profession and gained a level of respect around the world that few politicians have ever enjoyed. He was very proud to be President of the United States of America. His work had just begun. He had many important plans for his second term.

DULLES AND COMPANY

Allen Dulles enjoyed total respect whether he walked the halls of Congress or the Pentagon. From his very effective days as an official in the Office of Strategic Services, he had developed respect within the military community. From his background as a lawyer on Wall Street, he had developed powerful contacts with Banking and Big Business. He was intelligent and well-mannered with the look of a college professor. Calm, personable and deadly. This man could sign a death warrant with the ease of someone going out for a Sunday drive.

During the Eisenhower Administration, John Foster Dulles was Secretary of State and Allen Dulles was Director of Central Intelligence. These two brothers pretty much ran foreign policy during this period and they did it with a self-righteous arrogance that left a lot of people dead. Foster Dulles liked to say, "There were two kinds of people in the world. There are those who are Christians and support free enterprise and there are others". He might have added, others who we will call communists. If you were the leader of a small country and you would not accept bribes and allow your country to be ransacked by American corporations, you would be labeled a communist and you would be overthrown by our CIA. That's what the Cold War meant to the Dulles Brothers.

Russia was aggressively looking for satellites and their influence had to be opposed. All Americans agreed on that. Too often, however, one of these Third World countries would have to turn to Russia for help because of CIA interference. It was the chicken and the egg deal. Would these countries have gotten involved with communism if we had not interfered with their governments? In most cases, these countries did not like Russia any better than the United States. They were put in a position where they had to choose between what they considered two evils.

One month after John Kennedy was assassinated, former President Harry Truman issued a public statement. He said he was worried about the increased power of the Agency that he had created. He said that it had become a policy-making arm of the government. He went on to say that the CIA had become a symbol of sinister and mysterious foreign intrigue. The actions of the CIA were casting doubt on our ability to maintain a free and open society. Truman had gotten the message with the death of John Kennedy. The Central Intelligence Agency was out of control.

So let's review for a moment. When he left office in 1960, Dwight D. Eisenhower warned America to guard against the ever increasing power of the military-industrial complex. This was a former military man. Shortly after John Kennedy was killed, Harry Truman felt compelled to warn this country about the uncontrolled power of the CIA, which Truman had created. He said that their sinister activities had become a threat to our free society. Shortly before his death, Lyndon Johnson said that he thought a rogue element of the CIA was involved in John Kennedy's assassination. This from the man who became President as a result of Kennedy's death. Three former American Presidents were calling attention to the uncontrolled power of the military industry and the CIA.

Allen Dulles always said that Central Intelligence was like any other agency. It acted on behalf of its clients. Originally its clients were the President and the American people. Under Dulles, the CIA's clients became major corporations, oil companies and large defense contractors. These were our benefactors. They put up the money for our covert activities all over the world. Dulles had established a network of powerful eastern bankers. These guys controlled the purse strings of every major industry in the country. The Shadow Elite. These guys dictate policy, even to presidents. The major banks and corporations control every aspect of our lives. These were the only men that Allen Dulles respected. He answered to them and no one else. By 1963, they all agreed that Kennedy was bad for business. He was not going into Vietnam and he was going to destroy the CIA.

During his stay with the OSS, Dulles had developed a working relationship with the Pentagon and defense contractors. He might have been the only guy in the country who could have set up the CIA to run the way it did. His loyalty was always with his business associates, the bankers and the military. He saw presidents and congressmen as uninformed men who got in his way. Kennedy was a particular pain in the ass. He was rich and independent. He followed his own ideas. Most politicians could be bribed or intimidated. Kennedy was the exception.

Dulles wasn't content to have a free hand to raise and spend money. The amounts never had to be disclosed. Any covert operation could be denied in terms of National Security. He had a bigger plan. He wanted his own people throughout the news media. This way he could control public opinion. Every fall, Dulles would host a dinner in Virginia. Members of the print and television media would be invited. The idea was to put fear into the hearts of our guests that the world was a dangerous place and the Agency was doing everything in its power to make it a little safer. Dulles was a very sophisticated guy. He used all his charm to win the loyalty of these journalists. Some of them, like Bill Buckley, had been assets of ours for years.

Not everyone in the news media sold his soul to the Agency. Two months before John Kennedy was removed in Dallas, a reporter for The New York Times by the name of Arthur Krock tried to warn this country about the growing power of the CIA. He recounted several situations in Vietnam where the Agency had disregarded President Kennedy's instructions communicated through Ambassador Henry Cabot Lodge. Krock called the CIA a malignancy that even the president could not control. Many called Krock's statements irresponsible and even un-American.

Krock predicted that if the American government was ever to be victim of a coup, it would be at the hands of the CIA. He said that the methods and tactics of the Agency were not accountable to anyone. This was an insightful man with the courage to print the

153

truth. His prediction came true seven weeks later in Dallas.

Bribery and intimidation were our bread and butter, but we had another approach to winning people over to our agenda. We would recruit journalism major or a law student fresh out of college and put them on the Agency payroll. A monthly stipend. Then we would encourage them to go out and pursue a career in journalism or law enforcement or politics. We would use all of our connections that we had developed over the years to open doors for them. In this way, we had key people to do our bidding in government, law enforcement and the media. David Phillips used to say that a typewriter is much more deadly than a gun.

In 1963 we had made inroads into the media, but we had nowhere near the control that the Shadow Elite has today. With all of your major news outlets being part of some huge multi-national corporate umbrella, you only get the most watered down version of the news. AP, UPI, Time-Life. All are part of some great conglomerate. It's not in the interest of these huge corporations to stir up controversy. They're busy making the world safe for their companies.

Here's why you don't get much honest news coverage these days. Westinghouse owns CBS. Westinghouse is a major defense contractor. They also own power production plants all over the world, especially in Third World countries. In the mid-eighties, Westinghouse built the Bataan nuclear power plant in the Philippines for more than a billion dollars. It was supposed to cost half that much. The problem was that the plant was built too close to an active volcano and never generated one kilowatt of power.

Where did the Philippine government get the money to build this plant?   From the American taxpayer supported Export-Import Bank.   Why was this loan approved?   Because the head of the council that approved the loan was also a CEO at Westinghouse.   I keep telling you it's an insider's game.   The people of the Philippines are still paying something like seventy million dollars a year in interest on a loan for a power plant that never worked.   The American people are out the billion dollar loan.   Who benefitted?   Westinghouse.   Do you think CBS news is likely to run a story on this fraud?   Not on your life.   This corporate takeover of the news has continued to accelerate in recent years.

After John Kennedy was killed, The New York Times and Life Magazine ran serious challenges to the Warren Commission.   They had set up their own investigative teams.   They knew that the official version of Kennedy's death was nowhere near the truth.   Anyone who has seriously looked into the events in Dallas knows that the Warren Report is silly.   Anyone who has that knowledge and supports the official version has sold his soul to the Shadow Elite.   This includes everyone from Dan Rather and Bill Buckley to Robert Blakey.   The new poster boy is Gerald Posner with his silly little haircut.   I think he was some failed attorney from Philadelphia who found he could make a nice living by trying to clean up the business in Dallas for us.   When he had misrepresented everything about the assassination of John Kennedy, he turned his attention to Memphis.   You guessed it.   James Earl Ray acted alone.   Anyone who says otherwise is a conspiracy nut.

155

A guy like Oliver Stone can do more damage to the official version with one movie than can be offset by all of our paid hacks combined. It must be frustrating to Posner and Blakey. Oliver Stone has so much credibility even though he had the entire force of our Shadow Government doing everything in its power to shut him down. Have you ever heard of a movie being torn apart in the press before it was even edited into a final version? That's a dead giveaway that the Shadow Elite is worried. As long as we can keep Americans mentally lazy and uninformed, our job is easy. The independent press has been eliminated so all we have to worry about is troublemakers like Mark Lane, Jim Garrison and Oliver Stone. I would say that the hardest thing to find in America these days is a person who can think for himself. It's difficult to arrive at the truth when all the information you receive is twisted and distorted.

The CIA was not alone in creating imaginative plans for subversion during the Kennedy years. The National Security Agency, which these days has a budget much greater than the CIA's, came up with an idea in 1962 called "Operation Northwoods". The idea was to implicate Cuba in terrorism against the United States. Among the violent acts considered were blowing up a ship at Guantanamo Bay where the casualty list would cause a national outcry for revenge. We could sink boats with Cuban refugees or stage a terrorist attack in Miami. They even considered shooting down the rocket that would send John Glenn into space. The entire package was approved by the Joint Chiefs.

When the proposal reached Kennedy, he was furious. He said absolutely not. We were not about to kill Americans for an excuse to get back at Cuba. Once again it was Kennedy against the military. One sane man against these powerful fanatics. He told the Joint Chiefs that we weren't going into Cuba. Period. Army General Lyman Lemnitzer was head of the Joint Chiefs who had submitted this bizarre proposal to McNamara. Kennedy immediately transferred his fat ass to a lesser position. The military was trying to dictate American foreign policy. Kennedy, alone, stood in their way. Despite the President's rejection of this harebrained idea, the Joint Chiefs continued to scheme about ways to stage events for an excuse to invade Cuba. Kennedy had merely become an obstacle for the military and the CIA. There was tremendous relief in those circles when that obstacle was removed in Dallas.

After the Warren Report was issued, Dulles used to joke with his friends that the conspiracy buffs were going to have a field day with what happened in Dallas. He thought it was funny that he had been in Dallas a few weeks before the event. He said that history showed that every president who had been assassinated had been the victim of a deranged loner. More recently, Martin Luther King and Bobby Kennedy as well as George Wallace had fallen at the hand of a lone nut. He thought the formula was irrefutable. It worked every time. He knew there would be a few troublemakers, but he said that the American people didn't read much. There were so many layers of false information to dig through that it would be years before anyone got close to the truth. Anyone who reached that point could easily be discredited by our whores in the media.

J. Edgar Hoover's name has taken quite a beating in the years since his death, but Dulles will suffer a worse

157

fate in the long run. He was a sociopath, pure and simple. Less than human the way I see it. A guy who brought planeloads of Nazis to this country after the war and used them in all kinds of experiments on unsuspecting victims. A guy who could issue a death warrant on a foreign leader as easily as another man would sit down to breakfast. Dulles did the bidding for his circle of wealthy friends completely without conscience. With a nod of the head to his right-hand man, Ed Lansdale, Dulles set in motion a plot to kill a president who had the courage to stand up to him and his kind.

DAG HAMMARSKJOLD

We talked earlier about Patrice Lamumba who was a popular leader of the Congo whom Dulles decided to eliminate. Since that time, the people of that country have rotted in poverty while Joseph Mobutu became the richest man in Africa. There's a little more to that story. You might not believe what I'm about to tell you. Lamumba had just been elected in the Congo when the Belgians decided that they were in danger of losing their mineral investments in Katanga Province. So they encouraged a greedy crook by the name of Tsombe to stage a revolt against Lamumba in Katanga. Lamumba respected the concept of private property but he wanted the people of the Congo to share in these tremendous mineral riches. Gold, silver, diamonds, uranium. One of the richest pieces of ground in the world. England, Belgium and the United States were already heavily invested in mining operations there.   Two major American investors were Douglas Dillon and his good friend, Nelson Rockefeller. The talk of nationalizing or heavily taxing those mines was unacceptable to everyone concerned.

Lamumba made a trip to New York where he asked for our help in driving out the Belgians. Eisenhower was President at the time.   When he got no encouragement, he turned to Russia for weapons to fight the Belgians himself. He made it clear that the West was going to have to pay for the privilege of mining the Congo's resources. At this point the Agency encouraged Tsombe to declare Katanga an independent province. Lamumba had no choice but to fight the rebellion or lose the most valuable part of his new country. He asked the United Nations for help. They agreed to send in a peace keeping force. The civil war was on.

Our first order of business was to get rid of Lamumba. Executive Action. Allen Dulles felt that we were on solid enough grounds that he went to President Eisenhower for his approval. He convinced Ike that Lamumba was already accepting aid from Russia. Dulles explained that the situation would be much worse than Cuba because of the Congo's wealth and their influence on surrounding African countries. Ike agreed.

Dulles cabled our station chief in the Congo, Lawrence Devlin, that two assassins under the code names; QJ/WIN and WI/ROGUE were being sent to carry out the assignment. This was in the fall of 60. John Kennedy was running for President. He asked Averill Harriman if he thought it would be wise if he made a speech in support of Lamumba. Harriman advised him not to publicly come out in support of Lamumba. What Kennedy didn't know was that Harriman traveled in the same circle as Allen Dulles and Douglas Dillon. The fix was in.

With Tsombe benefitting from our help as well as the Belgians, The UN was powerless to protect Lamumba or keep his country together. Dulles and Company were worried that if Lamumba wasn't dead before Kennedy was inaugurated, all hope to salvage the mining interests in Katanga might be lost. After the Agency backed rebels had successfully cut off all of Lumumba's escape routes, the Tsombe forces finally caught up with him. They beat him to a bloody mess, but he was still alive. They put him in a cage and kept him suspended in air with a crane. He was killed on January 17th which was three days before Kennedy's inauguration.

During Kennedy's first week in office he did not realize that Lamumba had been killed. Our new president had no idea what our Shadow Government had done. He made a speech saying that the United Nations was our best hope for shielding the new and the weak nations of the world. He was referring to the Congo. When Kennedy learned of Lumumba's death, he sent word to Russia that he wanted to negotiate a peace so the Congo would remain united. When word got back to Dulles, he said that Kennedy had sold out to the communists. Dulles had eliminated Lamumba and began to lay the groundwork for Kennedy's removal. Remember, if you wouldn't play ball with the Colonialists, you were a communist. In his first week in office, John Kennedy had taken on the Cold Warriors. He had laid down the gauntlet. In trying to do right by the Congo he had put himself at risk. Dag Hammarskjold, the Secretary General of the UN, predicted that there would be a powerful backlash against Kennedy.

Kennedy's new policy on the Congo called for all the warring factions to be brought under control and the country to be neutralized. Katanga would not be allowed to secede. While Kennedy was trying to implement this new policy, Ambassador Timberlake, who was in the Agency's hip pocket, and station chief Devlin were working behind Kennedy's back. The Agency was pouring money and arms into the Tsombe camp. They were so ridiculous that they sent Navy gun boats up the Congo River in a show of support for Tsombe. When Kennedy got word of this open disregard for his policy, he dragged Timberlake's ass back to Washington. He made a statement that an ambassador was to carry out the President's policy and maintain authority over the CIA station chief. This was JFK's first public run-in with the Agency. He had only been in office a few weeks. Kennedy took a lot of criticism in the press for reversing Eisenhower's policy in Africa, especially from our lackeys like William F. Buckley. Less than one month into his new administration, Kennedy had incurred the wrath of the Shadow Elite.

Kennedy sent word to the British-Belgian mining company called Union Miniere that unless they quit bankrolling Katanga's war effort and Tsombe agreed to a unified Congo, the United States was going to join the UN peacekeeping effort with all the force that was required. Tsombe was ready to back down until Senators Thomas Dodd and Barry Goldwater sent word to Tsombe to try and hold out until the 64 election. When Tsombe attempted to visit the United States to drum up conservative support, Kennedy denied him a visa. The President was playing hardball, but he was outnumbered and outflanked.

Kennedy sent word to the new premier of the Congo to keep the faith. He said that he was seeking an end to the arms race with Russia as well as an agreement that would end the fighting in the Congo. Both of these objectives offended those of us who made our living from the Cold War. When Katanga attacked a UN helicopter outpost, the UN unleashed the dogs. Operation Grand Slam. Within a month, the capital of Elizabethville had fallen and Tsombe had fled to Rhodesia. The UN was going to withdraw its peacekeeping forces until John Kennedy addressed the General Assembly and convinced them to keep the UN troops in place for one more year.

When Dag Hammarskjold died in a plane crash in Africa in the fall of 61, Kennedy became more determined than ever to see a united Congo. He openly lined up against the old colonialists who were interested only in protecting their investments. Some of Kennedy's harshest critics, like Dean Rusk, were members of his own administration. Kennedy was surrounded by people who had no loyalty to him or his policies. Follow the money. People will sell their souls for money and power. Kennedy was different. He had his own idea of justice in the Third World and he was ready to fight. From his first month in office, his fate was sealed. He was like the Chinese kid standing in front of the tank in Tiananmen Square.

The reason that John Kennedy gained so much respect around the world during his three years in office was his concern for these developing countries. He understood our neo-colonialism for what it was. He was offended by it and he put himself at risk to try and change it. Kennedy wanted these small countries to be neutral. He wanted to give them a chance at self-government. The Shadow Elite wanted their resources. Russia was determined to counteract our influence. This was the essence of the Cold War. It was never about communism and democracy. It was about who would control the resources of these Third World countries. Kennedy's policies might have been honorable, but they were going to cut into corporate profits. The people in control of this country were not going to allow that to happen.

What I'm leading up to is our involvement in the death of Dag Hammarskjold. The American people now know that the Agency was behind the murders of any number of foreign leaders who were labeled as dangerous communists. How do you think they would react to the news that the Central Intelligence Agency had killed a Secretary General of the United Nations? Once again, it was Allen Dulles who signed the death warrant.

With Lamumba out of the way, we thought we were in control of the Congo. With our hand-picked guy Mobutu, who we had already made a millionaire, it would be business as usual. The only thing standing in our way was Kennedy and Dag Hammarskjold who was a hands-on Secretary General in these Third World countries. He had been in office for eight years and was probably the most effective Secretary General that the UN has ever had. He was a Swedish intellectual, but he had tremendous energy for his job. I think he had descended from some kind of Swedish royalty. We spread rumors that he was homosexual to slow him down a little. You know, neutralize him. He was an extremely hard worker and he was doing everything in his power to maintain a united Congo.

In September of 1961, Hammarskjold was to fly in a private plane to Ndola. This was a city in Northern Rhodesia on the border with the Congo. He was to meet with Tsombe and broker a deal for the reunification of the Congo. His flight plan was supposed to be secret to avoid any attempt on his life. The Agency leaked word of his destination to the press.

Late that night the pilot of Hammarskjold's plane radioed the airport at Ndola that he could see their lights and asked for permission to land. Then the plane disappeared. Dropped out of the sky. The wreckage was found the next morning about ten miles from the airport. The bodies in the plane were riddled with bullets. Several witnesses came forward. They said that a second plane was following above and slightly behind Hammarskjold's plane before it went down. A witness on the ground said he had seen two land-rovers rush to the crash site right after he heard the crash. A short time later they rushed away.

Because of Hammarskjold's unpopular involvement in efforts to reunify the Congo, there was a lot of suspicion about the crash. Most of the accusations were directed at England and Belgium. No one suspected the CIA of any involvement even though Allen Dulles had spoken openly in National Security Council meetings about Dag Hammarskjold becoming a real problem concerning our African policies. Behind the scenes, Dulles was collaborating with Britain's MI5 in something called Operation Celeste, which was the plan to eliminate Dag Hammarskjold.

Union Miniere was to supply a bomb that would be placed in the wheel bay of Hammarskjold's plane by our man whose codename was Dwight. When the plane took off and the wheels retracted, the bomb was supposed to explode. It didn't. The Company doesn't leave anything to chance. There was a backup plan that involved one of our shooters named Culligan. None of this would have ever seen the light of day if Culligan hadn't been thrown in jail on phony bad check charges. Supposedly it was for his own protection, but after several years in jail, Culligan was fed up with his protection plan. He wanted out, but he couldn't get anyone to listen to him.

Culligan had kept a journal of his work for the Agency over a twenty-year period. He was an assassin who knew a lot of dirty secrets. He brought in an attorney and gave him an outline of his activities. The attorney was supposed to take the message to Langley and use the information to leverage the Agency to get him out of jail. He figured he would rather take his chances on the outside than rot in prison. Culligan knew he might be killed, but he was going crazy in jail.

When the attorney read the outline, two lines jumped out at him: "1961-EA-Hammaeskjold-Rhodesia...1963-EA-Kennedy-Dallas." There were a total of six Executive Actions on Culligan's list. The attorney couldn't believe what he had read. He pressed Culligan for details. Culligan would not talk about Dallas, but he agreed to discuss the Hammarskjold murder. He said that he had flown from Tripoli to Abidjan and then to Brazzaville. He had intercepted Hammarskjold's plane near Ndola. When he was above the plane he had fired a semi-automatic weapon until the other plane went down. Culligan told his attorney that he didn't want to take the Hammarskjold job. He had tried to turn down the assignment, but you could not say no to the Agency.

The only thing Culligan was willing to relate about Dallas was that he was paid by the Agency to kill the

Cubans that were involved in the Kennedy assassination. This was done at our camp in Guatemala. He also said that after Nasser, he refused to do another job for the CIA. That's when Culligan fell out of favor with the Agency. Nasser was the last name on the list of Executive Actions.

No matter how hard The Agency tries to keep this stuff under wraps, occasionally a story like Culligan's leaks out. The press won't touch it and you're not going to see it on the evening news. Americans don't want to believe that we would kill our own president, let alone the head of the United Nations. Lyndon Johnson tried to warn us before he died, but no one took him seriously.

MK-ULTRA

The poison that was taken to the Congo as the first option to eliminate Patrice Lamumba was hand delivered by Dr. Sidney Gottlieb. He was one of the German doctors that Allen Dulles had blackflighted over here at the end of WWII. He was put in charge of our labs that developed undetectable methods to eliminate people. Barbiturate suppositories. Injections containing uranium or plutonium. He also helped organize our experiments in mind-control called, MK-ULTRA. We had working agreements with about two dozen hospitals, universities and prisons where they would receive Agency money for allowing us to conduct our experiments. Our program was kept apart from the rest of the institution so we wouldn't attract unnecessary attention. This program lasted two decades from the mid-fifties until Richard Helms left office as DCI in 1974.

I think there are a few lawsuits pending in Canada from our use of Alain Memorial Institute in Montreal. The mind control experiments were run by Dr. Ewen Cameron. Patients who were suffering from depression or a more serious psychosis would be transferred to our unit where they would be treated to our less conventional methods. Probably the most severe procedure was electroconvulsive shock therapy where a person would be given doses of electricity twenty times the amount normally used. We needed to know at what level of repeated voltage it would take to break a person's spirit and resistance. We could then try to program their thinking for use in assassinations, etc. Sounds pretty farfetched, but this stuff went on for almost two decades. And believe me, these people weren't volunteers.

We experimented with hallucinogens like LSD, which we also tried on enlisted men in some of our remote outposts. One of the places where we used some of these experiments was Astugi, Japan, where Oswald was stationed during his hitch in the Marines. I've often wondered if he was subjected to hypnosis or LSD during that period. Richard Helms called our agents who had been exposed to LSD, "enlightened operatives". He was a bundle of laughs, that Helms. A coldhearted little bureaucrat. The idea was to brainwash the guy to do whatever we wanted him to do with no memory of why he did it. This is exactly what happened with Sirhan Sirhan. He had worked with Dr. William Bryan in Los Angeles. Bryan was a hypnotist who had worked with the Agency for years. When Sirhan was charged with shooting Robert Kennedy, he said he had no memory of the event and he had no dislike for Senator Kennedy. Dr. Bryan might have also worked with Arthur Bremmer, who attempted to assassinate George Wallace.

Ewen Cameron also used paralytic drugs that amounted to an induced coma. Or he would experiment with sleep deprivation or sensory deprivation where a person would be locked away in the dark for days or even weeks to break down normal resistance and create disorientation. All this started back in the forties with Wild Bill Donovan at OSS. He was determined to find a chemical to induce truth from someone under interrogation. One of the best truth drugs they found was a clear liquid extract from marijuana which had no taste or odor. We fooled around with heroin and cocaine and other narcotics. Mescaline from peyote cactus was also experimented with. We got that idea from the German experiments at Dachau. Of everything tested, LSD had the most potential. Subjects were more apt to tell the truth and they would have no memory of the interrogation. We thought we had hit the mother load. In the fifties, we shifted from interrogating or brainwashing the enemy, to programming our own people. We hoped to create the perfect fall guy.

A lot of the funding for Cameron's work came from the Rockefeller Foundation funneled through the Agency. At the time, Cameron was a very respected guy. I think he was president of the American and Canadian Psychiatric Association. Fifty or sixty patients at the Alain Institute were given sleep therapy where they might be knocked out for months at a time. Then the good doctor would begin a depatterning phase using doses of LSD and massive amounts of electroshock to try to clear out past behavior patterns. Then it was back to the sleep room for the psychic driving phase where tape recorders would replay messages, maybe a hundred thousand times. Cameron protected us by using mental patients, prisoners, minorities, etc.

The Addiction Research Center in Lexington, Kentucky, was another one of our clinics. Dr. Isbell had free reign over about eight hundred inmates. He could use them to test any new pharmaceuticals or hallucinogens. There was a group of black inmates that was given LSD for about seventy-five straight days. It would build up to double, triple, and quadruple doses. We had other programs like that in Atlanta and New Jersey. We had a whole network of guys like Cameron and Isbell and Jolly West at the University of Oklahoma. Experts in their fields and all on the Agency payroll under the supervision of Richard Helms. To show you the extent of our research, in 1953, we paid over four million dollars for ten kilos of LSD. That's some serious drugs. Imagine four million dollars in 1953. What in the hell were we thinking?

Allen Dulles had only been DCI for a short time in 53, when he made a speech at Princeton which I happened to attend. It was a chance to see the Master in action. The Brains of The Beast. Dulles warned the audience that the Russians were developing mind perversion techniques that would be abhorrent to our way of life. Victims of these Russian experiments could not state their own thoughts, Dulles told the audience with a grim expression on his face. These poor souls could only repeat what their masters had implanted in the minds. A couple of days after the Princeton speech, Dulles approved MK-ULTRA. This was a massive expansion of the old ARTICHOKE program. To Allen Dulles, everything was a house of mirrors.

Our friend, Dr. Gottlieb, was put in charge of research. Old shoot-em-up Sid had this huge quantity of LSD on hand. He wanted to see what effect small amounts of the drug would have on someone at a political rally. This would be a way to discredit a politician who was not sympathetic with the Agency's scheme of things. The Kennedys of the world. So Gottlied encouraged his technical services staff to administer small amounts of LSD to their colleagues when they least expected it.

That fall, Gottlieb conducted a work retreat at some hunting lodge in Maryland. He spiked the after-dinner cocktails with with LSD. After the fact, he was decent enough to inform the group of what he had done. Some of the folks didn't handle the drug so well. A guy by the name of Frank Olson went into a deep depression. We were caring human beings. We sent Olson to New York to see Dr. Abramson of Columbia University. He was another one of our guys. Abramson couldn't help him so we were going to move him to Chestnut Lodge. This was a sanitorium in Maryland staffed by Agency psychiatrists. On his last night in New York, Frank Olson jumped out of a ten story window. He never bothered to open the window. Makes you wonder if he had been assisted. Most people would not dive through a pane of glass. If the Olson situation had tracked back to Gottlieb and the Agency, there would have been a scandal.

Gottlieb got dressed down pretty good by Allen Dulles for the Olson incident, but his experiments were allowed to continue. Sid's mind was ever resourceful. He recruited a narcotics officer named George White who set up an apartment in New York's Greenwich Village. We fixed it up like a safehouse with two-way mirrors and surveillance equipment. White posed as an artist and lured young people back to his apartment. He'd slip them LSD and record their reactions. We were so pleased with this experiment that we set up two more similar apartments in San Francisco. Of course there was nothing in our charter that allowed us to undertake this type of covert operation in this country, but we figured there wouldn't be any outcry if we messed with the heads of a few hippies.

White's next move was to set up Operation Midnight Climax. No kidding. This was Agency stuff at its finest. Prostitutes were paid to pick up men and bring them back to a hotel that had been set up with two-way mirrors and film equipment. The girls were happy because we protected them from the law and they were paid double for every trick. Such a deal. It was during Midnight Climax that we developed techniques for setting up subjects for sexual blackmail. An extension of this would be Linda Tripp and that Lewinsky gal with Clinton. There were any number of ways to compromise our adversaries.

The safehouse experiments came to an end in 1963 when John McCone found out about them. Kennedy had fired Dulles after the Bay of Pigs, but Richard Helms had failed to tell McCone about all of our ongoing experiments. Guys like Dulles and Helms never felt the need to answer to a higher authority. It was the nature of our business to mislead people. It was all about deniability. McCone concluded that these experiments had put U.S. citizens in jeopardy. To Dulles and Helms, McCone was weak. When George White was run off he sent his pal, Dr. Gottlieb, a letter saying that he had no hard feelings. He asked, where else could a red-blooded American boy lie, cheat, kill, rape and steal with the blessing of the U.S. Government? This was our boy, White.

At the time McCone shut down our safehouses, Castro and Nasser were at the top of our hit list. It was at this time that we began to study hypnosis more seriously. We needed to know if someone under a hypnotic trance could be programmed to kill with no later memory. One of our top psychiatrists was Dr. William Bryan who had worked with the military to train troops in methods to avoid brainwashing if captured by the enemy. This was at the time of the Korean War. Afterwards, Dr. Bryan settled into private practice as a hypnotist while still doing work for the Agency. He gained some notoriety when he worked with Albert de Salvo in the Boston Strangler case. He later got busted in LA for having sex with his female patients while they were under hypnosis. I know that he worked with Sirhan Sirhan and probably Arthur Bremmer. My guess is that he was preparing them for the assignments on Robert Kennedy and George Wallace which paved the way for Richard Nixon in 1968 and 1972.

COCAINE

In July of 1980 the most astounding coup in the history of Latin America took place. A cocaine cartel violently took over the government of Bolivia. Although the Drug Enforcement Administration had plenty of warning that the coup was in the works, the overthrow was accomplished with the blessing of the CIA. Three Bolivian drug kingpins had been released in Miami and the cocaine epidemic in the United States was about to begin. A former DEA official and deep cover agent by the name of Michael Levine detailed the events in a book called, THE BIG WHITE LIE. He had been fighting with his superiors to prevent the release of Roberto Suarez, Alfredo Gutierrez and Jose Gasser, while he sent repeated cables from Buenos Aires warning that the government overthrow in Bolivia was about to take place. Had Levine not had the courage to tell his story, the details of the coup in Bolivia would never have been fully understood.

On July 17, 1980, a caravan of masked assassins rode into the town of Trinidad and began killing everyone in sight. This elite squad had been put together by former Nazi Klaus Barbie, The Butcher of Lyon. In addition to their black ski masks, the shooters wore combat fatigues with swastika armbands. The government of elected President Lidia Gueiler was under siege. Gueiler had worked with the DEA to get Suarez arrested and now the tables were turned. Marcelo Quiroga, who was head of the socialist coalition and an outspoken critic of the drug cartel, called for a general strike. In La Paz, leaders of the worker's unions were soon under attack by the paramilitary goon squad. Quiroga was arrested and tortured under supervision of experts on loan from Argentina's Mechanic School of the Navy. This was a secret police force that was responsible for the torture and assassination of 25,000 suspected left-wing dissidents in Argentina. Quiroga's castrated body was found several days later south of La Paz.

On July 18, Bolivia's boarders were sealed off and the country was declared a military zone. Within a day, two dozen trade union leaders were tortured and killed. Political activists, clergymen, journalist and students were herded into stadiums where they could be selected for torture and execution. The formula had been developed and polished by the CIA in Chili in 1973. By mid-August the resistance to the coup was over. General Garcia Mesa was installed as President and Colonel Arce-Gomez was sworn in as Minister of Interior. These men took their orders from the cocaine cartel. The CIA justified the new government because a socialist coalition had been removed, but a nightmare had begun for the people of Bolivia. The secret police would make certain that anyone opposed to the cocaine government would be tortured and killed.

1980 happened to be a presidential election year in the United States. It did not reflect well on President Carter that cocaine suppliers had taken over the government of Bolivia. Unlike Nixon's orchestration of the overthrow of Salvador Allende in Chili, Carter had no knowledge of the Agency's involvement in the coup in Bolivia. This was the work of the Shadow Government. Carter was an outsider. Ronald Reagan was not burdened with the details of this plot although he would be the beneficiary.

Michael Levine's head was spinning as he heard the details of the mayhem in Bolivia. The years of hard work done by the DEA had been rendered useless and Levine suspected that the CIA might be responsible. He went to see a man known in Argentinean intelligence circles as "The Doctor." Levine had come to respect the man for having sensitive information unknown even to the DEA. What he learned caused him to question his decorated career as a crime fighter.

The Doctor began to explain the history of the Gasser family. They were an extremely wealthy Bolivian family that was actively involved with the CIA's Anti-Communist League. This tracks all the way back to Guy Bannister in New Orleans. The elder Gasser had financed a coup in 1971 that put a General Benzer in power. At the time, Gasser was protecting the drug smuggling of Roberto Suarez. Levine had helped set up the arrest of both Jose Gasser and Roberto Suarez in Miami. The CIA had also assisted in the government overthrow in Bolivia in 1971. Several large U.S. banks including the Bank of America had made substantial loans to the new Bolivian government which allowed it to develop its new cocaine economy.

Many of the key players in the 71 coup were involved in the 1980 overthrow in Bolivia. Klaus Barbie had been a security advisor for General Benzer and had organized the secret police. The Doctor concluded that the timing of the recent coup was the Agency's attempt to influence the 1980 presidential election. He said that Jimmie Carter was not very popular with the CIA. Carter had reduced the manpower at the Agency. Carter showed his disdain for the new government of Bolivia by cancelling two-hundred million dollars in foreign aid and ordering the DEA to close its offices there. Arce-Gomez, the new "Minister of Cocaine", warned that Bolivia was going to flood the United States with the drug. Gomez made good on his threat.

Six months later, word of the Bolivian coup began to be reported in America. As Levine followed the stories he concluded that, "Everything I read or saw was so completely uninformed, poorly investigated, or carefully edited not to expose special interests that it would have been better for the American people if nothing were reported. The media coverage was so incomplete that anyone watching would come away with the impression that our leaders were really trying to win the drug war." Sadly, Levine said that the only honest account he found of what had happened in Bolivia was published in HIGH TIMES, in an article titled: Cocaine Colonialism--How the Fascists Took Over Bolivia. Levine's statement would apply to the failure of the American media to provide honest and accurate reporting during the entire Cold War period. The Shadow Government had gained enough control over the news media and key high officials that Americans were told only what they wanted us to hear. At the turn of the new century, their control over the news media is greater than ever.

In frustration, Michael Levine made a big mistake. He wrote a long letter to Newsweek Magazine as he attempted to set the record straight on the coup in Bolivia. He never received a reply from Newsweek and his career at DEA began a rapid decline. He was transferred from Argentina to Washington where he could be watched more closely. What Levine feared more than the suits at DEA were CIA plants in the DEA. He had exposed them in his letter to Newsweek and his primary drug targets in Bolivia had turned out to be CIA assets.

In 1985, two associated press reporters named Barger and Parry issued a report detailing CIA cocaine shipments to America to fund an illegal war in Nicaragua. AP watered down their report and there was little media response. Two years later during the Iran-Contra hearings in Washington, the notebooks of Oliver North revealed hundreds of references to the drug trade including specific amounts for some operations. Congress was reluctant to tie the Agency to drug smuggling and the news media dropped the ball as usual. Finally, Senator John Kerry released a report that clearly exposed the CIA and its drug dealings, but the media was not interested.

In 1988, an accountant for the Medellin Drug Cartel named Ramon Rodriguez, testified in the Manuel Noriega trial that he had laundered hundreds of millions of dollars of Columbian drug money through U.S. banks in Panama. These included Bank of America and Citicorp. He said he had also laundered millions of dollars for the CIA that was transferred to the Contras in Nicaragua. This was done through numerous dummy corporations set up by the cocaine cartel and the CIA.

179

One of the dummy companies was a shrimp processing warehouse that also received $237,000 from the State Department in humanitarian aid. An interesting footnote to Rodriguez's testimony was that he had worked for the CIA in the early 1960s during its anti-Castro activities and he had delivered hush money to the families of the Watergate burglars for the Nixon Whitehouse.

Eight years later an obscure daily called The San Jose Mercury News blew the lid off the case. In a series of three articles printed from August 18 through August 20, 1996, a staff writer named Gary Webb provided us with the first detailed account of the CIA's involvement in America's cocaine epidemic. He established the connection between the South American drug cartels, the Central Intelligence Agency, the Contras and the street gangs of South-Central L.A.

The distributor was Freeway Rick Donnell who distributed the cut-rate cocaine to gangs across the country. His connection was a former anti-communist guerilla leader and dope dealer, Oscar Danilo Blandon Reyes. He was authorized by a CIA asset named Bermudez. Blandon worked the border with another Nicaraguan named Juan Norwin Meneses Canterero who owned homes and businesses in Northern California. U.S. Customs and the DEA complained that efforts to prosecute Meneses were compromised by the CIA. There was a picture taken in Meneses's San Francisco home with CIA asset Adolpho Calero, who was a high profile Contra leader. When Nicaraguan police arrested Meneses in 1991, the judge was astonished that he had traveled unmolested in the United States for the previous seventeen years. When

Blandon's arrest fell apart in Los Angeles, public defender Barbara O'Conner said, "The cops always thought that the investigation had been compromised by the CIA."

About a month after the Mercury News broke the cocaine story, The New York Times, the Washington Post and the Los Angeles Times went after the smaller newspaper. They quoted intelligence officials as saying that none of what Gary Webb reported was true. The lonesome reporter had challenged the dignity and integrity of a fine institution. When Webb was told that current CIA director John Deutch had said that he knew of no Agency connection to the crack-cocaine trade in the United States, Webb replied, "What else would they say?" The major papers had backed off from a confrontation with the CIA, but they pounced on the Mercury News like playground bullies. "It doesn't matter what they say about me," Webb explained. "I love a good fight." Independent journalism was alive and well in America if only for three days in a small independent newspaper in Northern California.

Webb had follow-up reports that would have clarified the first three articles but his editor decided to sit on them. "I turned in four more stories that advanced the story further," Webb explained. "They talked about the relationships between the members of this drug ring and who they were working within the federal government and which government agencies were aware of their operations. We have other stories about related drug trafficking in Central America that was condoned by the U.S. government."

In the way of background, Webb said, "You look at what happened to Bob Parry and Brian Barger back in

181

the eighties and you look at what happened to the Kerry Committee. The people on the Kerry Committee were telling me going into this that they were subjected to these fierce campaigns to discredit what they were doing, they were under federal investigation and their witnesses were harassed. This was a story that the government has tried very hard to keep under wraps and until we published this stuff...."

If nothing else, Gary Webb had succeeded in creating a controversy about the CIA's illegal operations. It was certainly plausible that the Agency would not turn its back on a huge source of revenue even if it were illegal. Since its inception, the Agency had been above the law. The ends justified everything. The means could never be discussed due to national security.

Next to come forward was a former pilot named Rodney Stich who wrote an article titled: Defrauding America--Forty-Five Years of drug trafficking. Stich first encountered the CIA moving drugs when he flew out of Tokyo and Beirut in the early 1950s. Many other pilots that he talked to also described CIA operations where they had transported drugs. It was common knowledge among pilots in those days. Some of the pilots had flown for Air America which was a well known CIA subsidiary. For the past decade Stich had interviewed former pilots as well as CIA and DEA operatives and military personnel who had firsthand knowledge of the Agency's drug smuggling activities. His sources included a former FBI agent who had reported these activities to his superiors and to Congress, a former head of a CIA proprietary airline who described how the Agency had set up and funded a

182

drug import operation, a CIA operative who ran a covert financial institution that looted the HUD program, military personnel who described drug shipments to a military base where they were stationed and a New York City vice squad detective who had reported CIA drug trafficking to his superiors. Stich's point was that the Agency's involvement with drugs was common knowledge, but nothing was ever done about it.

Stich reminds us that anyone who knows of a criminal act and fails to report it is guilty of a crime. Where does that leave government officials who have been informed of these transgressions and have done nothing to stop them?   Stich claims that there is a pattern of silencing those who seek to report these crimes. The most common method is to charge the informer with a federal offense. You can't call CIA officials to testify because they will decline and invoke national security. That leaves the informer pissing into the wind.

In the late eighties, Lawrence Zuckerman, who was a staff writer for Time, had uncovered the same Contra-cocaine connection. Zuckerman's article was pulled by his superiors. He was told by a senior editor, "Time is institutionally behind the Contras. If this story were about the Sandinistas and drugs, you'd have no trouble getting it in the magazine." Less than two years later, Ollie North, National Security Advisor John Poindexter and ambassador Lewis Tambs were barred from entering Costa Rica. On advice from his congress, President Oscar Arias decided that these men were running a drug smuggling ring out of the White House.

UGLY AMERICAN

The good news was that Major General Edward Lansdale had a novel written about him. The bad news was the novel was titled, THE UGLY AMERICAN. Lansdale was a former Madison Avenue advertising executive who Allen Dulles recruited to invent cover stories for the CIA. He was steeped in the art of deception and became the master of government overthrows in Southeast Asia. He retired from his storied career in intelligence one month before Dallas to concentrate on the most important cover story of all. When it came to the removal of an American President, there was no room for error.

In the early days of the Kennedy Administration, General Lansdale was the briefing officer for Secretary of Defense Robert McNamara. When McNamara went on a fact finding tour of Vietnam, Lansdale was at his side. It had been arranged ahead of time that McNamara would see only what the Agency wanted him to see. Events would be staged if necessary. A village would be worked on for days to become a model of combat devastation and McNamara would be taken there. The report that he would submit to President Kennedy was laid out ahead of time. When the report was discussed, Kennedy, McNamara and Secretary of

State Dean Rusk would be surrounded by career military men and public officials whose first loyalties were with the Agency and its wealthy benefactors. These men included; William Bundy, brother McGeorge Bundy, John McNaughton, Mike Forrestal, Joseph Califano, Generals Maxwell Taylor, Richard Stillwell, Victor Krulak, and the three Bills; DuPuy, Peers, and Rosson. These were members of the Shadow Government who sought to control the President by making sure that only their side of the agenda was represented. As the direct conduit to McNamara, Lansdale was a key player.

In defense of these military officers, if one dared to disagree with the Agency on a covert operation on which he had been briefed and then discuss the matter with the President, he might be charged with a security violation and lose his clearance. The Agency played hardball and made up the rules as it went along. If you were discredited and kicked off the team, your future was bleak. Oddly, there is a parallel to being a member of the Communist Party in Russia. It paid to be on the inside where the opportunities were plentiful. It didn't pay to waver from the party line. America's secret apparatus could be every bit as deadly as the Soviet Union's.

In matters of foreign policy, the President has to rely on the National Security Council and the Joint Chiefs of Staff for information and recommendations. When these groups are dominated by men whose allegiance is to the CIA and the Shadow Elite that it represents, the President often makes bad decisions based on poor information. When President Kennedy was misinformed about the requirements and the chance of success of the Bay of Pigs, he tried to reorganize the CIA, but he was still surrounded by men who answered to the Agency. If you were an insider and part of the Shadow Government, you would know what was going to happen in advance and you were sure to be on the winning side. When it came to defense budgets and overseas investments, this was a powerful elixir. Apart from their public careers, these men were well-healed investors.

Allen Dulles, the master manipulator, had begun to work his slight of hand from the inception of the Agency under President Truman. Congress had set up the National Security Council to direct and coordinate the activities of the new CIA. The NSC consisted of the President, Vice President, Secretary of State, Secretary of Defense and the Director of Central Intelligence. After Truman left office, Dulles succeeded in establishing a Special Group which consisted of briefing officers for the President and secretaries of State and Defense and the CIA director. Everything changed. By placing CIA assets as briefing officers, Dulles could devise an operation and then send his men to get approval. The key men in the administration would only have the information that Dulles provided for them. They would have to stop a planned operation after being sold the Agency position. Instead of the Security Council recommending an idea to the CIA, it was left only to approve or disapprove a suggested operation without all the background information. This was how Dulles cultivated the power to develop and control clandestine operations.

Ed Lansdale's specialty in the area of secret operations was to create an incident that would bring a predictable reprisal. Then the situation could be escalated to the required level. If a president, like Richard Nixon, was sympathetic to the methods of the Agency, then he would be privy to most of the dealings of the Agency. If a president, like Truman, Eisenhower or Kennedy, was suspicious of the tactics of the CIA, he would usually be left out of the information loop. Most of the activities that interfered with the internal affairs of foreign governments were taken to defend or promote American business interests. Communist insurgency was the handy explanation.

In the Philippines, General Lansdale perfected the art of the coup d'état. He succeeded in elevating a little known military officer by the name of Magsaysay to take over the reins of government. Lansdale actually disguised government troops as leftist Huk rebels and staged an attack on a remote village. When all appeared lost, Magsaysay's troops arrived on the scene and drove off the insurgents. It was nothing short of a miracle in the eyes of the villagers. The incident was reported throughout the country and Magsaysay's popularity was on the rise. The CIA would use the incident to call for more military support for our hand-picked leader. Magsaysay was sympathetic to our interests. He was controllable. American investments would be safe and increased military expenditures were good for business.

A similar situation took place in 1964, when the Gulf of Tonkin incident was staged by Lansdale who then handed the ball off to McGeorge Bundy so he could goad Lyndon Johnson into a massive new war effort in Vietnam. Brown and Root received a billion dollars to dredge Cam Ranh Bay and half a trillion dollars was spent on the war in Vietnam. The Shadow Elite found the situation very profitable. With its sanctimonious crusade against communism, the Agency could write the script and then activate the U.S. government to take up the cause. This scenario was repeated throughout Asia, Africa and Latin America. The American people and sometimes its leaders were the last to know what had actually taken place. It might be said that the war against communism, real or imagined, was the most profitable industry ever developed in this country.

Another example of the Agency managing government was the Bay of Pigs invasion. The Eisenhower Administration had only approved a modest version of the plan when it left office in January of 1961. Secretary of State Thomas Gates had been given his first thorough briefing one week before he left office and was not able to communicate the details to the new administration. By the time the Kennedy Administration began to get bits and pieces of the plan, it had greatly escalated. Finally, Kennedy made it clear that he would sign off on the operation only if there was no American involvement. Only Cuban volunteers were to be used. When Kennedy was pressured during the morning of the landing to use U.S. air support, he refused. From that point, he was blamed by the Agency and the anti-Castro Cubans for the failure at the Bay of Pigs. Kennedy and the CIA remained eyeball to eyeball from the Bay of Pigs until Dallas.

The key to the Bay of Pigs failure was CIA Director Allen Dulles being out of the country at the time of the invasion. He was on vacation in Puerto Rico to address a group of young businessmen. Why would he choose

188

to not be at his command post at such a critical time? Was it possible that the invasion was set up to fail in order to discredit President Kennedy? The Russians knew when and where it was going to occur. Was this Dulles's way of distancing himself from a guaranteed failure?

The day before the invasion most of Castro's air force had been wiped out in an air raid by Cuban pilots. Three T-33 fighter jets remained at an air strip near Santiago. The plan was to send five modified B-26 bombers from Nicaragua in the pre-dawn hours to arrive at dawn with the sun to their backs to eliminate the remainder of Castro's air force. The success of the beach landing depended on the removal of these three planes. The Cuban pilots were in their planes with the engines running but they never got the green light. They knew that their comrades would be helpless on the beach unless the T-33s were wiped out. At one point there was talk of not waiting for orders, but in the end they shut off their engines and climbed out of their planes. Their failure to fly was a death warrant for their fellow Cubans in the landing force.

In the early hours in Washington an argument had taken place. Deputy CIA Director Charles Cabell and Deputy Director of Plans Richard Bickell wanted authorization for the raid. McGeorge Bundy, President Kennedy's National Security Advisor, said no raid would take place without the approval of the President. He refused to call the president and the two Agency men did not have the authority. A Mexican standoff ensued. By the time General Cabell called Kennedy in Virginia it was too late. Kennedy would have to authorize air support from Florida. Kennedy refused.

He had stipulated that no U.S. military could be used. The Cubans were dead ducks and Kennedy was the villain.

Why the confusion? Cabell, Bickell and Bundy were all insiders. How could this critical mission have failed? Could the three have conspired to force Kennedy to use military air support? The president would have been condemned for aggression against a neutral country. Russia might have retaliated against West Berlin. Either way Kennedy would be seriously compromised. It didn't take Kennedy long to smell a rat. He fired Dulles, Cabell and Bickell. From that point his chances of survival were about as good as the brave Cubans who lost their lives at the Bay of Pigs.

After General Lansdale had propped up the Magsaysay government in the Philippines, he moved on to Saigon in 1954. He had made numerous trips to that city during the period when the French were being defeated in French Indo-China. The defeat of the French at Dien Bien Phu left a vacuum that the CIA was anxious to fill. The starring role in this production was given to Ed Lansdale. His behind the scenes work during the fifties laid the foundation for the Vietnam War. It was not a war that any president wanted. The American people were not anxious to send their boys to the humid jungles of Southeast Asia. On the other hand, the CIA and its benefactors, which included defense contractors, bankers and oilmen, knew that a sustained event in Vietnam would be immensely profitable. After WWII and Korea, there was a great military capability that was searching for an outlet. Southeast Asia was the unfortunate target of this massive military exercise.

Lansdale's first task was to get rid of the French puppet, Bao Dai. Lansdale had established a personal relationship with Ngo Dinh Diem and he was chosen by the Agency to lead the country. Lansdale whipped up a Madison Avenue style promotion to hail Diem as "the father of his country." It was always an important first step to groom the new hand-picked leader as a hero in his country. Lansdale established an elite bodyguard to keep Diem alive and the Agency sent thousands of covert troops to assist him. Not until the Marines landed in 1964, was there an American military presence in Vietnam. Up to that point, it was all Agency.

By 1964 the conflict had escalated way beyond the CIA's capability. Oddly, when the Pentagon Papers were published, the CIA was made the hero of the story. It was the failure of leaders in the U.S. government who had not heeded the warnings provided by the Agency. It was as if the documents had been written by Lansdale. Perhaps it was only a coincidence that Daniel Ellsberg had worked with Lansdale in Vietnam. Ellsberg had also studied under Henry Kissinger who was never more than a front man for the Agency and the Shadow Elite. Ellsberg's Pentagon Papers were simply another example of the CIA leading the news media by the nose in its effort to control foreign policy.

A perfect example of how Allen Dulles and the Shadow Elite were able to control the inner workings of government was what occurred in the Kennedy Administration before and after the Bay of Pigs. The outgoing Eisenhower Administration had been briefed on the details of the Cuban invasion one week before it left office. Most of this information was not passed on to the incoming administration. Then Dulles created a "slot" for General Maxwell Taylor as a special military advisor to the new president. This assured Kennedy of being told by General Taylor only what Dulles wanted him to hear. He also installed Ed Lansdale as the briefing officer to Robert McNamara. Later that position was taken by CIA asset Bill Bundy.

After the embarrassing failure at the Bay of Pigs, Kennedy set up a committee to determine what had gone wrong. On that committee were Maxwell Taylor and Allen Dulles along with Robert Kennedy. The hearings were controlled by Dulles who brought in only the witnesses that he wanted to testify. He would later control the intelligence related testimony during the Warren Commission hearings in the same manner. Robert Kennedy had no chance of seeing clearly through this smokescreen, but he concluded that a failure of leadership was primarily responsible for the Bay of Pigs fiasco.

President Kennedy acted on his brother's assessment and fired Dulles, Bickell and Cabell. These were the three highest ranking officers in the Agency. Kennedy then issued National Security Action Memos 55, 56 and 57. These directives placed responsibilities for covert operations during peace time with the Joint Chiefs of Staff. General Lemnitzer, who was chairman of the Joint Chiefs, was a measured man who was not inclined to employ cloak and dagger solutions. He decided that the best way to avoid embarrassments like the Bay of Pigs was to put an end to them. This temporarily eliminated the power of the CIA.

Dulles was out of a job but not out of power. He angled behind the scenes to have General Lemnitzer promoted to Allied commander of Nato Troops in Paris. This left a slot open for Maxwell Taylor to become chairman of the Joint Chiefs. His slot as advisor to the President was then filled by Bill Bundy's brother, McGeorge Bundy. These three men could be counted on to promote the new counter-insurgency policy which could control governments throughout the Third World. Dulles was still the conduit between the Shadow Elite and the Agency and he had a stronger team in place. Kennedy had worked hard to try and beat back the CIA, but he had been outflanked by the Master.

Major General Lansdale officially retired one month before John Kennedy was killed in Dallas. He was the most creative cover story man the Agency had ever found. His theatrics in the Philippines became a model that was used to change governments in many Third World countries. Lansdale continued to work with Allen Dulles to develop covert operations even though both were officially retired. Photographs taken in Dealey Plaza after the murder of President Kennedy showed Lansdale in the background. What could he possibly have been doing in Dallas, Texas? He was a long way from his home in Virginia.

LITTLE JOE

Richard Nixon's rise in politics was like the flotsam that comes to the surface in a sewer. There was a bad smell that followed the guy everywhere. He would have liked us to believe that he was some kind of great international statesman. That characterization is a complete fraud. It was always about Nixon and nothing else. The ends justified the means and the ends were always what was best for Nixon. After John Kennedy had watched Nixon's acceptance speech at the Republican National Convention in 1960, he told a friend that he owed it to the country to keep that guy out of the White House. Kennedy was embarrassed to watch Nixon with his arms waving out of control and that fake smile plastered across his face. Kennedy saw no humanity in the man. He thought Nixon was shallow and predictable. Kennedy would have felt humiliated to lose to a man of such low stature. He felt that Nixon was as transparent as any politician he had ever observed. Kennedy won the 1960 election by a narrow margin and spent less than three years in office. Nixon was the victor in the long run until his fascination with dirty tricks put an end to his second term in office.

194

On January 20, 1924, Nikolai Lenin lay sick in the city of Gorky. Joseph Stalin dispatched two doctors to assist the head of the Communist Party. A few hours later, Lenin was dead of a stroke. It is not clear if Stalin's physicians had a hand in Lenin's death but the timing could not have been better for Stalin. Leon Trotsky, who was assumed to be Lenin's heir to Russia's highest position of power, was on a train on his way to the Black Sea. When the word of Lenin's death reached Trotsky, he left the train and called Stalin. Trotsky was told that he could not return to Moscow in time for the funeral and was encouraged to continue to his destination. Stalin had lied. The funeral was later than Trotsky was told. While nearly a million common people migrated to Red Square to mourn the loss of Lenin, Stalin was working behind the scenes to seize control of the Russian government.

General Secretary Stalin had made certain that openings in key posts were filled by his supporters. Once in power, Stalin went on a systematic purge of those who opposed him in the Politburo. Show trials were held in which leading Bolsheviks were forced to confess to crimes they had not committed. Some were executed while others, like Trotsky, were banished from the country. Military leaders were murdered until Stalin could be sure that he was in absolute control. For three decades a rigid police state ensured that anyone suspected of opposing Stalin would disappear or be sent to a slave labor camp.

While Richard Nixon operated on a smaller scale, he employed the same techniques of false accusations and the elimination of political opponents. Like the Russian tyrant, Nixon was loyal only to himself. When

Watergate was closing in on him, Nixon dispatched his close friends and advisors, Haldeman and Ehrlichman, like a man throwing a pair of dirty socks into the laundry. Political expediency was the end. The means did not matter. In all the recorded conversations between Nixon and his henchmen, not once did the question of right or wrong come up. Would an operation work? Could they deny involvement? These were the only issues that concerned Nixon.

If you read biographies about Nixon as a boy, two images emerge. Determined and calculating. His high school debate coach was impressed that he could take either side of a debate and win easily. No one ever doubted Richard Nixon's intelligence. By working long hours in his father's grocery store and then studying late into the night, Nixon developed that bulldog tenacity that would take him all the way to the presidency. He saw himself as an underdog who would have to be clever in order to overcome his financial handicaps. He spent six weeks one summer as a carnival barker at the Prescott Fair. He found that he could talk people into anything and his wheel of chance became the most profitable booth at the fair. He later specialized in separating his inebriated Navy pals from their money in poker games. It was always about winning and control.

Nixon was an excellent student at Whittier College where he excelled in debate and acting while he majored in history. His acting background stood him in good stead years later when he teared up during the "Checkers" speech. Eisenhower was of a mind to dump Nixon as vice president for the second term, but Americans rallied to his support after the display of shameless sentimentality never before seen in this country's politics. Nixon went on to graduate third from the top at Duke Law School. He and two buddies broke into the dean's office to get the results before they were announced.

Nixon applied for a Navy commission even though he could have avoided WWII with an exemption as a Quaker. Nixon dusted off the military background for the desperate "Checker's" speech. He told a national audience that he probably deserved a few battle stars himself as he was in the South Pacific while the bombs were falling. The record shows that Nixon was a supply officer far from any area of combat. He did receive a citation for efficiency in getting supplies through to those who were fighting the war. Those long hours marking cans in his father's grocery store had paid off. After the war, when he was pumping up some major financial backers for his initial run for Congress, Nixon assured his audience that he had talked with many soldiers in the foxholes. What?

As he threw himself into the campaign against maverick Democrat Jerry Voorhis, Nixon would actually show up in his old Navy uniform to make speeches until he found out that many GIs resented the look of the officer. It is believed that the name for the Old Navy chain of clothing stores might have originated with Dick Nixon's early campaign appearances. Once again in civilian attire, Nixon hit the campaign trail as he denounced "Voorhis and his Communist friends" on any platform that was willing to have him. Nixon admitted years later that Voorhis was not a Communist and in fact had some impressive anti-Communist credentials, but the issue always drew a good response from the audience. Kind of like the wheel of chance at the carnival in Prescott. The idea was to win at any cost. Candor was much lower on the list of priorities.

Congressman Voorhis had managed to offend the banking industry, insurance companies and Big Oil, but he was popular in his district. He had been elected by sizable margins five times. Nixon was the unknown and it was his job to probe for a weakness in his popular opponent. Nixon's monied supporters had brought in a lawyer named Murray Chotiner to handle the campaign. Chotiner's formula was to discredit your opponent, associate him with an unpopular group and then stay on the attack. Nixon, always a quick study, accused Voorhis of being a communist sympathizer and accepting support from a communist labor group. When Voorhis challenged his young attacker to provide proof of his charges, Nixon strutted across the stage and handed a paper to Voorhis.

"Here is your proof," Nixon announced to the audience in the finest Shakespearean tradition.

Voorhis looked at the document and shook his head. It was a meaningless opinion paper that offered no proof at all. Nixon had tricked the audience and put the incumbent on the defensive.

For the duration of the campaign, Nixon hammered hard at the Congressman's imagined communist associations. On election-eve a telephone campaign warned those who answered, "I think you should know that Jerry Voorhis is a Communist." It was politics conducted on an elevated level. To make matters worse, the Voorhis camp said the L.A. Times, which had given its editorial support to Nixon, had failed to run their campaign ads just before the election. The last slight of hand was the Nixon Republican campaign sending letters to registered Democrats which began, "As one Democrat to another...." and going on to explain how Voorhis had sold out his own party. It was a first glimpse at Nixon and his sewer politics. The smell of victory was in the air.

In 1947, "Peewee", as Helen Gahagan Douglas referred to Nixon, was off to Congress. He landed on the House Committee on Un-American Activities where his legal background was expected to upgrade a group that had distinguished itself with racism and wild accusations. Nixon did bring reason to the band of eccentrics until he encountered the testimony of a morose journalist by the name of Whittaker Chambers. This suicidal editor for Time Magazine told a strange tale of working underground for the Communists in the 1930s. He had since experienced a Republican conversion and had decided to dedicate himself to the conservative cause by ratting out former associates whom he knew to be Red sympathizers. On his list submitted to the FBI and the HUAC was the name of Alger Hiss.

This entry caught Congressman Nixon's eye. Hiss had worked in the State Department for FDR and he had accompanied the President to the summit meeting at Yalta following WWII. Hiss had also presided over the first meeting of the United Nations. According to Chambers, Hiss had been a Russian agent throughout this period. While it turned out to be impossible to substantiate these charges, Nixon decided to work another angle.

After Hiss had testified before the HUAC, the committee members were of a mind to drop the investigation. Hiss had denied knowing anyone named Whitaker Chambers. On the other hand , Chambers had a history of depression and was an admitted city park homosexual. This made the committee reluctant to pursue the matter. All except Nixon. Nixon thought he had seen through the Harvard intellectual facade of Alger Hiss. He thought they ought to pursue the matter of perjury as to whether Hiss had ever known Chambers. Nixon arranged a meeting between the two men. Hiss inspected Chambers closely. He asked his accuser to speak in different tones of voice. The proceeding turned somewhat comical when Hiss demanded to inspect Chamber's teeth. Hiss then announced that he might have known Chambers fifteen years before as a man named George Crosley but denied ever participating in communist activities with the man.

Ahah, Nixon thought. This could be the breakthrough. Nixon was receiving national publicity on the matter so he continued to badger Alger Hiss. Hiss retaliated by filing a lawsuit against Chambers. Finally, some microfilm was found hidden in a pumpkin on Chamber's farm. It supposedly had been photographed from documents that Hiss had given to Chambers in the mid-30s. It was questionable that the technology was available at the time, but no matter. Nixon won a perjury conviction against Hiss that sent him to prison for four years. Nixon was now the darling of reactionaries everywhere. Whether or not Alger Hiss was guilty is still a matter of debate, but Dick Nixon had made a name for himself.

Nixon's run for the Senate in 1950 was made easier by three factors. Three weeks after the Alger Hiss conviction, Wisconsin Senator Joe McCarthy launched his communist witch-hunt. Americans in and out of government became the targets of wild accusations and guilt by association. The Democratic primary in California split the party and left Helen Gahagan Douglas on the defensive. On June 24, North Korea invaded South Korea and Americans feared a confrontation with Russia and China. Although Nixon had practically no competition in his primary, he could not resist sending out the "as one Democrat to another" mailer which got him labeled as "Tricky Dick." Next, of course, was to insinuate that Douglas was a Communist. In fact, Nixon claimed that Douglas was "pink right down to her underwear". Just because an easy victory is within reach is no reason not to savage your opponent. Why abandon the Red-scare tactic when it had always paid off?

In desperation, Douglas tried to compare Nixon to Hitler and Stalin, but the voters were not yet ready for those comparisons. Douglas was ahead of her times. In frustration, she said that if Nixon were ever elected President, "God help us all." Her problem was that she was worried about civil rights when the rest of the country was concerned with Communism. When she voted against the McCarran Bill that would have ferreted out communists in government related jobs, she saw Nixon grinning at her from the other side of the aisle. She knew that voting her conscience would be used against her. She also knew a fascist when she smelled one. When Nixon heard later that Douglas had referred to him as a "pipsqueak," he became enraged and vowed to "castrate" her. While the biology of the threat was somewhat of a problem, as some of Nixon's

201

later opponents would learn, it did not pay to anger Tricky Dick.

As the nasty campaign neared its end, the Nixon camp revived the telephone gimmick where the listener was bluntly told that Douglas was a Communist. This time there was a new wrinkle. They were told that her husband was a Jew. The creative Nixon team kept coming up with new schemes. Douglas countered by bringing out heavyweights like Sam Rayburn, Lyndon Johnson and Eleanor Roosevelt to campaign for her. Nixon called them "carpetbaggers" and trumped them with the Red-scare poster boy, Joe McCarthy. Nixon never failed to ask his audience, "Why does Helen Douglas support the Communist line?" The carnival barker knew how to work a crowd. In the end, Nixon almost blew his advantage when he made one remark too many about Douglas being married to a Jew. Nixon had come to enjoy slander as some men might enjoy a fine cigar. Ethnic attacks were particularly satisfying. Later, we'll hear these things straight from the horse's mouth in recorded conversations at the White House.

The 1952 Republican ticket was a done deal. At the top was Dwight Eisenhower, the revered general. He would be backed up by Dick Nixon, the rising star of the Republican Party. Ike was wary of Nixon's heavy-handed tactics, but he had been convinced that the young senator from California was the perfect balance to the ticket. You had the wise World War II hero and the tough young communist fighter. It didn't take the carnival barker long to swing into action. He started to publically refer to Adlai Stevenson as "Side-saddle Adlai". Nixon said that both of Stevenson's feet were on the left side of the saddle. It was also an implied

202

homosexual reference. Stevenson appeared effeminate to some observers and Nixon couldn't resist playing the homo card. Nixon teamed up with Joe McCarthy to work the commie angle and the Republicans won the presidency in a landslide. Now Ike would have his ambitious young vice president to deal with.

In 1954, the Army-McCarthy hearings were shown on television. The Wisconsin Senator and his right-hand man, attorney Roy Cohn, were made fools of by an attorney named Joseph Welch. When McCarthy attacked one of Welch's young assistants and implied that the man might mave communist leanings, Welch explained that the aide was secretary of the Young Republicans. Welch went on to expose McCarthy as a rude bully before the American audience. The Wisconsin demigog's reign of terror in Washington was over. It was then up to Nixon to carry out the Red-baiting. When Nixon blamed Dean Acheson and the Democrats for the Korean War, Eisenhower publically repudiated him. Ike said something to the effect that the attacks on communism had become an attack on Americanism. Nixon backed down and meekly told an audience in Baltimore that he hadn't meant to question the patriotism of Democrats. All Americans want peace, the contrite vice president explained.

While President Eisenhower had just about had his fill of Nixon's campaign tactics, Nixon had been working as the liaison between the White House and the CIA. Allen Dulles had found in Nixon a kindred spirit. Both men would use communism as an excuse to promote a favorite cause such as making the Third World safe for American corporations. Neither man would ever reject an operation in terms of morality.

Both men were willing to mislead Congress and the American people in order to please their benefactors. It was during this period that the CIA began to conduct its own foreign policy with or without the consent of the President. Dulles and Nixon would not hesitate to remove foreign leaders who did not cooperate with American business and military interests. From Arbenez in Guatemala and Lamumba in the Congo to DeGaule in France, the aim was to get rid of anyone who stood in the way of American control. It was easy to excuse these operations as opposing communism, the primary motive was always profits. While Truman, Eisenhower and Kennedy were reluctant to get involved in the murder of foreign executives, Nixon and Dulles saw the option as sensible and convenient. This was a common denominator from Nixon's early days as White House action officer through the removal of his political opponents and into his presidency with the murder of foreign leaders such as Salvador Allende. Shades of Stalin. If Nixon wasn't the planner, he was the approver and the beneficiary.

In 1958, President Eisenhower decided to send Nixon on a good will tour through Latin America. While his countrymen had seen one side on Nixon's face, Latin Americans had seen the other. People in poor countries had always been aware of the corruption and bribery of their government officials by American businesses. They can smell the CIA in the background. The people of the United States were always the last to know about these abuses. When Nixon arrived on the scene, the frustrated masses were waiting. At San Marcos University in Lima, Nixon was confronted by a mob that threatened his entourage and threw rocks at them. Nixon slowly backed off and then shouted insults at the students as his limo sped away.

In Bogotá, Columbia, there were death threats. In Caracas, Venezuela, an angry mob spit in Nixon's face and nearly overturned his car. "Muera Nixon," the crowd shouted as they began to throw rocks and break windows. A Secret Service agent was about to open fire when Nixon talked him down. Had there been gunshots, Nixon knew that he was probably a dead man. The motorcade retreated to the American embassy where riots took place in the streets that lasted late into the night. Nixon saw this as an opportunity to lecture the Venezuelan officials on the evils of communism.

Several years later President Kennedy traveled through Latin America. Everywhere he was received like a hero. His pictures could be seen in factories and schools. Many people pinned his newspaper photo to the walls of their makeshift shacks. When Mrs. Kennedy addressed the crowds in Spanish, the applause went on for minutes. Why? How could these uneducated people so clearly tell a friend from an enemy?

Nixon returned to Washington as a heroic survivor of communist riots south of the border. He was now the ultimate warrior. His anti-communist credentials were so impressive that he was sent to Russia to meet with Premier Khrushchev. In a preview to the famous "kitchen debate" Khrushchev made a comment to the effect that a particular American policy smelled like fresh horse manure. Nixon knew that the Russian Premier had been a pig farmer in his earlier years, so Nixon wisecracked that the only thing that smelled worse that horse manure was pig shit. This was Nixon's idea of international diplomacy conducted on a high plane. The two men argued again in front of a kitchen exhibit. Years later Khrushchev confided that he thought that Nixon was unbalanced. He called Nixon unpredictable and unstatesmanlike. Regardless of Khrushchev's opinion, Nixon received favorable publicity for standing up the Russian bully. The man Helen Douglas referred to as "Peewee" had become an international tough guy.

Richard Nixon was the obvious presidential choice for the Republican Party in 1960. With an eight year apprenticeship under Eisenhower, Nixon could claim experience in foreign affairs and ride the coattails of Ike's popularity. The problem was that Eisenhower had reservations about Nixon and never really endorsed him. In fact, he encouraged several other Republicans to challenge Nixon for the nomination. At one point Eisenhower confided to an acquaintance that he thought it strange that Nixon had no close friends. Later, during the campaign, Eisenhower was asked to describe the contributions that Nixon had made to his administration. "Give me a week and I may think of one," was not the kind of answer that was going to help Ike's former vice president.

John Kennedy and Nixon had come to Congress together in 1947. They were on friendly terms and, in 1950, Kennedy delivered a thousand dollar campaign contribution to Nixon on behalf of his father. Four years later, when Nixon was told that Kennedy had been given last rites after a back operation, Nixon broke down and cried. This was an odd show of emotion from the self-proclaimed tough guy, but apparently

Nixon had a real affinity for his colleague. During the entire 60 campaign, Nixon never reverted to his established practice of challenging his opponents' patriotism. He also avoided the easy target of Kennedy being Catholic. No Catholic had ever been elected president and the consensus was that no one ever would. For once Nixon took the high ground and lost. After that his feeling toward Kennedy changed. In Nixon's estimation, JFK became just another privileged rich kid whose father had bought him the election. He was what Nixon likes to call a "personality boy," meaning all show and no substance. In private he accused Kennedy of stealing the election with voter fraud in Illinois and Texas. He failed to mention that in some counties in southern Illinois, there were more Republican votes than there were registered voters.

Nixon took up life as a Wall Street lawyer, but his bitterness over Kennedy continued to fester. As Kennedy's popularity grew, Nixon's chance of ever becoming president grew dim. To make matters worse, there was a growing fear that after JFK had served eight years, Bobby Kennedy would follow. Then there was Teddy. Twenty-four years of Kennedys in the White House was too much for the Shadow Elite to bear. President Kennedy was uncontrollable. He had developed a personal dialog with Khrushchev and intended to wind down the Cold War in his second term. The Cold War was a source of huge profits for these icons of business. Nixon was part of this Elite during the Kennedy years. There was a consensus that Kennedy had become a danger to America's overseas interests and this country would be better off without him. There was no talk of killing the President, but the

CIA had accomplished that feat many times throughout the Third World. When America was in real danger, the Agency could be counted on to accomplish whatever was necessary.

Richard Nixon was the political beneficiary of John Kennedy's death. It parted the waters for him. His career was reborn. In June of 1968, on the night when Robert Kennedy had won the California primary to become the frontrunner for the Democratic nomination, he was killed by a bullet that was fired from within inches of the back of his skull from a man that was being wrestled to the ground six feet in front of him. Once again the Shadow Elite had eliminated a man they could not control. The investigation into Senator Kennedy's murder was handled by two L.A. detectives who were on the Agency's payroll. Once again, Nixon's path had been cleared by a tragic event.

In 1972, Governor George Wallace had split the polls three ways between himself, Nixon and George McGovern. The vote would have gone to the House of Representatives which was controlled by the Democrats. The Elite would have been saddled with a president who disdained military solutions of any kind. McGovern was a populist with no affinity for large corporations. McGovern might have been a more frightening prospect than the Kennedys. When a would-be assassin crippled the Alabama Governor in Virginia, the problem was solved. There were more wounds to Wallace and others than could have been inflicted by Arthur Bremer's gun, but no matter. There had been a resolution to the problem that would allow Richard Nixon to win the election in a landslide. Upon hearing news of Wallace's near fatal attack, President

Nixon suggested that McGovern campaign material be planted in Bremer's apartment. Why? Did the Nixon White House think that this could have been an attempted political assassination? Ben Bradlee, editor of the Washington Post called his senior editors together and asked, "Could this be the ultimate dirty trick."

Whether Nixon had a hand in the planning of these three events is unclear but he travelled in the same circles with men who knew how to carry out these kinds of operations. "For the good of the country," can be a powerful justification for the elimination of a man. Politics and foreign affairs are not for the squeamish. Sometimes one has to overlook unpleasant means to achieve a necessary end. Who would stand in the way of an act that could save this great democracy from a soft-headed extremist like George McGovern?

Even though the polls showed that Nixon could put his feet up on the dashboard and coast home in the 72 presidential election, he wasn't satisfied. At Nixon's request, Charles Colson had set up an extensive "dirty tricks" apparatus and had enlisted the expertise of a slippery Californian named Donald Segretti. With the help of such intelligence giants as Howard Hunt, plans were made to discredit Democratic candidates. Nixon had fought a clean fight against Kennedy and had lost. He now put on the brass knuckles for his type of contest. Under consideration was everything from hooker-spies to spiking the punch at Democratic fundraisers with LSD. The least of the Demo's worries was Nixon's plan to go after them with the IRS. One again, this was politics at its finest.

Nixon had reached a point where he needed not only to win the election but to crush the opposition. His enemies list had expanded to include not only the opposition party but most of the major newspapers and weekly magazines. He was hunkered down in a bunker of his own making. He was striking out wildly in all directions which led to the Watergate break-in. Nixon was on vacation when the news reached him. When he learned that Howard Hunt and the same Cubans who had been involved in Agency operations from the Bay of Pigs to Dallas had been arrested, Nixon must have felt that someone had left the door open and the wrong dogs had come home.

Nixon repeatedly warned Haldeman and Ehrlichman that Hunt was a potential powder keg. He said that Hunt tracked back to the "Bay of Pigs thing." Haldeman later realized that the "Bay of Pigs thing" was Nixon's code for the Kennedy assassination. How did Nixon know that Hunt was connected to the Kennedy assassination? Was Nixon also aware of a wider CIA involvement? Hunt was an agent of the CIA with the highest clearance. He had also ghostwritten Allen Dulles' autobiography. Even if all that was true, what was Nixon afraid of? What was his connection to Hunt and the "Bay of Pigs thing"? The eighteen minute erasure on one of the Oval Office tapes had to do with this subject. What did Nixon know about Dallas that caused him so much concern?

LIST OF CASUALTIES:

(1) Congressman Jerry Voorhis--Congressional career ends in 1946 when Nixon falsely accuses Voorhis of being a communist sympathizer.

(2) Alger Hiss--Convicted of perjury and does prison time after Congressman Nixon leaks information to press. Although Hiss is acquitted of communist charges, his trial makes Nixon a national figure and hero of Red-scare fanatics.

(3) Senator Helen Gahagan Douglas--Defeated in 1950 senatorial campaign when Nixon accuses her of being a communist and slanders her husband for being a Jew.

(4) John F. Kennedy--After defeating Nixon in 1960 presidential campaign, Kennedy is killed three years later by the same CIA-Mafia apparatus that Nixon had helped set up to assassinate Castro.

(5) Robert F. Kennedy--Eliminated after winning the California Democratic primary with a fatal shot to the back of his head by a first-night security guard with mafia connections. Investigation is controlled by two CIA operatives on L.A. police force. Death of Kennedy allows Nixon's election as president.

(6) Governor George Wallace--During the 72 primary campaign Wallace is shot by another lone nut with no motive. Wallace is crippled but survives.

211

Instead of a three-way voter split, Nixon wins reelection in a landslide.

(7) J. Edgar Hoover--Refuses to resign at Nixon's request. Refuses to conduct illegal wiretaps to help Nixon White House. Has reams of incriminating evidence on Nixon in his secret files. Hoover dies unexpectedly in his home. Neighbors see men carry boxes out the back door of Hoover's house before his body is discovered.

(8) Dorothy Hunt--Dies in a plane crash with a suitcase full of money. Howard Hunt's wife was fed up with her role as bag lady to distribute hush money to families of Watergate burglars. Also angry about Nixon's failure to assist her husband and threatening to go public with her story. Charles Colson tells reporter, "They've killed Dorothy Hunt."

The Shadow government

NIXON ON NIXON

If the above characterization of Richard Nixon's career in politics seems heavy-handed, the reader has only to read transcripts of conversations recorded in the Oval Office to get a sense of the man. When the Watergate investigation was closing in on Nixon and there was talk of impeachment, Nixon agreed to release about sixty hours of edited conversations in a desperate effort to save his presidency. While "expletive deleted" eliminated most of the profanity, the tone of the discussions was a shock to most Americans. The presidency had always been held in high regard until we read about burglaries, hush money and a vindictive determination to get even with enemies. Nixon's attempt to save himself became the last nail in his political coffin.

In 1996, an historian named Stanley Kutler went to court to gain the release of several hundred more hours of taped conversation. Kutler edited them into a book called, ABUSE OF POWER. The excerpts that follow will give the reader a sense of Nixon's view of the political world around him.

Charles Colson had been hired as a personal advisor and given the duty of managing "dirty tricks" against Nixon's political opponents. These were clandestine operations that were never supposed to track back to the

White House. Nixon had taken a page out of the CIA's plausible denial handbook. All activities were acceptable as long as you didn't get caught. As a hands on guy, Nixon wanted to be briefed on the details of these illegal activities. One of the most outrageous ideas was to firebomb the Brookings Institute which was a "think tank" that was thought to possess many sensitive government documents. These conversations take place in the fall of 1971 as the primary season approaches.

KISSINGER: Now Brookings has no right to have classified documents.
NIXON: I want it implemented....Goddamnit, get in and get those files. Blow the safe and get it.

The Nixon White House seemed to be obsessed with campaign contributions. They had to have a bigger war chest than the enemy. One fine way to raise cash is to sell ambassadorships.

NIXON: Ambassador Raymond Guest will give a half a million or what do you suppose he wants to hear about that? Well, anyway, I'm sure that he's talking about a quarter of a million because he gave 100,000 last time out in '65....Now he can't be the ambassador to Brussels....My point is that anybody that wants to be an ambassador, wants to pay at least 250,000.
HALDEMAN: I think any contributor under 100,000 we shouldn't consider for any kind of thing except just some nice--
NIXON: That's right. Like Fred Russell who was a big time contributor we know. But from now on, the

contributors have got to be, I think, and I'm not going to do it with quote, political friends and all the rest of this crap where we've got to give them to good old Bill....Now when he goes, I want him bled for a quarter of a million, too. He's got that kind of money.

HALDEMAN: It ought to be more than that.

NIXON: You're talking about 100,000. That's ridiculous. We play his game. It'll be worth a quarter of a million just to listen to him that long.

As a means of discrediting the Democrats, Nixon decided to engage in an effort to leak government documents.

NIXON: Well, we're going to expose them. God, Pearl Harbor and the Democratic party will--they'll have gone without a trace if we do this correctly. Who would you put in charge, Bob?

HALDEMAN: That's what I'm trying to figure because--

NIXON: You've got Colson doing too much, but he's the best. It's the Colson type of man that you need....Don't go back to World War II, this first. The first things I want to go back to--I want to go back to the Cuban missile crisis and I want to go to the Bay of Pigs.

Here is more on Nixon's obsession with the Brookings Institute.

NIXON: They have a lot of material....I want Brookings, I want them to just break in and take it out. Do you understand?

HALDEMAN: Yeah. But you have to have somebody to do it.

NIXON: That's what I'm talking about. Don't discuss it here. You talk to Hunt. I want the break-in. Hell, they do that. You're to break into the place, rifle the files, and bring them in.

HALDEMAN: I don't have any problem with breaking in. It's a Defense Department approved security--

NIXON: Just go in and take it. Go in around eight or nine o'clock.

HALDEMAN: Make an inspection of the safe.

NIXON: That's right. You go in and inspect the safe. I mean, clean it up!

More on the plan to discredit the Democrats.

NIXON: I have a project that I want somebody to take it just like I took the Hiss case, the Bentley case, and the rest....we won the Hiss case in the papers. We did. I had to leak stuff all over the place. Because the Justice Department wouldn't prosecute it. Hoover didn't even cooperate....It was won in the papers....They were all too worried about the Manson case. I knew exactly what we were doing on Manson. You've got to win some things in the press.

More Brookings.

NIXON: Did they get the Brookings Institute raided last night? No. Get it done. I want it done. I want the Brookings Institute's safe cleaned out and have it cleaned out in a way that makes somebody else responsible.

More on the Alger Hiss trial.

NIXON: Let me show you what happened....If I were called before a grand jury in New York and told to give up the fucking papers, I refused....I said I will not give up the papers to the Department of Justice because they're out to clear Hiss. I played it in the press like a mask. I leaked out the papers. I leaked everything, I mean, everything that I could. I leaked out the testimony. I had Hiss convicted before he ever got to the grand jury.

More conversation about leaks against the Democrats.

NIXON: I need one man directly responsible to me that can run this....I need a man--a commander-- an officer in charge here at the White House that I can call when I wake up, as I did at two o'clock in the morning and say I want to do this, this, this and this. Get going. See my point?....You need a guy in Congress. I agree. Rousselot will be fine. He's mean, tough, and ruthless. He'll lie, do anything. That's what you need.

HALDEMAN: That's the advantage of Johnny. You know he's conservative.

NIXON: He's a Bircher.

COLSON: Conservative.

NIXON: How about that fellow Crane? Can he do it? No. He's a talker....

COLSON: He's not a doer. What about Ashbrook?

217

NIXON: No. He's not reliable.

HALDEMAN: We trust Ashbrook. You can trust Rousselot.

NIXON: Mainly because he wants to get ahead. Well, you can use both Rousselot and the other for that matter. But he gets hot.

HALDEMAN: Can't really worry about that. If the guy is saying sensational enough stuff, it's trying to get stirred up in the papers. You're in the old McCarthyism business.

NIXON: That's right. We want somebody to be a McCarthy. Is there a senator?

KISSINGER: There's no one.

NIXON: Dole could have done it if he were still here. Is there another Dole?

COLSON: Brock comes the closest.

NIXON: No. Brock is not another McCarthy.

HALDEMAN: A congressman has such a great opportunity with this.

NIXON: That's right. Bob is right.

HALDEMAN: You take a pipsqueak like McKevitt or Rousselot that nobody has ever heard of, you can make--sonuvabitch could make himself a senator overnight.

NIXON: I said I wanted to give the Kennedy private notes so they have to....The networks--That's really real juicy stuff to them....I've got to talk to him very frankly about things that we want to do and I don't want him to go out and make a record and go out and blast it later, well, the President ordered--do you know what I mean?...I don't want some guy who's going to try and second guess my judgment on this because I know more than any of them. I've forgotten more than they'll ever learn. This is a game. It's got to be played in the press.

HALDEMAN: I like this guy Colson's talking about, the former CIA guy, get him in....You've got to have somebody that knows the business....Helms describes this guy as ruthless, quiet and careful, low profile. He gets things done....

NIXON: I wonder if Tower could take this and do it on the side?

HALDEMAN: Sure he could if he wanted to.

NIXON: Is he too damn lazy?

HALDEMAN Got to have a committee.

NIXON: Got to have a committee....I think Ichord is the man....Republicans have two Birchers....Don't you see what a marvelous opportunity for the committee. They can really take this and go. And make speeches about the spy ring.

EHRLICHMAN: Televise the hearings.

NIXON: Right....but you know what's going to charge up an audience. Jesus Christ, they'll be hanging from the rafters....Going after all these Jews. Just find one Jew, will you....

TIMMONS(on phone): And your Congressman, John Schmitz.

NIXON: Oh, boy, Bircher. John Schmitz, good.

A month later the talk turns to the IRS as an attack dog.

NIXON: John, but we have the power but are we using it to investigate contributors to Hubert Humphrey, contributors to Muskie, the Jews, you know, that are stealing every--....

EHRLICHMAN: I know.

NIXON: And John Wayne, of course, and Paul Keyes. After 1964 he does one stinking commercial....Made him a Goddamn martyr. What the hell are we doing?

EHRLICHMAN: I don't know.

NIXON: You see, we have a new man over there. I know the other guy didn't do anything, but--.

EHRLICHMAN: Oh, you mean at IRS?

NIXON: Yeah. Why are--are we going after their tax returns? Do you know what I mean....

EHRLICHMAN: IRS-wise I don't know the answer. Teddy, we are covering--.

NIXON: Are you?

EHRLICHMAN: Personally, when he goes on holidays....

NIXON: Do anything?

EHRLICHMAN: No. No. He's very clean. Being careful now....

NIXON: What's Muskie doing? What kind of a life is he living?

EHRLICHMAN: Very close group, very monkish....Yeah. Big family. He's got six kids. And very ordinary type of life....

NIXON: Now here's the point. Bob, please get me the names of the Jews, you know, the big Jewish contributors to the Democrats....All right? Could we please investigate some of the cocksuckers? That's all.

In May of 1972, Governor George Wallace of Alabama was shot several times by another lone nut named Arthur Bremer. The would-be assassin was an unemployed dishwasher from Wisconsin who had been traveling all over the country and staying in expensive hotels. The American people were never told who was behind Bremer. Where had he gotten his bankroll? As the conventions grew near, the popular vote was being split three ways between Wallace, Nixon and McGovern. If the election had gone to the House of Representatives which was controlled by the Democrats, McGovern would have been the next president. The attempt on Wallace's life had given the election to Nixon as he figured to pick up nearly all of the Governor's reactionary support. As Wallace fought for his life, Nixon and Colson discussed the matter.

NIXON: Is he a left-winger, right winger?

COLSON: Well, he's going to be a left winger by the time we get through, I think.

NIXON: Good. Keep at that, keep at that.

COLSON: Yeah. I just wish that, God, that I'd thought sooner about planting a little campaign literature out there (in Bremer's Milwaukee apartment).

NIXON: (Laughs)

COLSON: It maybe a little late, although I've got one source that maybe--

NIXON: Good.

H.R. Haldeman let the American people in on a secret in his biography based on his tenure as President Nixon's Chief of Staff. In THE ENDS OF POWER, Haldeman says that whenever Nixon mentions the "Bay of Pigs thing" it is his code for the Kennedy Assassination. In light of this information, the following conversation that took place one week after the Watergate break-in provides the reader with an idea

221

of Howard Hunt's involvement in Dallas and Richard Nixon's knowledge of the plot to murder John Kennedy.

NIXON: Of course, this....Hunt,....that will uncover a lot of, a lot of--you open that scab there's a hell of a lot of things in that we just feel that this would be very detrimental to have this thing go any further. This involves these Cubans, Hunt, and a lot of hanky-panky that we have nothing to do with ourselves. What the hell, did Mitchell know about this thing to any much of a degree?

HALDEMAN: I think so. I don't think he knew the details, but I think he knew.

NIXON: He didn't know how it was going to be handled though, with Dahlberg and the Texans and so forth? Well, who was the asshole that did? He must be a little nuts.

HALDEMAN: He is.

NIXON: I mean he just isn't well-screwed-on, is he? Isn't that the problem?

HALDEMAN: No, but he was under pressure, apparently to get more information, and as he got more pressure, he pushed the people harder to move harder on....

NIXON: Pressure from Mitchell?

HALDEMAN: Apparently....

NIXON: All right, fine, I understand it all. We won't second-guess Mitchell and the rest. Thank God it wasn't Colson.

HALDEMAN: The FBI interviewed Colson yesterday. They determined that would be a good thing to do....An interrogation, which he did, and that, the FBI guys working the case concluded that there was one of two possibilities: one, that this was a White

House, they don't think that there is anything at the Election Committee--they think it was either a White House operation and they had some obscure reason for it....Or it was a--

NIXON: Cuban thing--

HALDEMAN: Cubans and the CIA. And after they're interrogation of--

NIXON: Colson.

HALDEMAN: --Colson, yesterday, they concluded that it was not the White House, but are now convinced it's the CIA thing, so the CIA turnoff would....

NIXON: When you get in with these people....say: "Look, the problem is that this will open the whole, the whole Bay of Pigs thing, and the President just feels that"--without going into the details--don't, don't lie to them to the extent to say there is no involvement, but just say that this is sort of a comedy of errors, bizarre, without getting into it. "The President's belief is that this is going to open the whole Bay of Pigs thing up again. And because these people are plugging for, for keeps, and that they should call the FBI and say that we wish for the country, don't go any further in this case," period....Hunt....knows too damn much and he was involved, we have to know that. And that gets it out....this is all involved in the Cuban thing, that it's a fiasco, and it's going to make the FB--ah CIA--look bad, it's going to make Hunt look bad, and it's likely to blow the whole, uh, Bay of Pigs thing, which we think would be very unfortunate for the CIA and for the country at this time, and for American foreign policy, and he's just gotta tell 'em "lay off"....

A week later, Nixon still seemed to be obsessed with Howard Hunt.

NIXON: And I can't be sure, but I would say this. One thing I think you should know, I can't be sure that Hunt was not involved with the Cubans, because the Cubans--

HALDEMAN: They had his name in their address book....

NIXON: The point is he headed the Goddamn Bay of Pigs thing and these people worked with him....

COLSON: ....Hunt is a fellow who I would trust. I mean he's a true believer, a real patriot. My God, the things he's done for this country. It's just a tragedy that he gets smeared with this. Of course, the other story that a lot of people have bought is that Howard Hunt was taken out of the country by the CIA. Well, he's certainly done a lot of stuff....Oh, Jesus. He pulled a lot of fancy stuff in the sixties.

NIXON: Well I don't agree. If anything ever happens to him, be sure that he blows the whistle, the whole Bay of Pigs.

COLSON: He wrote the book.

NIXON: Blow their horn.

COLSON: He tells quite a story, coming in here during that period crying and pleading with Kennedy....

After the arrests of individuals on the White House payroll at the Watergate Hotel, Nixon was anxious to deflect media attention away from Watergate. One way to do this was to release documents that would incriminate past Democratic presidents. Howard Hunt had forged officials cables that would incriminate John Kennedy in the deaths of the Diem brothers. Kennedy had been told that the Diems would be flown out of Vietnam to Paris. Kennedy's aides said that he was sickened to find out that the brothers had been murdered. It was not out of bounds for the Nixon team to falsify documents to blacken the name of President Kennedy. Nixon was also prepared to release documents that would show illegal wire-tapping on the part of the Johnson Administration.

When LBJ got wind of this slander campaign, he sent word to Nixon that he would consider releasing evidence of Nixon and Kissinger's efforts to delay peace talks in Vietnam until after the 1968 election. While President Johnson was putting the arm on South Vietnam to engage in serious discussions with North Vietnam to try and end the war, Kissinger was working behind the scenes to resist the peace efforts. The incoming Nixon Administration would guarantee several more years of unlimited military support if South Vietnam would resist Johnson's pressure to talk peace with the North. In other words, if the prospect for peace in Vietnam was encouraging as Johnson left office, it could only help the Democratic candidate. Nixon would not allow that even if it meant the deaths of many more Americans. This conversation takes place on January 11, 1973 as Nixon prepares for his second term. Eleven days later, LBJ dies.

NIXON: Well, what I want is this from DeLoach. We know he knows who is in charge of that, probably still in the Bureau, a bugger. Do you know what I mean? The point on that is that Gray gives him a lie detector test, calls him in, or asks him--do you see what I mean....? That's what I'd like to do. I'd like to get so it's nailed down in terms of evidence, rather than DeLoach told Mitchell or that Hoover, a dead man, told Mitchell, because Johnson would lie about this, if necessary, if we have to use it. My only view is that I would not want to use this story at all. This is something that I would use only for the purposes of--

HALDEMAN: Dean's idea also goes the other way, which we may want to figure out a way to play around with, which is to use it on Johnson, because a lot of the problem we're dealing with on the Hill stuff, and all you get Califano and some of those people into, and if Johnson turns them off, it could turn them the other way. In other words--

NIXON: Why doesn't somebody go down and tell Johnson?

HALDEMAN: Well, here's the other side of it. The STAR is back on the story again.

NIXON: Yeah

HALDEMAN: See, the STAR had it during the campaign. There back on it also.

NIXON: On the Johnson bugging?

HALDEMAN: Mm-hmm. And that'll stir Johnson up, and that gives us a way to get back to Johnson on the basis that, you know you've got to get this turned off, because it's going to bounce back to the other story and we can't hold them--and scare him. And at this stage with his attitude right now, he's strutting around like crazy....

NIXON:....This story has been a great problem. Don't you think so?...Well, get Christian in, would you, today, like today, or whenever you can, or tomorrow and say that they're on this damn story again and are on DeLoach, and he's going to tell Johnson that we're trying to keep an eye on it. We'll do our best, but he'd better get a hold of Califano and Humphrey and anybody else he knows and tell them to pipe down on this thing....We'll use it without question, Bob, if it comes to nut time. Do you agree?

HALDEMAN: Sure.

Nixon and Ehrlichman discuss Howard Hunt's forged cable to falsely incriminate John Kennedy. Nixon denies any knowledge, as usual, but he and Colson had discussed the details of all of Colson's operations. Nixon then lies about knowing that Hunt worked for Colson. He even denies ever having heard of Hunt although Nixon had known him since his days as vice president. Hunt's involvement in the "Bay of Pigs thing" seems to be Nixon's biggest concern.

NIXON:....the plumbers operation, the papers said it was something regarding some letter that Hunt prepared from, allegedly a fake letter from Kennedy on Diem thing or something.

EHRLICHMAN: Yeah.

NIXON: But that, of course, is totally out of your ken. Have you ever heard of such a Goddamn--

EHRLICHMAN: Yes, sir. That leads directly to your friend Colson....

NIXON: Goddamn it, I never heard of it, John. What, that a fake letter was--

EHRLICHMAN: No. It's a cable.

NIXON: But a fake one?

EHRLICHMAN: Yeah.

NIXON: From John F. Kennedy?

EHRLICHMAN: Well, that is what it is alleged to be.

NIXON: Oh, my God, I just can't believe that. I just can't believe that. The whole--you remember, you were conducting for me--you and Young were conducting a study of the whole Diem thing and the Bay of Pigs thing.

EHRLICHMAN: That's right. That's correct.

NIXON: But John, you will--if my recollection is correct, I just said get the facts.

EHRLICHMAN: Well, I don't know where Colson got his inspiration, but he was very busy at it.

NIXON: And he had told you that there was a fake letter or a fake cable?

EHRLICHMAN: Yes....

NIXON: I should have been told about that, shouldn't I?

EHRLICHMAN: Well, I'm not so sure but what you weren't.

NIXON: By whom?

EHRLICHMAN: I don't know....

NIXON: No. I wasn't told anything, a mistake. I mean, the only thing I was ever told about, you remember I said the thing that you did for LIFE MAGAZINE?...That's the only thing I ever heard about the Diem thing.

EHRLICHMAN: Well, that's a part of that transaction.

NIXON: But was the fake thing in that?

EHRLICHMAN: Right. That's what I believe. I could be wrong on this.

NIXON: You didn't know there was anything fake in that, though, did you? You didn't tell me anything about that, John.

EHRLICHMAN: Well, I'd have to go back and check my notes. But my recollection is that this was discussed with you.

NIXON: Well, I'd be amazed at that. I mean, I must say that I knew that a lot was done. I mean, I knew we were making a study, but I didn't know that we were putting together something totally fake to send to LIFE MAGAZINE or something like that on Kennedy and Diem.

EHRLICHMAN: Well, I could be wrong on this. I'll try and get the time to check my notes tomorrow before I come up.

NIXON: Yeah, yeah. Well, I've got to know about that.. If I'm in--I mean if I'm in that kind of a position....my God, I didn't know they were faking stuff involving that on Kennedy....

EHRLICHMAN: Yeah, that whole thing, that Hunt--and it was mostly a Hunt-Colson thing--ran off in a lot of strange directions....

NIXON: You know the thing about that is that Colson never told me about Hunt, that he knew Hunt, until after the Watergate thing.

EHRLICHMAN: Is that right?

NIXON: I never heard of heard of E. Howard Hunt, no, sir, no. No sir....

More Nixon denial in a conversation with William Rogers.

NIXON: Good God, when they today indict that poor damn Maury Stans and John Mitchell for the most utter stupidity and insanity in that Vesco case. You know when I stop to think what in the world is the matter with those guys, Bill, why in the name of God, Vesco is a cheap kike, it's awful.

ROGERS: Yeah....

NIXON:....these guys, you know, they took the contributions and screwed around and so forth, and, Goddamn it, well, in this case they should have told me at least.

ROGERS: I know it.

NIXON: Told me. But they didn't.

Ron Ziegler asks Nixon about possible White House involvement in Chappaquiddick where Mary Jo Kopeckne died in an automobile accident with Edward Kennedy. Nixon doesn't deny the possibility.

ZIEGLER: Did those Plumbers take anything that if not illegal could be embarrassing--the whole Kennedy Chappaquiddick thing....

NIXON: That's Colson, and I'll be Goddamned if I know....Colson can answer that. I didn't tell you. I don't know anything. I had never heard who Hunt, Liddy, et cetera, were--you know what I mean? The only people I ever talked to were Krogh and Young, and about national security. Colson talked to me about all kinds of political activities. You know what I mean? We ought to investigate Chappaquiddick and all that sort of thing, but he never talked about anything illegal--never, never, never, not to me. But Colson should be asked....

BEBE AND THE BOYS

From the time Murray Chotiner appeared on the scene in California in 1946 to manage Richard Nixon's first congressional campaign, the Mafia played a prominent role in the political ascendency of Nixon. Chotiner's clientele was heavy on underworld types as he represented mobsters in over two-hundred prosecutions. Chotiner's political specialty was the creative defamation of Nixon's political opponents. It began in 46 and continued through Nixon's final campaign in 1972. He was always in the background and he had his own office in the Nixon White House. It was through Chotiner that arrangements were made to commute Jimmy Hoffa's sentence and release him from prison. Hoffa was five years into a thirteen year sentence for jury tampering and misuse of Teamster's funds. A federal parole board had unanimously rejected Hoffa's release before Nixon stepped in.

Through Chotiner and the CIA- Mafia arrangement to assassinate Fidel Castro, Nixon had met Johnny Rosselli and other prominent mobsters. As the action officer and go-between while he was vice president, Nixon had been on the inside while the CIA developed executive actions against foreign leaders. Nixon had worked with Howard Hunt as early as 1954 in the government overthrow in Guatemala and had employed Hunt eighteen years later to handle illegal break-ins and plant false evidence to discredit the Democrats. It was the fear that Hunt would spill his guts concerning the assassination of John Kennedy that caused Nixon to become involved in the cover-up of the Watergate burglary.

Bebe Rebozo, who was probably Nixon's only close friend, was heavily involved in anti-Castro activities and had many ties to the Mafia. Rebozo's Key Biscayne Bank was reported to have laundered millions of dollars of mob money as well as illegal Nixon campaign donations. Nixon was led to a number of cut-rate real estate investments by Rebozo. Eugenio Martinez, who was involved in everything from the Bay of Pigs invasion to the Watergate break-in, was vice president of the Keyes Realty company which was partially financed by mafia kingpin Meyer Lansky.

A long time campaign donor and associate of Nixon's was C. Arnold Smith who had a controlling interest in the U.S. National bank. The bank collapsed in 1973 after Smith had reportedly lost nearly four-hundred million dollars in questionable loans to mafia controlled businesses. The IRS hit Smith with a huge tax lien, but the damage was already done. Smith was convicted of tax evasion as was his associate, John Alessio. A connection turned up between Alessio and Thane Eugene Cesar. Perhaps it was only a coincidence that Cesar was a part-time security guard who was on his first night of work at the Ambassador Hotel when Robert Kennedy was killed. Cesar stood directly behind Kennedy with his gun drawn as Sirhan blazed away from the front. It was determined by coroner Thomas Naguchi that the fatal shot had been fired from within inches of the back of Kennedy's head.

A FRAGILE LEGACY

Upton Sinclair made a statement in1919 that indicated he must have had foreknowledge of the Bush family, "You will float upon a wave of prosperity, and in this prosperity all of your family will share; your sons will have careers open to them, your wife and daughters will move in the best society. All this, of course, provided that you stand in with the powers that be, and play the game according to their rules."

To understand the Bush family, you have to go back to the turn of the century. In the presidential campaign of 1900, Wall Street bankers forced William McKinley to take Teddy Roosevelt on the ticket as Vice President. McKinley was the last of the Lincoln Republicans, and he wasn't willing to take orders from the bankers and industrialists who were anxious to exploit the resources of undeveloped countries. TR was a man the colonialists could work with. Within a year, McKinley was assassinated and the Shadow Elite had their hand-chosen boy in the White House. For the rest of the century, America ran roughshod over the political and financial affairs of Third World countries. After World War II, the Elite found the perfect tool to control these small countries. The CIA.

When Prescott Bush finished school at Yale, he went to work for the Brown Brothers and Averill Harriman, running their New York office. Besides banking and railroad interests, Harriman owned the Hamburg-America Line of ships. Two of his lawyers were Allen Dulles and John Foster Dulles. Besides Harriman, the Rockefellers and Duponts were cutting a fat hog supplying the Nazi war machine. This lasted right up until America's entry into the war after Pearl Harbor. This is why the Shadow Elite has always been opposed to peace. Military expansion is very profitable. The world's poor people are cannon fodder while the wealthy reap the rewards. These powerful individuals are not about to let mere presidents stand in their way. The rest of us are a kind of sub-species. We're tolerated because we are needed as consumers, workers and soldiers.

During the Eisenhower presidency, John Foster Dulles became Secretary of State and Allen Dulles became Director of the CIA. The Elite had two of its own in control of foreign policy. The Dulles Brothers answered only to this network of bankers and industrialists. Their inner circle included Prescott Bush and Douglas Dillon. With these stalwart Americans leading the way, the fifties and sixties would become the finest hour of the Beast.

Like his father, George Bush went to Yale and was a member of Skull and Bones. This was a secret society in which the members swore loyalty to each other above all else. Over the years, Skull and Bones boasted an impressive group of members such as Averill Harriman, Robert Lovett, Richard Bissell, Harvey Bundy, who was the father of Bill and McGeorge

Bundy, Henry Luce of Time-Life, William Sloan Coffin, Amory Bradford who ran the New York Times, William F. Buckley who was close to our old friend Howard Hunt, and David Boren who was chairman of the Senate Intelligence Committee. All of these men were part of a network that was involved in government or intelligence work. They all worked toward a common goal to promote the interests of one another. These "bonesmen" were often willing to circumvent our system of government to benefit this inner circle of powerful businessmen.

Prescott Bush became a legend in Skull and Bones in 1918 when he and two friends went out West on Easter vacation and broke into the tomb of Geronimo. They stole the great chief's skull and returned to a hero's welcome at Yale. The skull was a little messy so they cleaned off the flesh and hair with carbolic acid. For years, the skull of Geronimo was used in the secret ceremonies at Skull and Bones. When an Apache Indian group went to court to get the skull back, they were given the skull of a child. The bonesman thought the exchange would fool the ignorant Indians. What was the big fuss? They had stolen the head of some old Indian.

From the time George Bush finished school at Yale and went to Texas to get his feet wet in the oil business, he was an asset of the CIA. Bush set up Zapata Oil and Zapata Offshore so the Agency could locate drilling operations anywhere we were involved in covert activities. If you look for Zapata's filings with the Securities and Exchange Commission from 58 through 66, you'll find that most years are missing. Due to national security, of course. Like Oswald's tax returns.

235

Or Ruth Paine's. The beautiful thing about the Agency is that we can hide anything we choose for reasons of national security. On the other hand, when we refuse to release someone's tax returns, we might as well admit that they are involved in intelligence work.

Prescott and George Bush never had much luck in getting elected. They were both so indebted to the Shadow Elite that they had difficulty sounding sympathetic to the working man. Prescott finally got elected in Connecticut when his opponent died shortly before the election. When George lost the Senate race to Lloyd Benson in 1970, Nixon appointed him U.N. Ambassador so he could learn a little neo-colonialism from Henry Kissinger. In 1973, George became head of the Republican National Committee. Later, he was appointed as Director of Central Intelligence. The point is that George always had more luck getting appointed than getting elected. Maybe he looked and sounded more like Yale than Texas. But he was a man who could follow orders.

From Prescott Bush all the way down to the boy governors, the only way to describe the entire Bush family would be lap dogs to the wealthy. The whole talent-challenged bunch is always ready to answer the call of their benefactors. This family was desperate to become part of the wealthy elite and they would never disobey instructions from their handlers. Tractable and obedient. The Bushes.

When George Bush assumed his duties as Vice President under Reagan, a strange thing happened. In the first place, Reagan did not care for Bush. He was not Reagan's first choice for Vice President. The two men had engaged in a bitter primary fight and there were some questionable tactics used by the Bush camp which was staffed with two dozen operatives with intelligence backgrounds. Like McKinley and Teddy Roosevelt at the turn of the century, Reagan had his running mate forced upon him. Reagan had confided to an aide that he had strong reservations about Bush and worried about turning the country over to him. Two months into his new administration, Ronald Reagan was the victim of an assassination attempt.

Maybe John Hinkley was exactly what they said he was--a lonely man obsessed with actress Jody Foster. They say he was trying to get her attention when he attempted to assassinate President Reagan. But when they arrested him, he was talking about other people who were involved. Now he's locked up so deep in St. Elizabeth's mental hospital that he'll never see the light of day. Of course, he's forbidden to talk to journalists.

What is curious about the attempt on Reagan was that Hinkley's father was a Colorado oilman who had worked with the Agency over the years. Religious treks into poor countries were his cover. Guatemala, Zimbabwe, South Africa. Jack Hinkley was doing relief work for World Vision which was financed primarily by the State Department and had always been a vehicle for intelligence operations. A Catholic organization had called World Vision "the Trojan Horse for U.S. Foreign policy." After the attempt on President Reagan's life, Nancy Reagan became so troubled that she began to rely on advice from her astrologer, Joan Quigley. This put the American president in the strange position of relying on his wife for advice while she relied on a clairvoyant for direction.

Another troubling connection was that John Hinckley's brother, Scott, was a friend of Neil Bush's and was supposed to have dinner with him the night following the shooting. This would indicate that Neil Bush had no foreknowledge of the situation, but the connection between the two families was troubling to some investigators. Neil's wife, Sharon, had let the cat out of the bag when she said that the Hinkleys had given a lot of money to the Bush campaign. Maybe it was all a coincidence. Or maybe the Shadow Elite had a man in George Bush who would support their agenda with enthusiasm.

Would the Elite rather have Reagan, who treated the Presidency as a personal crusade and was difficult to control, or George Bush who had never said no to his benefactors. Reagan was seventy when he assumed office and his assistants complained that his mind would drift during briefings. He required afternoon naps and delegated most decisions to his cabinet members. Beyond these shortcomings, Reagan was an honorable sort of guy who relied heavily on his own personal impressions.

When you have one per cent of the people controlling half the wealth of the country, it's essential to have a president who follows orders. The greatest fear of the Elite is a popular president who is able to rally support for causes that threaten their wealth or power. That is why men like Kennedy and Clinton are so dangerous. In Kennedy's case, the solution was to shoot him in Dallas. With Clinton, the effort was made to destroy his character. Clinton made things much easier with his womanizing and I must say, a poor selection process. He made himself an easy target.

Some Americans are able to see through this. They could understand the threat that Clinton's national health reforms posed to the AMA and the pharmaceutical companies and the insurance companies. Once Clinton was on the run, these initiatives died a quick death. He spent the rest of his presidency defending himself against a flood of personal accusations. Bubba had been effectively neutered.

If you want some insight into the Shadow Elite, check into a place called Jupiter Island, off the coast of Florida. It's a guarded fortress where all workers are screened and fingerprinted. Sensors track moving vehicles. Reporters are not allowed past the gates. Over the years, the residents of Jupiter Island reads like a who's who in America. Averill Harriman. Douglas Dillon. Prescott Bush. Robert Lovett. Gordon Gray. Robert Wood of Sears-Roebuck. Paul Mellon. Nelson Doubleday. Walter Carpenter of DuPont. These men gathered together to plot the direction this country would take. They didn't want to leave it up to riff-raff like presidents and congressmen.

Another thing to look into is the Bohemian Club that used to meet every summer on a large preserve on the Russian River in Northern California. These sessions are held secretly and are attended by some of the most powerful people in the country. As bizarre as it sounds, I'm told that much of the time these men are nude. I guess this creates a bond that helps assure secrecy, but seeing Henry Kissinger au natural could cause long lasting emotional problems. Bush was president of the Bohemian Club. He wasn't rich or powerful, but he could follow orders and he was anxious to please. It looks as if his boys are following his lead. Their political futures have a tremendous upside as handpicked candidates of the wealthy.

George Bush has a pretty good idea where all the bodies are buried. He was the first Texan called by J. Edgar Hoover after the Kennedy assassination. He was Director of Central Intelligence during the mid-seventies when there was a lot of heat on the Agency from the Church Committee's investigation of CIA plots against foreign leaders. The Senate was in a mood to get tough with what Frank Church called "the rogue elephant" until some of them were implicated in ABSCAM and Koreagate. Bush had helped turn the tables of Congress and protect the secrets of the Agency.

The Bush nomination for DCI received considerable opposition in Congress. When he was appointed by President Ford, he was being considered as a possible running mate for Ford in the upcoming election. Bush wanted to keep his options open. He had failed to get elected to the Senate in 1964 and 1970 and he had been passed over for vice president in 68 and 72. Time was running out. There was also a possible problem with money that Bush had raised in Texas for President Nixon. The money was laundered in Mexico and used to pay the Watergate burglars. When Bush agreed not to run for vice president, he was finally confirmed. One of his biggest critics in Congress was a young Senator named Gary Hart who was also an opponent of the covert activities of the CIA. Hart was later rendered impotent when he was caught with a young model named Donna Rice. Don't mess with the Agency. We have a hundred ways to compromise you.

Gary Hart, Patrick Leahy and Frank Church were putting considerable heat on the Agency to disclose details of foreign assassinations when an event in Greece put the damper on the investigation. Richard Welch, the CIA station chief in Athens, was gunned down as he returned home from a Christmas party. The Agency blamed Welch's death on the hysteria created by the Church Committee's investigation. The mainstream press took the cue and began to attack Congress as being irresponsible. Church tried to explain that his committee had never mentioned Greece or Richard Welch. No matter. The tables had been turned.

A month later, the Pike Commission had finished its investigation and was waiting to release a report that contained a condemnation of Henry Kissinger for lying to Congress. The report was leaked to Daniel Schorr at CBS. Kissinger went into a rage and accused Congress of a new kind of McCarthyism. Otis Pike assured the nation that his committee had not released the report but said a copy had been given to the CIA. By leaking the report, the Agency had put Congress on the defensive.

When Bush assumed his duties as DCI, he brought some familiar faces with him. Ted Shackley was put in charge of covert operations. His resume included the plots to assassinate Fidel Castro, including the illegal Operation Mongoose. He had worked with the likes of Howard Hunt and Frank Sturgess. In the late sixties, Shackley worked his magic in the Far East including Operation Phoenix which was a forced informant program where South Vietnamese villagers were required to turn in a quota of Viet Cong sympathizers. The numbers that were demanded were so high that thousands of innocent citizens were tortured and killed. This was exactly the man that Bush needed to run illegal covert operations. Shackley later turned up as a speechwriter for George Bush's 1980 presidential campaign.

The Deputy Director for Science and Technology was Carl Duckett when Bush took charge at the Agency. Duckett offered some insight into George Bush as an administrator. He said he never saw Bush feel the need to understand the depth of an issue. Bush was not a man dedicated to causes or ideas. He said Bush went with the flow, mainly concerned with how something would play politically. This was the case in Jamaica where Bush went along with a plan to destabilize the island with the intent to overthrow Prime Minister Michael Manley. Illegal arms were sent to Jamaica to create violence during the election and several million dollars was provided for assassination attempts on Manley.

The blackest episode to mark George Bush's tenure as DCI was the murder of Orlando Letelier in the embassy district of Washington D.C. Letelier and a man from the Washington Institute for Political Studies named Ronnie Moffitt were killed when a bomb strapped to the underside of their car exploded in midday on Embassy Row. It was a ruthless act of terrorism which took place with the blessing of the Agency.

Orlando Letelier had been a minister in the government of assassinated Chilean President Salvador Allende. He had come to Washington to provide evidence that would implicate Nixon, Kissinger, and former DCI Richard Helms in the plot to overthrow Allende. Letelier's testimony was feared in intelligence circles. An Agency asset named Vernon Townley and another agent were granted entry to the United States using Paraguayan passports. Townley had been working with DINA, which was the Chilean secret police who was working overtime to prop up the dictatorship of Augusto Pinochet Ugarte. Townley was a top assistant of our old friend, David Phillips, who was in charge of Western Hemisphere operations at the time. With the approval of George Bush at the CIA and Henry Kissenger at the Ford White House, Townley and his accomplice eliminated Letelier in the heart of the nation's capital.

There was an immediate public outcry for an investigation. A foreign diplomat was blown-up on American soil. U.S. Attorney Eugene Propper was given the hopeless task of trying to get the Agency to cooperate in the investigation. When Propper met with Bush, he ran into a wall of doubletalk. "Look, I'm appalled by the bombing," Bush whined. "Obviously we can't allow people to come right here into the capital and kill foreign diplomats and American citizens like this. It would be a hideous precedent. So, as Director, I want to help you. As an American citizen, I want to help you. But, as Director, I know that the Agency can't help in a lot of situations like this. We've got some problems here."

Bush flew to Miami for a meeting in Little Havana and the fix was in. Bush had worked with these ant-Castro Cubans since his days with Zapata Oil when he was running guns to Cuba. That's why J. Edgar Hoover called Bush in Houston immediately after the assassination of John Kennedy. He wanted Bush's insight into possible Cuban involvement. With the help of Bush, Vernon Townley plea-bargained and got off with a light sentence while a few low-level Cubans took the rap. Mission accomplished with minimal damage to the Agency.

In 1980, Ronald Reagan had fought the good fight to keep George Bush off the Republican ticket but in the end he was overwhelmed by Bush's wealthy supporters. Reagan didn't like Bush personally and he didn't trust him politically, but an unexpected benefit to Reagan's campaign for reluctantly taking Bush aboard was the addition of the Bush covert apparatus. It was in the dark corners of this intelligence group that the plan was hatched that later became known as the "October Surprise".

American State Department officials were being held hostage by the Ayatollah Khomeini in Iran. The Carter Administration had failed in April to obtain the release of the hostages with a military task force. As the election grew closer, the Reagan team worried that Jimmy Carter might pull off a last minute release of the hostages that would give him enough of a boost to win the election. While accusing Carter publicly of a hidden agenda, the Reagan forces under the coordination of George Bush and William Casey, worked behind the scenes to make sure that the hostages would not be released until after the election.

An Iranian arms dealer named Cyrus Hashemi who was connected to the secret police, was recruited by Casey as the go-between. Hashemi returned with a proposal that the Shah be removed from U.S. territory, the freeze on Iranian assets in the U.S. be removed, and a delivery of arms and spare military parts be made to Iran. Casey, who would become the new Director of

Central Intelligence, traveled to Madrid twice in the summer of 1980 to meet with Hashemi and representatives of the Iranian government. In the end, the Reagan-Bush ticket won the election and the hostages were released on Inauguration Day, 1981. When journalists began to get close to the truth, a disinformation campaign was initiated. Half-truths and false leads were leaked to the press and then discredited.

Barbara Honegger was an official in the Republican election campaign. She wrote a book in which she related an incident that had taken place in late October. Her boss, Stephen Halper, had boasted that they no longer had to worry about an October surprise from the Carter Administration because they had cut a deal with the Iranians. A few days later, Bush made a speech in Pennsylvania where he looked the audience in the eye and warned them that Iran did not want to see Ronald Reagan elected president. He promised that he wanted to see the hostages released as soon as possible. Of course, he was lying through his teeth.

The George Bush vice presidency was similar to Richard Nixon's vice presidency under Eisenhower. Both men had their own agendas which were carried out without approval of their presidents. In Nixon's case it was his close working relationship with the CIA and plots to assassinate foreign leaders. Also, there were behind the scenes efforts to sabotage Eisenhower's initiative for peace with the Soviet Union. In the case of George Bush, he was an active participant in cabinet meetings and National Security Council sessions. He also kept an office at the Senate. Bush would attend a weekly meeting of Republican committee chairman with Senate Majority Leader Howard Baker and then swing over to the weekly GOP luncheon hosted by John Tower. In an administration where the president had limited participation, Bush picked up the slack.

The Bush tenure as vice president will be remembered primarily for the Iran-Contra affair. While Reagan might have signed off on the scheme (he later couldn't remember), the details were handled out of the Vice President's office. Although the United States officially had an arms embargo against Iran, the Bush contingency decided that the money was needed to fund an illegal war in Nicaragua. This was the time when importing drugs into the U.S. became an acceptable means of financing covert activities. To carry on these activities, administration personnel were regularly required to lie to Congress. Iran-Contra became the biggest black eye to the executive branch in recent history, but George Bush danced through the scandal to become President.

To keep the lid on their illegal activities, Bush and his accomplices created new damage control mechanisms such as the Special Situations Group, the Standing Crisis Pre-Planning Group, the Crisis Management Center, the Terrorist Incident Working Group, the Terrorism Task Force and the Operations Sub-Group. These deception groups were organized between '82 and '86 for the sole reason of keeping these illegal activities from Congress and the American people. When a crisis began to develop, the Bush group would come up with recommendations for security and cover as well as plans to manipulate the media. When the details of these activities began to surface, President Reagan was lucky that he didn't have much recollection of the events. The poor old fella couldn't even remember some of his top assistants.

To handle the damage control, Bush brought in two former CIA employees, Donald Gregg and assassinations expert, Felix Rodriguez. Rodriguez had worked with Howard Hunt in Miami when mafia money had been made available for assassination attempts on Fidel Castro. Felix and his boys had carried out several terrorist raids against Cuba. Immediately after the murder of President Kennedy, Rodriguez was sent to Nicaragua where several participants in the event were eliminated. He later surfaced in Southeast Asia where he teamed up with Ted Shackley who was using the sale of opium to finance hit squads. This bloodthirsty little Cuban was Vice President Bush's trusted liaison during the illegal war in Nicaragua.

The Boland Amendment had declared that no money appropriated to the Department of Defense could be used by Defense or the CIA for military hardware or training for the purpose of overthrowing the government of Nicaragua. Enter Lt. Colonel Oliver North to run the operation as an employee of the National Security Council. A former CIA director of propaganda, Walter Raymond was brought on board to handle the media. In 1983 Bush and Ollie took a trip to El Salvador to get a first-hand account of what was going on in Nicaragua. Bush, the acting commander-in-chief, made a speech to the Salvadoran army officers. Ollie said it was one of the bravest things he had ever seen.

By 1983, the Bush group had gotten so confident that it decided to invade the small Caribbean island of

Grenada without bothering to get President Reagan's approval. The operation was handled by Bush's Special Situation Group. At some point, President Reagan must have wondered if he'd soon be out of a job. It is reassuring to learn that while Bush was conducting these meetings without Reagan's knowledge, he was actually sitting in the President's chair. In fairness, it should be said that Bush did notify President Reagan of the action against Grenada while Reagan golfed in Georgia.

About the same time that U.S. warships were surrounding the dangerous island of Grenada, CIA frogmen were setting charges to blow up an oil terminal and pipelines in three Nicaraguan ports. The Agency was not entirely happy with the resolve of the Contras so it brought in covert warriors with the assistance of CIA helicopters and speedboats. When a pipeline was blown up at Cortino, Exxon informed the Sandinista government that it would no longer transport oil to Nicaragua. This is how a covert action outside of the control of the U.S. government can undermine a foreign government. A year later, Congress tried to put an end to these illegal actions by tightening the Boland Amendment.

In the following months, Bush, Gregg and Rodriguez were working on the details of a new fund-raising scheme. Rodriguez would promise the Medellin cocaine cartel good will in exchange for cash that could be used to aid the Contras. Rodriguez told one drug runner that he had access all the way to the top of the American government. After putting out his feelers, Rodriguez reported back to the Vice President. Two months later, Bush and Rodriguez were off on a fact-finding trip to Honduras. The real reason was to bribe Honduras President Roberto Cordova to allow aid to the Contras to be filtered through his country. The Bush team continued to operate outside the law because they knew their cause was just.

It has been well documented that elements of the American government are willing to break the law in order to serve their own purposes. From CIA abuses overseas and in this country to Watergate to Iran-Contra to FBI cover-ups, Americans have learned to be suspicious of what we are being told. In the area of terrorism, it is sometimes difficult to separate the wheat from the chaff. While the Bush team was selling arms to Iran and ignoring drug smuggling to this country in order to fund an illegal war in Nicaragua, a rash of terrorism was occurring around the world. Were all these incidents exactly what they appeared to be or might some of them been staged to deflect attention from the illegal activities of the Reagan-Bush administration? By 1986, the Bush Terrorism Task Force had drawn up a report requesting the appointment of an anti-terrorist czar. The man proposed for the new position was none other than Oliver North.

In October, 1986, the bubble burst when a cargo plane carrying arms and ammunition to the Contras was shot down as it entered Nicaraguan air space. The cargo handler parachuted to safety but the other crew members died in the crash. The survivor was surrounded and taken into custody by Sandinistan troops. He immediately gave up Felix Rodriguez as the project coordinator. Rodriguez made a single phone call to Vice President Bush. The jig was up. Oliver North was sent to El Salvador to prevent the story from getting out and to arrange death benefits for the victims. The three amigos had their fannies in a jam. The next day Congressman Henry Gonzalez called for an investigation. A few days later, the captured cargo handler provided details of the supply line to the Contras. The Washington Post ran a headline that read, "BUSH IS LINKED TO HEAD OF CONTRA AID NETWORK." Rodriguez had given up Bush to save himself. Bush immediately denied that he was running the illegal operation. He said the story was absolutely untrue.

Three weeks later a Middle East newspaper broke the story that America was secretly selling arms to Iran. Things were beginning to unravel. In mid-December, CIA Director William Casey checked into the hospital for removal of a brain tumor. He died six weeks later without ever telling his side of the story. Former National Security Director Robert McFarlane attempted suicide. He survived. The Tower Commission blamed Chief of Staff Donald Regan for the Contra scandal while it praised Bush for his vigorous opposition to terrorism. When Bush later rode in on the coattails of Ronald Reagan and was elected President, he appointed John Tower to be Secretary of Defense, but the Senate wouldn't buy it. They refused to confirm Tower. Bush then sent up the nomination of Dick Cheney who had helped whitewash the Contra affair during a House investigation.

As Tower and Cheney had learned, if you play ball with the Bush team and you don't let ethics get in the way, you'll be taken care of. Donald Gregg, who along with Bush and Rodriguez had run Iran-Contra, was nominated by President Bush as ambassador to Korea.

When Senate confirmation hearings began to take Gregg's story apart he continued to stonewall even though a pile of evidence contradicted him. At one point Senator Cranston remarked that it was incredible that Gregg told his story with a straight face. Cranston summed up the Senate's frustration by saying that the National Security Agency rejected its inquiries, the CIA's access was so restricted that it was laughable, the Department of Defense was unresponsive and the Bush administration's actions were contemptuous. This is how a shadow government operates. Amazingly, the Senate voted to confirm Gregg. Senator Stanford explained that he was afraid that the investigation would lead to President Bush. So much for Congressional oversight. Bush publicly declared that Americans were bored with the Iran-Contra affair.

Ronald Reagan refused to support his own vice president in the 88 presidential campaign. He didn't like the guy. Bush attempted to put the best foot forward by attending a dinner in New Hampshire in honor of the late William Loeb, who had put fear in the hearts of politicians for years with his mean-spirited editorials. Loeb had called Bush "a preppy wimp, part of the self-appointed elite." Bush had to swallow what left of his pride and attend the Republican gathering. Afterwards, the Widow Loeb rewarded Bush with words of praise to the effect that Bush had been Ronald Reagan's errand boy for seven years but he would surely revert back to the old Bush. She then recommended Republicans should avoid the Bush presidential candidacy as if it were the black plague itself. This was the kind of warmth and affection that Bush often inspired in people.

251

Once his nomination was secure, Bush chose to gain the confidence of America by choosing political featherweight J. Danforth Quail as his running mate. Quail was to meet his new commander at the docks in New Orleans where the Natchez paddle wheeler would arrive with Bush. One observer noted that Quail arrived at the dock in a state of inebriated euphoria. He grabbed Bush's arm while he pranced and capered about. He added that Quail seemed to exhibit some of the mental impairment that is known to overtake long-term marijuana users. His grades at Indiana had been so poor that his only access to law school was through an affirmative action program that had been established for minority students.

Bush and Quail, an academically challenged ticket if ever there was one, were able to devise the perfect strategy to defeat Massachusetts Governor Michael Dukakis. They seized on an event where a black convict who was out of prison on a furlough program committed rape and murder. The fact that many other states had similar programs was not important. The lowest common denominators of fear and racism would reap rich rewards for the small-minded duo. Throw in a few accusations of the alcoholism of Kitty Dukakis and the election was a done deal. American presidential politics had been elevated to a new plateau. The Shadow Elite had their dull tools in place.

Big Oil has always had a friend in the Bush family. From Prescott to George to the two blank-faced governors, oil companies have lubed their campaigns. In turn, the Bushes have always made Big Oil and defense spending their top priorities. In 1986 there was concern in the Bush camp for the falling prices of oil due to a glut of Middle East petroleum. Vice President Bush embarked of a trip to discuss security matters in the region and conveniently found time to meet with his long time friend, King Fahd of Saudi Arabia. A few weeks later, the United States bombed Libya and Saudi Arabia decided to reduce its oil exports. Later as president, George Bush rewarded his defense contractors with Operation Desert Storm. It was a fine little war where the U.S. tried to bomb Iraq back to the Stone Age. Saadam Hussein was never really threatened and there were a pile of civilian causalities, but the main objectives were met. New weapons systems were tested in near battlefield conditions and tons of military hardware was used. After President Bush left office, his first act as a private citizen was another trip to the Middle East for talks with the ministers of oil.

CRIME DOG

J. Edgar Hoover was probably the most mean spirited man I've ever met. He would have been laughable if he wasn't so deadly the way he used the power of the FBI. It was always about revenge. Joe McCarthy was nasty, but he was a drunk and he burned out in a hurry. Hoover spent his entire career getting back at anyone who crossed him. I guess he never got over the fact that he was short and queer. With a mug like that there's certainly no percentage in cross-dressing. You know, he used to stand on a box when he would welcome the graduating class from the FBI Academy. The new men were warned not to look down at the box or they never would be hired by the Bureau. He would reject one guy because of acne scars or another guy because he didn't like his ears or another fella because his hairline made him look unintelligent. That's the kind of little tyrant he was.

Melvin Pervis made the FBI famous when he took down John Dillinger and the other big-time gangsters in the thirties. Pretty Boy Floyd. Baby Face Nelson. Hoover would show up after the fact to take the credit. Purvis didn't care. He didn't crave publicity the way Hoover did. He was more of a regular guy. There was a rumor that Hoover had a crush on Pervis and there were some suspicious notes sent by Hoover during this period. Evidently, romance was in the air.

The crush turned to jealousy when Purvis became a national hero and failed to mention Edgar every time he opened his mouth. When Pervis retired and wrote his biography, Hoover was infuriated that he didn't get a more glowing evaluation. He hated that Pervis was so much more popular with the press. So Hoover set out to destroy the man who brought so much favorable publicity to the FBI. Whenever Pervis was offered a prime job, Hoover would make sure that he wasn't hired. In the end, Pervis shot himself. That was the final reward for the man who had brought glamour to the FBI. Pervis' wife wrote a letter and thanked Hoover for not attending the funeral.

Hoover's bizarre sexual weaknesses were always the subject of rumors in Washington. The Agency had compromising photographs of Hoover and Clyde Tolson. So did the Mob. They also had information about Hoover's fondness for ladies clothing. He liked to call himself Mary. They say he or she felt most beautiful in black satin. Hoover never admitted the existence of organized crime because he couldn't prosecute the Mob. The Agency and the mob used the same type of blackmail to control Hoover that he used to control politicians. Hoover would regularly send over compromising material on the Kennedys to Attorney General Robert Kennedy as a way of protecting his job. The Kennedys couldn't stand the little pervert, but they were afraid to fire him.

Edgar used to send over bets on the horse races with Frank Costello. If Hoover won, he was paid off. If he lost, no money changed hands. This is the way Hoover worked the system. He ate for years in a restaurant called Harvey's at the Mayflower Hotel in Washington and never picked up the tab. He called his regular Cuban waiter, Castro. Hoover considered it an inside joke. Apparently, that was the only Cuban name that he knew. That shouldn't be surprising for a man who had never been out of the country. That's true. In all his years in power, he never set foot out of the country. At Harvey's, he was conscious about not being seen with liquor so he would have Clyde hold his drink in his lap. There were many other perks. He had FBI agents paint his house and do all his yard work. It seems that our little crime fighter was totally corrupt.

Hoover kept a dossier on everyone in Congress. It was "secret and confidential" and would include any incriminating information on a politician or any member of his family. Hoover's form of arm-twisting was sending one of his agents, such as Gordon Liddy, to a congressman's home with a copy of all the dirt that Hoover had on the man. The agent would assure the congressman that everything possible would be done to keep the material from becoming public. Hoover got tremendous cooperation with this form of blackmail. Every president from FDR to Nixon was afraid of Hoover. He was a vindictive little man with a lot of power.

Hoover and H.L. Hunt were the force behind Lyndon Johnson becoming vice president in 1960. When John Kennedy was nominated, he held out the olive branch to Johnson knowing that Johnson would want no part of the vice presidency. H. L. Hunt then convinced Johnson that a number of Presidents had not survived their term in office. When Johnson finally agreed, the Kennedys were shocked. They were looking for a way to withdraw the offer when Hoover stepped in. He warned Kennedy that he had very damaging material on his extramarital affairs. He suggested that Johnson stay on the ticket. Kennedy's hands were tied. The one positive was that with Johnson stepping down as Senate Majority Leader, Kennedy would have his favorite senator, Mike Mansfield, in charge of the Senate.

Hoover and Johnson had been neighbors in Washington for years. They walked their dogs together. Hoover's only chance to remain Director of the FBI after his 70th birthday was for Johnson to become President before January 1,1965. Win or lose his reelection, Kennedy had made it clear that he was going to force Hoover to retire. He was killed just in time to save Hoover's job. J. Edgar didn't participate in the plot to kill Kennedy, but he was aware of it and did nothing to stop it. Afterwards, he rushed in with the full force of the Bureau to control the cover-up. H. L. Hunt's scenario that Kennedy might die in office just happened to take place in the city that Hunt ruled with an iron fist.

Imagine what would have happened if Hoover had been forced to retire by Kennedy in 65. Without the power of his office, the stories of his homosexuality and corruption would have begun to surface. A lot of people he had abused would have jumped at the chance to smear him. He could not afford to let that happen. It was no surprise that Hoover made no effort to protect Kennedy when information about the assassination came across his desk. He had received numerous accounts of death threats from mobsters like Carlos

Marcello as well as right-wing fanatics. By not passing that information on the Secret Service as he was required to do, Hoover became an accomplice in the murder.

The bad blood between Hoover and the Kennedys started when Bobby Kennedy told Hoover that he no longer had direct access to the President. He would have to go through the Attorney General. For thirty five years Hoover had enjoyed the privilege of walking into the Oval Office whenever he decided to. Bobby further humiliated the Director when he had a direct line installed from the Attorney General's office to Hoover's desk. When Hoover had the phone moved to his secretaries desk, Bobby marched into the office and told Mrs. Gandy to get that phone back on Edgar's desk. This was unacceptable to a man who had not been challenged for nearly four decades.

Hoover detested everything about Bobby Kennedy. The first time Hoover went to visit the new Attorney General, Bobby threw darts at the wall while they talked. In truth, this was disrespectful. Hoover hated Bobby's casual style with his wrinkled pants and rolled up sleeves. He hated Bobby bringing his dog and his kids to work. He hated Bobby working on Saturdays and requesting sensitive files which meant Hoover would have to be in his office on Saturdays. That meant he had to miss the races at Bowie or Pimlico with Clyde. Hoover was a very proper man with rigid routines. Even in his weaker moments, he wouldn't think of being seen in anything less than black satin.

It was all about appearances with Edgar. His office was furnished with American flags and huge FBI emblems. The walls were covered with honorary plaques from every conceivable organization in the country. His desk was on a raised platform that would allow him a superior position with any visitors in his office. Behind the oak walls of his office was an inner sanctum with couches and a television. This is where he and Clyde could get comfortable. What Clyde did to keep the Director happy all those years is unclear, but a considerable amount of discomfort may have been involved.

Hoover and the Kennedys were on a collision course. Hoover would make one of his speeches right out of the 1930s about the insidious danger of Communism in America. The next day, Bobby would issue a statement to the press saying that communism no longer was as great a danger as organized crime or right-wing extremism. He would further anger the Director by saying that a large portion of the communist party was composed of FBI infiltrators. The Attorney General would suggest that we had more to fear from poverty than Communism. To Hoover, this clearly meant that the Kennedys were soft on Communism and a danger to this country.

When Hoover sent surveillance tapes of Martin Luther King having affairs with other women to President Kennedy, JFK immediately called King and warned him that he was a target of Co-Intel-Pro. He told King that his home and motel rooms were being bugged. Hoover considered King to be a dangerous communist and Kennedy was warning King about the Director's invasion of his privacy. Another instance of Hoover and Kennedy's cross purposes was the presidential pardon of Julian Scale who had gone to prison on Hoover's trumped up charges that he was a communist. When Kennedy turned Scale loose, Hoover was spitting nails. Hoover was so ridiculous with his accusations that he called President Truman a dangerous communist. Truman retaliated by calling Hoover America's greatest threat to civil liberties. When Kennedy decided that it was time to enforce civil rights laws in the South, the FBI was a very reluctant participant. It was another example of Hoover having his own agenda and not letting a president stand in his way.

Hoover actually referred to his FBI headquarters as SOG or the Seat of Government. This was a supremely arrogant man who had seldom been opposed. Any criticism of the FBI was taken personally. A favorable article in a newspaper or magazine would bring a thank you note from the Director. An unfavorable comment would send the publication to the no contact list. Hoover had his loyal group of newsmen that he would leak stories to. Or he would have them in his office when a major story broke. Friends were rewarded. Enemies were harassed. There was no middle ground with Edgar. He was just like the Dulles Brothers in that regard.

As a symbol of his self-importance, Edgar would order a new black Cadillac limousine each year. It was bullet-proof and the most expensive car in Washington. He and Clyde would ride in the back seat together to work or to their free restaurant meals. They would often get out and walk the last few blocks to work to project the image of two strong, virile crime fighters. Actually, their virility was only known to each other.

While the FBI had about six thousand agents in the field, much of their work was done by private investigators and informants. If a private investigator would break into an office or a residence, he would only be guilty of trespass. A federal agent wouldn't have that latitude. An informant, such as Lee Oswald, would be paid a small monthly stipend for information. Many worked both sides of the street between the CIA and FBI. There were Potential Criminal Informants and Security Informants. Oswald was the latter. All sensitive information would go directly to Hoover. He would decide whether to act on the information or place it in his secret files.

As Bobby Kennedy stepped up the pressure on Carlos Marcello, Sam Giancana and Jimmy Hoffa, Hoover's surveillance apparatus received more information about death threats to the Kennedys. Hoover merely filed this information away. If one of these threats was successful, it would solve all of Hoover's problems. The fact that he was breaking the law by not passing this information on to the Secret Service was a small price to pay. He had to maintain his position of power at any cost. In this case, it was the life of the President. Kennedy was like the college professor walking along with his head down, lost in thought, while a huge black cloud gathered overhead.

Here's an example of how Hoover would use any means available to discredit the Kennedys. In his meetings with steel executives, John Kennedy had been promised that they would not raise the price on steel. In the early sixties, the steel industry and the automobile industry were the backbone of the economy. Any serious price hikes could set off a serious round of inflation. When the major steel companies announced an across the board price increase, Kennedy was furious. He went on television and condemned them for being irresponsible. He told Bobby to ask Hoover to conduct interviews with all the major steel executives to see if there was evidence of price fixing.

Hoover saw a chance to alienate John Kennedy from some of his powerful supporters. So Edgar sends in his agents in the dead of night to roust these men out of bed and interrogate them. All under the orders from Attorney General, Robert Kennedy, of course. These powerful men of business never forgave the Kennedys. They caved in to Kennedy's pressure and rolled back their prices, but the incident was not forgotten. Along with the mafia and the CIA and segregationists and the military contractors and the Joint Chiefs of Staff, steel executives could be added to the growing list of those who would be much happier without President Kennedy.

While Hoover was busy squirreling away information about death threats to the President, he was also monitoring Lyndon Johnson's problems with regards to Bobby Baker and Billy Sol Estes. Baker was a Johnson protégé and a key fund raiser for the Vice President. He had set up an apartment with some professional girls that he would use to entertain congressmen and wealthy campaign donors. He was also involved in some hotel deals with some well known mobsters who answered to Meyer Lansky. Estes worked the state of Texas for LBJ. He was being investigated for fraud and some suspicious murders in the Lone Star State. This had become a serious concern for Johnson and his political future. The news surrounding Baker and Estes were also becoming an embarrassment for the Kennedy Administration.

262

In his typical self-serving fashion, Hoover was using these scandals to compromise Lyndon Johnson for maximum leverage, should he become president. Edgar was fairly confident that John Kennedy would not survive his first term in office and he wanted be certain that the new president would set aside his mandatory retirement on January 1, 1965. Although Hoover and Johnson had been neighbors for years, Edgar knew that any help that he gave the Vice President to sweep the political scandals under the rug would result in Johnson's undying gratitude. That is exactly what happened. After John Kennedy was killed, LBJ extended the Director's term in office. Hoover, in turn, used the considerable power of the Bureau to make the Baker and Estes investigations go away. They say that every president going back to Franklin Roosevelt lived in fear of Hoover and Lyndon Johnson was no exception.

Hoover was well aware of the rift developing between LBJ and the Kennedys. Fred Korth, who was Lyndon Johnson's choice as Secretary of the Navy, resigned when he was accused of graft. This was a black eye for the Kennedy administration. About this time Kennedy told his advisors that Johnson was a riverboat gambler who often had difficulty telling the truth. Johnson, in turn, began to show loyalties toward Hoover. He appeared at the FBI academy and lavished the Director with gushing praise. He then criticized the President for selling wheat to the Soviets. Hoover knew that his best chance for avoiding retirement was for something to happen to Kennedy and for Johnson to become president. Kennedy had waived mandatory retirement for men like Admiral Rickover, but he had made it clear that Hoover was going to have to leave his position on 1-1-65.

When Oswald was arrested for the murder of President Kennedy, Hoover could not have been more pleased. A communist. It couldn't have been more perfect. Edgar had been preaching the evils of Communism for thirty years. This was his vindication. His only concern was that word would get out that Oswald was an FBI informant and he had been in touch with the Dallas office during the weeks prior to the assassination. He immediately ordered Gordon Shanklin to sanitize Oswald's files so he could deny any Bureau contact with him. Hoover also strongly denied that Oswald had been an informant. This was a lie. Oswald had a Security Informant's number. The Warren Commission soon had to deal with this matter.

With the fall guy in place, Hoover rushed into the cover-up with a vengeance. He warned the Dallas Police to step aside. He even told Chief Currey that he would have to muzzle Captain Fritz who was openly updating the press on developments in the case. He even forced Agent Shanklin to lie about the paraffin tests on Oswald. The first press releases stated that Oswald showed traces of nitrates on both hands, but not on his face or neck. The nitrates could have come from the cartons of books that Oswald had moved earlier that day. Besides, a man who had fired a pistol would be expected to show nitrates on the hand that had fired the gun. The fact that there was no trace of nitrates on Oswald's face meant that he hadn't fired a rifle that day. Period. So Hoover made Shanklin go on record and say that nitrates were found on Oswald's face and hands. This was obstruction of justice, pure and simple.

Hoover's problem was finally solved two days after Oswald's arrest when he was shot dead by Jack Ruby in the basement of the Dallas Police Station.

Before the President's casket had landed at Andrews Air Force Base, Hoover had issued written statements that Oswald was guilty and that he had acted alone. Then Hoover took complete control of the investigation in Dallas. He knew that Oswald was connected to David Ferrie because Oswald had Ferrie's library card in his wallet. Hoover also knows through surveillance in New Orleans that Ferrie is tied to the CIA and the Mob. Edgar is not interested in following any of these leads. He is determined to shut down the investigation and get on with the business at hand. That would be an executive order from President Johnson extending his tenure as head of the FBI beyond the mandatory retirement age. In return, Hoover would do everything in his power to contain the Bobby Baker and Billy Sol Estes scandals.

As soon as Johnson appoints the seven members of the Warren Commission, Hoover begins to compile incriminating information on each member so he can exert control when it becomes necessary. He then cuts a deal with Congressman Jerry Ford to provide daily information on the workings of the commission. During the period following the assassination, Hoover unleashes a huge propaganda effort where the press is given only evidence that incriminates Oswald. Any contradictory evidence is buried and witnesses who come forward with this type of information are harassed. Members of the Warren Commission see this disinformation for what it is, but they are powerless to fight it. J. L. Rankin, the commission's chief council, wanted to try and trap Hoover while he was under oath, but he was overruled. Everyone on that commission was afraid of Edgar.

If you look at Hoover's speeches to the Boy Scouts or the American Legion, they were full of references about moral fiber and honesty. He would say that telling the truth is the key to responsible citizenship. This from the man who would leak false information to the press to compromise his enemies. He would stress the importance of restraint while he accepted free meals in Washington or free vacations in San Diego. He would speak of virtue and honor while he framed a person he knew was innocent. He would curse the evils of soft living and immorality, but he would have teenage boys brought to him at La Costa. He would call for God-loving people to shoulder their responsibilities while he committed obstruction of justice. The man was a fraud in every sense of the word.

In the end, Hoover died under suspicious circumstances. He had sensitive information involving Charles Colson's involvement in the attempted assassination of George Wallace. He also had information about Nixon's involvement in political murders dating back to his days as Vice President. It was not a coincidence that some of the men involved at Dealey Plaza were on the White House payroll at the time of the Watergate break-in. These were loyal soldiers from the anti-Castro campaign who could be counted on to do Nixon's dirty work. At one point Colson's plumbers were going to burn down the Brookings Institute to get rid of incriminating evidence. To say Nixon was paranoid would be a gross understatement. He knew what was in Hoover's files. Not only could this information end Nixon's presidency, it could ruin his place in history. Also, Hoover was refusing to give Nixon any help in the form of the illegal surveillance of Nixon's enemies. Nixon tried to force the Director to retire without success. Nixon was desperate for a new FBI Director who might be willing to help. He had to get his hands on any incriminating evidence that Hoover possessed. Timing was crucial.

There was a burglary of Hoover's home the day before his death. Rumor was that a thiophosphate toxin was put on some of Hoover's toiletries. Before he was found dead the next morning, neighbors saw two men carting a long box out the back of Hoover's house to the alley. A file cabinet? There were a lot of people in Washington who would have wanted to get hold of Hoover's blackmail files. Nixon was probably the most desperate. He was up to his eyeballs in suspicious deaths. He was like the dog that gets into the neighbors chicken coup. Once he gets a taste for it, he keeps going back. The only way Nixon could be sure that his legacy of murder and deceit would remain secret was to remove Hoover and seize his files.

THE TEXAN

Lyndon Johnson was never known as a big thinker, but he was a world class back slapper and arm twister. When it came to politics, he knew how to get things done. Ethics and legalities always took a back seat to expediency. John Kennedy's death could not have come at a better time for LBJ. His protégée in the Senate, Bobby Baker was about to be indicted on charges of influence peddling. Baker had entered into business deals with the Mob and was taking kickbacks from all directions. Johnson's longtime assistant, Billy Sol Estes, had already been charged with fraud in manipulating the cotton market in Texas. Johnson was beginning to look like a liability on the ticket for 1964. Kennedy maintained that LBJ would stay as vice president although there was a rumor that Senator George Smathers of Florida might replace him. Kennedy needed to win Texas and Florida in 64 and he apparently thought it would be safer to keep Johnson.

All this trouble ended on November 22, 1963, in Dallas. J. Edgar Hoover, who was a neighbor and longtime friend of Johnson's, effectively suppressed the Baker indictment. Billy Sol Estes's problems in Texas were forgotten amidst the sorrow over John Kennedy's death. Lyndon Johnson had fulfilled his desire to be

President. There were two heavy obligations. One was to the Shadow Elite who had sponsored Kennedy's death and put LBJ in office. Johnson could not say no to a massive escalation in Vietnam. The other was to Hoover for protecting him from scandal and shutting down the investigation into the murder of President Kennedy. Instead of being forced to retire in January of 1965, Hoover was given a lifetime appointment as Director of the FBI.

Whether because of guilt or a sense of loyalty, Lyndon Johnson dedicated his presidency to the pursuit of John Kennedy's favorite causes. JFK was gone but the New Frontier was alive and well as Johnson pushed through legislation at a pace not seen since the days of Franklin D. Roosevelt. Civil Rights Legislation, Medicare, Medicade, low income housing, the Freedom of Information Act, the Corporation for Public Broadcasting, consumer protection laws, pollution laws, food stamps for the poor, increased funding for all levels of education including pre-school, affirmative action and land preservation were enacted. While LBJ concentrated on these domestic programs, the Vietnam War was being shoved down his throat by the same players who had succeeded in subverting Kennedy's foreign policy.

After McGeorge Bundy went on a fact finding trip to South Vietnam, Johnson reluctantly agreed to bomb North Vietnam. Then General Westmoreland requested two battalions to protect the U.S. airbase at Danang. Then came a request for more troops and approval for search-and-destroy missions against the Vietcong. Then came an urgent cable from General Maxwell Taylor who was the U.S. Ambassador in Saigon, that

269

the situation had deteriorated to the point where American ground forces were necessary. Finally, the Joints Chiefs requested 150,000 troops. When Johnson gave in to their request, he lost any chance of limiting the war in Vietnam. The Beast had won the day and more than fifty-thousand American men would pay the ultimate price.

While Bundy, whose primary loyalty had always been to the Shadow Elite and the Agency, used every means available to persuade LBJ to approve a massive military buildup, there were a few voices of dissent. George Ball told the President that sending more men to Vietnam was like giving cobalt to a terminally ill cancer patient. Johnson said that he was faced with the option of being boiled in water or fried in oil. Senate Majority Leader Mike Mansfield agreed. He told Johnson that we were getting too deep in a war that neither the survivors nor the rest of the world would thank us for, even if we won, which he doubted. Mansfield worried that the war would cause a rift in the American people and correctly predicted that civil rights leaders might join with an anti-war movement. He concluded that the United States did not have any tangible national interest in fighting a war in Vietnam.

The Shadow Elite prevailed over a few voices of moderation and the massive military effort began. As the machinery of war was cranked up, the aluminum, copper and steel companies announced price increases. LBJ called the executives greedy bastards and war profiteers. He finally went public and complained that these companies were profiting off the sacrifices of our boys in Vietnam. In getting price rollbacks, Johnson was the champion arm twister. He succeeded in getting price reductions including Anaconda Copper in Chile. Kennedy had fought the same fight but it was an uphill battle with a war going on. Kennedy had called steel executives "sons-of-bitches" in 62 and it had ruined his reputation with Big Business. Johnson would have been in a similar position except that he had given the military industry its war in Vietnam. That bought him time to pursue his Great Society program.

In the summer of 1967, racial frustration boiled over in Newark, Detroit and Watts. Dozens were killed and thousands were injured in the riots. LBJ said that the hardest thing he had ever had to do was to send the National Guard into these cities with a chance that they might have to shoot at American citizens. He warned Congress that unless something was done in these inner cities to create jobs there was sure to be more violence. He said that the clock was ticking on Washington D.C. Instead of wringing his hands, Johnson did three things. He pushed Congress and Southern Democrats to pass legislation to establish home rule in Washington D.C. Johnson then appointed Walter Washington to be the first black mayor of a large American city.

LBJ then appointed Thurgood Marshall as the first black Supreme Court Justice. While others in his administration were worrying about getting rid of trouble makers like Stokley Carmichael and Rap Brown, Johnson was addressing the causes of frustration.

Next, Johnson called fifteen of the most influential businessman in the country to the White House for a dinner. LBJ told these powerful men that this country had been very good to them and he wanted them to create 100, 000 new inner city jobs within a year and half a million jobs within two years. The National Alliance of Businessman (NAB) was formed and it met its first year's goal.

In 1968 Lyndon Johnson's presidency began to unravel. There were anti-war demonstrations on college campuses across the country. There was no progress in Vietnam. No matter how many men or how much military hardware was sent to Southeast Asia, there was no encouraging news. Johnson decided that the best way to get America out of Vietnam was not to run for re-election, but he kept the decision to himself. He began to increase pressure on the South Vietnamese to engage in serious peace talks with North Vietnam. Unknown to LBJ, Henry Kissinger was working the back channels to encourage the South Vietnamese not to agree to peace talks. On behalf of Richard Nixon, Kissinger was promising South Vietnam several more years of unlimited military support if Nixon were elected President. While Lyndon Johnson was desperately trying to end the war, Nixon and Kissinger were condemning thousands of American soldiers to death in order to win an election.

In March, Eugene McCarthy who was running on an anti-war platform nearly beat Johnson in the New Hampshire primary. Four days later, Bobby Kennedy opportunistically announced his candidacy. Even though there was no love lost between LBJ and RFK, Johnson told aides that Kennedy could be trusted to carry out the Great Society programs. He also thought that Kennedy might be better able to heal the divisions in the country than Richard Nixon. This was a selfless evaluation from a man who had never been treated with respect from Bobby Kennedy. On March 31, Johnson told the nation that he would not run for re-election.

Four days later Dr. Martin Luther King, Jr. was shot to death in Memphis, Tennessee. President Johnson feared that the assassination might set off another round of urban riots, but Kings' death solved two problems. First, King had become an outspoken opponent of the Vietnam War. Blacks had been refusing to show up for draft inductions and had been deserting the military at an alarming rate. J. Edgar Hoover was convinced that King was under the influence of communists. Hoover also had personal reasons for wanting to see the civil rights leader out of the way. The FBI Director had been on a vendetta to discredit and undermine King's reputation for years.

The second problem that was solved by the assassination of King was the collapse of the Poor People's March on Washington that was planned for that summer. It was feared throughout the Johnson Administration that the march of possibly a million people might be joined by a similar number of anti-war protesters. The federal government would be under siege. The assembly that occurred in May was a paltry excuse for the multitudes that would have followed King into Resurrection City.

Two months after Martin Luther King was shot in Memphis, Robert Kennedy was killed in Los Angeles. Lyndon Johnson had not liked or trusted RFK from the time he had worked for Senator Joseph McCarthy. He thought that Bobby Kennedy had none of the attributes that Johnson admired in John Kennedy. Where John was considerate, Bobby was arrogant. While John was confident, Bobby was brash. While JFK's humor was often at his own expense, Bobby was intense and self-centered. Johnson had always felt that Robert Kennedy resented his sitting in John Kennedy's chair in the Oval Office. Johnson's affection for Jacqueline Kennedy was the main source of his grief in the death of his adversary.

Johnson had several meetings with Ted Kennedy after Robert Kennedy's death. He expressed a liking for the youngest Kennedy. He thought he had a little of the Populist about him and a respect for Congress. LBJ tried to achieve a positive out of the deaths of King and Kennedy by pushing gun control legislation. He was furious when the gun lobby was able to water down his proposals.

Lyndon Johnson spent his final days in office pushing legislation for national parks and wilderness areas. Although the graduate from Southwest Texas State Teachers College had passed more legislation than any president since Franklin Roosevelt, his legacy would always be tarnished by the Vietnam War. In that sense, he had been a victim of the Shadow Elite not unlike John and Robert Kennedy. The man who probably deserved better lies in an unnoticed grave in the hill country along the Pedernales River.

STRANGE BEDFELLOWS

In 1963, H.L. Hunt was considered to be the richest man in the world. Oil and military defense were his line. He was a notorious tightwad, but he always had money for the John Birchers or the Minutemen or right wing radio programs. For years he had worked with the Agency to make the world safe for Big Oil. He was our biggest cheerleader when we needed to overthrow an uncooperative leader in some poverty wracked Third World country. Hunt loved to say, "Patriotism has always been profitable."

Over the years, Hunt spent a lot of money on politicians who would do his bidding for him. Richard Nixon and Lyndon Johnson were two of the biggest beneficiaries. His stable also included the notorious commie hunter, Joseph McCarthy. If you were pro-military and ant-communist and you didn't let your conscience get in the way, you were just the kind of guy H.L. Hunt was looking for. After McCarthy burned himself out and fled the scene in disgrace, Hunt continued to employ the senator's cutthroat attorney, Roy Cohn. Hunt was willing to overlook Cohn's homosexual angle for the services of the ruthless and vindictive lawyer.

Hunt's financial empire was headquartered in Dallas. Hunt controlled a citizens committee that decided who would run for mayor or sheriff or any important civic office. They kept the lesser employees in line with a system of low wages plus bonuses. If you cooperated and followed orders, you could expect a nice bonus at the end of the year. If you had a sense of ethics like Deputy Sheriff Roger Craig, you quickly fell out of favor and were replaced. That's how Hunt, Clint Murchison and Syd Richardson controlled the city of Dallas.

The hand-picked mayor of Dallas in 1963 was Earl Cabell. He was instrumental in changing the motorcade route so it would pass beneath the Texas School Book Depository. His brother was General Charles Cabell. You'll remember that John Kennedy fired General Cabell after the Bay of Pigs failure. From that day, Cabell openly accused Kennedy of treason. He believed that Kennedy's push to end the Cold War was a dangerous path for America. A real patriot would try to stop Kennedy by any means possible. One means was to involve his brother who was the mayor of Dallas. There was an absolutely perfect ambush sight at Dealey Plaza.

Charles Cabell had been Allen Dulles' right hand man at the Agency for years. Cabell helped carry out a number of Executive Actions for Dulles and the Agency. Along with Ed Lansdale, Dulles had his two most trusted assistants available for Dallas. An EA in our own backyard to remove the President of the United States required the best planning and preparation that these three men could muster. There was no room for failure. Had John Kennedy survived, Bobby Kennedy would have gone on a vendetta that would have shaken the foundation of our government. That's why the arrest of Oswald was a frightening moment for the men behind the coup. If Oswald had spilled his guts to reporters about his intelligence background, some powerful men would have had to run for cover.

In addition to his ties to the Agency, H.L. Hunt was a friend of New Orleans mafia boss, Carlos Marcello. Powerful men tend to gravitate toward one another. I'll guarantee you that the problem of John and Bobby Kennedy was discussed by these men. There is an account by a former FBI man who went to work for Hunt who said he once observed a poker game at one of Hunt's ranches in East Texas. At the table were Hunt, Carlos Marcello and J. Edgar Hoover. Think about that for a minute. The richest man in the world, a mafia kingpin and America's most notorious crime fighter.

Hoover associated with other mobsters like Frank Costello, who would lead him to fixed horse races. Another of Hoover's closest friends was Hunt's buddy, Clint Merchison, who owned the Dallas Cowboys. He also owned Del Mar Racetrack near San Diego and a resort called Del Charro. Hoover and his significant other, Clyde Tolson, would spend a month in San Diego each summer compliments of the old wildcatter. Murchison liked to say, "Money is like manure. Spread it around and good things happen." He spread around plenty of it with the FBI Director.

On the evening before John Kennedy lost his life in Dallas, Merchison held a little get-together at his ranch in Texas. According to LBJ's former mistress, Madeline Brown, those present at the Merchison Ranch Summit included; J. Edgar Hoover, Richard Nixon,

Prescott Bush and his ambitious son, George. All these men had two things in common. They intensely disliked John Kennedy and they would all benefit from his death.

There was a world-class golf course at Del Charro that was frequented by upscale mobsters as well as Dick Nixon. Frank Fitzsimons, the guy who replaced Jimmy Hoffa as the head of the Teamsters Union when Hoffa went to jail, was another frequent guest of Murchison's. The reason that Hoffa may now reside in the end-zone at Giants Stadium is that Fitzsimons had a more liberal loan policy than did Hoffa. The mob found Fitzsimons an easier guy to do business with. Anyway, Del Charro was a place where real men could get together and discuss their problems. You can bet that the Kennedys were a popular topic of conversation on the lush green links. The Kennedys had prosecuted organized crime on a level that had never been attempted. These upstanding citizens also had a serious desire to get back to Cuba where so much money had been made in the fifties.

Murchison had secured loans for his many business ventures from Jimmy Hoffa and the Teamsters' Fund. Hoffa had also done business with Carlos Marcello, Sam Giancana and Santos Trafficante. Giancana and Trafficante were involved with the Agency in our efforts to assassinate Fidel Castro. The oilmen and the Mob had always given generously to Nixon's campaigns. As vice president, Nixon had worked closely with Allen Dulles and General Cabell in a number of Executive Actions. I remember the testimony of an ex-Agency guy named Cooper. He describes a meeting in the mid-fifties somewhere in

Honduras.   Vice President Nixon took part in a discussion with a team of hired shooters. Mechanics, we called them.   They talked about the removal of Panama's President, Jose Ramón. Nixon flew back to Washington and the next day Ramón was assassinated. Nixon also flew out of Dallas shortly before President Kennedy was killed.

Our old friend George DeMohrenschildt was also an employee of Murchison's. He had worked for the Nazis in France during WWII and had been recruited by Dulles after the war. He was the conduit for donations from H.L. Hunt and Merchison to the Agency for projects that benefitted them.   One such project occurred in Dealey Plaza. Hunt was a tight fisted old buzzard.   I'm told that he warned that we should not overpay for John Kennedy because it would drive up the price on Bobby and the others. There was such a hatred of the Kennedys by these right-wingers that they talked openly about killing them.

So DeMohrenschildt worked for the Agency as well as the oilmen. He became Oswald's handler when our fall-guy returned to Texas from Russia.   The two actually became friends. DeMohrenshildt was working on a manuscript that defended Oswald at the time of his alleged suicide.

Nixon's political future required the removal of John Kennedy. He was looking at four more years of John Kennedy followed by possibly eight years of Bobby. Then maybe eight years of Teddy. Dulles and Cabell often discussed that possibility. Twenty-four years of Kennedys. The mob was desperate for relief from Bobby Kennedy's Justice Department. Hoffa was going to jail and Marcello was going to be deported.

Trafficante wanted Cuba back. Those two mobsters anteed up for Dealey Plaza. The Agency was running scared from President Kennedy's public criticism and his intention to gut its power. The old guard at the CIA had a working mechanism in place to accomplish the job in Dallas. Operation Mongoose. By removing John Kennedy, Dulles could insure the future of the Agency. He could also provide help for his political and business allies as well as his circle of military contractors. Plus, he could throw a bone to the Mob. Everybody wins.

DAMAGE CONTROL

THE FALL GUY

Lee Harvey Oswald's run of bad luck started two months before he was born when his father died. Lee and his two brothers were in and out of orphanages while his mother continued to look for work. By all accounts he was an affectionate kid who was close to his brothers. When Lee was five, his mother married for the third time and they moved to Fort Worth, Texas. His two older brothers were left in a military school.

Lee got through second grade with good marks. Then his stepfather divorced his mother. The next four years, Lee bounced around from school to school as Marguerite looked for less expensive places to live. When Lee graduated from elementary school, they loaded up the '48 Dodge and headed for New York City.

A basement room was the best the mother and son could afford in the Big Apple. From there it was one cheap room after another. When Lee was put in his third middle school in less than a year, he decided that he would rather watch TV or go to the public library. His loner period had begun. As he rode the subway one day, a woman gave him a pamphlet titled, SAVE THE ROSENBERGS. As he considered the fate of the accused communists, he checked out a copy of Karl Marx's DAS KAPITAL. From that day forward, Lee Oswald was a socialist. Not a communist. He would always draw that distinction.

Two years in New York were just about enough for the Oswalds so they loaded up there meager belongings and headed home to New Orleans. Lee enrolled at Beauregard High and started to do well in school again. That summer he enrolled in the Civil Air Patrol and met a man who would play a big part in his future. Captain David Ferrie was an instructor and confirmed pedophile. Ferrie later confided to a friend that he had taught Lee Oswald about man and boy relationships. So we have the confused kid being turned out by the child molester. It was exactly what Lee did not need at this point in his chaotic life.

In the fall of '55, Lee Oswald decided that he wanted to join the Marines like his brother Robert. He dropped out of school and falsified some documents and tried to join the Marines. He was rejected because of his age, but his mind was set. He would wait until he was seventeen. He read books and got a job as a message runner on the New Orleans docks. He used his first paycheck to buy his mother a new coat. He wrote a letter to Robert explaining that happiness is not based on concern for oneself. Quite a statement from a man who was later accused of committing one of the most selfish acts in American history.

Oswald enlisted on his seventeenth birthday and was sent to boot camp at Camp Pendleton near San Diego. He got through basic training although he was uncoordinated and the joke of the firing range. The Marines decided to disregard his physical shortcomings and sent Oswald to Jacksonville to study aviation electronics. He was then sent to Biloxi to become a radar operator. At this point, the Marines obviously considered Lee Oswald to be a useful recruit. He was given a confidential security clearance and sent to Atsugi Air Base in Japan.

The plot thickened at Atsugi. The base was the start-off point for spy flights over China and the Soviet Union and was also a center for mind-control experiments. Arriving on the same ship as Oswald was the man behind the picket fence, Roscoe White. There is a real question whether both of these men were subjected to experiments with LSD and hypnosis. Oswald in particular would seem to disappear for days at a time. One thing was clear. He had become a proficient radar operator and he had firsthand knowledge of the U-2 flights.

The Marines interviewed by the Warren Commission had some favorable things to say about Oswald during his stay in Japan. One man said that Oswald was totally honest, the kind of guy he would trust completely. Another Marine recalled Oswald loaning him money until payday. Another said that Oswald was the kind of friend you could count on if you needed a pint of blood. Others talked about how Oswald would spend his entire day off reading books on his bunk. This hardly squares with the image of the violent loner.

During this period, Oswald began to learn the Russian language and would meet with an attractive Russian woman at a local night club. When he came down with gonorrhea, his medical record noted that the disease had been contracted in the line of duty. This was a giveaway that his intelligence career had begun. In December of '58, Oswald was transferred to Marine Air Control Squadron Nine in Santa Ana, California.

Oswald's first roommate at MACS-9 was a Puerto Rican kid named Nelson Delgado. He taught Oswald Spanish while they joked about becoming officers in the Cuban revolution. Delgado said that Oswald began receiving mail from the Cuban Embassy along with his Russian newspapers. When a man in a suit arrived at the barracks and talked with Oswald outside for two hours, Delgado decided that it must have been part of some official business. Delgado later got in trouble with the FBI for testifying before the Warren Commission that Oswald was such a bad shot that he often missed the target altogether. Maggie's drawers, he called it. That was with an M-1, which was a lot more accurate than the Mannlicher-Carcano.

Oswald's next roommate in Santa Ana was Jim Botelho who liked Oswald well enough to invite him home to meet his family in San Juan Bautista. When Oswald applied for a family hardship discharge, Botelho was surprised that it was granted so quickly. Oswald told him that he was really going to Cuba to train troops. A month later when Oswald defected to Russia, Botelho and Oswald's other fellow Marines decided that he had gone to the Soviet Union on official business and wasn't a real defector.

When Oswald was discharged from the Marines, he was given a Department of Defense I.D. This entitled him to medical care, PX privileges, etc. Discharged Marines aren't given this type of I.D., but it would be given to a civilian working for the government overseas. The question is, why was Lee Oswald given this type of identification on the same day he was given his military discharge? The answer is that he was going overseas on a government assignment. Intelligence operatives carry this form of I.D. This is crucial to understanding Oswald's movements from the time he left for Russia until he was shot in Dallas. Predictably, this information was hidden from the Warren Commission by the FBI and the CIA.

Jim Botelho later became a judge. A very respected man. To this day, he refuses to believe that Lee Oswald shot John Kennedy. He maintains that Oswald was a pacifist. Botelho calls him a gentle person. He says that if Oswald was involved in the assassination in any way, it was as an informant. Botelho guessed that Oswald would have tried to prevent the assassination. He says that during the time he knew Lee Oswald, he saw him as sort of a heroic figure. Certainly not a killer.

So Oswald leaves the Marines on a hardship discharge due to his ailing mother. Lee visits Marguerite in Texas where she is fine. He then heads for New Orleans with his passport and Department of Defense I.D. He catches a freighter and arrives in France three weeks later. He goes directly to London and takes a flight to Finland the same day. From there he takes the train to Moscow. He immediately announces that he wants to give up his American citizenship and become a citizen of the Soviet Union. To sweeten the deal, he offers to give Russia military secrets from his experience as a radar operator.

You have to realize that Oswald had considerable knowledge that he could pass on to the Soviets. He knew the size and strength of all west coast air defense squadrons. He knew the range of their radio and radar. He knew the authentication codes. He knew the height, range and radar codes of the U-2 flights from Japan. This would seem to be useful information to the Soviets, but they didn't seem to be interested. Perhaps they were aware that he was part of a false defector program. They would have looked foolish if they had embraced the defector and came up empty. Oswald's defection seemed all too public, like it had been rehearsed. They ordered Oswald to leave Russia at once.

This is when Oswald resorts to his feeble suicide attempt. He cuts his wrist, but not too deeply, and is taken to a hospital. While recovering, he is visited by someone from the American Embassy who is possibly connected with the Agency. Oswald's activities should have set off all kinds of alarms, but the CIA does not start a file on him for another year. This is difficult to explain unless he is already working as an operative for the Agency.

The Soviets issue a one year work visa and send Oswald to work in an electronics plant in Minsk. In 1959, Minsk was practically a new city. The Russians had used German POWs to rebuild the city before sending them back to East Germany. The facility where Oswald worked and lived had its own restaurant, gym and museum. The Russians considered it a showpiece of the Worker State. The thinking might have been to create a favorable impression for the defector before his return to the United States. Oswald is given an apartment with a balcony overlooking the Svisloch river. His salary is matched by a monthly stipend from the Russian Red Cross. This put Oswald in a position to meet a number of attractive Soviet women.

A little more than a year after his arrival in Minsk, Oswald meets nineteen year old Marina Prusakova at a dance. Like Oswald, she was raised without a father. A month later, they decide to get married. Two months later, Marina is pregnant and Oswald decides he wants to return to America. The next spring, June is born and the Oswalds leave Minsk on a train for the Netherlands. They board a ship and arrive in the United States two weeks later. The New York State Department of Welfare, which has loaned them the money for their return passage, puts the Oswalds up for the night in a hotel in Times Square. A hero's welcome for an alleged traitor and his Russian wife.

The next day the Oswalds are put on a commercial flight to Fort Worth, Texas, where they will stay for a month with Lee's older brother, Robert. Lee then finds work in a sheet-metal plant and moves his family into a rundown apartment on Mercedes Street. At this point, George DeMohrenschild stops by to introduce himself at the request of CIA asset, Walter Moore. DeMohrenschildt is not too impressed with Marina's intellect, but he takes a liking to Lee. They spend considerable time together arguing politics and foreign affairs. Later, DeMohrenschildt's testimony to the Warren Commission is twisted by attorney Albert Jenner to paint a very negative picture of Oswald. Before his death, DeMohrenschildt was working on a manuscript that would exonerate Oswald in President Kennedy's death. I'M JUST A PATSY would depict Oswald as an intelligent, sincere person who greatly admired the President. Oddly, the man sent to handle

Oswald by the CIA was probably the best friend he ever had.

The next spring, it was on to New Orleans where Oswald would function as an undercover operative for the Agency and an informant for the FBI. Oswald spent so much time hanging around the parking garage where the local FBI men parked their cars that he ended up losing his job at the Reilly Coffee Company. The garage was where he received his envelopes of cash from the FBI. He was also receiving cash from Clay Shaw. By establishing a one man Fair Play for Cuba Committee, handing out leaflets and appearing on radio talk shows, Oswald was firming up his credentials as a Castro sympathizer. This was essential to later convince the American public that he had a motive to kill John Kennedy. At the same time, he was informing the FBI of the activities of the anti-Castro Cubans in New Orleans and at their training camp at Lake Ponchatrain. If Oswald had not been working for Shaw and Guy Bannister, he never would have gotten near those Cubans. All the while, Oswald thought he was laying the groundwork for an undercover assignment in Cuba.

The next step was to send Oswald to Mexico City to set up the story of his intended defection to Cuba. While Oswald was holed up in a hotel room, our impersonators went to the Russian and Cuban embassies to try and secure entry visas. Had Oswald actually gone to the embassies, he would have been photographed and the pictures would have been used later to incriminate him. Lansdale figured it was enough to have Oswald in Mexico. Howard Hunt was stationed in Mexico City at the time and he oversaw the arrangements there. Years later a note was found from Oswald to Hunt asking for more details about his assignment.

When Oswald returns to Dallas, his wife is living with Ruth Paine. This was critical to keep communication about Oswald's movements to a minimum between husband and wife. It was also necessary to have a secure location like Ruth Paine's garage to plant all the incriminating evidence against Oswald after the assassination. When Mrs. Paine suggested that Lee inquire about a job at the Texas School Book Depository, everything was in place. While Marina Oswald defended her husband immediately after the assassination, she later condemned him during her Warren Commission testimony. In the interim, she had been isolated in a hotel room and interrogated more than forty times by the FBI.

Americans accepted pretty quickly that Lee Oswald was the lone assassin of President Kennedy. There was damaging evidence everywhere. Where the evidence wasn't damaging, Hoover suppressed it. Lansdale and the Agency had done their finest work of fiction. With important members of the press in our hip pocket, Americans got a steady diet of Oswald as the deranged malcontent. When an honest law enforcement officer, like Roger Craig, spoke publicly against the official version, all the powers of the FBI were brought to bear against him. Like Craig, a number of dissenters wound up dead. Remember, Ed Lansdale was a former Madison Avenue guy who was trained in the art of deception. He had perfected his trade while overthrowing governments in the Far East. He was the master and he set up the Executive Action in Dallas very well. Hoover was overjoyed to be rid of the Kennedys. He was absolutely determined to keep the lid on the story so the Bureau would not be embarrassed by its use of Oswald as a security informant.

Lansdale first isolated the perfect fall guy. He then firmed up his communist credentials in New Orleans. The reason for first trying to tie Oswald to Castro and Cuba was to give our military another chance to take back Cuba. That's why our Cubans were so willing to participate in the plot to kill Kennedy. They blamed him for the Bay of Pigs failure and not attacking Cuba during the missile crisis. When Kennedy promised Khrushchev that we would end our attacks on Castro, our Cubans were angry and demoralized. They wanted to get rid of Kennedy as much as our military and our overseas investors wanted to get rid of him. It was clear to all of us that he was going to try to end the Cold War in his second term. That would have left us exactly nowhere.

For the finishing touches on Oswald the Commie, we had two of our Cubans take a pot shot at General Walker, the red-necked Minuteman. We needed to establish a violent side to Oswald because he had never shown that tendency. We had John Masen, who was a dead-ringer for Oswald, all over Dallas in the two months leading up Kennedy's visit. We had him at gun shops and firing ranges and car dealerships saying things that would later incriminate Oswald. He told people at the firing ranges that he was practicing for Kennedy. He told the car salesman that he might have to go to Russia to buy a car. We even had Masen at Redbird Airport a few days before the assassination trying to rent a plane for a flight out of the country. Everything had to point to Cuba. In hindsight, it might have been too heavy-handed.

You have to understand that Oswald was supposed to be shot and killed at the Texas Theatre. There was never supposed to be a midnight press conference at police headquarters where Oswald could proclaim his innocence. We intended to have a massive amount of evidence to prove his guilt even though he was dead. It would have been a lot cleaner that way. We find the gun and the shells on the sixth floor of the book depository. We find the incriminating photographs in Ruth Paine's garage. We begin to release background information on his defection to Russia and his loyalty to Cuba. Witnesses start to come forward from the gun shops and the firing ranges. It would have been neat and clean.

J.D. Tippit was probably told to be looking for Oswald in the residential area west of Oswald's rooming house. He was told to take Oswald to the Texas Theatre. He had met Oswald several times in the Carousel Club with Jack Ruby. Tippit was aware of the plot to kill Kennedy, but he had no direct involvement in it. He also knew John Masen and was aware of his acting as Oswald's double. Tippit worked for Ruby during the gun running operations. This was just another side job where a cop could pick up some extra cash.

Oswald was told to go to the Texas Theatre where Chuck Rodgers would supposedly take him to Redbird Airport and fly him out of the country. Oswald decided to take the bus to the theatre and was probably already in the theatre when Tippit was shot. Oswald thought he had infiltrated the group in New Orleans that was planning the assassination. Then he had spent time with Jack Ruby and had informed both the CIA and the FBI about the whole operation. That was his assignment as an informant.

The mistake Oswald made was calling too much attention to himself by going into the theatre without paying. Our original idea was to shoot Oswald behind the theatre for resisting arrest. Nobody would have cared. They would have applauded the police. Who could blame them for not taking a chance with a man who had just shot the President of the United States and a Dallas policeman. The whole thing would have been over. Oswald wouldn't have had a chance to talk to police or the press. We could have avoided the complication of getting Ruby involved. This chapter in American history would have been closed. No Warren Report. No Ruby trial.

When you read about a particularly vicious crime, it usually involves a suspect with a history of similar offenses. Whether it's murder or rape or aggravated assault, there is ordinarily a background to go along with the crime. The guy has been arrested before or he is on parole. Oswald had no such history. I believe his only arrest was in New Orleans for a shoving match with some anti-Castro Cubans who were upset with his distribution of pro-Castro leaflets for his Fair Play for Cuba Committee. Oswald was the only member of the New Orleans branch. The arresting officer said for the record that he thought the scuffle had been staged.

So that's Oswald's criminal record. A misdemeanor fine for disturbing the peace. If you go through the appendix volumes of the Warren Report and you read the testimony of Oswald's fellow Marines, you will be amazed at the unanimity of their characterizations. Not one of the eighty or ninety guys interviewed described Oswald as violent or troublesome. Not One. When Oswald was arrested in Dallas, his wife said he was innocent and he was a good husband. Weeks later, after she had been grilled repeatedly by the FBI and quarantined with Pricilla Johnson, who was an asset of the Agency, she changed her statements to make Oswald appear to be violent. Then we throw in the General Walker deal. It had been a stressful negotiation where Marina was threatened with deportation with only one of her children. She had no choice but to go along with the official version.

From the time Lee Oswald entered the Marines, he was just the kind of guy we were looking for. Fairly high IQ. Kept to himself. Always followed instructions. Checked out as loyal to this country despite his knowledge of Marx and socialism. He was a natural candidate for our defector program. There were a couple dozen men who defected to communist countries and returned to the United States. Most of them went undercover to infiltrate radical groups as card carrying communists. It never had anything to do with information the Agency expected to receive while these guys were in Russia or Eastern Europe. The important thing was to establish their credibility as communists. If John Kennedy had been killed in Chicago or Miami, there would have been a different fall guy. When Lansdale and Howard Hunt discovered the perfect ambush site of Dealey Plaza, Oswald was the guy.

The gunshot wound into the gut in the basement of police headquarters was the final slap in the face endured by Lee Oswald. He had survived a lousy childhood as his mother moved from man to man and job to job. Like so many other kids, the solution for Oswald was to withdraw. Instead of becoming angry and striking back in criminal ways, Oswald turned to books. When he cut school, he could usually be found in the public library. That's how he made sense of his disappointing circumstances. When his older brother, Robert, joined the Marines, he became a hero in Lee Oswald's estimation. He counted the days until he could become a U.S. Marine.

It was Oswald's bad luck to be an intelligent loner. He was recognized by men with no conscience as a person who could be used. From that point, he was moved around like a chess piece from Japan to Russia to New Orleans and finally to Dallas. For all his trouble, he was shot to death by a Dallas pimp. He was the second victim in Dallas during that weekend in November of '63. He became the fall guy in the removal of a president and his name became synonymous with deranged loner. He broke ground for James Earl Ray, Sirhan Sirhan, Arthur Bremmer, and John Hinkley. All men with no apparent motive whose violent act would solve a problem for the Shadow Elite.

THE PIMP

Two days after John Kennedy was killed in Dealey Plaza, Jack Ruby shot Lee Oswald in the basement of the Dallas Police Department. What if the next morning's papers had reported that one FBI informant had killed another FBI informant? Or a CIA agent had been killed by a man who had run guns to Cuba for the CIA? Or that Jack Ruby had been an errand boy for the Mob since he was a teenager? Or that he had left Chicago in 1947 because of his involvement in the murder of a union organizer? Or that he counted as personal friends about half the Dallas Police Department?

The press didn't investigate most of these details in the aftermath of the bizarre weekend in Dallas. They were more concerned with Oswald's alleged connections with Castro and Cuba. So were the new president and the Warren Commission. That's precisely the way the Agency had set it up. The military needed another reason to invade Cuba. President Johnson worried that an attempt to overthrow Castro would have led to a Russian takeover of West Berlin and the real possibility of nuclear war. There were two objectives in Dallas. Get rid of Kennedy and get back Cuba.

Johnson avoided a confrontation with Russia by agreeing to escalate our involvement in Vietnam.

Ruby was nothing but a pimp and a bagman. He had arrived in Dallas to set up illegal gambling operations for the Chicago syndicate. He later ran narcotics into Texas for Carlos Marcello. When Castro made his push to take over Cuba, Ruby and a guy named Davis got involved in a gun running operation. The mob wanted to gain favor with Castro so they could continue their gambling, prostitution, money laundering and drug trafficking through Havana.

When Castro seized control in 59, he threw out the Yankee capitalists, including Meyer Lansky. It was a dark day for our Sicilian brothers. Santos Trafficante had used Cuba to funnel drugs from Laos to the United States. Rumor was that Pepsi had a plant in that country that did nothing but process heroine. Castro jailed Trafficante. Jack Ruby made several trips to Cuba in an effort to free Trafficante and several other mobsters. It was suspected that Trafficante cut a deal with Castro to inform him of attempts to overthrow him in exchange for distributing illegal contraband for Castro in Florida. That might have been the reason that the CIA and mafia arrangement for a contract on Castro never worked.

After it was clear that Castro was communist, the Mob and the Agency worked together to run guns and military equipment to the anti-Castro rebels in Cuba. That's when Ruby became involved with some of our covert assets like Chuck Rodgers, David Ferrie and Howard Hunt. This unusual alliance of anti-Castro Cubans, the Mafia, and the CIA continued right up until the time of the Watergate break-in when Howard Hunt and a handful of his most dependable Cubans were arrested. At the time, they were on the payroll of the Nixon White House. Nixon had known these men since his years as vice president when he and Dulles had planned some of our adventures in Africa and Latin America. It was no accident that Nixon's car was stoned in Caracas. People in the Third World knew all about the Beast.

Even with these powerful connections, Ruby engaged in one failed business venture after another. At the time he silenced Oswald on orders from Marcello in New Orleans, Ruby's claim to fame in Dallas was the Carousel Club. This was a strip joint a few blocks from the police department where off-duty officers drank free. To ingratiate himself with the authorities, Ruby would provide his strippers for after-hour dating. If a girl refused, Ruby might have to rough her up a little. Above anything else, Jack Ruby was a bully who chose his victims with care. He was known to beat up drunks and once was arrested for pistol-whipping a customer. The word was that Ruby was queer and he hated himself for it. He was much like J. Edgar Hoover in that respect.

Despite all the conjecture about how Ruby got into the basement of the police station where he shot Oswald, the word among the police was that Ruby entered the building on the main floor and saw two local TV cameramen trying to wheel a bulky camera toward the elevator. Ruby ducked his head and helped the men get the camera into the elevator and down to the basement. Ruby had been tipped off by Detective Blackie Harrison when Oswald would be moved. Once he was in the basement, Ruby stood behind the larger

Harrison until Oswald was brought out of the jail. Then Ruby merely stepped around Harrison and shot Oswald point blank while seventy police officers watched with their mouths open.

Sergeant Patrick Dean had been responsible for security of the basement. He pulled Ruby aside upstairs and told him to say that he had come down the Main Street ramp. Ruby did not want to endanger any of his police friends so he ran with that story. During their first meeting that afternoon, Ruby's attorney, Tom Howard, told him that the reason that he shot Oswald was to spare the grieving widow Kennedy the agony of returning to Dallas to testify. Those two falsifications held up through the Warren Commission hearings and Ruby's trial. How many of the Dallas police were involved in the arrangement to silence Oswald, we'll never know. But it was more than a couple.

When Ruby fired Howard and hired Melvin Belli, his murder trial took on a carnival atmosphere. Belli seemed more interested in publicity for a book he intended to write than providing a viable defense for Ruby. In the end, Belli got Ruby the death sentence. Belli told one amusing story after the trial. He had gone to a downtown barbershop for a trim. As the barber fixed the apron on him, Belli heard some of the resident bullshitters complaining about Ruby being a Jew and bringing in his goddamn Jew lawyers. When Belli figured he had heard enough, he jumped to his feet while still in barber towel and yelled "Auktung! Hiel Hitler!" as he stiff armed a Nazi salute. Belli was a large man with a big courtroom voice. As he left the barbershop, he said he had the full attention of those good ol' boys.

Ruby became more psychotic than ever as he wasted away in his isolated cell. There were no windows and his only company was a bible toting officer who was assigned to watch him. In exchange for instruction on religion, Ruby taught the man card tricks. Ruby had long since given up on the fame and fortune that he thought the Oswald murder would bring him. At one point, he got so desperate that he ran the length of his cell and rammed his head into the concrete wall. Like everything else in his life, Ruby's attempt to kill himself was a failure. All he got was a large knot on his head and the amusement of the police force.

Jack Ruby died of an accelerated cancer of the lungs, liver and brain. That's a lot of cancer in a man who prided himself on being healthy. Shortly before his death, Ruby had been attended to by Jolly West, who was one of our Agency specialists. A few days later, he was visited by another of our so called doctors named Bob Stubblefield. A trace of pure plutonium added to an injection will do the trick every time. Remember when James Earl Ray looked like he might get a new trial at the request of the King family? He came down with cancer of the liver and died shortly thereafter.

There seems to be many deaths in several circumstances.

300

GOOD NEIGHBORS

You could hardly ask for nicer friends than Michael and Ruth Paine. They were the kind of people who would volunteer to separate so a young Russian woman and her two children could be comfortable. The fact that her husband had been a defector to the Soviet Union and had offered classified military secrets to the Russians was no big deal to the Paines. They just liked to help out whenever they could. If that meant a little personal inconvenience, hey, what are friends for?

When Lee Oswald and his young Russian wife returned to the United States and set up housekeeping in Fort Worth, the first guy on their doorstep was CIA asset, George DeMohrenschildt. After becoming fast friends with this poverty stricken and intellectually inferior couple that was half his age, DeMohrenschildt introduced them to the Paines. Mrs. Paine had studied Russian at the Berlitz School which was a known recruiting center for intelligence agencies. What better way to brush up on her conversational Russian than to become best friends with this poor Russian girl?

Now Michael Paine was employed by major defense contractor, Bell Helicopter. At the time, one of the corporate heads at Bell was none other than former Nazi General, Walter Dornberger. It only seemed natural that Mr. Paine would strike up a friendship with a young traitor. Not only would he become Lee Oswald's friend, but he would help him get a job at Jaggars-Chiles-Stovall, which happened to do top secret photographic work for the U.S. government. It seemed like a natural fit for the former defector to the Soviet Union. Paine's father and brother were involved with the Agency for International Development which was a CIA front that operated in Third World countries. The entire Paine family was well-connected.

In the spring of 1963, our lonely Marxist decides to try his luck at employment in the Crescent City. While in New Orleans, Oswald happens to spend a lot of time talking to FBI agents in a parking garage. He is sometimes given envelopes by these agents. When Oswald is not busy rubbing shoulders with Hoover's men, he hangs around the office of Guy Bannister with David Ferrie. Bannister is a former FBI agent who is spearheading Operation Mongoose which is an illegal training camp for anti-Castro Cubans on the shores of Lake Ponchatrain. While President Kennedy has ordered these exercises to desist, the CIA overrides the President's wishes and continues to fund the program. David Ferrie is a training instructor at the facility as well as a pilot for the Agency and the Mob. At their request, Oswald opens a Fair Play for Cuba office in which he is the only member. When the young Marxist is arrested handing out pamphlets, he succeeds in further establishing his communist credentials.

During the summer, Marina decides to join her husband in New Orleans. Life isn't easy on an informant's salary, but just as Marina is about to sink into a deep depression, she catches a tremendous break.

Ruth Paine writes a long and personal letter indicating that Marina probably understands her better than her own husband. Then she offers Marina a deal that she would be a fool to refuse. Mrs. Paine practically demands that Marina move in with her in late September. She is very specific about the time. Then Mrs. Paine suggests that Marina can stay for two months or two years. Michael will move out. Ruth will sleep in a room with her children. Unbelievable. Not only does Ruth want Marina to stay there at least through the fall, she offers to jump in her station wagon and come pick her up. Now that's a friend.

Of course, Marina is helpless to turn down such a generous offer. While Ruth is emphasizing two months, Marina is probably thinking two years. So off Marina goes with her great and good friend while her husband is left to deal with the likes of Bannister and Ferrie. Kennedy has announced his trip to Dallas and there's not much work left for Oswald in New Orleans, so he has little choice but to follow his young and impressionable wife back to Dallas. But before Oswald heads for Dallas, he is sent to Mexico City to wait in a hotel room for several days for reasons which must seem unclear to him.

Back in Dallas, there's the ever present problem of finding a job. Once again, Ruth Paine comes to the rescue. It just so happens that her neighbor, Linnie May Randle, thinks Lee might be able to get a job at the Texas School Book Depository. The pay is minimum wage and the work is back-breaking, but it's practically right on the motorcade route. And if Lee can find living quarters near his fine new job, he is welcome to store all his incriminating evidence in Ruth Paine's garage. That will surely simplify things at the time of his arrest.

Well, it all worked out just fine. The motorcade was changed at the last minute so it would go past the book depository. Lee was not on the street to watch the parade because he was waiting in the lunchroom for a call that never came. And while the police were not able to find the doctored-up photographs of Lee posing with his Mannlicher-Carcano in one hand and his communist newspapers in the other with his pistol stuffed in his belt, another search of the garage on the second day produces the photos. Oswald was not supposed to have survived his arrest at the Texas Theatre to be able to protest the authenticity of these pictures. In any event, the commie photos clinched the deal.

THE COP

I can't tell you who pulled the trigger on J.D. Tippet, but I think he was sacrificed to incriminate Lee Oswald. Trying to figure out who killed him is like trying to pick up a live fish. You think you have it, but it slips away. The idea was to strengthen the image of Oswald as a psycho. A crazed killer. After all, if a man had just shot the President, why would he hesitate to shoot an arresting officer? On the other hand, if a man would shoot a police officer, wouldn't he be capable of shooting the President? The idea was to eliminate any doubt of Oswald's guilt in the public's mind.

Oswald was probably already in the Texas Theatre when Tippet was shot. He had nothing to do with it. I believe that whoever shot Tippet was known to him. If Tippet had pulled over to question a suspect in the murder of the President, he would have gotten out of the patrol car with his gun drawn. Instead, he let the assailant lean in the passenger window and carry on a conversation. When Tippet got out of the car, he walked around front with his firearm still holstered. He was taken by surprise when the man opened fire and killed him with four shots. Tippet hadn't taken any precautions that would be expected if it were an arrest situation. It's clear that Tippet was taken by surprise.

305

J.D. Tippet was no choir boy. He was your typical red-neck, right-wing, Dallas cop. He was a member of the Minutemen and a friend of Jack Ruby's. He was a regular at the Carousel Club and he had been involved with Ruby in some gun running activities. A witness by the name of Thayer Waldo told Mark Lane that Ruby, Tippit and a right-winger named Bernard Weissman had met at the Carousel Club for two hours one week before the assassination. Whether Ruby set up Tippet or someone from the Agency planned it, I don't know. It wasn't an accident. The killer was in the Oak Park area to carry out an assignment.

Here is my best guess as to what happened. Roscoe White and J.D. Tippit were close friends. Tippit's wife had been a bridesmaid at Roscoe White's wedding. Geneva White had worked at the Carousel Club and had heard Jack Ruby and White talking about assassinating the President. Supposedly, Ruby wanted to get rid of her, but White talked him out of it. Anyway, Tippit and White were friends and if White and Ruby were plotting to kill President Kennedy, Tippit was probably aware of it. He might have known too much and was considered unreliable by the conspirators. Plus his death would further incriminate Oswald.

Earlene Roberts, Oswald's landlady on North Beckley, said she saw a police car with two officers inside pull up in front of the house while Oswald was in his room. It was 1:00 o'clock. They honked twice and then drove off. Maybe White told Tippit that they were supposed to meet Oswald near Tenth and Patton and take him either to the Texas Theatre or Redbird Airport. They Agency used that small airport for trips in and out of Dallas. It wasn't far from the safehouse over on

306

Harlandale where our Cubans were holed up. While Tippit and White are patrolling that part of Oak Cliff, White changes out of his uniform. Part of a second Dallas police uniform was found in the back seat of Tippit's car after he was shot. Meanwhile, Oswald is taking the bus to the theatre where he is supposed to meet his contact.

While driving up Patton Street, they see a guy up ahead that looks like Oswald. It might have been John Masen who had been impersonating Oswald all over Dallas in the weeks leading up to the assassination or it might have been Bill Seymour who was involved with Alpha 66. It might have been someone else known to White and Tippit. So Tippit pulls over and gets out to talk to the man. As he gets around to the front of the car, the man pulls a gun and shoots Tippit. Roscoe White may also have fired because two types of shell casings were found at the scene. Three from a revolver and one from a pistol. Several witnesses said they saw two men leave the scene of the crime in different directions. Later, at police headquarters a disagreement was overheard where an officer had said, "You didn't have to kill a cop." This is all hearsay and conjecture but it might explain why two cops pulled up in front of Oswald's rooming house and why two types of shells were found at the scene of Tippit's murder.

As was the case with the evidence at Dealey Plaza, the evidence in Oak Park did not point to Oswald. The gun taken from Oswald at the Texas Theatre was a revolver with a defective firing pin. It couldn't shoot anybody. The slugs removed from the body of Officer Tippitt were three copper-coated and one lead. The shell casings sent to the FBI lab in Washington were two made by Western and two made by Remington. The first officer to arrive at the scene of the Tippitt murder called in an eyeball witness who described the assailant firing a .32 black finish automatic pistol. None of this indicates a single shooter with a defective revolver.

SEEING DOUBLE

Although he is seldom mentioned, John Masen was right in the middle of the plot to assassinate President Kennedy. He was a Dallas gun-shop owner who was a dead ringer for Lee Oswald. He ran guns with Jack Ruby and traveled in and out of Mexico. Masen had associations with oilman H.L. Hunt's two sons and was a member of the Minutemen as were many members of the Dallas Police Department and the Dallas Sheriff's Office. He was involved in supplying arms to anti-Castro groups including Alpha 66 whose members included the likes of Frank Sturgess. Masen was also an acquaintance of Major General Edwin Walker whom the plotters staged an attack on that would later be blamed on Oswald.

When Oswald was set up to take the fall, Masen became the impersonator. With his right-wing convictions, Masen was more than willing to help in the removal of John Kennedy. In the month leading up to the assassination, Masen was busy all over Dallas establishing the cover story of Oswald as the bloodthirsty Marxist. At a rifle range, a car lot, a gun-shop and Red Bird Airport, Masen provided the background for the frame-up.

Treasury Agent Frank Ellsworth followed Masen around Dallas and into Mexico while he investigated Masen's gun-running activities. Ellsworth finally got an arms violation conviction against John Masen, but the Oswald lookalike was never implicated for his efforts in the plot to kill John Kennedy.

Possibly a more sinister impersonation of Lee Oswald occurred in 1961 when Kerry Thornley used Oswald's name to ask for a bid on some trucks at Bolton Ford in New Orleans. The FBI sent out a memo at the time suggesting that someone may be trying to impersonate Oswald. At the time Oswald was in Russia. Thornley was directed in this activity by Guy Bannister who was spending most of his time infiltrating leftist groups and training Cuban troops to overthrow Fidel Castro. The question is, was Oswald being established as a patsy in the effort to get rid of President Kennedy as early as 1961? Kennedy had been in office for only a few months when the Bolton Ford incident occurred. Had Dulles and the Shadow Government already decided that the young president was a threat to their agenda? Dulles and Kennedy were clearly on a collision course from day one of the new administration. Actions in the Congo were most revealing. While Kennedy was trying to shield Patrice Lamumba and assist his government, Dulles had given instructions to have him killed.

Kerry Thornley had actually finished a manuscript on Lee Oswald before he was accused of killing President Kennedy. Thornley and Oswald had met in 1959 at El Toro Marine Base in California. The two men later served together at Atsugi Air Base in Japan. The CIA was conducting mind control experiments at

Atsugi as part of the MK-Ultra program at the time. There is suspicion that both men might have been involved in these experiments. Although the two Marines were casual acquaintances, their interaction seems to have been limited to off-hand conversations. Why had Thornley written a novel about Oswald? During the Warren Commission hearings, Thornley was the only Marine to make damaging remarks about his fellow soldier, but he admitted that Oswald had never shown any tendency toward violence. While the media called Oswald paranoid, schizoid, and homosexual, Thornley said he had never seen any of these traits.

Thornley and Oswald lived in New Orleans in the summer of 63. They had post office boxes near each other and were seen together by a number of witnesses. Like Oswald, Thornley was well acquainted with Guy Bannister and David Ferrie. Thornley was told that summer that John Kennedy and Martin Luther King would be assassinated. Thornley identified the source of this information as Howard Hunt. After telling this story, Thornley was attacked and beaten by men in ski masks while he attended a friend's birthday party. The intruders stole Thornley's identification. Was it the same type of intelligence identification that Oswald carried? Years later a letter from Thornley surfaced that expressed his hatred for Kennedy and a desire to piss on his grave.

William Seymour was another individual who may have impersonated Oswald. The Warren Commission figured him as the guy who was introduced to Silvia Odio as Leon Oswald. Seymour was a mercenary who had taken part in the training of Anti-Castro Cubans in Miami and New Orleans.

The last of the Oswald lookalikes was Charles Rogers who was responsible for the scenes in Mexico City at the Russian and Cuban embassies. He was an agency pilot who could have gotten in and out of Mexico without difficulty. The tipoff was the woman in the Cuban consulate who described Oswald as about five-feet-six with a thin face and sharp features. She said the man spoke with a stutter. That would be Rogers.

What makes this casting call to impersonate Oswald more than just window dressing is the planning that went into it. Who would be capable of such an elaborate scheme? The Mob? Not a chance. The oilmen? Not likely. The CIA? Bingo. Their Plans Division was filled with men employed to develop cover stories for situations like Guatemala and Chile and Dallas. The smoking gun in the murder of John Kennedy was the extensive plot to incriminate Lee Oswald.

THE SHOOTER

Roscoe White never graduated from any police academy, but he was in uniform near the Texas School Book Depository when John Kennedy was shot. White and Police Sergeant Patrick Dean were behind the picket fence during the shooting. White probably used a long barreled pistol with high velocity frangible bullets. His first shot hit the President in the throat and probably traveled down into his chest cavity. With that type of ammunition, Kennedy's insides were probably torn up pretty bad. The slug is designed to break up at the point of impact. That's why the head shot caused such extensive damage.

White had joined the Dallas police force two months before the assassination. Other members of the police department said that they weren't quite sure of White's job description because he never had to make out reports. White's son later said that he had seen coded messages that his father had received during the two months before the assassination. White left the police force after the murder of John Kennedy but stayed in Dallas for about a year. He was probably responsible for some of the cleanup work. If White hadn't been so useful, I'm sure he would have been terminated shortly after his role in Dealey Plaza. Our Cubans who took part in the shooting were flown to a camp in Guatemala where they were killed. The Agency couldn't have too many people wandering around with firsthand knowledge of the murder of a president.

As White lay dying from the burns he received in an explosion in 1971, he confessed his involvement in the Kennedy assassination to a minister named Jack Shaw. White also said that he had committed many contract murders for the government. It's been my experience that dying men usually tell the truth. There is not much percentage in lying at that point, especially when you are incriminating yourself.

Roscoe White's wife, Geneva, had worked as a stripper at Jack Ruby's Carousel Club. Years later she admitted that she had heard her husband and Ruby discussing the plot to kill President Kennedy. She had found a diary where White laid out the plan in detail. Her husband's intelligence code name was Mandarin. He claims to have fired two shots from behind the picket fence, one hitting Kennedy in the throat and one hitting the President in the head. In the diary, he also confessed to the murder of J.D. Tippit. The diary was turned over to the FBI and never seen again. Geneva White and her son were hounded constantly after their public statements concerning Roscoe White's diary. They finally said that the whole thing was a hoax just to get the FBI off their backs.

Mrs. White also found in her husband's possessions a photo similar to the two backyard photos published in LIFE MAGAZINE. It was a third pose in the same series. This photo had never been seen before. The incriminating pictures of Oswald were not found the afternoon of the assassination when authorities searched

314

Ruth Paines garage. By some miracle, police found the photographs when they returned the next day. It seems unlikely that they had not looked very carefully the first day. Time was needed to make the composite photos. Mrs. White pointed out that in the photos Oswald showed a lump on his wrist. Roscoe White had a lump on his wrist. Oswald did not. It was clear to Geneva White that Oswald's face had been superimposed on her husband's body.

Roscoe White and Lee Oswald had been recruited in the Marines for intelligence training about the same time. Oswald became an informer. White became an assassin. He was brought down to Dallas two months before Kennedy's visit and he left a year later. It was another example of Dulles' tentacles that reached into areas that were supposed to be out of bounds for the CIA. Five years later in Los Angeles, two Agency assets who were employed as LA police detectives handled Operation Senator. That was the inquiry into the death of Robert Kennedy.

A PIECE OF BONE

Thirty feet to the left and rear of where President Kennedy suffered the fatal head wound, a piece of his skull was found by Billy Harper. The chief pathologist at Methodist Hospital indentified the fragment as a piece of the occipital bone. That is the bone at the back of the skull and would verify what all the doctors at Parkland Hospital had said. There was a fist sized hole in the back of the President's head. The official autopsy photos show a neat little hole near the cowlick.

Deputy Seymour Weitzman found other pieces of bone in the same area. The pieces of skull must have exited John Kennedy's head with considerable force to have traveled thirty feet in the air. If you draw a line from where the skull fragments were found to the point of the fatal head shot, it would point directly to the corner of picket fence.

BABUSHKA

Beverly Oliver was a nineteen year old singer at the Colony Club which was next door to Jack Ruby's Carousel Club. She said that two weeks before President Kennedy was shot, Ruby introduced her to a man that Ruby called, Lee Oswald of the CIA. She also said that David Ferrie was in the Carousel Club so often that she thought he was the manager. She later recognized Oswald on TV after his arrest at the Texas Theatre.

On November 22, Oliver filmed the motorcade near the sidewalk on the south side of Elm Street. Because of the large scarf she wore, she became known as the Babushka Lady. She was one of the closest witnesses to the President at the time of the fatal head shot. She ran across the street and up the embankment toward the railroad yard. When she reached the area between the book depository and the picket fence, she encountered Roscoe White and Patrick Dean in their police uniforms. Oliver knew White because his wife was a stripper. What were White and Dean doing in that area right after the shooting? Officially, there were no officers assigned to that area.

Three days later, Beverly Oliver was taken aside at the Colony Club by FBI Agent, Regis Kennedy. He demanded that Oliver turn over her film. It had not been developed, but Oliver said it would have shown the book depository and the picket fence at the time of the ambush. When one of Oliver's fellow strippers disappeared, she decided it was time to leave Dallas.

Oliver married a Texas hood with mob connections named George McGann. During the 1968 election, Oliver says that McGann met for two hours with Richard Nixon in a Miami hotel room. McGann was murdered a year and a half later in West Texas. Oliver kept her mouth shut and stayed out of sight until the mid-70s when she told her story to a researcher named Gary Shaw.

BLOODBATH

Motorcycle officer Bobby Hargis is the key to understanding the Kennedy Assassination. He was riding to the left, rear of the presidential limousine. When John Kennedy was hit with the fatal head shot, his head snapped back toward Hargis. Blood and brain tissue left the President's head with such force that when it struck Hargis, he thought at first that he had been shot. He was covered in a sheet of blood. A piece of the President's skull was stuck to his lip.

Hargis knew the direction of that final shot. He parked his motorcycle and ran up the grassy knoll toward the picket fence. There was no way that shot could have come from the book depository.

B.J. Martin was the motorcycle officer directly behind Bobby Hargis. He was partially shielded by Hargis, but he was also covered with blood, flesh and brain matter.

THE TEACHER

Jean Hill was a Dallas school teacher. On November 22, she and a friend decided to go watch the presidential motorcade and flirt with a few Dallas cops. They sweet-talked one officer into letting them stand on the south side of Elm Street so they could take some pictures of the President. Miss Hill had just waved and shouted to the President when the shots commenced. Her friend dropped to the ground, but Hill stood and watched as someone fired from behind the picket fence. She could clearly see the muzzle and the smoke.

Miss Hill tried to get her friend to go across the street to the railroad yard, but her friend wouldn't move. As Hill began to cross the street, she felt a hand digging into her shoulder. When she looked back, a man in a suit flashed a Secret Service badge. Then he reached into her pocket and took her camera. He said, you're coming with me and led her across Dealey Plaza to the fourth floor of The County Records Building.

They entered the room which had a birds-eye view of Elm Street. There were other agents in the room and it appeared from the ashtrays that they had been there for some time. These suits began to grill Miss Hill about what she had seen. When she told them that she had heard four to six shots, they told her she had heard three.

Hill explained to these agents that her father was a forest ranger and he had taught her about guns at an early age. She repeated that there were at least four shots. The agents grew more angry and warned her to keep her mouth shut.

Who were these men who interrogated Jean Hill? There were no Secret Service Agents in Dealey Plaza that day. What were they doing in a room overlooking the ambush site? Minutes after the assassination, how did they know that the police would find only three empty cartridges on the sixth floor of the book depository? Why would they demand that Miss Hill go along with their version of what had happened? There was no official version at that time. What connections did these men who were posing as Secret Service Agents have in order to secure an office in a government building overlooking Dealey Plaza?

BYSTANDER

If James Tague had not been standing near the center of the triple underpass, the Warren Commission would have had a much easier time explaining the five wounds in President Kennedy and Governor Connelly. A bullet hit the curb in front of Tague and cut him on the chin. Nowhere in the Warren Report does it explain that a shot fired from the Oswald window would have been at least twenty feet over the President's head in order to have injured Tague. If you draw a line from where Tague was standing to the President, it points to a side window of the DalTex Building.

The necessity to explain how only two shots could have caused all the wounds to Kennedy and Connelly, resulted in the magic bullet theory. A shot hits Kennedy in the back, six inches below his collar and turns upward and comes out his throat. It then turns downward and hits Connelly in the shoulder. It comes out Connelly's chest and turns and shatters his right wrist and finally becomes embedded in his left thigh. The bullet is later found on a stretcher at Parkland Hospital looking like it had never been fired.

UPSET STOMACH

Jack Lawrence was a right-wing fanatic who moved to Dallas in the fall of 1963. A number of witnesses placed him in Jack Ruby's Carousel Club in the days before the Kennedy assassination. Lawrence had gotten a job at Downtown Lincoln-Mercury, where a man posing as Lee Oswald had gone on a reckless test drive. Against the wishes of his fellow employees, Lawrence insisted on calling the FBI.

The night before the motorcade, Lawrence had borrowed a car from his employer. He did not show up for work the next morning. Half an hour after the assassination, Lawrence ran into the dealership and began vomiting. He was in a sweat and his feet were muddy. The car he had borrowed was found parked next to the stockade fence by the grassy knoll. Lawrence was arrested later that afternoon for his suspicious behavior, but was released the next day.

THE AVENGER

Jim Garrison might have made a fine Shakespearean actor. He was a big guy with a booming voice. His size and demeanor were made for the courtroom. The Jolly Giant. His claim to fame in New Orleans was taking on a bunch of corrupt judges. It took some nerve to expose these judges. Anyone else would have adapted to the status quo. Not Big Jim. He was an ex-military pilot and he'd spent a couple years with the FBI. He was a tried and true patriot, but he found work with the FBI so boring that he ended up running for District Attorney in Orleans Parrish. He was pretty well liked around New Orleans, but he had an ornery streak. No one knew much about him until he decided to get involved in the Kennedy assassination.

Garrison heard that Oswald had been in New Orleans in the summer of 63, so he sent out his assistants to find any connections that might be pertinent to the murder investigation. He turned over his findings to the FBI and considered the matter closed. He went about his life as District Attorney until a conversation with Russell Long made him begin to question the findings of the Warren Commission. Big Jim ordered all 26 volumes of the Warren Report. He read them and reread them. He probably knew that report better than the guys who wrote it. Garrison found so many discrepancies and omissions that he decided to conduct his own investigation, at least as far as the connections in New Orleans were concerned.

As soon as the Agency got word that Garrison was looking into connections of Oswald to Guy Bannister, David Ferrie and Clay Shaw, they unleashed the hounds. All of their in-house journalist whores began to saturate the news with stories about Garrison's egomania and corruption. They even hinted at homosexuality. Discredit, entrap and destroy. Instead of assassinating the man, you can assassinate his character. It's a much more civilized approach. The target may not feel that way while his life is being picked apart by the so-called news media. To this day most Americans think of Garrison as some sort of publicity seeking goofball. Nothing could be further from the truth. It took great courage to stand up to the CIA and the FBI.

The CIA couldn't get Garrison to back down so a contract was put out. A street punk from Philadelphia by the name of Whalen was offered the job in a New Orleans bar by Shaw and Ferrie. Ten thousand up front. Another fifteen thousand when the assignment was completed. Whalen went to Garrison with the information. That's when Big Jim got mean. He actually subpoenaed Allan Dulles and Charles Cabell. They politely declined. The government was not about to let those holy cows be dragged into what they referred to as "that circus" in New Orleans. Garrison wanted to prove that Clay Shaw worked for the Agency, which he did, but the CIA wasn't going to admit it. Shaw was our cut-out in New Orleans. If there was any sign that he was going to crack, he would have been eliminated. That way it couldn't have tracked back any higher than Shaw. He supplied the money to Bannister who kept our Cubans in training for another assault on Castro. This same group was then turned against Kennedy.

If Dulles had denied under oath that Shaw worked for the CIA, Garrison would have charged him with perjury. At some point the cover-up would have been in jeopardy. Dulles, Lansdale and Cabell could not be allowed to testify. So all of Garrison's extradition requests were denied. There was no legal basis to deny them. They were simply ignored. President Johnson was not about to support Garrison's investigation. His Warren Commission was being picked apart. There were many discussions at the highest levels of government during the Clay Shaw Trial. Richard Helms at Langley was also very concerned with how Shaw was doing. Helms repeatedly quizzed his assistants whether Shaw was being given enough help.

Garrison was very close to unraveling the whole plot. It looked like David Ferrie was about to go states evidence. The FBI had bugged all of Garrison's offices and had several moles working on his investigation staff so they knew exactly what was going on. Ferrie not only knew Shaw, but he had been used as a pilot for Carlos Marcello and he was aware of Marcello's involvement with the plot. Ferrie was a major player in the conspiracy and he was willing to talk to Garrison so the Agency had three of their Cubans take care of business. Ferrie was given an anal suppository laced with proloid. It was almost impossible to detect in an autopsy. In much the same way, Marilyn Monroe and Dorothy Kilgallen were given barbiturate suppositories.

By refusing Garrison's requests for extraditions and eliminating some of his key witnesses, he had no chance to win the case against Clay Shaw. Aladio del Valle was murdered about the same time as Ferrie. He had been a CIA paymaster for the anti-Castro Cubans in Miami, and he had a key role in Dallas. Guys who worked for the Agency at that level knew that every day above ground was a good day. A former CIA agent named Robert Morrow has admitted that a rogue element of the Agency out of New Orleans was responsible for John Kennedy's murder. He's careful to add that no one in the upper levels of the CIA had any involvement or foreknowledge. It's the limited hang-out position. If the Agency didn't approve of Morrow's theories, his books wouldn't be out there.

Without Garrison's investigation and the Clay Shaw trial, we would know a lot less about the plot to murder John Kennedy. He uncovered Oswald's connection with Shaw, Bannister and Ferrie. Once it was clear that Oswald was being set up to take the fall, the conspiracy became undeniable. Along with the phony trip to Mexico, the only reason for sheepdipping Oswald as pro-Castro was to establish him with a motive for killing the President. Shaw was the cut-out. An investigation could never go higher than the paymaster in New Orleans, but when DCI Richard Helms offered the Agency's unlimited assistance during his trial, the message was clear. The Agency was worried. There was a bad smell coming out of New Orleans and it led back to Langley.

Garrison also gave us our first look at the Zabgruder film. Time-Life had purchased the only clear film taken of the assassination in Dealey Plaza. It had been locked away in a vault allegedly to spare the American public from this vivid reminder of how our government had changed in Dallas on that sunny afternoon. The real reason that the film had not been shown to the public was that it showed John Kennedy being slammed violently backward from the impact of the fatal shot. Until Jim Garrison showed the Zapgruder film in the courtroom in New Orleans, all we had to go on was Dan Rather's breathless account that the President had been thrown forward from the final shot.

In addition to providing us with background information of the key conspirators in New Orleans, Garrison interviewed many witnesses whose statements differed from the official version. He also looked into the discrepancies in the Tippit murder. His conclusion was that not only had Oswald not acted alone but he had not been involved in either murder that day. This made the New Orleans District Attorney very unpopular in some circles of government. It was high stakes poker and Big Jim had the stronger hand.

Jim Garrison died recently. He was still calling for an honest investigation into the murder of John Kennedy. He was also looking into the involvement of the powerful individuals surrounding President Kennedy who benefitted from Cold War policy. Allen Dulles, Douglas Dillon, McGeorge Bundy, Dean Rusk, John McCloy and Walt Rostow all had strong corporate and banking connections. Their long view would have been better served with the continuation of a warfare state. Since its inception, the CIA had been at the beck and call of these powerful business interests. John Kennedy was making wholesale changes in the way America did business around the world. He intended to end the Cold War. This would have seriously threatened the profits of defense contractors and overseas corporations. In short, Kennedy's vision was at odds with the men who surrounded him. The CIA was the tool used by these businessmen to remove foreign leaders who refused to cooperate with American business interests. In Dallas, another troublesome leader was removed.

Jim Garrison gave the CIA more trouble than any other individual in keeping the lid on the events in Dallas. He was pilloried by Agency assets in the media. His investigation cost him his reputation and his marriage, but he wouldn't back off. At one point, Garrison was offered a federal judgeship if he would end the investigation, but he was determined to get to the truth. His efforts left him isolated and discredited. When the dust finally settles on the assassination of John Kennedy, there will be a few individuals like Garrison who will emerge with honor. To this point, the Shadow Government has won, but with so many researchers picking at the carcass of the Warren Report, that could change.

Shaws primary function with the Kennedy EA was as paymaster in New Orleans. He would collect money from Carlos Marcello and pass it on to a Guy Bannister who would use it to train anti-Castro Cubans up at Lake Ponchatran. Shaw also handled Oswald while he was in New Orleans during the summer of '63. He was the money guy. Without him, nothing moved forward. During that critical period of time leading up to Dallas, Shaw received his instructions from Lansdale. Dulles and Lansdale were officially retired so nothing could track back to the Agency.

In 1967, when District Attorney Jim Garrison began to investigate the connection between Shaw, Bannister, Oswald and Ferrie, everyone thought it was a publicity stunt. Newspapers from all over the world converged on New Orleans. European countries had always suspected a right-wing coup. They knew that Kennedy was at odds with factions of his own government. The problem was that Oswald and Bannister were dead which left only Shaw and Ferrie. Shortly after the story broke, Ferrie was eliminated. That left Shaw. Garrison was afraid that if he waited, Shaw might be terminated as well.

The entire force of the federal government was brought down on Garrison. The FBI had his offices bugged. Witnesses refused to answer subpoenas. Extraditions were denied by governors like Ronald Reagan in California. Our lackeys in the press carried out a character assassination against Garrison. A contract on his life was put out through Permindex in Canada. He was fortunate to have lived, but to this day, he's thought of as a deranged publicity hound. The truth is that Garrison was very close to solving the case.

THE SPOOK

If there was anyone who could have written the biography of the Beast, it was E. Howard Hunt. He did write the biography of the creator of the Beast, Allen Dulles, along with some spy novels. If a major event happened in the Western Hemisphere, Hunt was right in the middle of it. Guatemala in 54, the Bay of Pigs in 61, Dallas in 63 and Watergate in 72. He knew so much about these and other events that when he decided to blackmail the White House after Watergate, Nixon told his people to give Hunt whatever he wanted. The eighteen minutes of tape that Nixon erased contained a discussion of Hunt's involvement in Dallas. Nixon knew that the information could not be made public at any cost. The cost became his presidency.

Hunt began his colorful career as a war correspondent for LIFE MAGAZINE in 1943 and joined the Office of Strategic Services the same year. This was the forerunner of the CIA and Hunt found himself in Shanghai, China. After the WWII, Hunt wrote a novel in Mexico and tried his hand at writing screenplays in Hollywood. In 1948, Hunt was summoned by the new CIA and became a press aide for Averell Harriman who was ambassador to Mexico.

From that day foreword, Hunt's duties would involve black operations and cover stories.

In his role as confidant to Allen Dulles, General Charles Cabel and Richard Nixon, Hunt became an untouchable. He knew the whole story and all the players. In the late fifties, Hunt ran an operation at the direction of Vice President Nixon against Greek shipping tycoon, Aristotle Onassis. In 1954, Hunt was a key player in the overthrow of President Arbenez in Guatemala. It was the first of many governments that the Agency would topple in the Western Hemisphere and President Eisenhower was happy with the result. United Fruit had gotten its country back. Eisenhower's Secretary of State, John Foster Dulles, was a major shareholder in United Fruit.

The rumor was that Hunt had rewritten the diary of Lee Oswald to make sure of the proper incriminations. There is also a good chance that Hunt wrote Arthur Bremer's diary. Bremer supposedly traveled the country with no visible means of support while he stayed in fine hotels. His alleged target was Richard Nixon until he turned his irrational anger toward Governor George Wallace. Bremer had worked with Agency hypnotist William Bryan as had Sirhan Sirhan. When Arthur Bremer shot George Wallace, he handed the election to Richard Nixon. At the time, the election was a three-way split between Nixon, Wallace and McGovern. The election would have ended up in the House of Representatives which were controlled by the Democrats.

After Wallace was shot, Nixon's director of dirty tricks, Charles Colson, ordered Howard Hunt to burglarize Bremer's apartment and plant McGovern campaign literature. Hunt refused. If there was one thing the master spook had learned in thirty years of dishonesty and deception, it was timing. Why was it so important to the Nixon White House that Arthur Bremer would appear to be anti-Nixon and pro-McGovern? Ben Bradlee, the publisher of the Washington Post asked his top assistants at the time of the attempted assassination of George Wallace, "Could this be the ultimate dirty trick?"

The scope of Howard Hunt's duties for the Agency was in no way limited to writing second-rate spy novels and fake diaries. After John Kennedy's death, Hunt forged cables that would implicate Kennedy in ordering the murder of South Vietnamese President Ngo Dinh Diem. Actually, Kennedy had been assured that the Diem brothers would be flown to France. I was told that Kennedy's face turned white when he was told that they had been killed. This was a few weeks before his own death and Kennedy repeated that the CIA would have to be dealt with. The Agency could expect to be neutered in Kennedy's second term.

When Daniel Ellsberg published the Pentagon Papers, he became public enemy number one to the Nixon Administration. To Henry Kissinger's embarrassment, Ellsberg had once been his student. They were out to destroy this anti-war creep and to get incriminating evidence. They sent our boy Hunt to burglarize the office of Daniel Ellsberg's psychiatrist. Hunt liked nothing better than working in disguise but he returned without the files. In kind of a seedy way, this was the Agency's Renaissance Man. Undistinguished writer, black op officer and master of disguise. He was the CIA poster boy for the fifties and sixties.

In what was probably Howard Hunt's most humiliating episode, he lost a lawsuit to former Agency asset Victor Marchetti and Spotlight magazine. Marchetti's article placed Hunt in Dallas on November 22, 1963. Hunt claimed to be in Washington, D.C. with his children at the time of the assassination of President Kennedy. Marchetti's lawyer, Mark Lane, brought in Marita Lorenz who had been involved with Frank Sturgis and Alpha 66 which was a high-powered anti-Castro Cuban group. Lorenz said she saw Hunt deliver a package of money to Sturgis in a Dallas motel room the night before the assassination. Lorenz left the next morning, but Sturgis later boasted that she should have stayed around for the Agency's greatest success ever. Her testimony probably wouldn't have offset testimony by Hunt's children that would have provided him with an alibi, but none of them would testify. Lane had proven that Hunt was in Dallas. The jury was stunned. Hunt was ordered to pay twenty-five thousand in court costs.

Other than the fact that E. Howard Hunt helped bring down two presidents, the most shocking story about him concerns the death of his wife, Dorothy. She was an innocent bystander who got pulled into the Watergate scandal when she was asked to deliver hush money from the Nixon White House to the families of the Watergate burglars. The concern from the White House was that she was in possession of boxes of her husband's sensitive files that could have incriminated Nixon in everything from the deaths of foreign leaders to the shooting of Governor Wallace. There was also

336

information on the Executive Action in Dallas which Nixon was determined to keep under wraps. In addition to concern over Hunt's hidden files was a nervousness about Attorney General John Mitchell's wife Martha's willingness to go public about corruption within the Nixon Administration. With Congress at the door, Nixon was skulking around the Oval Office like a cornered rat.

In December, 1972, Dorothy Hunt boarded a United Airlines flight for Chicago with over a hundred thousand dollars in bribe money that she was to deliver. She was also carrying some of her husband's most sensitive documents. She was fed up with her role as bag-woman and her husband was angry that the White House would not guarantee him clemency if he was convicted for the Watergate burglary. Traveling with Mrs. Hunt was CBS reporter Michelle Clark who had confided to associates that the Hunts might be ready to go public. Howard Hunt had issued a warning that before he rotted in prison, he would bring down every tree in the forest.

As United flight 553 descended for landing, it was passed off by air traffic controllers at O'Hare Airport to Midway Airport which was about ten miles away. While Midway approved 553 for landing, they communicated to O'Hare that they were sending the plane around for a second pass. Midway Airport did not have glidescope or precision radar and relied on a localizer at the end of the runway to direct the landing path. As 553 descended, the localizer malfunctioned. The outer marker was also off and the plane came out of the clouds wide of the runway. A flight attendant screamed, "Get down in a crouch!" Then 553 stalled and fell over a mile to earth.

All this could be written off as bad fortune except for what happened immediately afterwards. Citizens in the working class neighborhood that surrounded Midway airport had noticed unmarked government cars with men in suits parked in the neighborhood before the crash. Others were arriving at the time the plane went down. Although the telephone lines went down in the area, these men arrived at the scene of the crash before firemen could get there. Within minutes, approximately two hundred FBI and DIA men had sealed off the area and not allowed National Transportation Board investigators access to the area. The FBI listened to the tower tapes and then confiscated them. For the first time, the FBI had taken over the investigation of a commercial airlines crash site. Why? The local FBI office was forty miles away. Local officials got there within minutes and were turned away by the FBI. They turned away a medical team even though screaming had been heard from the plane after the crash.

Were these men who they claimed to be or were they like the phony Secret Service agents in Dealey Plaza? As they separated the victims from their belongings, an aide to Congressman George Collins, who had died in the crash, got through FBI lines by using military I.D. As he watched the grisly scene he recognized one of the men who was systematically going through the belongings of the passengers as an employee of the CIA. In Washington, Charles Colson, who had masterminded many a ruthless and dirty trick, had apparently had enough. He told a reporter from TIME

MAGAZINE, "I think they killed Dorothy Hunt." Colson turned to religion after that night.

In an odd postscript to this story, Howard Hunt and Gordon Liddy had worked together on Operation Gemstone. Among the charts they had developed were designed manipulations of flight communications and electronic signals. This might have been the finest hour of the Beast. No wonder Howard Hunt's children would not come forward to assist him in his trial thirteen years later.

SIGNIFICANT OTHER

Marita Lorenz wrote a firsthand account of her wild years with Fidel Castro and Frank Sturgess. Between affairs with those two colorful types, Marita was married to a former Venezuelan dictator. Her father owned a German luxury liner, the MS Berlin, and her mother worked for the National Security Agency. She met Castro shortly after his takeover in Cuba when he boarded her father's ship in Havana Harbor. Although Marita was only nineteen which was half the bearded revolutionary's age, the two could hardly keep their hands off one another. Castro asked her to be his personal secretary, but Daddy said no. Whether capitalist or communist, the rise to power is apparently a strong aphrodisiac. The phenomenon even made Henry Kissinger some kind of sex symbol, although admittedly, that's quite a reach.

A month later Fidel sent for Marita and they set up light housekeeping in Havana. The ruler of Cuba was giddy with his new power, but his two main priorities were education and medical care for the poor. Fidel envisioned some kind of democratic socialism while his brother Raul was pushing hard for communism. When Fidel traveled to Washington to enlist support for his new government, he got a chilly reception from Vice

President Nixon. Castro had not yet identified himself as a communist so what were Nixon's motives? Nixon had always received assistance at election time from mafia types. These mobsters liked the business climate in Cuba under the corrupt Baptista. They had access to prostitution, drug running and money laundering. Castro was bad for business.

Before leaving Washington, Castro visited the Lincoln Memorial. The new Cuban dictator might have been giving himself too much credit, but he felt a kinship with Lincoln. Castro felt that he had also freed an oppressed people.

When Raul Castro began to shut down the casinos and arrest American gangsters, Marita convinced Castro to allow many of them to return to the United States. It was at this time that she met Frank Fiorini who would later be known as Frank Sturgess. Fiorini warned Marita that the Castros were making a big mistake by shutting down the gambling houses and arresting these mobsters. Like the Kennedys, the Castros were on a collision course with the Mafia and the CIA. Fidel's instincts were to compromise while getting rid of bribery and prostitution. Raul's agenda was much less tolerant of capitalists.

In Washington, Nixon and Dulles were already working on a plan to sabotage Cuba with crop destruction and embargos. This convinced Castro to seek help from Russia. This was a situation that occurred throughout the Third World during the Cold War era. If a government was not receptive to American corporations, the CIA would work their magic behind the scenes to undermine that government in any way possible. The leader would turn to the

Soviet Union for support. The United States would then be justified to take overt action against a communist regime.

As President, John Kennedy came to understand this formula and tried to control it by reining in the CIA. His efforts were met with the same treachery and disinformation that the leaders of these small countries had experienced. In the end, JKF suffered the same fate as Patrice Lamumba and Salvador Allende.

During her stay with Fidel Castro, Marita had become pregnant. As she neared the time to give birth, she was drugged in her hotel room and given an abortion. She was flown out of Havana to join her mother in New York. Although she was weak from a serious loss of blood, she was debriefed by the FBI and the CIA. She was then shown pictures of a dead and mutilated infant on a bedspread that matched the one in her room at the Havana Hilton. While she recovered in the hospital, Marita received word from Castro that he had nothing to do with the abortion and that he wanted her to return to Cuba.

Having carried out the abortion ploy, the CIA took control of Marita's hospital recovery. She was given special vitamins that caused disorientation and sleep deprivation while she was told repeatedly that Castro was responsible for her condition. She became the ideal pawn in a plan to assassinate the Cuban leader.

To galvanize public opinion against Castro, the Agency had one of its paid hacks publish a story in a sleazy tabloid called CONFIDENTIAL. The hatchet job was a complete fabrication with Marita's mother as the alleged author. The cover read, "An American Mother's Terrifying Story---Fidel Castro Raped My

Teenage Daughter!" To lend an air of respectability, the article listed Marita's mother as an employee of the U.S. Government and a cousin of Henry Cabot Lodge's.

The lurid tale had Castro raping the helpless girl against her will with such brutality that she suffered an injured disc in her back. Unwilling to even remove his combat boots, Castro repeatedly had his way with the victim. Months later he drugged her so the child could be aborted. The procedure was carried out so primitively that Marita was left sterile. At least the readers of this fine publication would surely hate Castro. It was a solid beginning for the disinformation campaign.

When the Agency thought Marita was properly prepared, they sent her back to Cuba to poison Fidel Castro. The concoction would paralyze Castro's vocal cords while he drifted into eternal sleep. She would be protected in Havana by intelligence operatives who were already on the ground. The plan was presented to Marita as foolproof. There would also be a six million dollar bonus compliments of appreciative mobsters. Frank Nelson was the bagman who worked out of his Manhattan apartment to coordinate the efforts of the Mob and the CIA. It was at Nelson's apartment that Marita was reintroduced to Frank Sturgess. She described him as a "predator that lived only for money and the thrill of violence." His handler and paymaster in Miami was none other than our old friend, Howard Hunt.

After an elaborate course in mental discipline and killing techniques, Marita was off to Havana with three poison pills. While agonizing over the decision to follow orders or return to her former lover, Marita made a curious mistake. She decided to hide the pills in a jar of cold-cream. When she arrived at her suite in the Havana Hilton, she discovered that the pills had dissolved so she flushed them down the toilet. When Castro arrived he asked Marita if she had been sent to kill him. When she said yes, he laid down on the bed and handed her his .45 revolver. He said that he was badly in need of sleep. Marita pulled off his boots and noticed that he was still wearing mismatched socks, but at least this pair had no holes in them. Thousands of dollars and months of preparation had given way to an old attraction. Castro patted the bed next to him. A few minutes later they were naked together. When Marita checked out of the hotel, she left all her cash for Castro to use for schools or hospitals.

When Marita returned to the United States she was told that she would have to work off her failure with gun running and boat stealing activities. The beautiful part of this operation was that the perpetrators never had to fear prosecution. After all, this was government work. The expensive speed boats were altered the night they were stolen. Personal items were sold to a fence. Fun and games, without concern for the law. Robbing armories was a more serious matter as a guard would sometimes be killed. Such an event would never make the papers. It was a messy business. The merry band of Operation 40 was prepared with everything from bazookas to hand-grenades.

As a busman's holiday, the group would prepare leaflet drops over Cuba. The exercise was useless but it helped justify the expenses for pilots and planes. A more serious form of sabotage was crop burning. Sugarcane was Cuba's main cash crop and nothing burned like a dry cane field. A favorite practice was tying a rag soaked with kerosene to a cat's tail. When the rag was set on fire, the burning cat would race through the cane field lighting everything in its path on fire. A good cat could take out a few thousand acres of cane. This simple and effective method was used against Cuba for years. Castro's protests to the United Nations fell on deaf ears and the cats were always in good supply.

At one point during a training exercise, Marita was stabbed in the neck by an unknown assailant. There was considerable resentment within the anti-Castro community for her failure to kill the Cuban dictator. She was taken to the home of Orlando Bosch who was a Cuban pediatrician turned psychopath. He later did a stretch in prison for bombing a Cuban airliner. To beat a path away from this bloodthirsty bunch, Marita hooked up with a man called Mr. Diaz or General Diaz.

Marita learned that Diaz was deposed Venezuelan President Marcos Jimenez. He had fled that country with seven hundred million dollars. Jimenez had been a textbook American puppet during his reign. He took kickbacks with all U.S. companies who were stealing Venezuela's resources. He set up a secret police to protect him and get rid of his opposition while he took marching orders from the CIA. The Venezuelan people lived in brutal poverty but this is a small price to pay. America could heartily endorse this type of democracy. In fact, Jimenez was presented the Legion of Merit award by President Eisenhower. Only a communist would attempt to clean up graft and poverty.

As a means of putting her guerilla period behind her, Marita agreed to become the mistress of Jimenez. She was set up in a fashionable condo with a yacht and a new T-bird at her disposal. She adapted to a new life of luxury as her bodyguards protected her from her former associates. Marita and Jimenez had a daughter before the former dictator was taken back to Venezuela to face his accusers. When her life of comfort came to this abrupt end, she turned again to Frank Sturgess.

Marita settled into the anti-Castro community in Miami when the Bay of Pigs invasion took place. Everyone in Miami blamed President Kennedy for the fiasco. There developed a hatred for Kennedy as great as the hatred for Castro. The Cuban exiles seem determined to see both men dead. The CIA did not break its back to discourage these anti-Kennedy sentiments. The Agency and the companies they represented would be better off with both of these trouble makers out of the way. When Kennedy made a speech in Miami to try and raise the spirits of the Cuban exiles, one of Marita's colleagues commented, "That fucker's going to die."

In November of 1963, Marita was at the home of Orlando Bosch when Frank Sturgess arrived with a map of Dallas, Texas. The men spread the map on the kitchen table and began to discuss plans for a trip to Dallas. Marita assumed it was another gun running adventure and left the house. When the two cars were ready to depart for Texas, she was surprised to see a skinny young man they called "Ozzie." She had seen him during training exercises in the Everglades, but she had never taken part in an operation with him. The man might have been Bill Seymour who was a mercenary and was suspected by the Warren Commission of impersonating Lee Oswald.

Sturgess was the man in charge of the group. He answered only to Howard Hunt and David Phillips. Sturgess was outfitted with disguises from hobo to Catholic priest. The trunks of the cars were filled with every kind of weaponry. When they reached the outskirts of Dallas, Sturgess announced, "This is the big one."

They registered for two rooms at the Cabana Motel which was mob owned and operated. Sturgess warned the group to avoid any outside contact during the weekend. The arsenal was then offloaded into the motel to be checked and loaded. Shortly after midnight, Howard Hunt showed up with an envelope of cash. He and Sturgess conferred in private for about an hour. After Hunt left, a stocky man in a business suit and black fedora arrived. When the man saw Marita in the room he objected to a woman being involved. Sturgess vouched for her but the man was unhappy with the arrangement. After the events of the weekend had played out, Marita realized that the man was Jack Ruby. She was disgusted with the situation and told Sturgess that she was going to fly back to Miami. She had not been told what they were doing in Dallas but her instincts told her that it was time to get out. The next afternoon she heard the news that President Kennedy had been killed.

In 1981, Marita Lorenz returned to Havana for one last meeting with Fidel Castro. He had always maintained that the baby that was taken from her twenty-two years earlier was still alive. The uncertainty had haunted her for two decades. When she met Castro in the hotel room, she was surprised to find that there was still a mutual attraction. She begged him to let her meet her son. He finally agreed. Andre said he was happy to finally meet his mother. Marita was relieved to discover that he was healthy and well mannered. He had graduated from medical school and become a doctor. She could never be sure if this was really her son or if Fidel Castro had invented him to put her mind at rest.

REAR GUARD

John Swinton, editor of the New York Tribune addressed a group of fellow newsmen at a Banquet in 1883. He was a transplanted Scot with a reputation for honesty. He had been decertified as a Civil War correspondent when he wrote a series of uncomplimentary dispatches concerning the ineptitude of General Ambrose Burnside. The topic of the evening was, An Independent Press. Here's what Swinton had to say, "There is no such thing in America as an independent press, unless it is in the country towns. You know it and I know it. There is not one of you who dare to write his honest opinions, and if you did you know beforehand that it would never appear in print.

"I am paid one hundred and fifty dollars a week for keeping my honest opinions out of the paper. I am connected with others of you who are paid similar salaries for similar things and any of you who would be so foolish as to write his honest opinions would be out on the street looking for a new job. The business of the New York journalist is to destroy the truth, to lie outright, to vilify, to fawn at the feet of Mammon, and to sell his race and his country for his daily bread. You know this and I know it, and what folly this is to be toasting an 'independent press.'

"We are the tools and vassals of rich men behind the scenes. We are the jumping-jacks; they pull the strings and we dance. Our talents, our possibilities and our lives are all the property of other men. We are intellectual prostitutes."

It seems that as early as 1883, the Shadow Elite had a firm grip on the press. What is troubling about this speech one hundred years later is the press is even less independent today. The small town newspapers are owned by chains such as Gannett or Scripps-Howard or Newhouse. There is little independent reporting left. Network television news is controlled by corporate conglomerates. The renegade publications like Mother Jones find their way into very few homes. Instead we get a watered-down, Reader's Digest type of account of world affairs. There have always been journalists who were willing to do the bidding of their wealthy masters and nowhere is this more apparent than in the continuing cover-up of the murders of John and Robert Kennedy and Martin Luther King, Jr.

At the head of the class would have to be Dan Rather. He arrived at Dealey Plaza shortly after President Kennedy was shot and later was sent by CBS to bid on the Zabgruder film. Having seen the best evidence of the murder, Rather went on network television and told the American public that the President's head snapped violently forward during the fatal head shot. Nothing could be further from the truth. In fact, John Kennedy was clearly thrown backward from the fatal shot. What was Rather's agenda? Had he been told that the official version would be that Kennedy was shot from Behind? Was he confident the Zapgruder film would never see the light of day? At the time, CBS was owned by Westinghouse which was a large defense contractor and a power producer in many Third World countries. Maybe the word had been passed down to CBS.

CBS conducted its own investigation of the assassination and was preparing a program which outlined evidence that pointed to a conspiracy. At the last minute, Walter Cronkite was given a text to read by CBS to the American people that contradicted its own investigation. Why? What pressures had been brought to bear on the management of CBS? Walter Cronkite was said to have had a puzzled expression as he read the new version that conformed to the Warren Report. Ever since that last minute reversal, CBS has led the rear guard in reassuring us that there is no new evidence to contradict the official versions of any of these crimes. There's Dan Rather in his trench coat, with the Washington Monument in the background, telling us that it all happened just like the FBI and the Warren Commission said it did. Then another CBS 'white paper' concluding, yep, James Earl Ray was guilty and without confederates. Or we are told that even though Robert Kennedy was shot from two inches behind his right ear and Sirhan was being wrestled to the ground six feet away, Sirhan had acted alone. The American people don't know all the details, but they know they are being lied to.

Next in line would be G. Robert Blakey who appeared on the scene when he replaced Richard Sprague as director of the House Select Committee on Assassinations. Sprague was calling for an all-out investigation into the deaths of John Kennedy and Martin Luther King, but when he showed a willingness to take on the CIA, he was replaced by Blakey. According to investigator Gaeton Fonzi, whenever a promising lead was developed that pointed toward the Agency, Blakey would point the investigator in another direction. It became clear that Blakey had made some sort of compromise with the CIA to steer the inquiry away from Agency involvement.

Blakey adopted the fall-back position that there was a conspiracy in the murder of John Kennedy, but it involved the Mafia. This was the Agency's second layer of the "onion skin." The first layer was Castro and Cuba. Second was the mob. The third layer was Lyndon Johnson and the Texas oilmen. The fourth layer as seen in the books written by Robert Morrow was a rogue element of the CIA acting independently of Langley. Blakey aided the cause in one respect. His report admitted that there was a second gunman that fired from behind the picket fence. This should have retired the Oswald acted alone conclusion of the Warren Commission.

Then along comes Gerald Posner. This guy has taken the investigation back to the dark ages by his shameless support of every detail of the Warren Report. He has fooled enough people with his dishonest manipulation of evidence that he has become an official spokesman for assassination research. You can't flip through the cable channels anymore without seeing Posner with his silly haircut and pencil-thin mustache telling the audience with a straight face that everything happened exactly as the Warren Report said it did. Even members of the Warren Commission admitted afterward that they knew parts of the report were untrue.

Posner became so giddy with his new position as number one prostitute for the Shadow Government that he whipped out a volume on the death of Martin Luther King, Jr. You guessed it. James Earl Ray acted alone and incriminated himself exactly like Oswald had by leaving evidence where it was sure to be found. Enough contradictory evidence had surfaced that King's wife and children befriended Ray and were calling for a new trial. No matter to Posner. His specialty was picking out only those bits and pieces of evidence that supported the official version. While critics of the government version often have to publish and distribute their own findings, Posner was guaranteed mass media support of his shiny hard-bound volumes. In the area of assassination research, selling one's soul has always been profitable.

In the thirty-five years since Dallas, members of the media have lined up like the girls at Mustang Ranch to be chosen for whatever disinformation their masters require. William F Buckley, James Phelan, Hugh Aynesworth, Walter Sheridan and other high profile journalists have misled the public for financial gain. Certainly the comfortable and profitable route for media types has always been to do as they are told. On the other hand, researchers who have refused to compromise have become the targets of FBI or IRS harassment. Jim Garrison found out the lengths the Shadow Government will go to keep its control intact. Billy Hunter, a writer for the Long Beach Independent Press Telegram, suffered the ultimate reprisal. He was accidently shot to death in a police station.

In recent years we have a situation where a U.S. Navy ship shoots down an Iranian passenger jet with 290 people aboard. The early reports blamed Iran as we were told that the plane was outside the commercial flight corridor at an altitude of 7,000 feet on an intercept path with the battleship Vincennes. Several days later when American public opinion has been galvanized to blame Iran for the incident, we learn that the Vincennes had placed itself under the commercial flight corridor and the plane was at 12,000 feet. Was the plane shot down in retribution against Iran? Americans had already learned to hate that country and the Ayatollah.

Psych warfare is not limited to foreign countries. The invasion of Panama was called, "Operation Just Cause." "Surgical strike" sounds clean and efficient. "A target rich environment" sounds positive unless civilians are killed. They become "collateral damage". We have "peacekeeper missiles" and "patriot missiles". Rebels attempting to overthrow an elected government in Latin America are called "freedom fighters". As the country is economically crippled, we're told that the people are disillusioned with their government. When a new fascist dictator is installed, we hear that democracy has returned. It has always been about which leader is willing to accept bribes and do business with the United States. They are the good guys. If a government wants to use its resources to improve the living conditions of its poor, the CIA will do everything in its power to prevent that from happening. Americans are left wondering why we are disliked in so many parts of the world.

354

We finish with a few quotes. Katharine Graham, owner of the supposedly liberal Washington Post, made a speech at CIA headquarters in Langley, Virginia, in 1988, "We live in a dirty and dangerous world. There are some things the general public does not need to know and shouldn't. I believe democracy flourishes when the government can take legitimate steps to keep its secrets and the press can decide whether to print what it knows."

Dennis McDougal, a former LA Times staff writer said of his editor, "He is the dictionary definition of someone who wants to protect the status quo. He weighs whether or not an investigative piece will have repercussions among the ruling elite, and if it will, the chances of seeing it in print in the LA Times decrease accordingly."

THE GRIM REAPER

TOWERMAN

Railroad towerman Lee Bowers had the best view of what happened behind the picket fence in Dallas. He was on the second floor of a building that was about fifty yards behind the fence. He told the Warren Commission that he had seen several cars casing the parking lot during the morning of the assassination. He said that one of the men was talking on a hand-held radio. For reasons already mentioned, the investigators did not want to hear any testimony that pointed to a conspiracy.

Bowers said that just before the shooting, he had seen several men behind the picket fence. At the time of the shots, he had seen a flash of light. Unfortunately for him, Bowers continued to tell his story. He received death threats. In 1966, he was killed when his car ran off the road. The coroner said that at the time of his death, Bowers was in a state of shock which he could not explain.

AN HONEST COP

One of the decent guys in the Dallas snake-pit was Deputy Sheriff Roger Craig. Craig testified that he had seen Oswald leave the book depository and get into a car driven by a latin man. Actually it was our boy, John Masen, who had been impersonating Oswald for a month. Lansdale's last touch was to have Oswald seen in the company of Cubans. We were trying to blame the murder on Castro to give this country another reason to invade Cuba. Johnson put an end to this when he set up the Warren Commission to stop the investigation with Oswald. Our military wanted to take back Cuba, but LBJ feared that a conflict with Russia might result. That's how he talked Earl Warren into limiting the investigation to Oswald. It was a compromise so we wouldn't turn the dogs loose on Cuba.

The Warren Report made Johnson look like part of the conspiracy, but he was really saying "no" to our military. Hoover and Dulles were anxious to help with the cover-up because Oswald had worked for them. Also, Hoover had done nothing about repeated warnings about an attempt on Kennedy's life in Dallas. Remember, Kennedy was about to force Hoover to retire which would have ended his power in

Washington and exposed him to embarrassment by his enemies. There were many.

Craig and two other deputies found a German Mauser on the sixth floor of the book depository. It was the first rifle found. It had been used by our shooter at the west end of the sixth floor. Later, the Manlicur-Carcano was found under some boxes. The deputies were told to forget about the Mauser, but Craig continued to tell his story. In 1962, Craig had been Man of the Year in the Dallas Sheriff's Office. He was honest to a fault, I guess you could say.

A guy by the name of Edgar Bradley was identified by Roger Craig as one of our Secret Service imposters outside the book depository during the assassination. He was a preacher from Southern California who had worked for the OSS during WWII and later became an asset of the CIA's. Bradley had no alibi for his whereabouts on November 22. The good preacher had been seen in a meeting with David Ferrie in the summer of 63 and Jim Garrison wanted to talk to him. California Governor Ronald Reagan refused to extradite Bradley, who later joined the sheriff's office in Los Angeles. Roger Craig said that he had received a number of death threats from Bradley.

It wasn't long before Craig was fired. He had been told to keep his mouth shut. In 1967, he agreed to testify in Garrison's trial of Clay Shaw in New Orleans. When he got back to Texas, the fun started. First, a bullet nicked his head as he was walking to a parking lot. He then injured his back when another car forced him off the road. When he began to appear on some talk shows, his car was bombed. Then he was nearly killed in Waxahachie by a shotgun blast. Finally, he died of what they said was a self-inflicted shotgun wound. Roger Craig insisted on telling the truth and it cost him his life.

In an odd footnote, Roger Craig's close friend, Deputy Hiram Ingram, also met with a strange death. In the spring of 1968, Ingram fell and broke his hip. Three days later he died of cancer. He was fifty-three years old. This quick form of cancer is sometimes referred to as "the CIA flu".

TOP SECRET

When the first news broke on the Kennedy Assassination, there was a story about a Secret Service Agent who had been killed. CBS, NBC and ABC all carried accounts of an agent who had been killed in the ambush. An agent at Parkland Hospital told a reporter that he had seen the news come over his teletype that another agent had been killed. The Secret Service refused to confirm the report and the story just went away. One reporter said that even in death they are secret. Years later there were still officials who were trying to figure out what had happened.

The account I heard was that a man named Chuck Robertson, who was an agent with the Dallas-Fort Worth Secret Service office had gotten wind of a plot to kill the President. He had watched the suspicious activity of several men with rifles in a Rambler station wagon shortly before the motorcade started. This is the same description that Deputy Roger Craig and another witness provided. Somewhere on Harwood Street, before the motorcade turned onto Main, Robertson jumped into the street in front of the limousine and yelled, Stop, I must tell you! Witnesses say that he was knocked to the ground and taken away. He hasn't been seen since.

361

Robertson's widow continued to receive his paychecks, but the Secret Service acted as if they knew nothing about the episode. Robinson had vanished with no explanation. Twenty years later, an agent by the name of Fox admitted that he had been ordered to get a detail together to retrieve the body of an agent in Dallas. He wasn't given the name, but it was likely the body of Robertson. The Secret Service refused to confirm the story.

There were other strange occurrences with the Secret Service in Dallas that day. Normally the press bus is right behind the Secret Service car, but they were moved five cars back just before the motorcade started. There were no motorcycle officers in front of the limousine and the officers in back were instructed to hang back further than usual. Motorcycles in front of the car would have made shots from the front much more difficult. Remember that Douglas Dillon was the Secretary of the Treasury which meant he was in charge of the Secret Service. Dillon was a close friend of Allen Dulles and a major investor in mining in the Congo. His circle of friends were the same Wall Street bankers that Allen Dulles traveled with.

ROSE CHERAMIE

Two days before John Kennedy was killed in Dallas, a heroin addict by the name of Rose Cheramie was admitted to Louisiana State Hospital in Jackson. While she was hitchhiking, she had been hit by a car near Eunice, Louisiana. When she reached the hospital she was going through heroine withdrawal and was talking out of her head. She was given a sedative and she began to make more sense. The story she told hospital officials was unbelievable.

She had left Florida with two Cubans who were on their way to Dallas to murder President Kennedy. Cheramie was part of a drug smuggling operation which involved moving heroine across the Mexican border. She had gotten into an argument with the Cubans at a bar called the Silver Slipper. They had abandoned Cherimie to hitchhike in the night.

Nurses who were later interviewed said that Cheramie not only predicted when the President would be killed, but also told them where it would happen. She had learned this information on her way from Florida with the Cubans. Later, she told these same nurses that she worked as a stripper for Jack Ruby and had seen Oswald in the Carousel Club on several occasions. When Ruby killed Oswald two days later, hospital officials contacted the FBI. Of course, the FBI suppressed the information. Hoover was determined not to let anything interfere with the official version.

A Lt. Fruge of the Louisiana State Troopers had first transported Rose Cheramie to the state hospital in Jackson. The day after Ruby shot Oswald, Fruge returned to Jackson for an in depth interview. He then checked out all aspects of her story and found them to be accurate. There was a room reservation in her name at the Rice Hotel in Houston. The man holding her child had mob connections. Her connection in Galveston had just gotten off a ship there. Fruge chartered a small plane and flew to Texas with Cheramie. When they reached Texas, Captain Fritz told Fruge that they didn't want testimony from Cheramie. The FBI had taken over the investigation. When asked to tell her story to the FBI, Cheramie declined because she felt that she had already said too much. Little did she know that the person running the cover-up was none other than J. Edgar Hoover.

Rose Cheramie's story was put on hold until 1965, when DA Jim Garrison began to look into the matter. He contacted Fruge and asked him to try and locate Cheramie. Fruge learned that Cheramie had been killed on a highway near Big Sandy, Texas. It appeared that the body had been run over several times. The death certificate said dead on arrival, but the time of her death was listed as 11:00 AM. She was found nine hours earlier. There was also mention of a gunshot wound close up. Had someone shot Cheramie and then run over her head several times to make it look like an accident? It turned out that Cheramie had been questioned by FBI agents a month earlier.

When Lt. Fruge learned of the circumstances of Rose Cheramie's death, he decided to question the manager of the Silver Slipper Bar. Fruge brought along a stack of photographs of known Cuban mercenaries. The manager quickly identified the two companions of Cheramie as Sergio Arcacha Smith and Emilio Santana. He said the two men had stopped at the bar a number of times and he was under the impression that they were running prostitutes. He said the bar was some sort of meeting place with other Cubans.

When Garrison looked into Aracha Smith's background, he found that he had attended law school and represented Ford and other American corporations in Latin America. He was also involved with Guy Bannister and Clay Shaw in Operation Mongoose, which was the plan to overthrow Castro that Kennedy had forbidden. Smith was the top Cuban in the New Orleans sector and he was handled by Howard Hunt. At the training camp at Lake Ponchatrain he worked closely with David Ferrie. Earlier, when Castro seized power in Cuba, Smith and his family were flown to this country in a Navy jet. Smith was known to have in his possession a clearance letter from the CIA which exempted him from prosecution in any illegal gun running activities. His office in New Orleans was in the same building as Guy Bannister's. Smith was also involved with Clay Shaw in money raising activities. This was the man who Rose Cheramie said was on his way to Dallas to kill President Kennedy.

THE BARON

With the possible exception of David Ferrie, the most unusual character in the whole fabric of the Kennedy assassination was George DeMohrenschildt. Born to Russian nobility, DeMohrenschildt wound up as a lieutenant in the Polish cavalry until that country was annexed by Germany in '39. During WWII, he was involved with French Intelligence and might have had ties to the Nazis through a cousin named Maydell. He spent the next few years in Mexico as a movie producer until that country expelled him as a suspected spy. He also had a run-in with the FBI when he crossed state lines with an underage Mexican girl. He was accused of committing unnatural acts with a minor, but Demohrenschildt said everything was very natural. The Baron was a free thinker. He moved to Texas where he received a degree in geology from the University of Texas.

While working the oil fields in Colorado, DeMohrenschildt becomes a US citizen and gets married for the third time. At this point he becomes involved with the Agency as his geological work takes him from Cuba to Venezuela and finally to Yugoslavia on behalf of the American government. When he returns to the United States, he's debriefed by an agent in the Domestic Contact Service named, Walton Moore who becomes his handler. The two men meet on a regular basis until Oswald returns from Russia in '62. Moore sends DeMohrenschildt to befriend the Oswalds and the Baron takes control of the young defector until Oswald moves to New Orleans in the summer of '63.

DeMohrenschildt's associations during this period read like a who's who in Texas. He's a member of the Dallas Petroleum Club and the World Affairs Council. His friends include billionaire H.L. Hunt, Clint Merchison, Syd Richardson and failing oilman, George Bush. His work for the Agency with his cover as a geologist takes him to every backwater of the globe. This is why the CIA has always worked closely with those in the oil business. It was a perfect front for any operation.

DeMohrenschild's strange associations included courting Jacqueline Kennedy's mother when Jackie was a girl. He was Uncle George to Jackie at that time. As a Russian nobleman, Mrs. Bouvier was interested. As a man without a fortune, she was not. DeMohrenschildt was also a friend of Ruth Paine's father and he once had a mistress in common with Allen Dulles. The Russian had found his way into some very important circles. He had the goods on the oilmen and the Agency. When the House Assassinations Committee called for his testimony, he became a significant liability.

When the Oswalds arrive in Fort Worth, DeMohrenschildt pays them a visit and convinces them to move to Dallas. He introduces the communist defector and his Russian bride to the radical anti-communist White Russian community. This would have been impossible if DeMohrenschildt's Russian friends did not know that Oswald was an asset of the Agency and he had been on a government assignment in the Soviet Union. Anyway, they all become great and good friends and Marina Oswald is introduced to Ruth Paine who also works for the Agency. At this point, Ruth Paine becomes Marina's handler. When Marina moves to New Orleans to be reunited with Lee in the summer of '63, Mrs. Paine writes Marina a very personal letter and practically demands that the Russian wife move in with her in late September. She is very specific about the time. She tells Marina that she can stay for two months or two years. The main thing is to have Marina in her home during the Kennedy visit so the garage can be used to plant all the incriminating evidence against Oswald.

Oswald and DeMohrenschildt actually become friends. DeMohrenschildt admires Oswald's honesty and his passion for the underdog. When they discuss politics, Oswald always offers a complimentary opinion of President Kennedy. He says Kennedy is more honest than most politicians and has a chance of becoming a great president. Oswald even says that Kennedy's facial expressions are more open and honest than other politicians. Later, during the Warren Commission hearings, DeMohrenschildt is pressured by Albert Jenner to say negative things about Oswald. The Baron later said that not only did Jenner lead him through his testimony, but his statements were altered. Whatever the case, Demohrenschildt felt badly that his recorded testimony helped to vilify Oswald in the minds of the American people.

In the mid-seventies, De Mohrenshieldt was working on a manuscript about Oswald and the Kennedy assassination that supposedly exposed individuals in the FBI and CIA. It also set the record straight on the kind of person he thought Lee Oswald was. He said Oswald was the kind of person who was always searching for the truth. He deeply wanted to see improved relations between the Soviet Union and the United States. In that respect, he was clearly a supporter of John Kennedy. Oswald also admired the President's courage to enforce civil rights laws in the South. DeMohrenschildt said that he had not defended Lee vigorously enough during the Warren Commission hearings. He said that had the situation been reversed, Lee would have defended him totally. The Baron felt that he had acted as a coward by not strongly defending his dead friend.

About the time word of DeMorenschildt's manuscript began to circulate, he was sedated and committed to a mental hospital where he was turned over to an Agency doctor named Charles Mendoza. DeMorenschildt underwent intensive therapy under Mendoza. His wife said that he was never quite the same afterwards. He would rant and rave for hours about WWII and the Jews. On the day that DeMohrenschildt agreed to testify before the House Select Committee on Assassinations, he was found dead of a shotgun wound in the mouth. His death was ruled a suicide. His family disagreed. They said he was looking forward to setting the record straight about his hillbilly friend.

DOROTHY KILGALLEN

The death of Dorothy Kilgallen was part of the damage control that followed the death of John Kennedy. There were a lot of innocent bystanders who lost their lives because they were in the wrong place at the wrong time. You might remember Kilgallen from that TV show, What's My Line. She was a freelance journalist and I think she also had a morning radio show in New York. She was smart and articulate. During the Sam Sheppard trial she had made a name for herself as a crime reporter. Despite the guilty verdict against Sheppard, Kilgallen continued to doubt that he had a real motive to kill his wife. When the verdict was reversed years later, Kilgallen's theories were vindicated.

After John Kennedy was murdered in Dallas, Kilgallen began to have her doubts about Oswald's motives and his ability to carry out the crime. She went to Texas and interviewed witnesses and became more convinced that this was much bigger than Oswald. She became friends with Mark Lane after he published, RUSH TO JUDGEMENT. They were trading information back and forth when she got what she thought was a major break. Jack Ruby agreed to allow her the only in depth interview he had given since he had been in prison. She went to Dallas and they spent several hours in conversation. Ruby kept warning her that the room was probably bugged.

When Dorothy Kilgallen left the interview, she told reporters that she was going to break the case wide open. Ruby had told her too much about the plot. A person with Kilgallen's visibility could stir up a lot of public interest. The dominos could start to fall. Ruby's statements could not be allowed to become public. Kilgallen went to New Orleans for additional interviews which indicated that she was on the right track. In her newspaper column, she wrote about government scientists conducting mind control experiments. All of these activities were carefully watched by the Agency. It was at this time that she met a mystery man from Ohio. They became romantically involved, although Kilgallen would tell her friends nothing about the man.

A short time after Dorothy Kilgallen arrived back in New York, she was found dead in her home. The investigators said it looked like the scene had been staged. The official cause of death was ingestion of alcohol and ten times the barbiturates that it would take to kill a person. There was an unusually high concentration of nicotine in her system, but she didn't smoke. She may have been given a barbiturate suppository like Marilyn Monroe and possibly David Ferrie. Once a person is subdued, say a sedative had been put in her drink, an anal suppository is the least detectable way to administer a fatal dose of whatever you want to appear on the death certificate. Two days later, Mrs. Earl Smith, who was Kilgallen's best friend and assistant, was also found dead. No cause of her death was given.

Kilgallen's family knew that she hadn't committed suicide. She had been very upbeat about the book she was writing about Jack Ruby and the Kennedy Assassination. Her husband quickly destroyed all of her notes on the Ruby interview. He was a reasonable man who wanted to stay alive. When asked by friends about what had been in his wife's assassination files, he said that the secret would go with him to the grave. Maybe that wasn't good enough. Several years later, it seems that he committed suicide.

As seen in many parts of the Third World, it's often easier to seize power than to maintain power. In other countries it involved setting up a secret police like we did in Iran and all over Latin America. In this country, it involved covert operatives who would eliminate someone on orders from their handler or paymaster. Often it was Cubans who were used. Not that they were particularly bloodthirsty, but they were completely under our control. They had nowhere to turn. We could move them anywhere in the world or eliminate them if we pleased.

The deaths of Kilgallen and Smith were not isolated incidents. I would estimate that about sixty people lost their lives after Dallas because they had first hand information that the Agency thought was dangerous. We didn't like the idea of killing Americans. It was much easier to rationalize murder in small foreign countries. Once the Executive Action in Dallas was carried out, we had to keep the lid on the story at all costs. We had contract agents on our payroll who would take care of these matters for surprisingly small amounts of money.

MARILYN MONROE

Marilyn Monroe was innocent until the day she died. You never heard of her doing anything mean or vindictive. Her mother was in and out of institutions and Marylyn ended up in the Vine Street Orphanage. After that, it was eight or ten foster homes. She never knew her father. It's not easy to overcome all that disappointment, but she was more of a fighter than most people think. When she got tired of the sex symbol routine, she went to New York to become a serious actress. Imagine those condescending Broadway types when this blond arrives to study acting. After her marriage to Arthur Miller failed, she was having health problems. She bought a fairly modest home in Ventura and became sort of a recluse. It was at this point that she met John Kennedy and she was temporarily revitalized. She was excited to spend time with such an important person. Unfortunately, Kennedy's intentions were less altruistic.

Marilyn was drinking heavily toward the end. I think she was taking a lot of sleeping pills and pain killers. The mob had their hooks into her at this point. She would drink too much and allow one of her body guards to sleep with her. It was pretty sad. She had become self-destructive. Her fixation with the

President was becoming a problem. She would repeatedly call the White House in a delirious state and beg to speak to the President. The situation was getting unmanageable, so Jack sent Bobby to Los Angeles to try and end the relationship. Of course, the Agency was aware of everything that was going on. There wasn't an important office in Washington that wasn't bugged or wiretapped by our people as well as Hoover's.

Sam Giancana was looking for a way to bring down the Kennedys and the Agency was anxious to help. Joe Kennedy had promised Giancana that he wouldn't have to worry about heat from the Justice Department if his son was elected President. Giancana and Mayor Daley had helped Kennedy carry Illinois in 1960. Joe Kennedy had also worked with Giancana by investing large amounts of his money in the Teamsters' pension fund. Mr. Kennedy realized a good return on his money that went out as high interest loans.

Giancana, Trafficante, Marcello and the rest of the bosses were not too happy when John Kennedy appointed his brother Bobby as Attorney General. John was an independent thinker who had the ability to get along with just about anybody. He was always more interested in hearing about the other guy. He had this drive to understand everything and everybody. Bobby, on the other hand, could be a mean little sonuvabitch. He was the fighter in the family. He had a personal vendetta against the Mob going back to the days of the Kefauver hearings. Bobby especially disliked Jimmy Hoffa and the feeling was mutual. Bobby wasn't happy just to prosecute these guys. He wanted to humiliate them. His arrogance and toughness made him hated not only by the mobsters, but by J. Edgar Hoover and Lyndon Johnson. Even though John Kennedy depended greatly on Bobby's loyalty, I often wonder if he would have had a much smoother administration without him.

Anyway, they all knew that Bobby was going out to L.A. to meet with Marilyn. Giancana comes up with the idea that when Bobby gets there, he finds Marilyn dead. It could be made to look like he was involved. The scandal might damage the political futures of both Kennedys. Marilyn's two bodyguards were mafia goons. They waited until she was drunk and then administered the suppository. The Agency supplied the prescription. Bobby got word of the situation before he got to Marilyn's home. He flew immediately back to Washington. The Agency and the mob didn't get the scandal they wanted and another innocent bystander had lost her life.

THE PEDOPHILE

The most unusual guy involved in the plot to murder John Kennedy was David Ferrie. Like Chuck Rodgers and George DeMohrenschildt, he was very intelligent. He had been trained in the priesthood, but he was rooted out because of his homosexual behavior. He had been a pilot for Eastern Airlines, but he lost his job because of an incident with a teenage boy. At that point, he became a pilot for the Agency and also for Carlos Marcello in New Orleans. He flew Marcello back from Guatemala after Bobby Kennedy had basically kidnapped him and dropped him off in the mountains of Honduras. It was not unusual in those days for an asset of ours to have mafia connections, but Ferrie was a very valuable guy. He was a bush pilot who could get in and out of the most remote areas in Latin America.

In the late fifties, Ferrie had been a platoon leader in the Civil Air Patrol in New Orleans. He helped train teenage boys which suited this predatory homosexual just fine. Lee Oswald was a member of Ferrie's Civil Air unit at this time. There is a possibility that he introduced Oswald to his brand of gratification during their summer camp-outs. I've often wondered if the reason that Oswald had guarded his intelligence background so closely after he was arrested in Dallas, was that the Agency might have had compromising sexual material that they would had used to humiliate him and his family. We had material like that on J. Edgar Hoover and it bought us a lot of latitude with the FBI.

Ferrie was a go-between with Carlos Marcello and Jack Ruby. Marcello controlled that part of Texas and Ruby had to have clearance from New Orleans for any new operation in Dallas. Ferrie spent so much time in Ruby's Carousel Club that some people thought he was the manager. Lee Oswald also spent time in the club while he was in Dallas. Ruby was connected to the Agency through our gun-running operation with Cuba, as was George Bush. That's why Hoover called Bush in Houston after John Kennedy was killed. He wanted a local Agency version of what had happened. He knew he wouldn't get any answers from Langley.

In 1967, Jim Garrison had heard from a number of witnesses that Ferrie had been seen in the company of Lee Oswald and Clay Shaw. Ferrie spent much of his time in New Orleans in the offices of Guy Bannister. Shaw and Bannister were running what we called Operation Mongoose which was at a training facility up at Lake Ponchatrain. We were training Cuban exiles for another invasion Cuba even though President Kennedy had told us to cease and desist. That gives you an idea how out of control the Agency was in those days. Kennedy promises Khrushchev that we will no longer try to overthrow Castro while the CIA is training men to do that very thing.

Garrison held several interviews with David Ferrie. Once it was clear that Garrison understood Oswald's intelligence background and his relationship with Guy

Bannister and Clay Shaw, Ferrie began to open up. He occasionally expressed some guilt and he seemed disgusted with the way the Agency manipulated him. He might have blown the case wide open, but he died just before he was scheduled to testify. It was ruled a suicide.

ELADIO DEL VALLE

On the same day that David Ferrie was found dead in New Orleans, his friend Eladio Del Valle was found with his head split open by a machete. Jim Garrison had been trying to locate Del Valle for questioning about the Kennedy assassination.

Del Valle had been a leader in Miami and New Orleans in training Cuban exiles for an assault on Cuba. He was a paymaster and had flown to Cuba several times with David Ferrie. He was in Dallas on November 22, 1963. He was said to be the shooter from the DalTex building, but that was not the case. The shooters from the DalTex and the book depository were two Cubans who were killed at our camp in Guatemala a few months after the assassination. I don't use their names because they were also victims of the plot. They followed orders and they paid with their lives.

Del Valle was on a level with Guy Bannister. He was familiar with all aspects of the plan to kill Kennedy and he could not be allowed to testify.

TOUGH GUY

If there was ever a person well-suited for the Cold War, it was Guy Bannister. He was mean and intolerant and he hated everything that was not one-hundred percent American. He worked with the Office of Naval Intelligence and the CIA and he had once been head of the FBI office in Chicago. He was a leading organizer in the Minutemen, which was a right wing, para-military organization. There's that picture you might have seen with Oswald in handcuffs where he's raising his fist. Most people assumed that it was a hostile gesture. What he's really trying to do is show you his Minuteman ring. He had infiltrated that group and he thought that the Minutemen and the anti-Castro Cubans were behind the plot. Oswald had no idea that the Agency was behind the murder. That's why he must have been shocked when he was told that President Kennedy had been killed. He had been passing warnings to everyone from the FBI to the Secretary of the Navy that there was a serious threat to Kennedy when he went to Texas.

In the summer of 63, Oswald was sent to Bannister in New Orleans to firm up his communist credentials so he could take the fall in the Kennedy murder. We had him handing out pro-Castro leaflets, getting in fights

380

with Cuban exiles and taking part in radio shows so we could paint a convincing picture of him as a communist. Once again Oswald thought he was involved in undercover work as an informant.

Bannister was the cut-out in New Orleans. After the Executive Action was successful in Dallas, he became a liability. The main problem was his drinking. We knew he was a guy who we could count on to keep his mouth shut, but a man who drinks heavily might say anything. He died less than a year after Dallas. The official report was a heart attack. I'm here to tell you, it was assisted. We had labs that did nothing but develop undetectable ways of killing people.

A MEETING AT RUBY'S

On the Sunday night that Jack Ruby shot Lee Oswald in the basement of the Dallas Police Headquarters, there was a meeting at Ruby's apartment. George Senator, who was Jack Ruby's roommate, had called the meeting. He thought it was important that others knew what he knew about Ruby's connection with the Kennedy murder.

Tom Howard was Ruby's attorney. He met with Ruby shortly after the point-blank murder of Oswald. It was at this time that Howard told Ruby to say that he had killed Oswald to save Mrs. Kennedy the anguish of returning to Dallas to testify at Oswald's trial. That was Tom Howard's creation and it's still the official version.

Bill Hunter was a reporter for a Long Beach newspaper. He was originally from Dallas and he knew the lay of the land. He understood the corruption at City Hall and he knew of Ruby's dealings with the police.

Jim Koethe was a staff writer for The Dallas Times Herald. He was a tough guy who often rubbed people the wrong way. He was more inclined to get a story out than make friends.

No one will ever know exactly what was discussed at that meeting. Five months later, Hunter was shot to death in a police station. Supposedly two officers were leaving the police station while Hunter sat in the press room. One of the officers dropped his gun on the floor. When he picked it up, the gun discharged and shot Hunter in the gut. The coroner questioned the angle of the wound, but it was ruled an accident. A few months after that, Koethe was strangled to death in his Dallas apartment. The following spring, Tom Howard died of a heart attack and George Senator dropped out of sight.

THE WRONG HAND

A man I had known since WWII died a few months after John Kennedy was murdered. Gary Underhill had been with the Office of Strategic Services during the war and he worked with the Agency on a number of projects during the fifties. A few days after JFK died, Gary made the mistake of telling a friend in New Jersey that he knew who had ordered the Kennedy assassination. An Executive Action does not take place without an order. Covert operatives do not do anything without being told.

Evidently Gary had told this person in confidence that the action had been carried out by a Far Eastern group in the CIA. He might have known Lansdale was involved. The Far East was Lansdale's background. Word must have gotten back to Dulles or Lansdale or Richard Helms.

Gary Underhill was found in his apartment with a bullet in his brain. There was one problem. The coroner's report said that the bullet entered his head from behind his left ear. Gary Underhill was right-handed.

TWO DOCTORS

Mary Sherman was a physician with Ochsner Hospital in New Orleans. She had gotten to know David Ferrie because of his interest in cancer research. Ferrie had a great mind, but he also talked a lot. After Jim Garrison had opened his investigation into the death of John Kennedy, he interviewed Mary Sherman. Shortly thereafter, she was shot and her body was set on fire. The corpse was found by a man named Valdez, who was a friend of Clay Shaw's.

Nicholas Chetta was the coroner in New Orleans during the Garrison investigation. He had performed autopsies on Mary Sherman, David Ferrie and Robert Perrin, who was an acquaintance of Jack Ruby's. All of these people died before they had a chance to testify. In turn, Dr. Chetta died of a heart attack before he could testify. A few months later, Chetta's assistant, Henry Delaune was murdered.

If anyone ever bothered to make a graph of witnesses who had died, he would find a cluster of deaths in the year and a half after the Kennedy assassination. You'd have another cluster during the Garrison investigation. There would be a third cluster a decade later during the investigation of the House Select Committee on Assassinations.

THE AUTOPSY

William Pitzer was a doctor at Bethesda Medical Center who had filmed the autopsy of President Kennedy. Everyone in the room that night had been warned not to talk about what they had seen. This was true at Parkland Hospital as well. Everyone who was present at either one of those hospitals will tell you that John Kennedy had a massive exit wound in the back of his head. In the official autopsy photos, there is a neat little entry wound in the back of the President's head.

When Pitzer was ready to retire in 1966, he was offered a job at a good salary with one of the television networks. This must have set off an alarm at Langley about unwanted publicity concerning the Kennedy autopsy. Pitzer was found in his office at Bethesda with a gunshot wound to the head. You guessed it. Suicide.

Pitzer's wife said that he had been warned a number of times not to disclose what he had seen when he filmed the autopsy. She thought his death might have been a warning to others to keep their mouths shut.

TREASON

There was a handbill passed around Dallas on the day of John Kennedy's visit. It accused the President of treason for selling wheat to the communists, welcoming President Tito of Yugoslavia to the White House, giving aid to Argentina and letting Latin America turn communist. It complained that Robert Kennedy had gone soft on communists while prosecuting loyal Americans. This was a reference to the Kennedy's enforcement of civil rights laws in the South.

Robert Surrey was the publisher of this handbill and he was an aide to Major General Edwin Walker. You'll remember that Walker was dressed down and arrested for his participation in the riot at Ole Miss. This made Walker an instant hero with the Minutemen and the John Birchers. Circulating this handbill during President Kennedy's visit to Dallas was an attempt to get even.

General Walker had been shot at in April of 63, by one of our Cubans in an attempt to portray Oswald as a violent man. In fact, Surrey had told police that he had seen two latin men casing General Walker's house several days before the shooting. He had followed the two men and noticed there were no license plates on

387

their car. Neighbors had also seen our Cubans in the neighborhood before and after the shooting.

In 1977, Surrey was being asked to testify before the House Select Committee on Assassinations because of his knowledge of the relationship between Jack Ruby and some anti-Castro Cubans. He was found dead of a gunshot wound. Suicide.

THROUGH THE GLASS

Hank Killam was a house painter in Dallas who found himself under a lot of scrutiny after John Kennedy was killed. His partner was a man named Carter, who just happened to live in the same rooming house with Lee Oswald. To make matters worse, his wife had worked for Jack Ruby. Federal authorities hounded Killam to the point that he moved to Florida.

In Florida the pressure was just as great. He was regularly visited by the FBI or Agency guys posing as Secret Service. Someone was worried that Hank Killam knew more that he was letting on.

In March of 1964, Killam was found with his throat cut in Pensacola, Florida. He was lying in a pile of glass in front of a department store window. The authorities ruled suicide, but the coroner said that he had never known of a suicide where a man had thrown himself through a plate-glass window.

TALK RADIO

During the House investigation in 1977, radio talk show host Lou Staples had received what he thought was reliable information from a trusted source. With great enthusiasm, he went on the air and told the audience that he was going to break open the JFK assassination case. He never got the chance. He was found dead of a gunshot wound to the head. Another suicide.

You wonder how all these killings could be carried out so easily right under the noses of the local authorities. In those days, there was a fine line between the Mafia and the CIA. Many of our covert assets had ties to the mafia. We had worked together since WWII. If the price was right on a contract, we'd have a line of guys willing to do the job. Afterwards, we could bring a lot of pressure to bear on the local investigators to close the case. If Posner wanted to write an honest book, he might look into the cases that were closed on these dead witnesses.

MORE CLEAN-UP

Carlos Prio Socarros had once been President of Cuba. He was a proud man with a deep hatred for Fidel Castro. He had forfeited a great deal of wealth when he was forced to flee from Cuba. He had more reason to want to see Castro overthrown than anyone I can think of with the possible exception of Santos Trafficante.

Carlos had become a leader in our anti-Castro activities. He was well known to operatives like Howard Hunt and David Phillips. He was also familiar with everything from the Bay of Pigs to Operation Mongoose. He counted among his friends, Eladio Del Valle, Guy Bannister, Clay Shaw and David Ferrie.

Oddly enough, the House Committee called on Socarros to testify not about his ties to CIA, but about gun-running activities involving Jack Ruby. This shows how well-intended investigators can get so far off track. A few days after George DeMohrenschildt was found dead, they found Carlos's body. He had died of a gunshot wound. Of course, it was a suicide.

OPEN SEASON

At one time during his career with the FBI, William Sullivan was thought to be the heir-apparent to J. Edgar Hoover. He had been promoted to number-two man in the Bureau after Hoover had gotten into a snit with Cartha De Loach. Remember, DeLoach was the one who would threaten publishers who intended to print controversial books like RUSH TO JUDGEMENT. He was a miserable little bastard, but that's another story.

Sullivan headed the FBI investigation into the death of John Kennedy and he was trusted enough that Hoover had put him in charge of COINTEL-PRO, which was the FBI's domestic espionage program. Mail was opened, telephones were tapped and radical groups were infiltrated. This was Hoover's idea of how to protect democracy.

By 1971, Sullivan was looking for support from the Nixon Administration for the opportunity to replace Hoover as Director of the FBI. He was spreading the word that the old crime czar was losing his mind. Nixon wasn't getting much cooperation from Hoover at the time and wanted to get rid of him. The problem was that Hoover had damaging information on Nixon going back to his days as vice president when he worked closely with the CIA in planning Executive Actions in

Africa and Latin America.   Nixon was still using operatives from the Kennedy assassination and he worried constantly that he might someday be tied to JFK's death.

When Hoover learned that Sullivan's loyalties were more with the Nixon Administration than to the FBI, he cut him loose. Sullivan had not only been in charge of the FBI's illegal domestic surveillance, he had also been in charge of all information concerning Oswald's FBI and intelligence connections after Dallas.   He was interested in writing a book to set the record straight. He reportedly had files on Hoover's stock portfolio and taxes.   He had been involved in arranging Hoover's misuse of Bureau personnel to paint his house and cut his lawn. Sullivan felt no loyalty to Hoover and wanted vindication. He was a man who knew too much.

In 1973, Sullivan did an interview with the Los Angeles Times in which he called J. Edgar Hoover "a master blackmailer." He said, "The weaknesses of the FBI have always been with the leadership in Washington, of which I was a part for fifteen years." In November of 1977, as the House Select Committee prepared to open its investigation, William Sullivan was shot by the son of a New Hampshire state trooper. The gunman said that he mistook Sullivan for a deer.

SAILING

John Paisley was a longtime agent of the CIA who was at one time involved with the defector program that sent Lee Oswald to Russia. He knew Oswald's background as well as anyone at the Agency. He had become a friend of KGB defector, Yuri Nosenko. Jim Angleton and others at the Agency thought Nosenko was a double agent and that put Paisley under suspicion. To make matters worse, Bernard Fensterwald, who had represented James Earl Ray, was Paisley's next-door neighbor. That might have given Paisley background information on the Martin Luther King murder.

Paisley was called before the House Select Committee and the word at Langley was that he might be inclined to tell what he knew. His body was found floating in Chesapeake Bay with a gunshot wound behind the left ear. Suicide while sailing. The body had been weighted down with two sets of diving belts. The corpse was in an advanced state of decomposition and it was determined to be four inches shorter than Paisley. His wife stated flatly that the body was not Paisley. If not, where was John Paisley?

A few years ago, former Director of Central Intelligence William Colby was also found adrift in Chesapeake Bay. His was a rowing accident.

WRATH OF THE LORD

Clyde Johnson was a preacher from Kentwood, Louisiana. He had once run for governor in Louisiana. His political agenda was that he was against everything that John Kennedy was for. He was a red-necked conservative who had the misfortune of witnessing a meeting between Clay Shaw, Lee Oswald and David Ferrie in Baton Rouge.

The day before he was scheduled to testify in New Orleans in Jim Garrison's trial against Clay Shaw, Johnson was so badly beaten that he could not appear in court. He was never able to testify which denied Garrison of an eyeball witness who could put Shaw and Oswald together.

A few months later, Johnson was killed in a shotgun attack near Greensburg, Louisiana. No suicide, this time.

MURDER INC.

The mid-seventies was a tough time for mobsters. Richard Cain was Sam Giancana's right-hand man in Chicago. He had worked with the Agency on a number of occasions including Dallas. He had funneled money to Jack Ruby to be used to bribe some members of the Dallas Police. This is where the Agency had to rely on the mob. We preferred not to have any of our operatives involved with bribing public officials. That was the Mafia's specialty.

In 1973, Cain and Giancana had a falling out and Cain offered to cooperate with the FBI as he had done with the Agency. In December, Cain was having lunch at a Chicago sandwich shop when everyone except Cain got up and left the table. Two men with ski masks entered the shop and lined the patrons up to one side. One man had a shotgun and the other talked on a hand-held radio. When the radio man gave the signal, the other man stepped forward and fired two shots at point-black range into Richard Cain's head. The radio man searched Cain's pockets and the two quickly walked away.

In Chicago's long history of gangland killings, there was never anything like this. The radio signal had the earmarks of an Agency job. It's possible that the CIA was worried that Cain would get too cozy with the FBI and tell them a little too much about his involvement in Dallas.

In June, 1975, staff members of the Church Committee arrived in Chicago to provide a safe escort for Sam Giancana to go back to Washington D.C. He was scheduled to testify before a congressional committee that was set up to investigate abuses of the CIA. That night, Giancana was murdered in his home in Oak Park even though he was under federal protection.

My sources tell me that Johnny Roselli was ordered to make the hit by Santos Trafficante. Chicago was out of his territory unless Trafficante had been given orders by the CIA. The following year, Johnny Roselli's remains were found in a sealed oil drum floating off the coast of Florida. Although his arms and legs had been severed, he died of suffocation.

Another casualty of the Giancana family at the time of the House investigation, was Charles Nicoletti. Before he could testify he was shot in the back of the head three times. Just for good measure, his car was firebombed. By coincidence, Nicoletti was murdered the same day that George DeMohrenschildt supposedly put the end of a shotgun in his mouth and pulled the trigger.

CHANGING TOO FAST

Mary Meyer was another attractive woman who was alleged to have had an affair with John Kennedy. In the years following Dallas, it was considered a slight if you were a woman who wasn't accused of having an affair with the former President. Meyer's brother in law was Agency big shot, Cord Meyer. She had met Kennedy while he was a young reporter covering the first United Nations convention in 1946. In Washington, she traveled in the same social circle as legendary spymaster, James Angleton. She also kept a diary.

The day after John Kennedy was killed in Dallas, Mary Meyer called her friend, Timothy Leary. She was crying and seemed to be in a panic. She blurted to Leary that they couldn't control Kennedy. He was changing too fast. He was learning too much. They'll cover everything up. I've got to come see you. I'm scared.

Then the line went dead. Leary learned several hours later that Mary Meyers had been murdered. The case has never been solved.

Mary Meyer's body was found along a path between a canal and the Potomac River. She had been shot twice about noon. One shot entered behind her shoulder blade and severed her aorta. The other shot was from behind her ear and entered her brain. Investigators said it looked like a professional hit.

The first group of people to reach Meyer's home after her death included James Angleton and his wife and Ben Bradlee and his wife. They were all personal friends of the victim. Angleton seemed obsessed with finding Meyer's diary. Bradlee's wife finally found the diary in a metal box that also contained letters. She turned the box over to Angleton. After going through the documents, he burned all of them.

What did Mary Meyers know that was so important that a top official in the CIA would rush to her home following her murder? Why would he destroy all of her personal notes?

In 1971, after the death of CIA officer Win Scott, Angleton immediately flew to Mexico City to meet with Scott's family. He demanded a manuscript that Scott had been working on that blew holes in the Agency's version of Lee Oswald's activities and his trip to Mexico in 1963. Angleton also seized the documents in Scott's safe. All of this material was destroyed.

James Angleton was an overseer of the false defector program in which Oswald had gone to the Soviet Union. He had also been involved in the cover-up of the Executive Actions against Lamumba and others. He was the author of the concept of plausible deniability. He said never use the word assassination and never put anything on paper. Better than anyone at the Agency, Angleton understood the urgency of damage control.

USED CARS

Albert Bogard had the bad fortune of being a car salesman at Downtown Lincoln-Mercury when a man posing as Lee Oswald came in to inquire about a used car on November 9, 1963. Oswald didn't drive, but his imposter test drove a Mercury Comet at high speeds on the Stemmons Freeway. Our look-a-like said he would have to come back in a few weeks when he expected to come into a lot of money. Bogart didn't take the man seriously until he saw him on television after the assassination of the President.

Bogard's next piece of bad luck came when he was asked to testify before the Warren Commission. His statements before that high tribunal must have made someone anxious because he was beaten within an inch of his life by a group of unknown assailants. After a long stay in the hospital, Bogard moved to Louisiana.

Two years later at the age of forty-one, Bogard was found dead in his car at a cemetery in Hallsville. The windows had been rolled up and a hose had been run from the exhaust pipe into the car. It was your typical suicide in the cemetery.

BEHIND BARS

When John Kennedy took office in January of 1961, he was disappointed to find such a small number of negroes employed in government service. He set out on his own affirmative action program and sought qualified black Americans for positions at all levels of the federal government. One beneficiary of this new push for equality was a young man named Abraham Bolden. He became the first black man employed by the Secret Service. He gained immediate notoriety and became a role model for ambitious young black men.

In the first week of November, 1963, Bolden witnessed the arrest of Eugene Vallee on Damen Street in Chicago. He was found with an M-1 rifle in his car on the route of John Kennedy's motorcade that day. Boden reported the incident to his superiors and also passed along an FBI report that there was a plot by four Cubans to kill the President in Chicago that day. To Boden's disappointment, the Secret Service did not investigate this information.

Three weeks later when John Kennedy was assassinated in Dallas, Boden told his story to a reporter in Chicago. Douglas Dillon and other officials in the Secret Service were offended by Boden's public criticism. He was soon charged with trying to sell government files.   Boden was convicted and sent to prison for six years.   America's black young poster boy had fallen out of favor.

It was learned later that the New York license plates on the car driven in Chicago by Eugene Vallee were registered to a Lee Harvey Oswald. Oswald didn't drive and he didn't own a car. He was also a long way from Chicago, but somehow he was going to be tied to this plot if it had succeeded.

QUICK FLIGHT

John Crawford was a lifetime friend of Wesley Buell Frazier, the man who drove Lee Oswald to work after his visits with Marina in Irving, Texas. Crawford had grown up with Frazier in Huntsville, Texas and was alleged to have been a homosexual partner of Jack Ruby's. Crawford was living in a trailer at the Huntsville airport in 1969. He died in a plane crash near the airport that year along with three other men, a woman and two children.

When officials got to the airport they found Crawford's stereo playing in his trailer. When they searched the cars of the other victims, they found that all three men had left their keys in their cars and the woman had left her purse on the front seat.

EXCESS BAGGAGE

Bud Fensterwald was a Washington D.C. attorney with a nose for the controversial. He was the founder of the Assassination Archives Research Center and the Committee to Investigate Assassinations. His clients included James McCord, the CIA man who worked for the Nixon White House and was arrested at the Watergate break-in and accused Martin Luther King assassin James Earl Ray. He also represented Richard Case Nagell who was an intelligence agent with foreknowledge of the plot to assassinate President Kennedy. Bud Fensterwald was carrying around a lot of sensitive baggage.

When Fensterwald developed information that a retired Air Force Colonel might have been the bagman for the murder of John Kennedy, he asked a friend who had worked for the Agency to set up an interview. The friend warned that Fensterwald was going to get himself killed. Fensterwald was persistent and an interview with him was arranged in Miami. A week and a half before the interview was to take place, Fensterwald was found dead. No autopsy was performed and his body was quickly cremated. His wife believed that he had been killed.

BAD KARMA

There were many right-wing fanatics, particularly in the South, who thought of little else than getting rid of John Kennedy. The young president was destroying their southern racist tradition. Since the Civil War, no white man had ever been convicted of killing a black man in the Deep South. Think about that. One hundred years of lynchings and burnings and not one conviction. It was open hunting season on Negroes. Then along comes John Kennedy and brother, Robert, and all hell breaks loose in the South. Civil rights laws are enforced. Black people are encouraged to register to vote. Bastions of higher learning like the University of Mississippi are invaded by black students with the protection of federal marshals. It was obvious to any clear thinking bigot that these Kennedys had to go.

One of the most outspoken and well informed of these good ole boys was a wealthy Georgian named Joseph Milteer. Two weeks before Dallas, Milteer told a friend named Willie Somerset that JFK was going to be killed by a sniper with a high powered rifle shooting from a high building. What Milteer did not know was that Somerset was an FBI informant and their conversation had been recorded. Because of this revelation, President Kennedy's motorcade through Miami was cancelled, but nothing was done to increase

406

protection in Dallas. J. Edgar Hoover had filed away dozens of similar threats without informing the Secret Service.

Among the items on Milteer's resume was the suspected bombing of a church in Birmingham, Alabama in which several black children were killed. He was so excited about the prospect of eliminating John Kennedy that he was photographed in Dealey Plaza when the President was killed. Milteer obviously had some inside information. When the House Select Committee on Assassinations began to interview witnesses in the mid-seventies, Milteer's life came to an untimely end. He was fooling around with a Coleman stove in his Georgia mansion when the thing blew up. Milteer went to the hospital with some serious burns which were not considered life-threatening. He improved steadily and then died. Chances are that nobody bothered to check the list of his visitors while he was in the hospital.

IMPROVED EYESIGHT

When Officer J.D. Tippit was shot in the Oak Cliff neighborhood of Dallas, Warren Reynolds saw the assailant run from the scene. He refused to identify Lee Oswald as the man that he saw flee the area. Before he could be called to testify before the Warren Commission, Reynolds was shot in the head. Fortunately, Reynolds recovered from the head wound. He was then able to identify Oswald as the gunman.

A local drunk by the name of Darrell Wayne Garner bragged about shooting Reynolds so he was hauled to jail. Garner was released when one of Jack Ruby's strippers, Nancy Jane Mooney, provided him with an alibi. A week later, Mooney was arrested for disturbing the peace. She died in jail. They said she had hanged herself with her toreador slacks.

A SURVIVOR

The most unusual story to come out of the clean-up operation that lasted for fifteen years following the Kennedy assassination was the case of Richard Carr. As the Kennedy motorcade passed through Dealey Plaza, Carr watched from a steel girder on the County Courts building that was under construction at the corner of Main and Houston Streets. Before the shooting, Carr saw a stocky man with a tan sport coat and horn-rimmed glasses on the sixth floor of the book depository. Carr was on about the same level and saw the man clearly.

After the President was shot, Carr saw this same man and two other men run from the back of the book depository and then walk quickly toward him on Houston Street. The men then turned east on Commerce Street and got into a Rambler station wagon on Record Street. Carr said that the Rambler was driven by a dark-skinned man and headed north on Commerce Street back toward the book depository. This was the same car that Roger Craig saw pick up our boy, John Masen, in front of the book depository. Do you think anyone involved in the murder of a president would be stupid enough to return to the scene of the crime unless they knew their movements were protected by a higher authority?

Richard Carr told his story to the FBI. He was told that unless he had seen Oswald in the window with a rifle, they weren't interested. That was J. Edgar Hoover's crackerjack crime-fighting team in Dallas. A few days later, Carr's home was raided in the middle of the night by twelve Dallas Policemen. One of his sons was arrested and held on charges of possession of stolen goods. Carr then received a call warning him to leave Dallas.

Carr didn't wait around for any more bad news. He packed up his family and headed for Montana. He thought he was a safe distance from Texas until one morning when he found dynamite hooked up to the ignition of his car. When he agreed to testify for Jim Garrison in New Orleans, someone tried to shoot him. To Carr's credit, he went ahead and testified.

Later, two men with knives attacked Richard Carr in Atlanta. He shot and killed one of them. The other got away. His life settled down after Clay Shaw was acquitted. When the House Select Committee on Assassinations began to interview witnesses, Carr again received threatening phone calls. The men he saw leaving the Texas School Book Depository in 1963 were obviously connected with the murder of John Kennedy.

Most of the work documenting the plight of all these witnesses who became victims was done by Penn Jones. He was the editor of a small newspaper in Mithlodian, Texas. Once he got involved in the case, he was like a dog with his teeth in your pant leg. There was no way to shake him loose. If it wasn't for Jones and people like Sylvia Meager, those who carried out the assassination of John Kennedy would have taken over

410

our government without so much as a slap on the hand. The real failure since 1963, lies with the American news media which has been lazy or compromised in the pursuit of the truth. It is now a corporate media with most of the news being watered down by the corporate masters.

THE PROPHET

In Penn Jones' collection of strange deaths, the strangest had to be that of Jack Zangretti. He managed a motel in Altus, Oklahoma. He had commented to friends the day after President Kennedy was murdered that three men, not Oswald, had killed the President. He predicted that Oswald would be shot the next day by a man named Ruby. Zangretti then predicted that a relative of Frank Sinatra's would be kidnapped to draw attention away from the assassination.

Two weeks later, Zangretti's body was found in Lake Lugert in Texas. He had been shot twice in the chest.

ECHOES

DEALEY PLAZA

Governor John Connelly, "We had just made the turn, well, when I heard what I thought was a shot. I instinctively turned to my right because the sound appeared to come from over my right shoulder, so I turned to look back over my right shoulder, and I saw nothing unusual except just the people in the crowd, but I did not catch the President in the corner of my eye, and I was interested, because once I heard the shot in my own mind I identified it as a rifle shot, and I immediately -- the only thought that crossed my mind was that this was an assassination attempt. So I looked, failing to see him, I was turning back to look over my left shoulder into the back seat, but I never got that far in my turn....then I felt like someone hit me in the back....the thought immediately passed through my mind that there were either two or three people involved or more in this or someone was shooting with an automatic rifle....I immediately when I was hit, I said, oh no no no. And then I said, my God, they are going to kill us all."

The Warren Report concluded that the first shot that Governor Connelly had heard was the shot that hit President Kennedy in the back, exited his throat, hit Connelly in the right shoulder, came out his chest, shattered his right wrist and lodged in his left thigh. Connelly said that he had time to look over his right shoulder and begin turning to his left before he was hit. He clearly would not have had time to do this if he had been hit by the first shot. He repeated many times in later years that he was certain that he had been hit by two shots that day.

S.M. Holland stood on the railroad bridge and looked directly up Elm Street, "I counted four shots and about the same time all this was happening, and in this group of trees, there was a shot, a report, I don't know whether it was a shot. I can't say that. And a puff of smoke came out about six or eight feet above the ground right out from under those trees....There were definitely four reports....I have no doubt about it. I have no doubt about seeing that puff of smoke come out from under those trees either....I definitely saw the puff of smoke and heard the report from under those trees." Holland watched as a dozen policemen and plainclothesman looked for shells behind the wooden fence. He said there was a station wagon parked near the fence and there was mud on the bumper where someone had stood for a better vantage point. There were many footprints between the car and the fence and two sets of footprints leaving the area to the west. He also noticed that the trunks of the cars in this area were never searched.

Ed Hoffman was a deaf-mute who watched the scene at Dealey Plaza from beyond the railroad tracks west of the parking lot. After the shooting, he tried to communicate what he had seen to a policeman, but was unsuccessful. "The first man, who wore a dark suit and tie, with an overcoat, ran west along the wooden fence with a rifle and tossed it to a second man who was dressed like a railroad worker. The second man hid behind a railroad switchbox, disassembled the rifle and put it in a soft brown bag." When Hoffman finally told his story to the FBI, he says they offered him a bribe to keep from going public with what he had seen.

James Worrell was walking south on Houston Street after the shooting had ended in Dealey Plaza. He saw a man in a brown sport coat run from the building and onto Houston Street ahead of Worrell. The description is the same as Richard Carr's. Worrell was killed on his motorcycle three years later.

Secret Service Agent Paul Landis, Jr. who rode in the car directly behind the presidential limousine, "I was not certain from what direction the second shot came, but my reaction at this time was the shot came from somewhere towards the front, right hand side of the road."

Ray Roberts was a Texas politician who rode in the motorcade, several cars behind the presidential limousine. He said as he passed through Dealey Plaza following the shooting, he could smell gunpowder. This would indicate that at least one of the shots came from street level.

Jean Hill was a Dallas school teacher. She had gone to Dealey Plaza with her friend, Mary Moorman, as much to flirt with a few Dallas policemen as to watch the presidential motorcade. She was standing next to the curb on the north side of Elm Street when President Kennedy was hit with the fatal head shot. She was probably the closest spectator to the President when he was killed. In her own words, this is her account of what happened.

416

"In 1963, I was a teacher in the Dallas school system, having recently arrived from Oklahoma City. I didn't know yet my way around Dallas, so a friend of mine, Mary Moorman, had said we should play hooky that day and head down to the motorcade. There were some policemen in that motorcade that we were particularly interested in, so we went to see the President as well. The friend of mine was riding on the President's wheel and I think that is one reason that Mary got the picture she got at the moment of the head shot. We had gotten down to the area in Dealey Plaza about an hour before the motorcade came around. We had been on the opposite side of the street, just in front of the School Book Depository and people were filling in and it was getting--there were too many people there, and we were afraid that these policemen weren't going to see us. We started across the street toward the triangle. We were stopped by a policeman on the corner and he told us that there was no one allowed in that area. After some flirting, though, Mary and I got him to let us go down there. Mary was rather short and we wanted to get a picture of this police officer's motorcycle as it came around. That area is sloping so when Mary reached up to take the picture, we did get a picture of the School Book Depository. We knew that, because we had a Polaroid camera, we were going to have to be quick if we wanted to take more than one picture. I would pull it out of the camera, coat it with fixative and put it in my pocket. That way we could keep shooting. When the head shot came, Mary fell down and the film was still in the camera. When the motorcade came around, there were so many voters on the other side that I knew the President was never going

417

to look at me, so I yelled, Hey Mr. President, I want to take your picture. Just then his hands came up and shots started ringing out. Then, in half the time it takes to tell it, I looked across the street and I saw them shooting from the knoll. I did get the impression that day that there was more than one shooter, but I had the idea that the good guys and the bad guys were shooting at each other. I guess I was the victim of too much television, because I assumed that the good guys always shot at the bad guys. Mary was on the grass shouting, Get down! Get down! They're shooting! They're shooting! Nobody was moving and I looked up and saw this man, moving rather quickly, in front of the School Book Depository toward the railroad tracks, heading west, toward the area where I had seen the man shooting on the knoll. So I thought to myself, This man is getting away. I've got to do something. I've got to catch him. I jumped out into the street. One of the motorcyclists was turning his motor, looking up and all around for the shooter, and he almost ran me over. It scared me so bad, I went back to get Mary to go with me. She was still on the ground. I couldn't get her to go, so I left her. I ran across the street and up the hill. When I got there a hand came down on my shoulder, and it was a firm grip. The man said, You're coming with me. And I said, No, I can't come with you, I have to get this man. I'm not very good at doing what I'm told. He showed me I.D. It said Secret Service. It looked official to me. I tried to turn away from him and he said a second time, You're going with me. At this point, a second man came and grabbed me from the other side, and they ran their hands through my pockets. They didn't say, Do you have the picture? Which pocket? They just ran their hands through my pockets and took it. They both held me up here where you could hurt somebody badly--and they told me, Smile. Act like you're with your boyfriends. But I couldn't smile because it hurt too badly. And they said, Here we go, each one holding me by the shoulder. They took me to the records building and we went up to a room on the fourth floor. There were two guys sitting there on the other side of the table looking out a window that overlooked the killing zone, where you could see all of the goings on. You got the impression that they had been sitting there for a long time. They asked me what I had seen, and it became clear that they knew what I had seen. They asked me how many shots I had heard and I told them four to six. And they said, No you didn't. There were three shots. We have three bullets and that's all we're going to commit to now. I said, Well, I know what I heard, and they said, What you heard were echoes. You would be very wise to keep your mouth shut. Well, I guess I've never been that wise. I know the difference between firecrackers, echoes, and gunshots. I'm the daughter of a game ranger, and my father took me shooting all my life."

The Dallas County jail was located on Houston Street on the block adjacent to Elm Street. John Powell was in a cell on the sixth floor which put him on a level with the sixth floor of the Texas School Book Depository where Lee Oswald allegedly waited in the sniper's nest to assassinate President Kennedy. Powell and other inmates said they saw two men in the "Oswald window" just before the shooting. He said they appeared to be adjusting a scope on a rifle and one of the men appeared to be latin.

419

Dallas police officer Tom Tilson was off duty on November 22, 1963, which seems strange considering the President was in town. Tilson's beat in Oak Cliff was covered by officer J.D. Tippit who did not survive the day. Was this a coincidence or was Tippit set up for some reason? Officer Tilson was driving east on Commerce Street toward Dealey Plaza with his daughter when he heard over his police radio that shots had been fired. Tilson told the Dallas Morning News this story, "I saw all these people running to the scene of the shooting. By that time I had come across under Stemmons. Everyone was jumping out of their cars and pulling up on the meridian strip. My daughter Judy noticed the limousine come under the underpass. They took a right turn onto Stemmons toward Parkland Hospital. Well, the limousine just sped past this car parked on the grass on the north side of Elm Street near the west side of the underpass. Here's one guy coming from the railroad tracks. He came down the grassy slope on the west side of the triple underpass, on the Elm Street side. He had this car parked there, a black car. And, he threw something in the back seat and went around the front hurriedly and got in the car and took off. I was on Commerce Street right across from his car fixing to go under the triple underpass going into town. I saw all this and said, 'That doesn't make sense, everybody running to the scene and one person running from it. That's suspicious as hell.' So I speeded up and went through the triple underpass up to Houston, made a left, and back on Main and caught up with him because he got caught on a light. He made a left turn, going south on industrial. I told my daughter to get a pencil and paper and write down what I tell you. By then we had gotten on the toll road going toward Fort Worth. I got the license number and the description of the car and I saw what the man looked like. He was stocky, about five -foot-nine, weighing 185 to 195 pounds and wearing a dark suit. If it wasn't Jack Ruby, it was his twin brother."

James Underwood on the north side of Elm Street, "Most of the people in the area were running up the grassy slope toward the railroad yards just behind the Texas School Book Depository Building. Actually, I assumed, which is the only thing I could do, I assumed perhaps whoever had fired the shots had run in that direction."

William E. Newman, Jr., "We were standing at the edge of the curb looking at the car as it was coming toward us and all of a sudden there was a noise, apparently gunshot....I was looking directly at him when he was hit in the side of the head....Then we fell down on the grass as it seemed that we were in the direct path of fire....everybody in that area had run up on top of that little mound. I thought the shot had come from the garden directly behind me....I do not recall looking toward the Texas School Book Depository. I looked back in the vicinity of the garden."

Deputy Sheriff A.D. McCurley, "I rushed toward the park and saw people running toward the railroad yards beyond Elm Street and I ran over and jumped a fence and a railroad worker stated to me that he believed the smoke from the bullets came from the vicinity of a stockade fence which surrounds the park area."

The Terminal Annex Building is located on the south side of Dealey Plaza. Jesse Price stood on the roof of the building to watch the motorcade. Half an

421

hour after the shooting, Price told the sheriff's office that after the volley of shots, he had seen a man about 5'6" tall and about 145 pounds run from behind the wooden fence toward the railroad cars with something in his hand. Price said the man was running very fast and thought he might have been involved in the shooting.

Deputy Sheriff I.C. Smith, "I heard a woman unknown to me say the President was shot in the head and the shots came from the fence on the north side of Elm."

Malcolm Summers hit the ground when he heard shots, "Then all the people started running up the terrace....Everybody was just running around toward the railroad tracks and I knew that they had somebody trapped up there....I stayed there fifteen or twenty minutes and then went over on Houston Street where I had my truck parked.....I had just pulled away from the curb and was headed toward the Houston Street viaduct when an automobile that had three men in it pulled away from the curb in a burst of speed, passing me on the right side, which was very dangerous at that point, then got in front of me, and it seemed then as an afterthought, slowed in a big hurry in front of me as though realizing that they would be conspicuous in speeding....They were in a 1961 or 1962 Chevrolet sedan, maroon in color."

Abraham Zaprgruder, who filmed the motorcade from on top of the cement wall in front of the stockade fence, "I remember the police were running behind me.....right behind me. Of course, they didn't realize yet, I guess, where the shot came from - that it came from that height.....Some of them were motorcycle cops.....and they were running right behind me, of course, in the line of the shooting. I guess they thought it came from right behind me.....I also thought it came from the back of me."

Emmet Hudson was standing on the cement steps that led up the grassy knoll toward the stockade fence, "The shots I heard definitely came from behind and above me."

Mary Woodward, reporter for The Dallas Morning News was standing on Elm Street in front of the stockade fence, "My first reaction was that the shots had been fired from above my head and behind me. My next reaction was that they might have come from the overpass which was to my right. I never looked at any time toward the Texas School Book Depository."

Frank Reilly, "The shots seemed to come out of the trees....on the north side of Elm Street, at the corner up there.....where all those trees are....at the park where all those shrubs is up there....up the slope."

Deputy Sheriff Harry Weatherford, "I heard a loud report which I thought was a railroad torpedo, as it sounded as if it came from the railroad yard....by this time I was running toward the railroad yards where the sound seemed to come from."

Secret Service Agent Forrest Sorrels who rode in the car ahead of the President, "The noise from the shots sounded like they may have come from back up on the terrace there. The reports seemed so loud , that it sounded like to me -- in other words, that was my first thought, somebody up on the terrace, and that is the reason I looked there."

Chief of Police Jessie Curry, who also rode in the lead car, said into his microphone immediately after the shots were fired, "Get a man on top of that triple underpass and see what happened up there."

Patrolman J.M. Smith who was standing in front of the book depository, "I heard the shots and thought they were coming from the bushes of the overpass.... A man standing behind the fence, further shielded by the cars in the parking lot behind him, might have had a clear shot at the President as his car began to run downhill on Elm Street toward the underpass....I caught the smell of gunpowder there behind the fence. I could tell it was in the air."

NBC cameraman Dave Weigman rode in the seventh car of the motorcade. As the shooting started he kept his film rolling as he jumped out of the car and ran toward the grassy knoll. When Weigman's film was analyzed frame by frame, in one of the frames smoke could be seen above the picket fence.

Earnest Ashkensky and Bernard Weiss were acoustics experts that studied the police dictabelt that had recorded the shots during the assassination. They testified before the House Select Committee on Assassinations that they were 95 percent sure that the final shot came from the direction of the grassy knoll.

Gordon Arnold tried to film the motorcade from behind the stockade fence, but he was told to leave by a man who showed Secret Service credentials. The problem was that there were no Secret Service Agents assigned to that area. Arnold went down to the grassy area below the fence and was filming the parade when the shooting started, "The shot came from behind me, only inches over my left shoulder. I had just got out of basic training. In my mind, live ammunition was being fired. It was being fired over my head. And I hit the dirt....you don't exactly hear the whiz of the bullet, you hear the shock wave. You feel it....you feel something and a shock wave comes right behind it."

Arnold said that he was then confronted by a hatless policeman who seemed very upset. The man kicked Arnold and then took the film out of his camera. Arnold decided it was a good time to move to Alaska.

Steven F. Wilson, Vice President of the Southwest Division of Allyn & Bacon, Inc., had an office on the third floor of the Texas School Book Depository, "It seemed the shots came from the west end of the building or the colonnade located on Elm Street across from the west end of our building. The shots really didn't sound like they came from above me."

After making that statement, Wilson said that he was continually visited by FBI Agents. "I couldn't get any work done at all. They were always here." When asked if he would agree to a filmed interview by Mark Lane, Wilson answered, "If I talk with you and you film my original impressions that the shots came from down there in the railroad yards and not from up there on the sixth floor, the agents will be back again and again, and I cannot go through all that again. My work would suffer and so might my health."

Buell Wesley Frazier was Ruth Paine's neighbor in Irving. He worked at the book depository and had given Lee Oswald a ride to work that morning. He watched the motorcade from the steps in front of the book depository, "Well, to be frank with you I thought it come from down there, you know, where that underpass is. There is a series, quite a few in number, of them railroad tracks running together and from where I was standing it sounded like it was coming from down the railroad tracks there....I didn't want to think what was happening, you know, but I wanted to find out so I went down to where the grassy slope is, you know, and I was trying to gather pieces of conversation of the people that had been close by there."

Delores Kounas, "Although I was across the street from the Depository building and I was looking in the direction of the building when the motorcade passed and following the shots, I did not look up at the building as I thought the shots came from a westerly direction in the vicinity of the viaduct."

Mrs. Avery Davis, "I took up a position on one of the lower steps of the building entrance to view the Presidential motorcade as it passed by on Elm Street. I thought the explosions were from the direction of the viaduct which crosses Elm Street west from where I was standing."

Dorothy Ann Garner watched the motorcade from the fourth floor of the book depository, "I thought at the time that the shots or reports came from a point to the west of the building."

Thomas Atkins, White House photographer, "The shots came from below and off to the right from where I was....I never thought the shots came from above. They did not sound like shots coming from anything higher than street level."

Billy Lovelady had watched the motorcade from the entrance of the book depository, "After he passed and was about fifty yards in front of us I heard three shots. There was a slight pause after the first shot and then the next two was right close together." The official version maintained that Oswald could have fired three times in

426

six seconds, but would have had to work the bolt action twice which would have spaced the three shots evenly.

Mary Ann Mitchell, There were three....the second and third being closer together than the first and second."

Lee Bowers had watched from the control tower in the railroad yard, "I heard three shots. One, then a slight pause, then two very close together."

Dallas Mayor Earl Cabell rode in the lead car ahead of the limousine, "There was a longer pause between the first and second shots than there was between the second and third shots. They were in rather rapid succession."

Robert Jackson, "I would say to me it seemed like three or four seconds between the first and second, and between the second and third, well, I guess two seconds. They were very close together."

Edward Shields, "I heard one shot and then a pause and then this repetition--two shots right behind the other."

Joe Molina, "Of course, the first shot was fired, then there was an interval between the first and second longer than the second and third."

Secret Service Agent Warren Taylor, "In the instant that my left foot touched the ground, I heard two more bangs and realized they must be gunshots."

Special Agent Forrest Sorrels, "There was about twice as much time between the first and second shots as there was between the second and third shots."

Special Agent William Lawson, "I heard two more sharp reports, the second two were closer together than the first. There was one report, and a pause, then two more reports closer together. Two and three were closer together than one and two."

Special Agent George Hickey, "At the moment he was almost sitting erect I heard two reports which....were in such rapid succession that there seemed to be practically no time element between them."

Special Agent Rufus Youngblood, "There seemed to be a longer span between the first and second shot than there was between the second and third shot."

Special Agent McIntyre, "The Presidential vehicle was approximately two hundred feet from the underpass when the first shot was fired, followed in quick succession by two more."

Dallas Mayor Earl Cabell who rode in the lead car, "There was a longer pause between the first and second shots than there was between the second and third shots. They were in rather rapid succession."

Congressman Ralph Yarborough, "By my estimate-- to me there seemed to be a longer time between the first and second shots, a much shorter time between the second and third shots."

Luke Mooney, "The second and third shots were pretty close together, but there was a lapse there between the first and second shot."

Arnold Rowland, "The actual time between reports I would say now, after having had time to consider was six seconds between the first and second reports and two between the second and third."

Deputy Sheriff John Wiseman, "I heard a shot and knew something had happened. I ran at once to the corner of Houston and Main Street and out into the street when the second and third shots rang out."

"Linda Willis, "Yes I heard one. Then there was a little bit of time, and then there were two real fast bullets together. When the first one hit, well, the President turned from waving to the people, and he grabbed his throat, and he kind of slumped forward...."

Ruby Henderson saw two men on the sixth floor of the book depository about five minutes before the presidential motorcade arrived. She described one of the men as having dark hair, dark skin and wearing a white shirt. She said he was "possibly a Mexican, but could have been a Negro."

PARKLAND HOSPITAL

Robert McClelland was the attending physician to President Kennedy when he was brought to Trauma Room One. McClelland said that there was no doubt in his mind the wound to the President's throat was an entrance wound and the fatal shot hit the President at the temple and blasted out the back of his head. He was surprised that none of this was shown in the official autopsy photos. In a British television documentary, Dr. McClelland said, "There was a jagged wound that involved the right side of the back of his head. My initial impression was that it was probably an exit wound. So it was a very large wound. Twenty to twenty-five percent of the brain was missing. My most vivid impression of the entire agitated scene was that his head had almost been destroyed. His face was intact but very swollen. It was obvious that he had a massive wound to the head. A fifth to a quarter of the right back part of his head had been blasted out along with most of the brain tissue in that area."

Dr. Charles Crenshaw, who attended President Kennedy in Trauma Room One, "The bullet that killed the President entered from the right side about the temple coming down and across. There was a huge blown-out hole in the back of his head....If the bullet had come from the back, the cerebellum would have been destroyed."

Dr. Ronald Jones, chief resident in surgery, describing President Kennedy's throat wound, "The hole was very small and relatively clean cut, as you would see in a bullet that is entering rather than exiting a patient. If this were an exit wound, you would think that it exited at a very low velocity to produce no more damage than this had done, and if this were a missile of high velocity, you would expect more of an explosive type of exit wound, with more tissue destruction than this appeared to have....there appeared to be an exit wound in the posterior portion of the skull....There was a large defect in the back side of the head as the President lay in the cart with what appeared to be brain tissue hanging out of this wound...."

Dr. Charles Baxter had assisted in performing a tracheotomy on President Kennedy' throat, "It was unlikely that the President's throat wound was one of exit. There was a large gaping wound in the back of his skull."

Dr. William Clark was chief of neurosurgery and the man who pronounced John Kennedy dead. In describing the throat wound, Dr. Clark said the bullet entered about the where the knot in the necktie was. "It ranged downward in his chest and did not exit. In the emergency room, Dr. Clark had said, "My God, the whole back of his head is shot off." When the official autopsy photos were released, the back of the President's head was intact.

Diana Bowron was a nurse at Parkland hospital who saw the limousine arrive. She helped wheel the gurney to the emergency room, "The President was lying across

431

Mrs. Kennedy's knee and there was blood everywhere. When I went around to the other side of the car, I saw the condition of his head....the back of his head....it was very bad....I just saw one large hole."

Fouad Bashour, associate professor of medicine in cardiology, was present when John Kennedy was treated in Trauma Room One. When he was later shown the official autopsy photos, he shook his head and said, "Why do they cover it up? This is not the way it was."

Audrey Bell was the supervising nurse when Governor Connelly was treated. She removed several bullet fragments from Connelly's wrist. "The smallest was the size of the striking end of a match and the largest was at least twice that big. I have seen the picture of the magic bullet, and I don't see how it could be the bullet from which the fragments I saw came."

BETHESDA

Jerrol Custer was a technician who x-rayed President Kennedy's body at the autopsy. Of the wound in the back of the President's head, Custer said, "I could have put both of my hands in the wound....Let me tell you one thing. If you have ever gone hunting you know that a bullet goes in small and comes out big. Okay? Well, that is exactly how the skull looked. Okay?...from the front to the back."

J.Thorton Boswell assisted Dr. James Humes in the autopsy of President Kennedy at Bethesda Naval Hospital. Describing the bullet wound in Kennedy's back, Thorton said it was "a penetration of one or two inches." This was the bullet that the Warren Commission said exited the President's neck, hit Governor Connelly in the shoulder and on and on. The reason the bullet had only penetrated a few inches was that the rifle fired from the DalTex Building had been equipped with a silencer or suppressor to reduce the number of shots that would be heard.

Robert Bouck was employed by the Protective Research Section of the Treasury Department which was in charge of the Secret Service. After the autopsy of the President at Bethesda, Bouck signed a receipt that stated, "One receipt from FBI for a missile

433

removed during the examination of the body." What missile would that be? The one that passed out of his neck and hit Governor Connelly? The final bullet that exploded the President's head? Or the bullet that lodged a few inches into his back? If it was the latter, the lone gunman theory collapses.

OSWALD

Dallas Chief of Police, Jesse Curry, "We don't have any proof that Oswald fired the rifle and never did. Nobody's yet been able to put him in that building with a gun in his hand."

After Lee Oswald was arrested, District Attorney, Henry Wade issued a statement that the police were tipped off to Oswald when all the other employees at the Texas School Book Depository were located after the shooting except Oswald. There were two errors in his statement. Several other employees had not gone back to work after the assassination and Lee Oswald wasn't identified by name until after his arrest. How could so many police officers be sure that the man who walked into the Texas Theatre without paying was the man who had shot the President and a police officer?

When Robert Oswald visited his brother after he was arrested in Dallas, Lee told Robert, "Don't pay any attention to this so-called evidence." Robert said that he looked Lee in the eye and he thought he was telling the truth. Later, Robert Oswald stated, "I still do not know why or how, but Mr. and Mrs. Paine are somehow involved in this affair."

A former CIA Agent by the name of Robert Morrow wrote a book called, BETRAYAL. His explanation of

Oswald's activities are as follows, "Oswald, who went to Russia for the CIA and was an FBI informant by the summer of 1963, was brought into the assassination plot led by CIA consultant Clay Shaw, using right-wing CIA operatives and anti-Castro Cubans headed by Jack Ruby in Dallas and Guy Bannister in New Orleans. This group, operating outside Agency control, manipulated events to insure Oswald being named the assassin. They also used an Oswald lookalike to incriminate the ex-Marine by firing shots from the Texas School Book Depository. Dallas policeman J.D. Tippit was killed by this Oswald substitute when he failed to go along with the group's scheme to have Tippit kill the real Oswald in the Texas Theatre. With the capture of Oswald, Ruby was compelled to stalk and finally kill the accused assassin."

A CIA finance officer named James Walcott testified before the House Select Committee on Assassinations that Oswald had been recruited by the CIA while he was stationed at Atsugi Air Base in Japan. It was for the purpose of a double-agent assignment in the Soviet Union. Walcott said that he had personally handled the funding for the assignment. Agency officials rushed forward to deny any knowledge of this assignment and the committee did not see fit to follow up on Walcott's testimony.

James Crowley was a State Department intelligence expert, "The first time I remember learning of Oswald's existence was when I received copies of a telegraphic message from the CIA dated October 10, 1963, which was information pertaining to his current activities." The Agency has always denied any involvement with Lee Oswald's activities after his return from Russia.

436

Oleg Kalugin was a former Russian major general who had been in charge of the KGB's foreign counterintelligence service. In 1990, he told a reporter for the New York Times that Lee Oswald had not been recruited by the KGB because "he was viewed as a CIA plant."

Forrest Sawyer is a reporter for ABC news who often appears on Nightline. In 1991, he spent several months in the Soviet Union where he was given access to a number of KGB files on Lee Oswald. Sawyer came to the conclusion that all of Oswald's woman companions during his two and a half years in the Soviet Union were KGB informants. The apartment that Lee and Marina shared in Minsk was bugged. After John Kennedy's death, KGB officials concluded that Lee Oswald was incapable of carrying out the assassination.

Sylvia Meagher is probably the most respected researcher to ever get involved in seeking the truth in the death of John Kennedy. She studied and cross referenced all twenty-six volumes of the Warren Report. She did a more thorough and honest investigation of the report that the Warren Commission had done on the original investigation. I believe she worked in the medical field and she did all of this in her spare time. In 1967, she published a book called, ACCESSORIES AFTER THE FACT, in which she single-handedly destroyed the credibility of the Warren Report. Here is how she summarized the ease with which Oswald re-entered the United States, "The State Department's extraordinary and unorthodox decisions and the decisions taken by other U.S. official agencies in regard to Oswald fall into several categories: (1)

repeated failure to prepare a 'lookout card' to check Oswald's movement outside the U.S.; (2) grant and renewal of Oswald's passport despite cause for negative action; (3) apparent inaction and indifference to Oswald's possible disclosure of classified military data; and (4) pressure exerted and exceptional measures taken on behalf of Marina Oswald's entry into the U.S."

C.A. Hamblen was the early night manager of the Dallas Western Union Telegraph Co. After the assassination, Hamblen told his superior that about two weeks earlier, Oswald had sent a telegram to Washington, DC, "possibly to the Secretary of the Navy." What reason would Oswald have to send such a telegram unless it was a warning about the plot to kill the President?

Carolyn Arnold worked at the Texas School Book Depository, "About a quarter of an hour before the assassination, I went into the lunchroom on the second floor for a moment....Oswald was sitting in one of the booth seats on the right-handed side of the room as you go in. He was alone as usual and appeared to be having lunch. I recognized him clearly."

Motorcycle patrolman Marrion Baker rushed into the Texas School Book Depository approximately one minute after the shooting ended. As he went up the stairs, he noticed movement in the second floor lunchroom. In his report, Baker said he encountered Oswald "drinking a Coke." From the time he was seen by Carolyn Arnold, this would have given Oswald fifteen minutes to get to the sixth floor, establish his position, shoot the President in the back, miss by thirty feet high and left, hit the President in the head, wipe the rifle clean of fingerprints, hide the rifle at the other end of the room, go down four flights of steps to the lunchroom, extract a Coke from the machine and be calmly drinking it when confronted by Baker. FBI paraffin tests showed Oswald had not fired a rifle that day. Was it more likely that Oswald had been in the lunchroom when John Kennedy was assassinated?

Lee Oswald's landlady at his rooming house on North Beckley was Earline Roberts. She told the Warren Commission that Oswald entered the rooming house about half an hour after the President was shot and he seemed to be in a hurry. Oswald stayed only a few minutes and left with his jacket. While he was in the house, there was a Dallas police car parked in front of the house with two uniformed policemen inside. They honked the horn twice and then drove off. Mrs. Roberts said that the last she saw of Oswald, he was waiting for a bus on the east side of the street. Less than ten minutes later, officer J.D. Tippit was killed about a mile away. The bus Oswald was waiting for would not have taken him in that direction. The question that has never been answered is; who were the two police officers and why had they honked the horn?

Eusebio Azcue was the Cuban consul in Mexico City at the time of Lee Oswald's alleged visit in September of 1963. When shown a photograph of Oswald, Azcue stated, "This gentleman is not the person who went to the consulate. The man was over thirty years of age, very thin faced....He was dark blond. He had a hard face. He had very straight eyebrows, cold, hard, and straight eyes. His cheeks were thin. His nose was very thin and pointed."

Silvia Duran was a secretary at the Mexico City Cuban Consulate when Lee Oswald supposedly visited

439

in September of 1963. She was arrested twice after the assassination on orders from the CIA. She was warned not to talk about her meeting with Oswald. The first request stated, "With full regard for Mexican interests, request you ensure that her arrest is kept absolutely secret, that no information from her is published or leaked, that all such information is cabled to us." What was the CIA afraid of if Oswald wasn't connected to the Agency? Duran described the Oswald in Mexico City as about thirty-five years old and barely over five foot tall. This was about ten years too old and half a foot too short.

Nelson Delgado bunked next door to Lee Oswald for a year at El Toro Marine Base in California. As to Oswald's ability with a rifle, Delgado said, "It was a pretty big joke because he got a lot of Maggie's Drawers, you know, a lot of misses, but he didn't give a darn....He wasn't as enthusiastic as the rest of us. We all loved--liked, you know--going to the range....He was mostly a thinker, a reader. He read quite a bit....he never said anything subversive." After the Warren Commission hearings, Delgado took his family to England. He explained, "The conspirators might think I know more than I do."

Sherman Cooley was a Marine Corps buddy of Oswald's who said they had called Oswald "Shitbird" when he couldn't qualify with his rifle. "It was a disgrace not to qualify and we gave him holy hell about it."

Godfrey 'Gator' Daniels met Lee Oswald aboard the USS Bexar on the way to Japan, "He was simple folk, just like I was....we were a bunch of kids--never been away from home before--but Oswald came right out and admitted that he had never known a woman....but he never was ashamed to admit it....He was just a good egg."

James Bothelho roomed with Lee Oswald at El Toro Marine Base in Santa Ana, California, "I shared a room with Oswald for about two months before his discharge. He was unusual in that he generally would not speak unless spoken to, and his answers were always brief....It was common knowledge that Oswald had taught himself to read Russian....Some kidded him by calling him, Oswaldovich....My impression is that, although he believed in pure Marxism, he did not believe in the way Communism as was practiced by the Russians....We both enjoyed classical music....Oswald played chess with both me and Call. Oswald was not a very good chess player, although he was better than I was....My impression was that Oswald was quite intelligent...." Bothelho later became a judge in California.

Zack Stout had known Lee Oswald in the Marines, "Oswald was honest and blunt. That's what usually got him in trouble. His diction was good. He seemed to think about what he was going to say. He was absolutely truthful, the kind of guy I'd trust completely."

Richard Call served on the same radar crew with Lee Oswald for one year, "I was probably one of his best friends....I played chess with him about once a week. He was studying Russian....We kidded him about being a Russian spy. Oswald seemed to enjoy this kind of remark....I had a phonograph record of Russian classic pieces entitled, Russian Fireworks. When I would play the record Oswald would come over and say, "You called?" Oswalds reactions to everything were subdued and stoic....I do not recall Oswald's making serious remarks about the Soviet Union or Cuba."

Peter Connor served with Oswald at the Marine base in Atsugi, Japan. "When the fellows were heading out for a night on the town, Oswald would either remain behind or leave before they did. Nobody knew what he did....Oswald had a reputation of being a good worker....I was of the opinion that Oswald was intelligent....I never heard Oswald make any anti-American or pro-Communist statements. He claimed he was named after Robert E. Lee, whom he characterized as the greatest man in history."

In September of 1963, John Manchester was the town marshal for Clinton, Louisiana. He testified during the Clay Shaw trial that he had seen Shaw, David Ferrie and Lee Oswald together while he supervised a voter registration drive. Manchester said that the three men "arrived in a big black car and the driver identified himself as a representative of the International Trade Mart in New Orleans."

Edwin McGhee was the town barber in Clinton, Louisiana, where Lee Oswald was driven by Clay Shaw and David Ferrie in the fall of 63 to look for work. Oswald came into the barbershop for a haircut and some information. When Oswald inquired about employment possibilities at the state hospital in nearby, Jackson, the barber informed him that it was a mental institution. McGhee said "Oswald appeared shocked when I told him this was a mental hospital."

John McVicker was a foreign service officer at the American embassy in the Soviet Union when Lee Oswald defected in 1959. When McVicker first spoke to Oswald after his arrival he said, "Oswald wanted to

442

renounce his U.S. citizenship and threatened to reveal the military secrets that he had. He appeared to be following a pattern of behavior in which he had been tutored by person or persons unknown."

Samuel Ballen met Lee Oswald through George DeMohrenschildt and tried to help him find work. Ballen said that Oswald was the kind of person he could like. He had that kind of Ghandi, far off look about him.

The Mikado Club was a competitor of Jack Ruby's Carousel Club in Dallas. In early November of 1963, a chef named Harold Williams who worked at the Makado Club was roughed up during a vice raid. He was shoved into the back of a patrol car and taken downtown. J.D. Tippit drove the car while Jack Ruby rode in the passenger seat. Williams said that Tippit referred to Ruby as 'Rube', which would indicate that the two men were well acquainted. After the assassination of President Kennedy, Williams said he was warned by members of the Dallas Police Department to keep his mouth shut about seeing Tippit and Ruby together.

Aquilla Clemons witnessed the murder of Officer Tippit from her porch across the street. She described his killer as "kind of a short guy and kind of heavy." She was warned by the Dallas police not to talk about what she had seen or she might get hurt. She was not asked to testify before the Warren Commission.

Shortly after officer Tippit was killed, Dallas patrolman H.W. Summers radioed from Oak Cliff that he had an eyeball witness to the assailant. The man running from the scene as having black, wavy hair. No one ever described Oswald as having dark, wavy hair.

443

THE BEAST

"It is the most bizarre conspiracy in the history of the world. It'll come out at a future date," Jack Ruby teased a reporter as he rotted in jail. When Lee Oswald was brought out for a brief press conference on Saturday night, District Attorney Henry Wade told reporters that Oswald was a member of the Free Cuba Committee. From the back of the room, Ruby piped up and told reporters that Oswald was actually a member of the Fair Play for Cuba Committee. How was he supposed to know that?

A night clerk at the FBI office in New Orleans named William Walter told District Attorney Jim Garrison of a telex he had received on the night of November 17, 1963. The memo was a warning of a plot to kill President Kennedy. The FBI had purged the memo from its offices and denied its existence. In 1976, Mark Lane pried loose the memo under the Freedom of Information Act. It read:

URGENT: 1:45 AM EST 11-17-63 HLF 1 PAGE
TO: ALL SACS
FROM: DIRECTOR
THREAT TO ASSASSINATE PRESIDENT KENNEDY IN DALLAS TEXAS NOVEMBER 22

DASH THREE NINETEEN SIXTY THREE. MISC INFORMATION CONCERNING, INFORMATION HAS BEEN RECEIVED BY THE BUREAS BUREAU HAS DETERMINED THAT A MILITANT REVOLUTIONARY GROUP MAY ATTEMPT TO ASSASSINATE PRESIDENT KENNEDYON HIS PROPOSED TRIP TO DALLAS TEXAS NOVEMBER TWENTY TWO DASH TWENTY THREE NINETEEN SIXTY THREE. ALL RECEIVING OFFICES SHOULD IMMEDIATELY CONTACT ALL CIS, PCIS LOGICAL RACE AND HATE GROUP INFORMANTS AND DETERMINE IF ANY BASIS FOR THE THREAT. BUREAU SHOULD BE KEPT ADVISED OF ALL DEVELOPMENTS BY TELETYPE. OTHER OFFICES HAVE BEEN ADVISED. END AND ACK PLS.

Three days after the assassination of the President, Deputy Attorney General Nicholas Katzenbach sent a memo to Lyndon Johnson's press secretary, Bill Moyers, "It is important that all the facts surrounding President Kennedy's assassination be made public in a way which will satisfy the people in the United States and abroad that all the facts have been told and that a statement to this effect be made now, 1) The public must be satisfied that Oswald was the assassin; that he did not have confederates who are still at large; and the evidence was such that he would have been convicted at trial. 2) Speculation about Oswald's motivation ought to be cut off....I think this objective may be satisfied by making public as soon as possible a complete and thorough FBI report on Oswald and the assassination. This may run into the difficulty of pointing to inconsistencies between the report and statements by Dallas police officials. But the reputation of the Bureau is such that it may do the whole job."

U.S. Army lieutenant colonel, Robert Jones of the 112th Military Intelligence Group in Texas, had been given orders to "stand down" and not provide protection for the motorcade. Several hours after the assassination, Jones received a report that an "A.J. Hidell" had been arrested. Jones looked up Hidell in his files and it cross-referenced to "Lee Harvey Oswald". While the CIA and FBI were denying any association with Oswald, Army Intelligence had a file on him. If Hidell was the alias that Oswald had used to mail-order the rifle from Chicago, how would the intelligence community be aware of the fact? A more reasonable assumption is that the rifle was ordered by a group within the intelligence community without Oswald's knowledge and planted as evidence. Oswald said he'd never seen the rifle and the FBI lab in Washington could find none of his fingerprints on the weapon.

Edwin Lopez was an attorney who worked for the House Select Committee on Assassinations. It was his job to investigate Oswald's alleged trip to Mexico City in September of 1963. He concluded that an imposter had made visits to the Soviet and Cuban embassies. Lopez told author, Anthony Summers, "It was very obvious, from dealing with people at the CIA for approximately ten years, which the CIA was covering something up. We weren't sure if it had to do with some element of the CIA having assassinated the President, but we knew at the very least they were covering up something they knew about the assassination. I came away feeling that we could not trust our government, that what we had been told all along was a sham. And I thought the American people deserved better."

Marion Cooper was an Agency informant who had attended a meeting in Honduras on January 1, 1955. The topic of discussion was the assassination of Panama's President, Jose Antonio Ramón. At the meeting, Cooper said, "were a team of hired assassins and Vice President Richard Nixon." The next day, President Ramón was killed by machine-gun fire.

An FBI memo from 1947, "It is my sworn statement that one Jack Rubenstein of Chicago, noted as a potential witness of the House Committee on Un-American Activities, is performing information functions for the staff of Congressman Richard Nixon, Republican of California. It is requested that Rubenstein not be called for open testimony in the aforementioned hearings." In 1948, Rubenstein changed his name to Jack Ruby and moved to Dallas. Fifteen years before Ruby participated in the murder of President Kennedy, he had provided another service for Richard Nixon.

Victor Marchetti was an assistant to the DCI Richard Helms. He wrote a book called, THE CULT OF INTELLIGENCE. The CIA censured the book by blanking out about a third of its contents. Marchetti says that the American people should not hold their collective breath waiting for documents to be released that would tie the Agency to the death of John Kennedy as all such documents have been destroyed. Before he left office, Helms also destroyed all sensitive documents involved with the Agency's MK-Ultra mind

447

control program. During the Clay Shaw trial in New Orleans, Helms constantly worried that the Agency was not giving Shaw enough help. Marchetti says that Shaw was closely connected to the CIA. He had worked on plans for the Bay of Pigs invasion with Allen Dulles' top assistant, General Charles Cabell. Also involved were Howard Hunt, Bernard Barker, Frank Sturgess, David Ferrie and Vice President, Richard Nixon. Hunt, Barker and Sturgess later ran President Nixon's dirty tricks operations and the three were arrested at Watergate. If the above cast of characters was also involved in the Kennedy assassination, it is no wonder that Nixon felt the need to erase a little tape here and there.

H.R. Haldeman was President Nixon's chief of staff. Explaining the Watergate tapes, Haldeman said, "In all those references to the Bay of Pigs, Nixon was actually referring to the Kennedy assassination....After Kennedy was killed, the CIA launched a fantastic cover-up....The CIA literally erased any connection between Kennedy's assassination and the CIA."

In his book, WITNESS TO POWER, John Ehrlichman describes a situation during the 1968 primary campaign when Robert Kennedy announced his candidacy for the Democratic nomination. Nixon watched Kennedy's announcement and continued to stare at the television after it was turned off. Finally, Nixon shook his head and said, "We've just seen some very terrible forces unleashed. Something bad is going to come of this....God knows where this is going to lead." Nixon had worked with these terrible forces throughout his political career. He understood their capabilities and was probably not surprised when RFK was murdered several weeks later.

Sammy Halperan was a CIA agent who initialed an internal CIA memo stating that the Agency was concerned that "E. Howard Hunt's presence in Dallas at the time of the assassination would be discovered."

George DeMohrenschildt spent time in Haiti, supposedly to run business operations for Texas oilman Clint Merchison. Soon after John Kennedy was killed, DeMohrenschild deposited close to a quarter of a million dollars in a Port-au-Prince bank account. According to an officer in the bank, the money was soon paid out. During his time spent in Haiti, DeMohrenschild had developed a friendship with Haitian President Papa Doc Duvalier. In a speech before the assassination, Duvalier said, "the big man in the White House isn't going to be around much longer."

One of Jim Garrison's star witnesses in the Clay Shaw trial was to be Richard Case Nagell. By the time the trial was underway, Nagell was nowhere to be found. Garrison had learned that Nagell was an intelligence agent who had stumbled onto the massive plot to kill President Kennedy in 1963. Nagell quickly sent a letter detailing what he knew about the conspiracy to J. Edgar Hoover. When Nagell received no reply from the FBI, he began to worry that he might be in a trap where he might be implicated in the conspiracy. Nagell decided that the best way to keep from being associated with the plot was to be in prison if John Kennedy was murdered. So Nagell went into an El Paso bank and fired two shots into the ceiling. He then walked outside and sat on the steps and waited to be arrested. He served three years of a ten year sentence. Nagell told Garrison that the three principles in the plot in New Orleans were, "Clay Shaw, Guy Bannister and David Ferrie."

McGeorge Bundy sent a message to Air Force One while it was en route from Dallas to Washington saying that, "There was no conspiracy. The assassination had been determined to be the act of a lone gunman." What was Bundy's hurry? What was his agenda? Oswald hadn't been charged with the murder yet. At the same time, Attorney General Robert Kennedy got a call from a Secret Service agent telling him there was evidence of "a massive plot in Dallas."

Fidel Castro, "Then too, after such a plot had been found out, we would be blamed--for something we had nothing to do with. I think it would have been an excuse for another invasion try....I think he was killed by U.S. fascists--right-wing elements that disagreed with him."

Eugene Hall was a Cuban exile who had been tied to the murder of President Kennedy in the Warren Report. While Hall admitted to anti-Castro gun running activities, he had an alibi for the day the President was shot. Years later he told a reporter for the Dallas Morning News that he was approached about a month before the assassination by "ultra-right-wing activists working with CIA operatives, who wanted me to take part in the JFK hit."

John Martino was a CIA contract agent with ties to the Mafia, "The anti-Castro people put Oswald together. Oswald didn't know who he was working for--he was just ignorant of who was putting him together. Oswald was to meet his contact at the Texas Theatre. They were to meet Oswald in the theatre and get him out of the country, then eliminate him. Oswald made one mistake. There was no way we could get to him. So they had Ruby kill him."

Chauncey Holt is the admitted eldest tramp of the three men arrested in a boxcar in the railroad yard next to Dealey Plaza. Holt says the other two men were Charles Harrelson and Richard Montoya. Montoya is thought to be Charles Rogers, who was wanted in Houston for the murder of his two parents. The three men were held briefly and released, probably due to Rogers' connections as a pilot for the CIA. Holt was also a pilot and a career criminal and master forger with ties to Meyer Lansky. He worked as an accountant for Lansky and later for the International Rescue Corporation Committee, which was a CIA front. Holt says he forged documents for the CIA. He claims to have produced the phony Secret Service documents that were used in Dealey Plaza as well as the fake I.D. in the name of Alek Hidell. Holt was under the impression that an incident was to be staged in Dallas that could be blamed on Castro. After the shooting, he went to the ninth boxcar from the engine as instructed and there he met Rogers and Harrelson who said they were with the Agency. When they were being arrested, it occurred to Holt that they might have become the patsies if Oswald had escaped. Holt said he arrived at Dealey Plaza in an Oldsmobile station wagon and parked next to the fence.

A November, 1967, edition of Life Magazine shows two pictures of Dealey Plaza from similar vantage points. Both photographs were taken within seconds of one another. One shows a boxcar beyond the parking lot. The other does not. The picture with no boxcar was in possession of the FBI for several weeks. Penn

Jones offered this explanation, "We think the boxcar was eliminated from the picture to try to erase all traces of three men who were arrested in a boxcar just after the shooting."

Pat Kirkwood was a friend of Jack Ruby's and the owner of The Cellar, which was a nightclub in Fort Worth, Texas. In the Fort Worth Star Telegram, Kirkwood described the scene at his club the night before John Kennedy was murdered, "After midnight the night before, some reporters called me from the Press Club, which didn't have a license to sell drinks after midnight. Said they had about seventeen members of the Secret Service and asked if they could bring them over to my place. I said sure. About 3:30 in the morning, these Secret Service men were sitting around giggling about how two firemen were guarding the President over at the Hotel Texas....We didn't say anything, but those guys were bombed. They were drinking pure Everclear." Supposedly, Kirkwood was known to wealthy oilmen H.L. Hunt and Clint Merchison as well as Meyer Lansky.

Raymond Broshears was a minister who shared an apartment with David Ferrie in 1965. When Ferrie drank too much he would talk about his role in the Kennedy assassination, "David admitted being involved with the assassins. There's no question about that." Ferrie also told Broshears that he would never consider suicide.

Vernon Bundy testified in the Clay Shaw trial that he had seen Lee Oswald and Clay Shaw together at Lake Ponchartrain in the summer of 1963. After a conversation between the two that lasted about fifteen minutes, "The older fellow gave the guy what I'm not sure, but it looked like a roll of money. The young guy stuck it in his back pocket."

Judge Edward Haggarty presided over the Clay Shaw trial in New Orleans. Afterwards, he told a reporter, "In my opinion, Shaw lied through his teeth."

Gaeton Fonzi worked as an investigator for the House Select Committee on Assassinations. He turned up a potentially explosive witness in Antonio Veciana who was a former accountant from Cuba. Veciana had founded a militant group called Alpha 66 which provided training for the assassination of Fidel Castro. Working with this group were the likes of Frank Sturgess and Howard Hunt. Get Castro became get Kennedy. Veciana said he had numerous meetings with a CIA operative who called himself Maurice Bishop. In the fall of 1963, Veciana saw Bishop meet with Lee Oswald in a hotel in Dallas. After John Kennedy was murdered, Bishop offered Veciana a large sum of money if one of his relatives would say that they met Oswald in Mexico City in September of 63. Veciana later identified Maurice Bishop as David Phillips who was a high ranking official at the CIA. It was the Agency's attempt to frame Oswald in Mexico that clearly tied them to the assassination of John Kennedy.

The mind control experiments conducted by the CIA were a black chapter in American history. Unsuspecting victims in the military or mental hospitals were used and often their lives were irreparably damaged. As usual, Allen Dulles was talking out of both sides of his mouth. He would make a speech accusing Russia of these abuses against its citizens while he had approved the same grim experiments at the Agency. One of the main players in this area was

453

Dr. Charles Mendoza. George De Mohrenschildt's wife, Jeanne, said that he developed extremely troubling behavior after he had spent time with Dr. Mendoza. She said that the sessions would last several hours and her husband would be given injections of an unknown substance. Afterwards, George would begin ranting about the Nazis and the Jews.

Another CIA mind-control expert, Dr. Louis "Jolly" West was sent to help Jack Ruby while he was in jail. Soon afterward, Ruby developed cancer and died. He had received mysterious injections. To insiders at the Agency, this was humorously called "the CIA flu."

This is a quote from a letter sent by Ruth Paine to Marina Oswald in New Orleans in July, 1963, "Think about the possibility of living with me. Marina, come to my home the last part of September without fail, either for two months or two years. And don't be worried about money." The time frame of late September for at least two months would guarantee that Marina would be under Ruth's guidance at the time of the assassination. It would also guarantee a garage full of incriminating evidence. In no other murder case did the accused go to so much trouble to incriminate himself as Lee Oswald supposedly did.

Word throughout the underworld during the month leading up to the assassination of John Kennedy was that there was a contract out on the President. A bar owner in New Orleans named Ben Tregle, who was a business associate of Carlos Marcello was talking with some of his friends when he saw an advertisement for a mail-order rifle. It was reported that he said, "This would be a nice rifle to buy and get the President. There is a price on the President's head and other members of the Kennedy family. Somebody will kill the President when he comes down south."

Just before his death, Santos Trafficante supposedly told his lawyer and longtime friend, Frank Ragano, "Carlos fucked up. We should not have killed Giovanni. We should have killed Bobby." Trafficante had recruited Cuban exiles for the CIA's Bay of Pigs invasion. He had been brought into the Agency's plot to kill Castro by Johnny Roselli and Sam Giancana. This was not a new concept. Twenty years earlier, Lucky Luciano had helped the FBI break the dock strike in New York City. With the mafia wanting JFK dead and the anti-Castro Cubans blaming the President for the failure at the Bay of Pigs, it was easy for the Agency to open the gate and turn loose Operation Mongoose. This was an unauthorized group trained to kill Castro which was simply redirected toward President Kennedy. The rank and file at Langley had no idea of what was taking place. A former head of the Agency like Allen Dulles could give the nod to a trusted assistant like Ed Lansdale who in turn could give approval to Clay Shaw who was the paymaster for Operation Mongoose. This way the plot could never track back to the Agency.

One of the key witnesses in the Clay Shaw trial was Perry Russo. He was a friend of David Ferrie's who greatly admired the pilot's intellect. He described a party he had attended at Ferrie's apartment during the summer before President Kennedy was assassinated, "Ferrie took the initiative in the conversation, pacing back and forth as he talked. He said the assassination attempt would have to involve diversionary tactics. There would have to be a minimum of three people

455

involved. Two of the persons would shoot diversionary shots and the third person would take the good shot. There would have to be a triangulation of crossfire....One of the people would have to be sacrificed." Two reporters from NBC attempted to bribe Russo to turn on Jim Garrison and destroy his case. Russo refused.

A career criminal from Philadelphia named William Waley told D.A. Jim Garrison that he had been offered $25,000 in 1967 in a bar on Bourbon Street for a hit on Garrison. The two men offering the contract were David Ferrie and Clay Shaw.

George Butler was a lieutenant with Dallas Police and a member of the Ku Klux Klan. He was in charge of the transfer of Lee Oswald on the Sunday morning that he was killed by Jack Ruby. A reporter by the name of Thayer Waldo who worked for the Fort Worth Star Telegram noted that Butler's cool demeanor seemed to fall apart at the time of the transfer, "....when I was standing asking him a question after I had entered the ramp and gotten down to the basement area, just moments before Oswald was brought down, he was standing profile to me and I noticed his lips trembling as he listened and waited for my answer. It was simply a physical characteristic. I had by then spent enough time talking to this man so that it struck me as something totally out of character."

In 1990, Jules Kimble was rotting away in El Reno Federal Penitentiary when he was interviewed by a couple of reporters from Covert Action Information Bulletin. He talked of his acquaintance with Clay Shaw and David Ferrie before the conversation turned to the death of Martin Luther King. Kimble surprised the reporters when he admitted being part of a widespread conspiracy that included the Mob and the CIA. He said that James Earl Ray did not shoot King and he had been set up to take the fall. Kimble said he had introduced Ray to a "CIA identities specialist" in Montreal in 1967. Ray has always maintained that he met a man named, "Raul" in Montreal that summer and that Raul had guided him in illegal activities from that time until the time of Reverend King's murder.

Ellen Ray was a documentary film maker. In 1967 she went to New Orleans to do a story about Jim Garrison. She later told a journalist, "People were getting killed left and right. Garrison would subpoena a witness and two days later the witness would be killed by a parked car. I thought Garrison was the great American patriot, but things got a little too heavy when I started getting strange phone calls from men with Cuban accents." After receiving several death threats, Ray abandoned her project and left the country.

"Anyone for whom democracy is more than just a word should be working to abolish the CIA," said Mark Zepezauer. The author of THE CIA'S GREATEST HITS, recounts how President Nixon sent Bob Haldeman to warn Richard Helms at the Agency to call off the Watergate investigation because it could "blow the whole Bay of Pigs thing". Helms got angry and said that Watergate had nothing to do with the Bay of Pigs. Haldeman explained that when Nixon and his advisors were engaged in taped conversations, he used "Bay of Pigs" as code for the Kennedy assassination.

DALLAS

LANDMARKS

I organized Jim Quinn's manuscript during the summer and fall. His theory of the Cold War era was beginning to make sense to me. Greed was the prime mover. Individuals were expendable. Morality was never part of the discussion.

In November, I decided that I would travel to Texas for the 35th anniversary of that dark day in Dallas. I arrived at Dealey Plaza late on a Thursday afternoon. I was not prepared for the beauty of this city park. There were acres of manicured lawns surrounded by tall buildings and a railroad bridge at the lower end. The brick School Depository Building looked orange in the afternoon sun.

I walked down to Elm Street where there were two red crosses painted on the road. These marked the two shots that had hit President Kennedy. I turned and looked at the corner of the picket fence. I was no more than fifty feet away. I walked up the grassy knoll and around to the back of the fence. When I looked over the corner of the fence, a sadness came over me. A marksman would have made this shot with sickening ease.

I walked back down to Elm and stood next to the first cross. A sniper from an upper floor of the Daltex Building, shooting at a severe downward angle, could easily have overcompensated and hit the President in the back. If he had overcompensated on his second shot and missed high, that would explain the bullet fragment that nicked James Tague by the railroad underpass. Likewise, the shooter behind the crook in the fence, also shooting downward, could have overcorrected and hit Kennedy in the throat.

I walked to the second red cross and looked back to the corner of the fence. This was a more level shot at point blank range. A frangible bullet at this distance would have destroyed the President's head. All the things that Jim had been telling me now became a clear picture. When I looked back through the trees to the Oswald window on the sixth floor of the depository, I understood the folly of The Warren Report.

Oswald would have passed up an easy shot when the President was right beneath him. He would have waited until the limousine was halfway down the block and picking up speed. He would now be looking through a row of Texas Live Oak trees. He then would have fired three shots in six seconds with a bolt action rifle at a sharp right angle and downhill. Absolutely impossible. Anyone who stands on the street where John Kennedy was killed will immediately see the folly of the official version.

On Friday morning I set out to visit a number of locations that I had marked on a city map of Dallas. It was another beautiful fall day. Clear skies. Maybe seventy degrees. I first drove to Oak Park to find the rooming house where Lee Oswald stayed at the time of the shooting. As I passed the red brick house at 1026 North Beckley, I was surprised that it was in such good repair after all these years. As I looked for a place to park, I saw a man who looked to be in his fifties come down the front steps and walk a few houses down to the bus stop.

I parked the car and walked to where the man was standing. I introduced myself and shook his hand. His name was Bob Birdwell, from Alto, Texas. I asked him if he knew which room Oswald had rented in the fall of 1963. He pointed to a window on the north side of the house that was equipped with a swamp cooler. It didn't have the air conditioning at the time, he explained. He knew because he had stayed in the house off and on since 1960. Earline Johnson, the landlady in 1963, was a close friend of Bob Birdwell's mother. They were both from Alto, Texas.

Birdwell explained to me that he was in the Navy in 63 and when he was on leave, he would spend time with the Johnsons at 1026 North Beckley. During his visits, he had met Oswald, and they had compared notes on the Marines and the Navy. He said Oswald had predicted a huge war in Southeast Asia.

Birdwell was a cautious man who looked you in the eye. I was inclined to believe his story. He said that three days before the President was shot, he had had coffee with Oswald and the subject of Kennedy's visit to Texas had come up. Oswald said he admired Kennedy's stand on civil rights and thought he might become one of our better presidents. This seemed like a strange statement from a man who intended to shoot the President. Birdwell's next comment struck me as more unusual. He said Oswald commented on how Kennedy's features were different from other politicians. They were more honest.

Birdwell said he was shocked when Oswald was arrested for the murder. In Birdwell's presence, Oswald had said only favorable things about John Kennedy. To this day, Birdwell refused to believe that Oswald had anything to do with the shooting. He said that Oswald seemed to be a passive individual who liked to read books and talk philosophy.

The city bus pulled up in front of us. I shook hands with Bob and thanked him for his time. I wished we would have had another hour to talk. As I walked back to my car on the warm November morning, I was impressed by the clean, working class neighborhood of Oak Cliff. Modest homes with well-kept yards. I wondered what the odds were of running into a person who had known Oswald at the time of the shooting.

Next stop was Tenth and Patton where Officer J.D. Tippet was shot. As I studied my Dallas map, I noticed something strange. If you drew a line from Oswald's rooming house on North Beckley to the Texas Theater where he was arrested, Tenth and Patton was about six blocks east of the line. What was he doing walking in a direction away from the Texas Theater if that was his destination? Also, how could he have traveled that distance of about a mile in less than ten minutes?

When I found the corner of Tenth and Patton, there was no one in sight. The area was of an age where some of the houses had been torn down which left grassy vacant lots. It seemed like too peaceful a neighborhood for a murder to have taken place. I walked along East Tenth to the place where the confrontation took place. I could see the black and white police car and Tippit lying on the ground. It was a stark picture in this quiet neighborhood.

462

If a President had been shot a half-hour earlier, what was Tippit doing patrolling a sleepy out-of-the-way residential neighborhood? On the same kind of a Friday, there was no one in sight. Jim Quinn said that Tippit was set up to take the fall. Maybe he was supposed to meet someone in this neighborhood. Oswald had no reason to be anywhere near here if he was on his way to downtown Oak Park. According to the Warren Commission, Oswald had reversed his direction and ran back the way he had come. According to witnesses, the shooter had run into the alley off Patton Street where he was picked up in a car. Once again, this seemed like a better fit.

I drove south to Jefferson Blvd. where I found the Texas Theater. It was a cream-colored stucco building with blue trim. It was much smaller than I had expected. The windows were boarded up, and trash had blown into the entry way. The neighborhood was Hispanic now, and I doubted that anyone paid much attention to this old landmark. Once again, I saw Oswald being led out of the theatre in his tee-shirt with hundreds of people gathered around. If he was innocent, it must have all seemed surrealistic to him. So many cops and a crowd of onlookers. It was something right out of Kafka. As I stood in the doorway of the abandoned theatre, mariachi music played in the background. 1963 was nothing like this.

I had to drive several miles south to find Harlandale Avenue where Jim Quinn said that the Agency had set up a safe house for the Cuban shooters. This area was very run down and entirely Black and Hispanic. I finally found the residence at 3126 Harlandale. It was

463

run-down and appeared to be vacant. I got out of the car to look around.

This was the perfect set-up. There was a long driveway on the right side of the house that led to a detached garage. To the right of the driveway was a five-foot high wooden fence. Anyone using the house could have driven to the end of the driveway and gone through the backyard to enter the house. None of the neighbors would have seen them.

I decided to drive back to downtown Dallas and look for Jack Ruby's Carousel Club. I was hungry, but I didn't want to waste time to eat. So far, Jim Quinn's story was doing better that the Warren Report.

As I turned up Commerce Street, I passed the Greyhound Bus Depot with the dispossessed scattered along the street. Several blocks up on the left was the Adolphus Hotel which had the most expensive rooms in town. In 1963, H.L. Hunt and Lyndon Johnson held court there. The address where I expected to find the Carousel Club was now a city bus stop. I was surprised to learn that it was only a block from the Adolphus.

Next stop was the city jail which was only three blocks north of Ruby's night club. No wonder all the cops dropped in after hours. It was a perfect location for a small-time mobster to cultivate the police.

There was a narrow ramp leading into and out of the basement. It didn't seem like a good idea to walk down the ramp so I used the main entrance to City Hall. There was an officer posted at the elevator. I figured that they probably did not want tourists wandering around the basement, so I walked up a flight of steps and then took the elevator down to the parking garage.

464

Across the room was the bottom of the ramp and the entrance to the jail where Ruby had shot Oswald. When I walked over to try to determine exactly where the shooting had taken place, I was approached by a young officer who politely told me that the basement was off limits to the public.

I introduced myself, and we shook hands. I told him that I had come all the way from Nevada to see where everything had happened in 1963. His name was Anthony, and he had only been on the force a short time. He showed me where the two men were standing at the time of the shooting. He explained how the entrance to the jail had been changed. He said that a few weeks earlier, 20-20 had been there to film a special edition that they were going to run on the Kennedy assassination. Anthony's job had been to escort the film crew through the jail. Most of what he knew about the event he had learned during this time.

I could not believe my good fortune when he offered to show me the cell where Oswald had been held. That part of the jail was no longer in use. There were many lights out in the corridors as we made our way to the holding cell. There were three cells in the small wing. Oswald's was the larger cell with wooden bunks on either side. I walked into the dimly lit cell and looked around. Metal, wood and cement were all Oswald saw during his last two days.

Then Anthony told me a curious thing. He said that James Lavell had been part of the 20-20 story. He was the officer handcuffed to Oswald's right hand when he was shot by Ruby. Lavell said that all the way through the jail and down the stairs to the basement, Oswald had repeatedly told him that his life was in danger. Oswald told Lavell that if anything was going to happen to him, it would be during the transfer. Oswald warned that an attempt might be made on his life that Sunday. Lavell said he had discounted Oswald's warning as paranoia until he was shot by Ruby.

If Oswald had shot the President, why would he think he was in danger? Who would want to silence him? If the official version was correct, what would be the danger of a trial?

I was tired and hungry as I left City Hall, but I had one last stop. I got onto the Stemmons Freeway and headed west toward Irving . With very little difficulty, I found that modest tract home at 2515 West 5th Street where Marina Oswald and her two children had lived with Ruth Paine. I sat in the car in front of the house and remembered what Jim Quinn had told me. He had indicated that Ruth Paine was an asset of the Agency. Her husband had moved out so that Marina and her two children could stay there. It was necessary that they could use the Paine's garage to plant incriminating evidence against Oswald. He said that Mrs. Paine had no foreknowledge of the plot to kill John Kennedy. Like so many others, she was just following orders.

THE SPOKESMAN

Saturday morning. Another sunny fall day in Dallas. I was disturbed by what had happened here in 1963, but I was beginning to like this city. The perfect fall weather. The grassy beauty of Dealey Plaza. The clean working-class neighborhoods of Oak Park. Also, everyone I had talked with was very polite. I hadn't come to Dallas to enjoy myself, but everything so far had been very pleasant.

I decided to spend the whole day in Dealey Plaza. On the weekend, there would be more people to talk with. I might be lucky enough to find another Bob Birdwell or Anthony the cop. The 35th anniversary of John Kennedy's assassination was on Sunday. There would surely be some knowledgeable people in town for the ceremony.

As I looked over the green expanse of the plaza, I saw a group of people gathered around a man who appeared to be in his late sixties. I approached the group. One of the onlookers told me that the individual who was answering questions was a retired deputy sheriff named Al Maddox. I eavesdropped as this soft-spoken, well groomed man patiently answered questions. Did he know Jack Ruby? Yes, he had spent a number of evenings as Ruby's guest at the Carousel Club. He considered Ruby to be a friend of law enforcement. Had Ruby ever told him why he shot Oswald? No, but as they took Ruby to the infirmary, he slipped a note into Al Maddox's hand. When Maddox was alone, he read the note. It simply said, "It's a conspiracy."

I thought about this new information as I stood in the warm morning sun. Jim Quinn had said that Jack Ruby was injected with a trace of uranium or plutonium which caused a fast developing cancer. This was after Ruby began to show an inclination to talk. Now this former deputy was saying that Ruby had passed him a note saying the whole thing was a conspiracy. Ruby silences Oswald and then Ruby is silenced.

The next conversation I had was with a man from Orange County whose Aunt's best friend is a woman named Milliscent Goggins who was a personal secretary to Allen Dulles for twenty years. The man told me that to this day, Mrs. Goggins is visited regularly by employees of the CIA. She refuses to discuss anything related to the Kennedy assassination. It was beginning to seem like everybody I met had a small piece of pertinent information. I sat down of the grass and thought about what I had already heard that morning.

As I propped myself up on my elbows, I noticed a group of people gathered near the cement steps in front of the grassy Knoll. As I approached the group, I recognized Mark Lane who had written several books on the assassination. He was talking about his experiences in Jonestown, Guyana. He had gone there at the request of several families and was unfortunate enough to arrive just before the mass suicide. He had fled to the airport where he was stopped by several of Jim Jones' guards who were under orders not to let anyone get out alive . He convinced the guards that he was a writer and a friend of civil rights and that someone would have to write the story of Jonestown.

I eased a little closer as someone asked him about his trial against Howard Hunt. Lane explained that he had represented Victor Marchetti, a former CIA operative, and Spotlight Magazine in a libel suit brought against them by E. Howard Hunt. Marchetti had claimed that Hunt was in Dallas to help organize the ambush. Hunt had always maintained that he was in Virginia on November 22,1963. Hunt said that he had picked up his children from school when the news of Kennedy's death was announced. Lane was afraid that any of Hunt's children could have provided him with an alibi that would have made Marchetti's case impossible to win.

Lane had found another witness who was willing to testify that Hunt was in Dallas on November twenty-second. Marita Lorenz was willing to swear that she had traveled from Miami to Dallas with Frank Sturgess and other members of Alpha 66, which was a select hit squad of CIA covert operatives that had been set up to assassinate Fidel Castro. Lorenz claimed that Hunt had met with Sturgess in their motel room on the night before the murder of John Kennedy. She said that Sturgess had received a bundle of money from Hunt. Lane said that Lorenz had put herself in danger by testifying against Hunt. Hunt was a CIA insider who had written Allen Dulles' biography and he was still well-connected at the Agency.

469

When the time came for Hunt's lawyer to call his witnesses, none of Hunt's children were called to testify. The jury was shocked. If any of Hunt's children had testified that their father had picked them up from school that afternoon, Hunt would have won the suit. Evidently, Hunt's children were unwilling to lie in order to provide him with an alibi.

The morning sun was comfortable as Lane continued to field questions from the circle of people. He had smiling eyes and seemed very content. Someone asked how he had first gotten involved in the Kennedy assassination. Lane looked tired as he thought about his answer.

He looked at the man and began to calmly explain that Marguerite Oswald knew that her son was innocent of the two murder charges. She knew that since his time in the Marines, he had been involved in government intelligence work. She was sure that he had gone to Russia on some sort of government assignment and he had returned when he was told to do so. She knew that his work for the government in Dallas and New Orleans had been to infiltrate radical Cuban groups. Marguerite Oswald had heard her son discuss John Kennedy with such high regard that she knew that he was being used in some sort of cover-up. When her son was shot in the basement of the police department by Jack Ruby, she knew his name would forever be tied to the murder of John Kennedy.

Lane agreed to help Oswald's mother. He would act as the dead man's defense lawyer before the Warren Commission. Lane said it quickly became clear to him that the Warren Commission had been set up to determine WHY Lee Oswald shot President Kennedy with very little thought given to IF he actually shot the President. Despite Lane's request, the Warren Commission wanted no part of his serious questioning of witnesses. They refused to let him participate.

Instead, the Commission chose Walter Craig, who was head of the American Bar Association, to protect Lee Oswald's interests. Craig attended two of the 51 hearings. It became very clear to Lane that the Commission did not want any balanced sort of inquiry.

"You see that square white building behind the picket fence?" Mark Lane pointed toward the parking lot west of the Book Depository. "Lee Bowers, who was a radio dispatcher for the railroad, sat in that window on the morning of November twenty-second. He observed several cars with out of state license plates drive slowly through the parking lot that morning. One man appeared to be talking on a hand-held microphone. The third time he saw this particular car, two men got out and walked to the picket fence. At the time of the shooting, Bowers noticed a flash of light or smoke under the trees behind the picket fence. Shortly thereafter, Bowers saw a train departure that he had not authorized. He stopped the train and three tramps were taken off.

"If you study the pictures of the three tramps being marched through Dealey Plaza, you will notice several unusual things. Dallas police are marching the suspects to the County Sheriff's office. When in the history of law enforcement has that ever happened? The two police officers are about ten feet in front and ten feet behind the three tramps. The officers seem to be paying little attention to the three men even though they are suspects in the murder of a President. The officers'

471

uniforms do not seem to fit right. The officer in back has pant legs that hit about six inches above his shoes. The officer in front has sleeves that are above the wrist and is carelessly carrying a shotgun. The problem is that shotguns were not used by police at the time. In his right ear is a listening device. Oddly enough, the older tramp also appears to have a similar device in his ear. The tramps appear to be clean and well dressed. No record has ever been found of their arrest.

Lee Bowers told this story to the Warren Commission, but they were not interested. Later he would grant interviews with writers like Mark Lane. In 1966, Lee Bowers was found dead when his car crashed into a bridge abutment near Midlothian, Texas. The pathologist who examined the body said that Bowers was in some kind of physical shock which he could not identify.

Mark Lane glanced around at the group of us that was gathered around him. He seemed to have gained energy as he turned and pointed toward the curb on Elm Street near the railroad underpass. "On the morning of November 22nd, Julia Ann Mercer was stuck in traffic as she traveled west on Elm Street. Ahead of her was a pick-up with its right two wheels parked up on the sidewalk. Miss Mercer was irritated that the truck, which had an air conditioning sign on the door, was partially blocking traffic. While she watched, the passenger in the truck got out and went around to the back of the truck. He reached over the tailgate and took out what appeared to be a gun case and walked up the grass toward the picket fence. As Miss Mercer passed the truck, she looked into the window and saw a heavy-set man that she later identified as Jack Ruby. It is clear that if the man who left the truck was really one of the shooters, he could have been dropped off behind the fence where no one could identify him. It is more likely that the man was another of our Oswald impersonators. Witnesses would be able to place Oswald in Dealey Plaza with a gun."

Lane pointed to the railroad bridge at the bottom of Elm Street. "S.M. Holland was standing right about there when the shots were fired. He heard four shots. He looked over toward the picket fence and saw a puff of smoke come out from under those trees. He immediately realized that an assassination was taking place. He believed that the assassins were behind the picket fence. He ran to the north end of the bridge and into the railroad yard to see who was behind the fence. A car parked third from the corner of the fence was a station wagon that was backed up to the fence. When Holland got to the car, he could see many footprints around it. There had been rain that morning. Holland noticed that there was mud on the bumper where someone had stood to look over the fence. There was also mud on the two-by-four supports of the fence. Between the car and the fence were dozens of cigarette butts. Someone had been waiting there."

Mark Lane swung around and pointed south across the plaza to the roof of the Terminal Annex Building. "J.C. Price watched the motorcade from that rooftop. Thirty minutes after the assassination, Price gave a statement to the Dallas Sheriff's Office. He said he heard a volley of shots and saw a young man run from the fence toward the parking lot with something in his hand. He was never questioned by the Warren Commission."

"Right about where we are standing, William Newman stood with his wife and two small children. He had been there about five minutes when the motorcade approached and turned onto Elm Street. He heard two shots and the President had this bewildered look on his face and then bam, another shot took the right side of his head off. He was knocked violently back against the seat like he had been hit by a baseball bat. Newman thought the shots had come over his head from behind fence. He yelled to his wife to get on the ground. Newman said that the limousine momentarily stopped. The driver had a radio up to his ear as if he was waiting on some word. Finally the car roared off. Newman later expressed disappointment that he wasn't asked to testify before the Warren Commission."

"Right across Elm from where we are standing, a school teacher named Jean Hill waited for the motorcade. She and her friend, Mary Moorman, were interested in some of the policemen as well as the President. They had a Polaroid camera, and they took a picture of the President as his limousine turned down Elm Street. The picture had the book depository in the background. They were ready to take the next picture when the President's hands came up to his throat. More shots rang out. Jean Hill looked at the picket fence and saw smoke under the trees. Her friend fell to the ground yelling, "They're shooting, get down," but Jean ran across the street and up the knoll toward the fence. Just then she felt a firm grip on her shoulder and a man in a suit said, "You're coming with me." He produced a Secret Service I.D. You have to understand that all the secret servicemen in Dallas that day were with the motorcade. Who were these men in Dealey Plaza with their false Secret Service I.D.s?"

"A second agent appeared and they went through Jean's pockets looking for photographs and then forcefully escorted her to the Record's Building across Houston Street. They took her to a room on the fourth floor overlooking Dealey Plaza where she was met by two more so-called agents. Jean told them she had heard four to six shots. They said she had heard only three. The rest were echoes. At that point, only minutes after the assassination, it became clear to Jean Hill that the official cover-up was already underway."

Mark Lane looked around at the circle of people to judge the effect of his words. "You see that red X on the street? That's where John Kennedy was hit with the fatal head shot. Just to the left and to the rear of the limousine, motorcycle officer Bobby Hargis was splattered so forcefully with blood and brain tissue that he thought that he had been hit. A piece of John Kennedy's skull was stuck to his face. If you draw a line from Bobby Hargis to the President and beyond..." Mark Lane swung his right arm from the street, "It points directly to the corner of the picket fence. That's where so many witnesses said that they had seen smoke from under the trees."

While we thought about that, Lane asked a question. "How many of you have seen a photograph of the motorcade just before the fatal head shot? Jacqueline Kennedy is leaning in front of her husband to see why he is clutching his throat. Now look up to the sixth floor window where Oswald is about to fire the fatal shot. Draw a line from that window to the X on the street. If the fatal shot had come from that direction, it may well have killed Mrs. Kennedy, too. At the very least, she would have been the one covered with blood."

A tall man began to ask a question, but Mark Lane raised his hand to stop the question. "I'd love to stay, but I'm late to another obligation. There's a symposium at the Terminal Annex Building this afternoon if any of you are interested."

TRAUMA ROOM ONE

When I entered the downstairs floor of the Terminal Annex I found myself in a cavernous Amtrak Depot. I was the only person in a room the size of a gymnasium. I followed the signs up an escalator to a reception area outside a large conference room. I looked through the brochure and found that the speakers for the afternoon session were:

1:00   Dr. Charles Crenshaw: Parkland Hospital

2:00   Mark Lane: Oswald on Trial

3:00   William Pepper: The Death of Martin Luther King

4:00   William Turner: Robert Kennedy.

My head was so full of information as I tried to sort out the facts in the Kennedy assassination that I was reluctant to get involved with the details of the murders of Martin Luther King and Robert Kennedy. I finally decided that I probably wouldn't have another chance to hear from individuals who had first hand information on these matters. As I filed in for the afternoon session

I was surprised to see that so many of the members of the audience were relatively young. These people had only heard of John Kennedy. Those of us who had experienced the shock of the assassination would never forget that day or the events that followed. I was curious why so young people had gotten interested.

Doctor Crenshaw was a round faced man with a crew cut who appeared to be in his late sixties. He looked like everyone's grandfather. He seemed reluctant to be at the podium as he began his speech. He explained that contrary to the recent articles in The Journal of American Medicine, everything he was about to discuss was true and common knowledge to all the doctors at Parkland Hospital in Dallas on November 22, 1963.

Dr. Crenshaw said he had walked past Jacqueline Kennedy who was bloody and distraught as he pushed through the doors of Trauma Room One. Dr. Jim Carrico and Dr. Malcolm Perry were feverishly working on the President. To this day, Crenshaw said he could remember every detail of the President's body. The two most obvious problems were the bullet hole in the throat that was bubbling blood and the massive damage to Kennedy's right temple and parts of his brain that were hanging from the exit wound in the back of his head. He remembered the blood dripping from the gurney into the kick bucket. He studied the massive head injury and glanced around the room at Doctors Baxter, Clark, McClelland, and Jones. Crenshaw could see there was no hope. Still Kennedy struggled to breathe. Finally it was over as Dr. Baxter went into the corridor and embraced Mrs. Kennedy. He informed her that her husband was dead.

478

The corridor was filled with Secret Service Agents who were aggressively maintaining security. They seemed intent on providing protection for the dead President. There was an arrogance about these men in suits that all the doctors found offensive.

As time passed, Dr. Crenshaw read whatever he could find on the subject of the Kennedy assassination. He became more and more offended by the untruths that were being circulated as the official version of what had happened. Years later, Crenshaw saw the official autopsy photographs. They looked nothing like what he remembered from Trauma Room One. He remembered a piece of skull missing from the back of the President's head that was big enough to put his fist into. In the official photos, the back of the President's head was intact with a neat bullet hole near the cowlick. Crenshaw concluded that either John Kennedy's head had been reconstructed or the photos had been altered. Also, the hole in the President's throat had been enlarged to a jagged wound that would resemble an exit wound. Crenshaw remembered a neat round wound in the throat that was enlarged by Dr. Malcolm Perry in order to perform a tracheotomy. The throat wound in the photos was a ragged mess.

Another thing Dr. Crenshaw had not been able to reconcile was a report that he read that indicated that Sheriff Bill Decker, whom he knew personally, had received orders from Washington that his deputies were not to take part in the security of the motorcade. That duty was the responsibility of the Secret Service. It had always seemed odd to Crenshaw that the President would not have wanted all the protection that Dallas could afford.

Dr. Crenshaw had just finished surgery when he was told that President Kennedy had been shot and was on his way to Parkland Hospital. As he sprinted toward Trauma Room One, he grabbed Dr. McClelland and informed him of the situation as they ran together. Dr. Salyer sensed their urgency and fell in behind them. As they passed the nurses' station, Dr. Crenshaw saw a man in a suit to their left running in the same direction. To his amazement, he saw another man in a suit jump into his path and smash a Thompson sub-machine gun into the man's face. The first man's eyes were glassy as he collapsed to the floor. Dr. Crenshaw was sure from the sound of gun to bone that the man's jaw was broken. His first instinct was to stop and assist the man, but he had to get to the trauma room. He later found out that a Secret Service Agent had hit an FBI man.

There was an air of unreality as Dr. Crenshaw saw Lyndon Johnson being escorted to a room behind the nurses' station. Johnson had recently suffered a coronary. His face was ashen, and Dr. Crenshaw feared that the Vice President might be having another heart attack. Behind Johnson was Senator Ralph Yarborough who was crying.

As Dr. Crenshaw entered the trauma room, he came face to face with Jacqueline Kennedy as she stood and clutched her purse. He would never forget the look of disbelief and despair on her face. It was his belief that these kinds of tragic circumstances stripped away all peripheral emotions from those close to the victims. In Mrs. Kennedy's expression, he saw a deep sadness as she stood in her bloodstained clothes.

In Trauma Room One, Crenshaw next observed the President. He was a larger man than Dr. Crenshaw had expected   He nearly filled the gurney. His gray suit and shirt were soaked with blood, but his face was unmarked. His eyes were open, but devoid of life. As he examined the President more closely, he saw that the entire right hemisphere of his brain was missing. Pieces of his rear skull that hadn't been blown away were hanging on a matt of bloody hair. Based on his experience with head wounds, Dr. Crenshaw knew that only a high velocity bullet could dissect a cranium that way. The cerebellum was dangling from the President's head by a single strand of tissue. It looked like a blood soaked gray sponge that would fit in the palm of your hand. Blood from the wound dripped from the gurney into the kick bucket.

Dr. Crenshaw was very pessimistic as he examined the wound in President Kennedy's throat. It was the diameter of a pencil at the midline of his throat and was consistent with an entry wound.   He guessed it was from a .30 caliber high velocity bullet consistent with the bullet that had hit the President above the temple and blown out the back of his head.

Dr. Crenshaw did not want Mrs. Kennedy to witness the procedure that they were about to undertake. He suggested that it might be better if she were to wait outside the room. She reluctantly complied. Crenshaw then noticed that Secret Service Agent Clint Hill was circling the trauma room with a loaded .38 pistol.

"What are we going to do about him?"   Dr. Crenshaw asked Dr. Baxter as he nodded toward the nervous agent.

About that time, Doris Nelson, who was in charge of the trauma room, turned to Agent Hill and snapped,

"Whoever shot the President is not in this room so put that gun away so we can get to work."

With that, Hill disappeared. Crenshaw realized that Hill was in shock. The Secret Service had failed to protect the President. Crenshaw later heard that Hill had been institutionalized with a nervous breakdown. He also heard that as the limousine had sped from Dealey Plaza to Parkland Hospital, Hill had repeatedly pounded his fist in frustration on the trunk of the car.

As they began to remove the President's clothes, Crenshaw noticed that there was a lift in the sole of his left oxford. He realized that Kennedy's left leg was about an inch shorter than his right leg. When they removed the back brace, it turned out to be a reinforced steel harness that Kennedy had to wear due to his series of back injuries. In respect to the dying President, they had left on his briefs.

Kennedy's skin had a bronze tint to it. To the casual observer the skin color was that of a suntan, but it was actually due to Addison's disease. Kennedy had been sickly as a boy, and he had contracted tuberculosis of the adrenal glands. This caused the skin discoloration.

The next procedure was to insert a tube in the President's windpipe. A bullet had entered his neck and pierced the windpipe. In all, three cut downs were made to give a rapid infusion of fluids intravenously. When blood began to bubble out of the President's neck wound, Dr. Perry decided to perform a tracheotomy on his throat.

At this point, Kennedy was on a breathing machine. Two chest tubes had been inserted to get air to his lungs. The cut downs were circulating vital fluids into his arm and two legs. The trauma care procedure was complete.

Dr. Crenshaw then inspected the head wound. The entire right cerebral hemisphere was missing. There was an empty cavity where the bullet had entered at the temple and furrowed through the brain and blasted brain matter out the back of the head. Crenshaw characterized this as a four-plus injury which no one survives. If by some miracle Kennedy had survived, he would never have opened his eyes or uttered a sound.

As Dr. Crenshaw looked around the cold, gray room, several of the doctors were weeping. The President's clothes were scattered around the room. When Crenshaw looked down at the kick bucket under the gurney, he almost broke down. There in the blood and brain tissue were Mrs. Kennedy's red roses. He looked up and someone had closed the President's eyes. It was 12:52.

After the priest had performed the Last Rights on John Kennedy, Dr. Crenshaw left Trauma Room One and entered the corridor. He saw Dr. Sternbridge and Dr. Stewart talking to a group of Secret Service Agents. They were explaining to the agents that an autopsy would have to be performed on the President before his body could leave the hospital. The men in suits said that they had orders to take the President's body back to Washington. There would be no autopsy. The discussion soon turned into a shouting match. Dr. Crenshaw sensed that the agents were under orders and there was an urgency to get the President's body back to Washington.

Shortly after this confrontation, Dr. Crenshaw was approached by a medical student named Evalea

Glanges. She seemed to be very upset as she told him of an incident that had taken place outside the emergency room entrance. Glanges and another student were looking at the limousine and discussing a bullet hole in the windshield and another bullet hole in the chrome above the windshield. Upon hearing the conversation, A Secret Service Agent got in the limo and drove off.

At the time, Dr. Crenshaw did not realize the significance of Evalea Glanges' observation, but when the Warren Report concluded that Oswald had time to fire only three shots, he realized that something was wrong. One shot had supposedly hit Kennedy in the back and exited his throat. Crenshaw knew this was false because the throat wound was one of entry. Oswald's second shot was thought to have missed the limousine altogether and struck a curb where bystander, James Teague, was struck by a bullet fragment. The Commission concluded that Oswald's third shot hit the President in the back of his head and exited his temple. Dr. Crenshaw had observed an entrance wound near the temple and an exit wound that had blasted out the back of the President's head.

What about the two bullet holes in the limousine? With Oswald as the lone shooter, there was no way to explain the damage to the limousine. Dr. Crenshaw later read that the limousine was taken to Ohio under helicopter escort and completely rebuilt three days after the assassination. Why the hurry? The limousine was the best single piece of evidence from Dealey Plaza.

Dr. Crenshaw's last duty that day was to oversee the placing of President Kennedy's body in a bronze casket. Two nurses put a plastic mattress cover inside the casket to prevent the white velvet lining from being stained. Crenshaw turned down the sheet and took a last look at Kennedy's head wound. He was overwhelmed with grief for the young man who lay before him.

They lifted the dead president into the casket and put his neatly folded clothes at his feet. Then the handles were turned, and the lid was tightened.

Years later, Dr. Crenshaw saw the autopsy pictures of John Kennedy that were taken at Bethesda Naval Hospital. It was then that he realized that something was very wrong in America in 1963. The back of the President's head had been reconstructed, and the hole in his throat had been enlarged and mangled. He also learned that President Kennedy had arrived at Bethesda in a metal coffin and wrapped in a gray body bag. What had happened from the time the body left Parkland Hospital until it arrived at Bethesda? Also, the remainder of the President's brain was missing. Who had decided that it was necessary to alter this vital evidence?

Dr. Crenshaw's last brush with history was on Sunday, two days after John Kennedy was assassinated. Late Sunday morning Parkland Hospital was alerted that Lee Harvey Oswald had been shot and was on his way to the emergency room. In deference to President Kennedy, Oswald was taken to Trauma Room Two.

Dr. Crenshaw's first observation of Oswald was that he was unconscious and deathly pale. His pupils were dilated, but he still had a heartbeat. From his swollen abdomen, it was apparent that he was bleeding internally. In a matter of minutes, the doctors had performed three venous cut downs and completed a massive blood transfusion. They had inserted a chest tube to keep Oswald's left lung from collapsing and they lowered the front end of the gurney to get blood to his heart and brain.

When Dr. Perry made an abdominal incision, nearly a gallon of blood exploded everywhere. The remaining blood in Oswald's body began to rush into his abdomen. A small piece of lead had shattered the spleen, pancreas, kidney and liver.

About this time, a nurse tapped Dr. Crenshaw on the shoulder and asked him if he could take a call. The doctor reluctantly agreed. When he reached the phone, he was shocked to hear Lyndon Johnson on the other end. He was more shocked when the new President said that he wanted a deathbed confession from Oswald. Johnson said that he expected Dr. Crenshaw's full cooperation on the matter.

An hour later, Lee Oswald's heartbeat had stopped. There would be no confession. Dr. Crenshaw felt a huge disappointment that he and his colleagues had not only failed to save the President, but also the man accused of his murder.

Dr. Crenshaw nodded his head and thanked the audience as he left the podium. He seemed to be a tired, dispirited man. Maybe the burden of knowledge that he had carried with him since 1963 had robbed him of his chance to be happy.

THE DEFENSE

When Mark Lane walked to the podium as the next speaker, he looked like he had been energized from his impromptu speech in Dealey Plaza. I guessed that he was close to seventy, but he had liveliness in his eyes and an energy to set the record straight. Mark Lane had been trying to get the word out for thirty-five years.

Lane started by explaining that he had gotten involved in the Kennedy assassination at the request of Marguerite Oswald, Lee Oswald's mother. She was convinced that he had worked for government intelligence from the time he had left the Marines and gone to Russia, until he was shot in Dallas. She said he had a military identification card that he used to cash government checks. Mrs. Oswald was afraid that with her son not alive to defend himself, he would become the scapegoat of the Warren Commission investigation.

Mark Lane was not allowed to participate in the Warren Commission hearings, but he gathered evidence and interviewed every witness that he could find as if he were constructing a defense for Lee Oswald. He began to write a legal brief which grew into his book, RUSH TO JUDGEMENT. The manuscript contradicted many findings of the Warren Commission.

487

When Lane looked for a publisher, a series of events began to be repeated. The manuscript would be well received. Contractual discussions would take place. Then the editor would abruptly have a change of heart and drop the project.

After fifteen such rejections, Lane signed a contract with Holt-Rinehart and Winston. When Lane joked to the editor that he would probably change his mind, the editor revealed that Cartha De Loach of the FBI had already called and brought pressure to bear to reject Lane's book. The editor and his associates agreed that they would all resign if their company refused to honor the contract. It took that kind of courage on the part of a few men to allow the publication of the first book that caused the American people to question the facts surrounding the death of John Kennedy.

Mark Lane said that he could best outline a defense for Lee Oswald in the form of questions. "For example, the November 22 issue of the Dallas morning news showed a map of the Kennedy motorcade that would have gone down Main Street through the center of Dealey Plaza and on to the Stemmons Freeway. There would not have been an opportunity to shoot from the book depository at that distance. How did Lee Oswald know that there would be a last minute change in the motorcade route that would place the President below the book depository at ten miles per hour? And if he was aware of the route, why didn't he shoot the President at point blank range as he came toward him on Houston and made the slow turn on Elm? Why did he wait until the President was well down Elm Street and partially hidden behind trees before he began to shoot?

"Oswald was seen in the employee lunchroom by a fellow worker just minutes before Kennedy was shot. Ninety seconds after the shooting ended, Patrolman Marion Baker encountered Oswald in the same lunchroom. Oswald was drinking a Coke. The motorcade was running about one-half hour behind schedule. If Lee Oswald did not know the exact time that the motorcade would arrive, could he have been so precise as to leave the lunchroom and get up to the sixth floor sniper's nest, fire three rapid shots with world-class precision, wipe the rifle clean of fingerprints, hide the weapon, hustle down four flights of stairs, go to the lunchroom, buy a Coke from the machine, and be calmly drinking the beverage in one and a half minutes? An adequate defense attorney might have convinced a jury that Lee Oswald was not on the sixth floor of the Texas School Book Depository at the time of the shooting."

Lane said that there was a more likely scenario. "Oswald studied Russian during his Marine duty. The Warren Commission had heard testimony to that effect. There was a defector program at that time run by the Office of Naval Intelligence in conjunction with the CIA. If Oswald had been given training in the Russian language, he might have been recruited for that program. The idea was to send the man to the Soviet Union with information that the Russians would find useful. In Oswald's case, he had been stationed at Astugi, Japan as a radar operator. Astugi was the take-off point for U-2 flights over Russia.

"Oswald was given a hardship discharge from the Marines so he could be with his ailing mother in Texas. Marguerite Oswald was not really sick at the time. A few days after visiting his mother in Texas, he departed on an expensive trip to Russia. At the time, he had two hundred dollars to his name. In Russia, Oswald renounced his American citizenship and agreed to provide the Soviet Union with American military secrets. He was rewarded with a job and a comfortable apartment in Minsk. He was then introduced to Marina Prusakova, the niece of a Soviet intelligence agent. They decided to get married and move back to the United States. Not only does the American government cut through red tape to allow Oswald and his Russian wife to return to the United States, they also provide them with money for the trip.

"When Oswald returned to the United States, was he arrested for treason for defecting to the Soviet Union and providing the Russians with secret radar codes? Absolutely not! He was allowed to settle down in Texas where he is placed under the guidance of George DeMohrenschildt, who not only is a covert intelligence operative, but also works for Texas billionaire, Clint Murchison. DeMohrenschildt then introduces the Oswalds to Ruth Paine who had gone to an eastern linguistics school from which many students were recruited for intelligence work. Michael Paine's family was also involved in intelligence work. At one point, Michael and Ruth Paine agree to separate so that Ruth can drive to New Orleans and take Marina Oswald and her child back to Texas to live with her. This is an incredible humanitarian gesture by any measure.

"None of what I've just told you makes much sense unless you believe what Marguerite Oswald had alleged. She fiercely maintained that from the time Lee

Oswald left the marines until he was shot in Dallas, he had been an agent of the U.S. government.

"Oswald was not sent to the Soviet Union as a spy. That's why he did not go through rigorous debriefing when he got back to this country. He was being sheep-dipped as a defector and communist sympathizer so he could return the United States and infiltrate radical socialist organizations. This continued in the summer of 63 when Oswald was sent to New Orleans to set up a chapter of the Fair Play for Cuba Committee under the watchful eye of Guy Bannister. From the time Oswald returned to the United States, he understood his role as a well-documented communist who could infiltrate radical groups. Imagine his amazement when he was arrested in the Texas Theatre and charged with the murder of a man whom he admired.

"When Kennedy made the decision to withdraw troops from Vietnam, the Cold Warriors, who were counting on that war as an outlet for military production, made a decision. Kennedy would be removed from office. The CIA had the perfect fall guy in Lee Harvey Oswald.

"The Plan was nearly foolproof. Send Oswald to New Orleans under the care of Guy Bannister to pose as a Castro sympathizer. Have him set up a chapter of the Fair Play for Cuba Committee in which he was the only member. Stage a publicity event where Oswald is arrested while handing out pro-Castro leaflets. Have Oswald appear on a radio talk show to establish his pro-Castro position. Bring Oswald back to Dallas where his wife is living with Ruth Paine. At Ruth Paine's suggestion, Oswald gets a job at the Texas School Book Depository. Make sure that President Kennedy's

491

motorcade is rerouted to pass by the depository. Tell Oswald to wait for a phone call in the lunchroom while the motorcade passes by so he will be out of sight. After Oswald is shot or arrested, have a secure area such as Ruth Paine's garage, where incriminating evidence against Oswald can be planted. Case closed.

"This is the way our covert apparatus worked during the Cold War period. It was fun and games at the highest level. Our CIA had perfected the art of overthrowing governments that would not cooperate with our strategic interests. John Kennedy was one of a long list of Executive Actions during that period.

"Why did fifty-seven witnesses in Dealey Plaza say that shots came from the railroad yard behind the picket fence? Why did so many people run up the grassy knoll right after the shooting? Why did so many people say that they had heard four to six shots? Why did witnesses describe rifle smoke above the picket fence and under the trees? Senator Ralph Yarborough was two cars behind the President in the motorcade. He said he smelled gunpowder. If all the shots had been fired from the sixth floor of the depository, you would not have smelled the smoke at street level.

"Who were the Secret Service agents in the railroad yard who turned back police and witnesses? All Secret Service agents in Dallas that day were with the motorcade. Who were these impostors?

"Bobby Hargis was the motorcycle escort to the right rear of the presidential limousine when Kennedy was shot. He was splattered with so much blood and brain tissue that he thought at first that he had been hit. How could a shot from the right rear cause brain matter to hit someone at the left rear? If you draw a line from Bobby

Hargis through John Kennedy, it points to the crook in the picket fence.

"When Oswald was arrested, the FBI conducted a paraffin test to determine if there were traces of nitrates on Oswald's face or neck which you would expect to find if he had fired a rifle three times earlier that day. J. Edgar Hoover announced that the results were inconclusive. Several years later, we learned that no traces of nitrates were found on Oswald's face. Conclusion? He had not fired a rifle that day. Where does that leave the whole charade of the Warren Commission Report? Oswald did not do the crime. He was in the lunchroom. Who did commit the crime? Because of our governments' reluctance to properly investigate the matter, we may never know."

MEMPHIS

William Pepper was a measured, soft spoken man. Like Dr. Crenshaw, he seemed reluctant to overstate anything. He said he had gotten involved in the Martin Luther King conspiracy totally by accident. He had originally accepted the official version of King's murder at the hands of James Earl Ray. He had personally known and admired King. He took the murder very hard and wanted to put the tragedy behind him. Like Crenshaw, Pepper had become aware of inconsistencies in the case against Ray during the next decade.

At the request of Ralph Abernathy, Pepper conducted a five hour interview with James Earl Ray. After that interview, Pepper decided to get to the truth in the matter of Dr. King's death. As Pepper studied King's life in the years leading up to his death in 1968, he realized that King was more than a civil rights leader. He was a non-violent revolutionary who was determined to change the social and economic fabric of the United States. His opposition to the Vietnam war and his plans for a poor people's march on Washington D.C. in the summer of 1968, were considered a serious threat to the Johnson Administration that was under siege from anti-war riots and urban unrest.

Officials in military intelligence and FBI director J. Edgar Hoover had decided that King was under communist control. With that conclusion, King had become an enemy of our country. Lyndon Johnson feared that a poor people's siege on the capitol could cause the federal government to crack. Without specific details, Johnson told his top aides that the matter would have to be handled. There could be no march on Washington. A riot in Detroit the previous year had resulted in eight hundred injuries and one hundred and fifty million dollars in property damages. With millions expected to follow Dr. King to Washington, the results could have been disastrous. The barbarians were at the gate.

As he studied the facts surrounding Dr. King's death, William Pepper concluded that our system of checks and balances no longer worked. Our country was being run by powerful special interests. Our government had become nothing more than a tool of these powerful groups.

Pepper believed that Martin Luther King became an enemy of the state one year before he was killed when he officially announced his opposition to the Vietnam War. In that speech on April 4, 1967, at Riverside Church in New York City, Reverend King called for conscientious objection and anti-war demonstrations. At that point, even some of King's long time supporters like Roy Wilkins began to openly distance themselves from King.

After the NAACP Board of Directors passed a resolution that condemned King's attempt to link civil rights and the anti-war movement, King addressed a crowd of a quarter of a million people and called for the government to end the bombing in Vietnam. In the eyes of the embattled Johnson administration, King had become a serious adversary.

Pepper did not learn until ten years after the assassination that a CIA program called OPERATION CHAOS had been put in place to undermine dissenting citizens groups by opening mail and placing informants in these groups. The FBI had a similar program called COINTELLPRO. The CIA and the FBI zeroed in on Dr. King when he began to call for an end to the Vietnam War. There was a real fear within the federal government of the riots that might result from King's poor people's march on Washington in the summer of 68. When King died in April of 1968, the plans for a march on Washington also died.

William Pepper then related the unlikely story of James Earl Ray. Weeks before Ray was arrested in London, the FBI had started a well planned series of leaks to the press that would convict Ray in the court of public opinion. He was portrayed as a racist and a drug user who was addicted to pornography and prostitutes. They even quoted a fellow convict as saying that Ray was interested in collecting a bounty on Martin Luther King that they had heard about in prison.

When Ray was extradited back to Memphis, he had retained the services of Arthur J. Hanes of Birmingham, Alabama. Hanes and his son and a local private investigator worked with Ray to prepare for his trial. Two days before the trial was scheduled to begin, Ray was visited by famous Texas attorney, Percy Foreman. Ray was convinced to drop Hanes in favor of Foreman. A five month continuance was granted, but Foreman's health was so poor that he was unable to spend adequate time with Ray. The court then appointed public defender Hugh Stanton to assist in the case. As it turned out, Foreman convinced Ray to plead guilty in order to save his life.

Actually, Foreman pressured Ray to plead guilty by threatening a less than vigorous defense. He said that Ray's elderly father would be sent back to Idaho on a forty year old parole violation. If Ray insisted on a trial, Foreman assured him that they were gonna fry his ass. Finally, Foreman offered a sum of money if Ray would plead guilty. Someone behind Percy Foreman did not want this case to go to trial. He had not come all the way from Texas to offer friendly advice. Foreman had a life-long working relationship with Big Oil.

James Ray's account of events that led to the evening of April 4, 1968 has remained unchanged over the years. In April of the preceding year, he had escaped from the Missouri State Penitentiary by hiding in a bread truck.

He made his way to Chicago where he got a job in a restaurant. Fearing that he would be apprehended, he obtained false identification papers and went to Canada. He hung around the docks as he looked for work on a freighter. He hoped to work his way to Africa or South America.

At the Neptune Bar, in August, he met a character named, Raul, who would control Ray's movements for the next eight months. Ray entered into a partnership with Raul in a smuggling operation that took him from Canada to Mexico and from California to Georgia. Raul made sure that Ray always had money in his

497

pocket and even bought him a car. Raul would lay out Ray's itinerary including phone numbers of contacts in different cities. He provided Ray with money to buy a rifle in Alabama. Raul then told him to bring the rifle to Memphis.

On April 3, 1968, Ray checked into the New Rebel Motel in Memphis. Raul appeared at the motel that evening and picked up the rifle. He wrote down the address of Jim's Grill in a rundown part of town and told him to meet him there the next day at three in the afternoon.

At this meeting, Raul told Ray to register for an upstairs room above the restaurant and purchase a pair of binoculars. Ray was given two hundred dollars for this. Ray was then told to leave for a few hours and go see a movie or something. Ray decided to drive to a gas station and have his spare tire repaired. The service station was busy but Ray was in no hurry so he waited. It was at this point that an ambulance raced by with its siren on.

As Ray drove back to his room, he encountered a policeman and a road block. The officer motioned for Ray to turn his car around. As an escaped prisoner, Ray decided to leave Memphis and take the back roads through Mississippi. Eventually, Ray made his way by bus out of the United States and into Canada. He obtained a false passport and flew to London where he was later arrested. As Pepper weighed the evidence to decide if he would help Ray get a new trial, many discrepancies with the official version became apparent:

1. King's Chauffeur, Solomon Jones, reported that at the time of the shooting, he had seen someone in the

498

brush behind the rooming house where Ray had rented his room. Ray was supposed to have shot from an upstairs window directly over the brushy area. The city of Memphis cleared out all the brush the next morning, thus eliminating evidence of cover for a possible shooter.

2. Martin Luther King had never stayed at the Lorraine Motel in a seedy part of Memphis. Not only had there been a last minute change from the Rivermont Hotel where King had usually stayed, but there had been a last minute room change where King would have access to the exposed balcony.

3. There were reports of a second white Mustang parked within 100 feet of where Ray had parked his Mustang. It was an unlikely coincidence. Could this have been part of a frame-up?

4. No fingerprints that matched Ray's were found in the bathroom where the shot was supposedly fired, and the FBI couldn't match the death slug to the alleged murder weapon.

5. There was a fire station directly behind the Lorraine Motel. The night before King's arrival, a black fireman from that station had been transferred across town.

6. Edward Redditt, a black detective who was involved in King's security detail, was also transferred from his post the day before the shooting.

The most alarming information that William Pepper encountered, however, was the discovery of a personal vendetta that J. Edgar Hoover had carried out against Martin Luther King. Hoover also had close ties to Army Intelligence.

Mark Lane had given Pepper an affidavit of a detailed conversation between Daniel Ellsberg and Brady Tyson, who was an aide to U.N. Ambassador Andrew Young. Ellsberg had asked Tyson if he thought that there was a conspiracy in the death of Martin Luther King.

Tyson answered that the conspiracy involved a group of off-duty and retired FBI officers working under the personal direction of J. Edgar Hoover. The group included a sharp-shooter who had fired the fatal shot. He said the facts had come to light in Walter Fauntroy's HSCA investigation. Tyson also asserted that when Fauntroy informed Speaker of the House Carl Albert of these facts and said that he would like to be on the committee to investigate Dr. King's death, Carl Albert turned him down. "Walter," Albert said, "You don't want that assignment. You will probably be killed." This was America in the 60s and 70s.

Pepper and Mark Lane decided to turn the information over to Robert Blakey who was in charge of the HSCA investigation. An argument followed in which Lane accused Blakey of not following any leads that pointed in any direction other than James Earl Ray. Blakey exploded and told Lane that if he kept it up, he would be taken care of once and for all.

During his investigation, Pepper uncovered a shadowy figure named Walter Youngblood who had been a government asset of both the CIA and Army

Intelligence. He had been identified by several witnesses as being in Jim's Grill during the week before King's murder. Jim's Grill was a focal point because it was downstairs from the rooming house where James Ray allegedly shot King from a bathroom window. Youngblood also had ties to organized crime and had told an acquaintance that Robert Kennedy would be next.

Pepper met with Youngblood twice. He denied any involvement in the King and Robert Kennedy assassinations. He said the individuals involved were living outside the country. Youngblood said he had an oil company plane at his disposal and, for a price, these men might be willing to talk. He said that they felt betrayed by Army Intelligence and that their lives were in danger.

Pepper learned that there had been several murder contracts on James Earl Ray while he was in prison. Also, the owner of the storefront where the bundle with the rifle and Ray's belongings had been dropped, had originally stated that the bundle was dropped off before he heard the shot. This would certainly indicate that Ray had been set up.

Recently, the King family had gotten involved to try and get James Ray a new trial. They were convinced that he was innocent. About this time, Ray developed cancer which made it doubtful that he would live long enough to have a new trial.

As William Pepper left the podium, I was struck with the similarities of the King and Kennedy assassinations. In the months leading up to the events, Ray and Oswald had been moved around like chess pieces. There were many inconsistencies in the cases

501

against them and the government seemed unwilling to follow leads that pointed away from the patsies. In their opposition to the Vietnam War, John Kennedy and Martin Luther King had become very unpopular with our military establishment. Most disturbing of all was Walter Younblood's statement that he was told that Robert Kennedy was next. That would have eliminated the last serious opposition to the war. Jim Quinn had spent six days trying to convince me of this exact scenario.

POWDER BURNS

William Turner looked like a former FBI man. Tall, athletic and clean-cut with a haircut to match. He could have been a banker or a stock broker. Very conservative and respectable. He spoke in a quiet voice as he explained his background with the FBI and his disenchantment with its director, J. Edgar Hoover. When it became clear to Turner that Hoover was using the FBI to attack his critics and reward his supporters, he decided to get out.

Turner went to work for Ramparts Magazine as a free lance correspondent. He was dispatched to Dallas when John Kennedy was killed in Dealey Plaza. His job was to investigate the breakdown of Secret Service protection. After Turner had finished his presentation and was answering questions in the lobby, I told him I had been out to Harlandale to look at an alleged safehouse. Turner confirmed that there had been a safehouse for the contract men on Harlandale. Turner had received a tip   two days after John Kennedy's death, but when he got there, the place was already cleaned out.

Turner said that Robert Kennedy's murder at the Ambassador Hotel on June 5, 1968, looked like an open and shut case. Sirhan Sirhan had fired at point-blank range a few feet in front of the Senator. Then Turner had heard from an old contact in the FBI that a number of slugs had been found in a door jamb and a ceiling beam. It sounded like twelve or thirteen bullets had been fired from a gun that held eight bullets.

Then came the news that Coroner Thomas Noguchi's investigation had shown that all three bullets that struck Robert Kennedy had been fired from the rear at an upward angle from right to left. It sounded as if Kennedy's killer had been standing behind him while Sirhan was firing away from the front. Noguchi also determined from the powder burns that the fatal head wound was fired from less than one inch from Kennedy's head behind the right ear. This would completely rule out Sirhan. He was never that close to Kennedy.

Turner remembered the picture of Robert Kennedy lying on the floor in a pool of blood with a clip-on tie near his right hand. The Ambassador Hotel security guard behind Kennedy is missing his tie. Could the Senator have reached back to protect himself and grabbed the man's tie?

As Turner looked into the case, other evidence pointed to a shooter other than Sirhan. The barrel of the .22 caliber pistol that was taken from Sirhan was so full of lead that it had to be cleaned out by firing jacketed bullets through it. If Sirhan had fired the bullets that were found at the scene, the barrel of his gun would not have had the heavy amounts of lead in the barrel. If, however, Sirhan had fired blanks, the lead deposits could be explained. Could Sirhan have been another actor in a scene like Oswald? The physical evidence clearly seemed to point in that direction.

Turner began to wonder why so much contradictory evidence had been suppressed. He had met two L.A. detectives who were in charge of Special Unit Senator, which was the name given to the investigation of Robert Kennedy's death. When Turner checked into the backgrounds of Manny Pena and Hank Hernandez, he found that both detectives had backgrounds with the CIA. Pena, who boasted of eleven suspects killed in the line of duty, retired from the Los Angeles Police Department in November of 1967 to take a job with the International Development Office of the State Department. He was going to take an assignment in a Latin American country to train police forces in investigative techniques. Turner knew from his FBI days that the Agency for International Development was a cover for the CIA's clandestine operations in third world countries. Inside intelligence circles, it was known as the Department of Dirty Tricks. It's primary functions were to teach interrogation techniques and assassination methods.

Turner learned through one of his contacts that Pena had left the LAPD for a special CIA training unit in Virginia. He was told that Pena had done special assignments for the CIA during the previous decade.

Turner's next statement made my blood run cold. He said Pena had worked in South America with a CIA operative named Dan Mitrione. I remembered Jim Quinn's account of how Mitrione had rounded up indigents on the outskirts of Montevideo and tortured them to death during his interrogation seminars. Was it a coincidence that an LA detective with a decade of experience with the CIA was put in charge of Special Unit Senator?

505

The next part of William Turner's discussion sounded like something out of the Twilight Zone. As he went through Sirhan's testimony, he was surprised to learn that Sirhan had always maintained that he could not remember shooting Kennedy. He claimed to have liked Robert Kennedy and felt grief when he learned that he had died. No matter how hard he tried, Sirhan could not remember the incident. The prosecution called Sirhan's condition a self-induced trance. Psychiatric experts said that this was very unlikely.

Several doctors who examined Sirhan while he was in custody thought that he exhibited symptoms of someone who had been under hypnosis, but they doubted that it could have been self-induced. Later, when Sirhan was on death row at San Quentin, he was examined for thirty-five hours by Dr. Edward Simson-Kallas. Dr. Simson concluded that Sirhan could have been programmed to kill Robert Kennedy. He described Sirhan as someone who was easily influenced, had no real roots and was looking for a cause. Dr. Simson said that the Arab-Israeli conflict could have been used to motivate him. The doctor felt that Sirhan was not devious enough to have planned the assassination. Dr. Simson concluded that Sirhan had been prepared by someone.

The idea that Sirhan was programmed to make an attempt on the life of Robert Kennedy might have been a dead-end had it not been for the strange case of William Bryan Jr., who called himself "America's Most Famous Medical Hypnotist." By coincidence, he was a technical advisor during the filming of The Manchurian Candidate, which was an account of a man who was programmed to carry out an assassination without

506

conscious knowledge. The idea came from two CIA programs. MK-ULTRA was an extensive experiment in mind control that included everything from hypnosis to LSD. Included in MK-ULTRA was a program called OPERATION ARTICHOKE that would determine whether a person could be programmed to involuntarily commit an assassination.

During the Korean War, Bryan had been chief of medical survival training for the U.S. Air Force which dealt with brainwashing. After the war, he became involved with the MK-ULTRA program.

Bryan set up a practice on the Sunset Strip in Hollywood which he called The American Institute of Hypnosis. His specialty was sexual disorders. He liked to get to know his clients on a deep emotional level. One method was through sexual intercourse. In 1969, the California Board of Medical Examiners found Bryan guilty of unprofessional conduct for having had sex with four women patients while they were under hypnosis.

After Robert Kennedy had been killed and before Sirhan had been identified, Bryan had commented to an LA radio station reporter that the killer had probably acted under post-hypnotic suggestion. Where had this conclusion come from? One of the pages in Sirhan's journal had the name Di Salvo written over and over. Bryan had helped crack the Boston Strangler case and spent the rest of his life bragging about how he helped convict Albert Di Salvo. Sirhan could not remember writing "Di Salvo" in his journal and had no idea who he was. Could that name have been mentioned to Sirhan while he was under hypnosis?

In 1974, writer Betsy Langham was granted an interview with William Bryan at his office on the Sunset Strip. After discussing Bryan's success in solving the Boston Strangler and Hollywood Strangler cases, Langham offhandedly asked Bryan if he thought that Sirhan could have acted under a hypnotic trance. Bryan replied angrily that the interview was over and quickly left the office.

Bryan's secretary was apologetic and agreed to go across the street with Langham for a cup of coffee. During their discussion, the secretary told a very unusual story. Minutes after George Wallace had been shot during his 1972 campaign, Bryan had gotten a phone call from Maryland. The secretary's impression was that the call had to do with the shooting. Arthur Bremer was another alleged loner who had shot a national figure with no apparent motive.

In 1977, Bryan was found dead in a Las Vegas motel room. Death from natural causes was declared before an autopsy could be performed. Shortly thereafter, William Turner interviewed two call girls who had been servicing Bryan twice a week over a period of four years. They would humor him by asking about the important people he had worked with. The first people he would discuss were Albert Di Salvo and Sirhan Sirhan. The girls told Turner they were sure about the names. Bryan had also told the girls to call an unlisted number at his office. If someone else answered, they were told to say they were with "The Company", which was an insider's term for the CIA. Bryan told the girls that he had been involved in many top secret projects with the CIA.

William Turner concluded his speech on an upbeat note. It had been an uphill battle to piece together the facts in the assassinations of John Kennedy, Robert Kennedy, and Martin Luther King and the attempted assassination of George Wallace. The number of people who continued to turn up information as well as the new freedom of information laws were beginning to complete the puzzle. Turner said we were getting close to a final resolution.

I knew all about Dr. Bryan and MK-ULTRA from my conversations with Jim Quinn. It was almost inconceivable that the CIA could have been involved in the murders of John and Robert Kennedy and the near murder of George Wallace. The possibility that a former CIA psychologist worked with both Sirhan Sirhan and Walter Bremmer was hard to dismiss as a coincidence. Lyndon Johnson said that in the 1960s, the CIA was running a "murder incorporated" in the Caribbean. Maybe it was more widespread than that.

DEPARTURE

      Sunday morning was bright and clear in Dallas. This was the 35th anniversary of the assassination of President Kennedy. I had a plane to catch, but I wanted to make one last visit to Dealey Plaza. I was obsessed with this beautiful park and the awful thing that had happened there.

      At 9:30 in the morning, there were about three hundred people wandering around Dealey Plaza. Flowers covered the lawn on both sides of Elm Street. As I approached a group of people, I could see that some of them had been crying. This group of mourners was speaking German. Could they have come all this way to pay their respects to the fallen president? West Berlin had given John Kennedy the greatest reception of his presidency.

      There was a convocation planned for 12:30. I wished that I could have attended. It was clear from observing the crowd that there was still a depth of feeling for President Kennedy. The crowd was growing larger, as people with flowers entered the park from all directions. Reluctantly, I said goodbye to Dealey Plaza and the memory of John F. Kennedy.

      As my plane took off for Salt Lake City and the flat Texas landscape receded in the distance, I realized that

I had not learned one thing in Dallas that contradicted anything that Jim Quinn had told me. The ambush site was clear. There were shots coming from at least two different directions and not from Oswald's 6th floor window. No matter how hard the Warren Commission tried to make everything point to Lee Oswald, their job was impossible.

When the presidential limousine turned right on Houston Street and approached the deadly turn on Elm, it seemed that America had also turned right. When John Kennedy was killed a few moments later, gone was his populist agenda and his pursuit of world peace. While the defense industry breathed a huge sigh of relief, people throughout the Third World were devastated. They had lost their champion. The man with the courage to stand up to the Pentagon and the CIA was gone.

Jim Quinn said that you can assassinate the man or you can assassinate his character. In the case of John Kennedy, it seems that both ends were accomplished. Thirty five years after his murder in Dallas, much of what the young president was trying to accomplish has been forgotten. A real chance to end the Cold War had been lost in a volley of gunshots. Had it not been for a day of fishing with an old man on Flathead Lake, I would never have understood any of this.

Made in the USA
San Bernardino, CA
11 February 2014